Praise for Anne Emery

Praise for *Death at Christy Burke's*

"Emery's sixth mystery (after 2010's *Children in the Morning*) makes excellent use of its early 1990s Dublin setting and the period's endemic violence between Protestants and Catholics."
— *Publishers Weekly*, starred review

"Halifax lawyer Anne Emery's terrific series featuring lawyer Monty Collins and priest Brennan Burke gets better with every book."
— *Globe and Mail*

Praise for *Children in the Morning*

"This [fifth] Monty Collins book by Halifax lawyer Emery is the best of the series. It has a solid plot, good characters, and a very strange child who has visions." — *Globe and Mail*

"Not since Robert K. Tanenbaum's Lucy Karp, a young woman who talks with saints, have we seen a more poignant rendering of a female child with unusual powers." — *Library Journal*

Praise for *Cecilian Vespers*

"Anne Emery has already won one Arthur Ellis Award for her first Monty Collins mystery, and this one should get her on the short list for another. *Cecilian Vespers* is slick, smart, and populated with lively characters." — *Globe and Mail*

"This remarkable mystery is flawlessly composed, intricately plotted, and will have readers hooked to the very last page."
— *The Chronicle Herald*

Praise for *Barrington Street Blues*

"The yin-yang of Monty and Maura, from cruel barbs to tender moments, is rendered in occasionally hilarious but mostly heartbreaking fashion. Emery makes it easy to root for Monty, who solves not only the mystery that pays the bills, but also the one that tugs at his heart."
— *Quill & Quire*

"Anne Emery has given readers so much to feast upon . . . The core of characters, common to all three of her novels, has become almost as important to the reader as the plots. She is becoming known for her complexity and subtlety in her story construction."
— *The Chronicle Herald*

Praise for *Obit*

"Emery tops her vivid story of past political intrigue that could destroy the present with a surprising conclusion."　　— *Publishers Weekly*

"Strong characters and a vivid depiction of Irish American family life make Emery's second mystery as outstanding as her first. "
— *Library Journal*, starred review

Praise for *Sign of the Cross*

"A complex, multilayered mystery that goes far beyond what you'd expect from a first-time novelist."　　　— *Quill & Quire*

"This startlingly good first novel by a Halifax writer well-versed in the Canadian court system is notable for its cast of well-drawn characters and for a plot line that keeps you feverishly reading to the end. Snappy dialogue, a terrific feel for Halifax, characters you really do care about, and a great plot make this one a keeper."
— *Waterloo Region Record*

"Anne Emery has produced a stunning first novel that is at once a mystery, a thriller, and a love story. *Sign of the Cross* is well written, exciting, and unforgettable."　　　— *The Chronicle Herald*

Blood
on a Saint

The Collins-Burke Mystery Series

Blood
on a Saint

A MYSTERY

ANNE EMERY

ECW Press

Published by ECW Press
2120 Queen Street East, Suite 200, Toronto, Ontario, Canada M4E 1E2
416-694-3348 / info@ecwpress.com

LIBRARY AND ARCHIVES CANADA CATALOGUING IN PUBLICATION

Emery, Anne, author
Blood on a saint : a mystery / Anne Emery.
(Collins-Burke mystery)

ISBN 978-1-77041-122-7 (bound)
Also issued as: 978-1-77090-412-5 (EPUB); 978-1-77090-411-8 (PDF)

I. Title.
PS8609.M47B56 2013   C813'.6   C2013-902493-X

Cover and text design: Tania Craan
Cover image: Medioimages/Photodisc/Getty Images
Author photo: Precision Photo
Typesetting and production: Troy Cunningham
Printing: Friesens   5   4   3   2   1

The publication of *Blood on a Saint* has been generously supported by the Canada Council for the Arts
which last year invested $20.1 million in writing and publishing throughout Canada, and by the Ontario
Arts Council, an agency of the Government of Ontario, which last year funded 1,681 individual artists and
1,125 organizations in 216 communities across Ontario for a total of $52.8 million. We also acknowledge
the financial support of the Government of Canada through the Canada Book Fund for our publishing
activities, and the contribution of the Government of Ontario through the Ontario Book Publishing Tax
Credit. The marketing of this book was made possible with the support of the Ontario Media Development
Corporation.

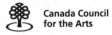
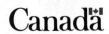

PRINTED AND BOUND IN CANADA

Chapter 1

Monty

"Burke fired her."

"Eh?"

"The wrongful dismissal file. She was hired as a secretary at the church. Turned out she couldn't spell, and she kept taking bogus sick days. So Burke sent her packing. Now she's suing for damages."

Monty Collins's law partner, Ronald MacLeod, pointed to one of the files on the desk, files that had piled up while Monty was out of town for the first week of a two-week trial.

"Oh." Monty picked up the folder. Befanee Tate. *Befanee?* When did they hire her? I remember seeing a new face over there. I said hello on the occasions I was in, but I never actually met her."

"She wasn't all that new. Four months ago."

"How much did they offer her as severance pay?"

"Month's salary."

"So what's she complaining about? That's more than a judge would give her if it went to court."

"She wants it all. Compensation for mental anguish, loss of reputation, punitive damages, you name it."

1

"Burke won't be too happy about that." Monty knew Father Burke well. The priest had a limited tolerance for this sort of aggravation.

"You got that right. He asked for you, and I told him I'd bring it to your attention as soon as you got back. I'll leave you to it."

"Thanks, Ron." This was the Saturday of the Labour Day weekend. A lost weekend, but not the kind Monty had enjoyed before becoming a partner at Stratton Sommers. He was in the office, and he would be flying back to Toronto Sunday night for the second week of the products liability trial. "I'll have a word with him next week."

"I'm sure he'll be fine with that," Ron said.

"Right," Monty answered. He was distracted by all the work in front of him. "Can't say this Befanee Tate matter is the most urgent case on my docket!"

"I hear you." MacLeod headed for the door, then turned back. "Oh, and she claims the Virgin Mary appeared to her in the churchyard."

Monty rolled his eyes and tossed the file aside. He would see Burke at some point and reassure him that he had offered Befanee Tate more than enough in compensation, Virgin or no Virgin, and he could put it out of his mind. End of story.

The following Friday night Monty boarded the plane in Toronto and flopped into his seat for the flight home to Halifax, exhausted but relieved. The trial had come to a successful conclusion, the fourteen-hour work days were over, and he was on his way back to a saner, kinder, gentler way of life. He fastened his seat belt and nodded yes to the flight attendant when she came by with the day's newspapers. He took the Halifax *Chronicle Herald* and proceeded to catch up on the news in his home town. On the front page, below the fold, was a photo of a crowd of people taking part in some kind of protest or gathering in a parking lot. He looked closer and saw some people kneeling, others carrying what appeared to be religious icons. One person was lying on a stretcher, with attendants at both ends. A bearded man in a long, belted robe appeared to be making a speech. A young girl with a round, pretty face and thin hair pulled back in a ponytail stood gazing at a statue. Monty recognized it as the figure of St. Bernadette in the churchyard on Byrne Street. There was often a group of people around the statue, devotees of the saint. But now there were tents on the site. And what was that? A cart — no, three carts — piled with goods of some kind.

Looking over all this was . . . he was shown from the back, but Monty would have known him anywhere. The caption read, "Father Brennan Burke looks out at the crowd gathered in his Halifax church-yard in response to the claimed sighting of the Virgin Mary." Neutral the prose may have been, but Burke's posture spoke volumes to Monty. He could tell that the priest's arms were folded across his chest; Monty could picture the profile, the hawkish nose, the lips clamped shut, the black eyes scourging the scene, the animosity emanating from him in waves. Monty let out a bark of laughter, which caused heads to turn in his direction. Then he read the piece.

Virgin Mary Appeared in Halifax, Woman Claims

A carnival atmosphere pervades the once-staid grounds of St. Bernadette's church, in the wake of a claim by a Halifax County woman that the Virgin Mary appeared to her above a statue of St. Bernadette. Pilgrims from as far away as Montreal and the eastern United States have travelled to the city, some of them sleeping in tents on the church grounds. There was a clash yesterday as two self-styled prophets strained to outdo each other in proclaiming the Word, and police were called when one tugged at the beard of the other and smote him with a homemade wooden sword. Souvenir vendors jostled for space in the parking lot and offered such wares as plastic rosaries, vials of "Lourdes water," and even "Bernie Bears," teddy bears garbed in the religious habit worn by St. Bernadette, the young French girl who, in 1858, reported receiving visions of the Virgin and then discovered a miraculous spring. Thousands claim to have been cured at Lourdes ever since.

Befanee Tate says her attention was drawn to the statue initially when she saw a homeless man staring intently at it. Befanee had seen him frequently during the four months she worked as a secretary at the parish office. One day, she decided to approach the statue herself and, after a few minutes of silent reflection, she saw a form materialize and hover above the figure of Bernadette. At first, she said, she refused to believe it was the Virgin Mary, but later she could no longer deny the presence of the Mother of God. Asked whether the apparition had spoken to her, Befanee said she would be making a statement at a later time. Another woman, interviewed after a spell of kneeling before the statue, said she could "feel the presence of the heavenly mother" and felt at peace for the first time in her life.

Father Brennan Burke, parish priest at St. Bernadette's, tersely refused comment on the situation. But the church's pastor, Monsignor Michael O'Flaherty, reached while on a retreat at Monastery in the eastern part of the province, said he would take a wait-and-see attitude to the hubbub surrounding his parish. "I hope and trust that people will comport themselves in a respectful manner until we see what is happening, and I will keep the pilgrims in my prayers until I return."

"Look at them!" Burke stood at the window of his choir school, the Schola Cantorum Sancta Bernadetta, glaring down at the motley crowd of pilgrims, seekers, gawkers, and hawkers. "Where did all these people come from?"

It was the Monday after Monty's return to Halifax, and Monty was waiting for Father Burke to wrap up his workday at the schola, where he taught traditional sacred music to church musicians from around the world. He and Monty were heading out for a draft or two at their local drinking spot, the Midtown Tavern. Monty's wife, Maura, would be joining them later.

"Many of them are well-known characters in the city, Brennan. Habitués of the courts and the wall in front of the library. And the mental health wards. You've given them a new home, Father."

"I've not given them any such thing. It wasn't my image that appeared above the statue, for the love of Christ."

"Is that a backhanded confirmation of the claims, Father, an acknowledgement that there was an image? Should I alert the press?"

"Oh, your bollocks, Montague. This is highly amusing to you, but highly aggravating to me. I can't walk from home to my church or my choir school without becoming part of this carnival of charlatans."

They left the choir school and headed out for the brisk ten-minute walk from the corner of Byrne and Morris streets to the Midtown on Grafton. It was ten minutes mostly uphill on the way there; sometimes it took longer on the way back, even with the downhill advantage.

"An Irishman walks into a bar," Monty said when they arrived at the door.

"And?" Burke prompted him.

"Just stating a fact."

"Two Irishmen walk into a bar. You're an Irishman yourself, yeh gobshite."

"Half."

"All right, a half-arsed Irishman walks into a bar. We're here. Anything else you have to say? No?" Catching the eye of the waiter, Brennan said, "Two draft, Dave, if you please."

"They're already on the table, boys. Saw you coming."

"They say the universe is fine-tuned to support life. Here's the proof," Burke said with a sigh of contentment. "Thank you, David."

They talked sports with the waiter for a few minutes and consumed their first draft with pleasure. But the mood did not last.

"I can't take much more of this bedlam," Burke remarked as he lifted his second glass to his lips. "The self-styled preachers in the churchyard, the hawking of the tawdry souvenirs, the transparently phoney claims of *Befanee* Tate that she's been unjustly dismissed and visited by the Blessed Virgin, the cacophony of noisy gongs and clanging cymbals. What the hell is wrong with people?" He sank half his draft in one go.

Monty had to feel sorry for the beleaguered priest — a man whose approach to religion was a melding of faith and reason, emphasis on the reason; a man who revelled in the complex intellectual gymnastics of the great philosophers; an intellectual who took the rational pathway to the irrational; a man who revered those who had reached the summit of human achievement: Plato, Aristotle, Mozart, Bach,

Newton, Einstein. Now, all he was seeing around him was the irrational, the absurd, the loud and the loony.

"This too shall pass, Father."

"Not soon enough." He signalled Dave for another round and thanked him when it arrived. He picked up his glass and took a mouthful. "I don't want to be associated with this, particularly if . . ."

"If what?"

"Well, nothing's cast in stone yet."

"What are you talking about?"

"There may be a well-known . . . musician coming to visit the choir school, if the fates allow."

"Who?"

"No point in telling you in case it doesn't work out. And this sideshow in our churchyard does nothing to enhance our reputation and our chances of being included on the tour. I'm thinking of disappearing until this blows over." He drained his glass and brought it down hard on the table. "I'm thinking of heading to Antigonish County for a spell in the monastery."

"What?" Monty halted the mouthward motion of his glass and stared at his friend. "You? A monk?"

Then someone else chimed in. "Did I hear you correctly, Father, or am I having a psychotic episode?"

Burke's head jerked up at the sound of the familiar voice. "Ah. The MacNeil."

Maura MacNeil took her place at the table and stared at Burke. Her mild appearance — a sweet face, soft shoulder-length brown hair with a bit of grey, and matching grey eyes — sheathed a sharpness of mind and of tongue.

Dave came by with a tray of draft, took a glass, and raised his eyebrows in inquiry.

"Normally I would," she said, "but I'm wondering what's in the stuff tonight. I'm hearing some crazy talk at this table. But sure, I'll have one. This pair of reprobates will ensure that I'm not drinking alone, so you might as well give us three."

Dave put three down and moved off.

"What did I hear you saying, Father? Please repeat it and I'll try to comprehend it as best I can."

"I'm going to enter the monastery."

"And thereby become the least likely monk in the history of the world."

The idea of the worldly, hard-drinking, sexually-been-there-done-that Burke removing himself from the world and living the life of a monk was inconceivable.

"Time to take Father to the detox," she said. "I wonder how many times that sentence has been uttered in this province, eh? Dad's off to the detox."

"I'll give you another sentence that's been uttered frequently in this province and elsewhere in the world," Burke replied, "and it's a lot shorter and to the point."

"Now, Father, don't be bitter. And don't worry. The monks have done wonders with hard cases before you. You may come back to us boasting of a miraculous cure!"

They did have a rehabilitation centre there, but that was not on Burke's agenda. Monty knew his drinking history well. Burke had a considerable tolerance for booze but could give it up for extended periods without any adverse effects. He liked a drink, certainly. But he was not addicted.

"Whatever it's like in there, it can hardly be worse than what is happening on the grounds of my church these days."

"Now, Brennan," she replied, "life should have taught you this much by now: there is always something worse." And there was. Duty called upon Father Burke before he could flee to the cloistered life.

He and Monty were walking across the churchyard two days after the session at the Midtown.

"Brennan, watch where you're — "

"Christ!" Burke stumbled and landed on his knees, hands flat on the ground. Monty could see his lips moving. A colourful string of curses, without question. He had tripped over a pair of crutches lying in the grass. He batted at the knees of his pants when he got up.

"Leave them, Father. Dirty knees will send the right message to your public; you've been kneeling in prayer at the shrine."

"Feck off."

"Isn't that a fine way for one of my priests to be talking!"

No! His Grace, the Most Reverend Dennis Cronin, Archbishop

of Halifax. But there wasn't a trace of embarrassment on the face of his priest.

"My apologies, Dennis. I allowed myself to be baited by one of my parishioners here, and failed to control my tongue. If you knew him, you'd understand. Your Grace, may I present Monty Collins. Not a bad fellow really, when all is said and done."

"Your Grace, it's an honour to meet you."

"Likewise, Mr. Collins. I have seen you and I know of your legal work, but this is the first time I've had the opportunity to be introduced. What do you think of all this go-ahead?" He made a sweeping gesture with his left arm, indicating the circus that had grown up around the church.

Monty just shook his head.

The archbishop was in his late fifties, tall, broad-shouldered, and handsome, with thick, fair hair going white and shrewd blue eyes behind a pair of stylish glasses. He wore a Roman collar and black shirt under a sports jacket.

"Are you here to take in the festivities, Bishop?" Burke asked him.

"No, I'm here to see you."

"Ah."

"How fortuitous that you should stumble into my path."

"Yes. I am here to serve in any way I can, on my knees or otherwise."

"Good man. Let me ask you this: have you ever heard of Pike Podgis?"

"Say that again?"

"Pike Podgis. Familiar to you at all?"

"No. What is it?"

"You don't know?"

Monty knew, but he was not going to help Burke out. More fun to see him floundering for a connection.

"I know what a pike is," Burke replied, "a long pole with a spearhead on it. You see them on monuments to the Rebellion of '98 in Ireland. That's 1798, Collins. Is that what you're talking about, Bishop? If so, why — "

"No," the bishop said, "it's not a *that*. It's a *he*."

"That's someone's name? Poor soul."

"You may want to reserve your sympathy. He's a talk show host."

"Ah. One of those blathering individuals who gets people all excited on the radio?"

"He used to be on radio. Now he has his own show on CTV. Nationally televised."

"Well, isn't that grand. I don't watch television, except for the odd football game or the World Cup. Or Midnight Mass from St. Peter's of course, Your Grace. So I've never seen this fellow's program."

"That's about to change."

"How's that, now?"

"The *Pike Podgis Show* is coming to town and I want you on it."

"Are you *well*, Dennis?"

"This man intends to run a show about religion and miracles."

"God help us."

"Exactly. Michael O'Flaherty is dying to take part, though he won't admit it. But I don't want him on there. Mike knows his stuff, but this Podgis creature will eat him alive. Do you know Rob Thornhill at Dal?"

"Yes, I've met him. Teaches in the sociology department."

"Well, he's your opponent. He's taking the atheistic position, and you're on for Holy Mother Church."

"This debate, will it be a reasoned, thoughtful — "

"I won't lie to you, Brennan; it will be the verbal equivalent of mud wrestling."

"Then why on earth would we have anything to do with it?"

"Because if we don't, it will look as if we are not willing to defend the faith."

"We defend the faith every day, in our liturgy, our sermons, our service to the poor . . ."

"A week from tonight, nine o'clock, ATV studio on Robie Street."

Burke bowed his head. "As you wish, Your Grace."

"Offer it up, Brennan. Sorry to stick you with this, but it has to be done. You should watch the show tonight to get some idea what it will be like."

"Life is short. I don't want to waste any more time on this than I have to."

"Suit yourself, my lad."

†

Burke might not be willing to lose an hour of the finite time he had left on earth watching the *Pike Podgis Show*, but Monty could not resist. And he had persuaded Maura to share the experience. Monty and Maura had been living apart for several years, but were spending a little more time together these days. So there was nothing unusual about Monty making himself comfortable in the den of the old family home on Dresden Row and calling Maura down to join him when he tuned in to the program for the first time in its six-year history.

"Remind me what it is we're going to be watching?" she asked.

"Perry 'Pike' Podgis, the Cicero of modern times."

"Podgis. I've heard of this clown, but I've never seen him."

"You've been lucky. But your luck is about to run out. As is Brennan Burke's."

"What do you mean?"

"He's going on the show next week."

She looked at Monty as if he had turned back into the toad she knew he really had been all along. "Brennan Burke would no more go on a TV talk show than I would march down Spring Garden Road in a short, sparkly skirt, twirling a baton."

"Bishop's orders. Told him to defend the faith in a debate with a non-believer. It's all because of the claimed Virgin Mary sighting at the church. Pike Podgis is coming to town to do a show on it."

Monty clicked the remote to make sure he was on the right channel. Didn't want to miss a thing. "Have you ever seen a pike, Maura?"

"No. What it is? Something you run through the guts of your enemy, isn't it?"

"Yes. But there's also a fish by that name, a voracious predator with a long snout and a great big mouth full of pointy teeth. They some-times call it a water wolf."

"Sounds lovely."

"Wait till you see this guy."

"I sound like Brennan here, but pour me a pint, would you?" She did a fair imitation of the priest's Irish accent. "I have to fortify meself with drink to get through this."

Monty sprinted up the stairs to the kitchen and returned with two cans of Keith's, which he poured into glasses. He handed one to his wife.

"You've never seen it before either?" she asked him.

"No. The clients talk about it."

"Your criminal clients, I suppose."

"Right. Example: 'Pike had these girls on that had, like, worms in their intestines when they moved here after working as whores in some really hot jungle country. And they showed these worms crawling around after they came out of their shit, and now they're here, and this guy was sitting there with a bag on his head 'cause he's got these worms that are like two feet long and he doesn't want his wife to know, but she probably has them now too because one time he was sick and had an accident in the bed, if you know what I mean, and the wife cleaned the sheets, so she's going to find out about the worms and the whores, and maybe have these worms herself and pass them along to other people, but he can't work up the nerve to tell her.'"

"You're making that up."

"You don't believe in the existence of intestinal parasites? You'll be shocked then to learn that these things abound in certain parts of the world and — "

"I know they exist, but nothing on this earth could compel me to go on television with or without a bag on my head and discuss them in public."

"Well, let's see what else people go on television and discuss in public."

He turned up the volume. Loud, insistent theme music crashed into the room. "And now, Pike Podgis!" This was met by a rhythmic pounding and a chant of "Pike, Pike, Pike!" There was a lot of high-volume prattle about ripped-from-the-headlines issues, fearless debates, run but can't hide, on and on, then viewers saw the head of a man with a thick-lipped mouth crowded with protruding, spiky teeth. The upper part of his head was recessed behind the enormous jaw, and the hair was dark, thin, and pasted to his skull.

"Hey out there! Lots to talk about tonight. Second half of the show we'll have cheerleader moms! Cheerleader moms who kill other cheerleader moms, or their daughters' rivals! Yeah! Girls, girls, girls! But first, pets in nursing homes! Nice idea, right? Herb Sproule says yes, Gladys Morton says no. I say, 'What's that under the bedsheets with Grandpa?'"

There was the sound of howling from the seats in front of the stage, and the camera panned the studio audience. The faces could have been painted by Hieronymus Bosch.

Podgis thrust his jaw at Gladys, a septuagenarian in garish makeup, sitting on his right. He leered at her and asked, "Gladys, whaddya say? What's wrong with Fluffy or Fido in the room with Granny?"

The old lady blinked at the host, then peered out towards the audience. "Nothin' wrong with it until they start doin' unnatural acts with each other, and then it's time for the dog catcher to be called in. Or the gerbil to be put back in the cage. Least, that's what they tell me. After a thorough disinfecting!"

"Ooooo!" Podgis mugged at the camera. "Unnatural acts. Do tell!"

"Well, excuse me for sayin' things that aren't polite, but I've always been one to tell the truth however I see it, and if that upsets some folks, well that's just too bad. There's this one resident we'll call Willie — "

Podgis wheeled on the elderly man at his left. "That's really you, isn't it, Herb? Come on, fess up. Whatever this is, and it ain't gonna be pretty, it's about you, right, Herb?"

"No!" the man squawked. "It's not me! I don't do nothing with dogs!"

"Dogs, eh? You know what they say, Herb. Lie down with dogs, you get up with fleas. I should know." Podgis put his right hand under his left armpit and made a big show of scratching himself, then pulled his hand away, put it up to his nose, and exclaimed, "Peeuuw!" He waited for the guffaws to subside, then continued, "But anyway, let's hear more, Gladys. Herb here said something about dogs. You said something about some guy called Willie. Is there a connection? What do you guys think?" He gestured to the audience and was rewarded with shrieks and wolf whistles.

"Yeah, well, old Willie," Gladys said, "he always says this dog, Bucky, reminds him of the dog he had on the farm when he was a little boy, and so he wants to be alone with his memories. But why he really wants to be alone with Bucky the dog is so he can feel his . . ."

Maura drew her hand across her throat: end it now. Monty pressed the remote and made it go away. They looked at each other. They were both thinking the unthinkable: the Reverend Father Brennan Xavier Burke, B.A. (Fordham), S.T.L. (Pontifical Gregorian), Doctor of Sacred Theology (Angelicum), making an appearance in such an arena.

Monty set the remote on the coffee table. "We'll turn it on again when the local news comes on. I heard that one of my clients had an entourage at the courthouse today. Someone I'm representing on a certificate from Legal Aid. I was still in the courtroom talking to the Crown when they staged a performance for the cameras."

Sure enough, Monty's client made the news as he left the courthouse following his bail hearing. The perp turned towards the camera, giving TV viewers the benefit of his pale but spotty face, patchy facial hair, and missing front tooth. He stuck his tongue out at the cameraman, then stepped back, grabbed his crotch and delivered himself of a string of invective that the broadcaster bleeped out. His hangers-on, male and female, got into the act then, with lots of crotch-grabbing, breast-squeezing, butt-crack-showing, and one incident of full-moon-pulling that was made blurry in the production studio.

"Their mothers must be so proud," Maura remarked.

"Don't get me started on their home life," Monty replied.

"No need."

Monty was about to turn the television off, possibly for all time, when he saw the statue of St. Bernadette and heard yet another story from the site of the claimed apparitions. He expected to see Befanee Tate in her usual pose before the statue: on her knees, gazing over the saint's head, ostensibly ignoring the cameras. But this time it was another girl being interviewed. Tall and slim with long, lustrous dark hair, Jordyn Snider was the latest to have seen the Virgin. Jordyn was decked out in a flowery dress with wide shoulders and a wide white collar. Her eye makeup had been applied with care, and not a hair moved out of place in the wind that blew the reporter's curly locks across her face.

"I saw a beautiful lady," Jordyn said, "floating up over the statue. She was dressed in blue and white, or more like aqua and cream, but that could just be the light. She didn't say anything but smiled down at me. Not just me. Us, everybody here."

"What do you take from this?" the reporter asked. "What do you think it means?"

"I think it means I was meant to be here."

"Will you be joining the pilgrims now?"

"Oh, yes. I never want to leave."

She turned gracefully, offering her profile to the camera, and looked out at the pilgrims assembled in the churchyard. "All these people. It's a beautiful thing."

The camera followed her line of vision. Here came Befanee Tate. A closer angle revealed that Befanee too seemed to have been granted the gift of a wind-proof hairdo. Her dark blue dress was plain but her makeup was more pronounced than in the earlier photos Monty had seen. She was holding a little blond girl by the hand. The child was wearing an ankle-length white dress.

"Befanee," the reporter called out, "are you still having the experience of seeing the Virgin Mary here?"

"Of course!" Befanee avowed. "She has been with me since the beginning. The first day." And not, presumably, with the gatecrasher in the flowered dress. "I am going to read a short statement."

"Is it a message from Mary, Befanee?" the reporter asked.

"Well, it's not like a message from her. I mean, she didn't tell me what to say. It's just . . ." She groped around in her handbag and withdrew a piece of paper, cleared her throat and proceeded to read. "It was the most amazing experience of my life. At first I could just see her and not hear, but then I felt she was communing . . . communicating with me. It was like her voice was inside me, and I knew what she wanted me to do. To love and support the poor. To give whatever I can, to give whatever we can, all of us, to make the poor's life better. And I should spread the word that this is what she wants, that anyone who can give should give."

"Was that it?" the reporter asked.

Befanee blinked and looked down at her paper. "Yeah. Yes. But she said . . . I got the feeling that she will keep coming back. To see me. And maybe give more messages."

The reporter bent down to the little girl and asked her name.

The child looked up at Befanee, who gave her a little nudge. The child said her name was Angelique.

"And why are you here today, Angelique?"

She looked uncertainly at Befanee, then at the ground.

"She's shy," said Befanee, "but she saw the Virgin too. I'm going to bring her here every day after school."

With that, Befanee darted a look at the newcomer, Jordyn. Jordyn directed a brief smile at Angelique, then looked straight at the camera and said, "Excuse me. It's time for me to go and give thanks again. Tomorrow I'm going to give more than that. Some of the children in my neighbourhood are making sparkly tiaras for Mary. They're really cute and . . ." Her voice petered out as she tried perhaps to come up with an adjective appropriate to a gift made specially for the Queen of Heaven. She turned her gaze to the statue of St. Bernadette and walked towards it.

Befanee too returned to her devotions.

Chapter 2

Brennan

Brennan Burke awoke on Wednesday, September 23 and almost immediately regretted coming to consciousness. There was something aggravating about this day, he knew, even before his left brain came fully awake and confirmed that this was the day he had to appear on that man's talk show. Whatever his name was, Pike something. So the evening would be shot. But that did not mean he could not be productive during the day. He had the early Mass at seven thirty, then a rehearsal of the Vivaldi *Gloria* at the choir school, and he was giving a lecture on Aristotle and John Duns Scotus at St. Mary's University in the afternoon. Get up and seize the day.

Several pairs of eyes fastened on Brennan when he emerged from the choir school after the Vivaldi rehearsal. A man charged forward and stood in front of him with an expectant look on his face. The fellow was stocky and balding and had an Alexander Keith's T-shirt stretched across an incipient beer belly. He seemed impervious to the chill in the air. Brennan had no idea what the man expected of him.

"What are you going to say to him, Father?"

"Em, say to whom?"

"That fellow. You know who I mean. Pike Podgis."

"Ah. Him."

"He's got a lot of nerve coming here from Toronto."

"Well, that's his job, I suppose," Brennan replied, coming to the defence of the talk show blatherer. "Something makes news; he makes it bigger news."

"He's coming here to laugh at us in the Maritimes. He thinks he's better than us."

"Well, we know he isn't. Right? What's your name?"

"George. He'll say we make up stories."

"And we do," an older man put in. "We're damn good at it."

Another figure emerged from the multitudes, and he was familiar to Brennan, though Brennan didn't know his name. Like some of the others who had migrated to the churchyard in recent weeks, this fellow was a fixture on the local scene. Brennan had noticed him in front of the library on Spring Garden Road, sometimes panhandling, sometimes just sitting on the stone wall watching the passing show. He had seen the man occasionally near the statue of St. Bernadette even before all this began, and perhaps at the church's lunch program for the disadvantaged people in the area. Here he was now in his long, soiled beige overcoat. He had thick, dishevelled white hair and deep-set blue eyes with crinkles at the corners. He came in Brennan's direction, and Brennan nodded to him.

"Blessings upon you, Father."

"Thank you. Blessings upon you as well. How are you doing?"

"Father, I can't complain. When I look at the hardship around me . . ." He shook his head in sadness.

Here was a man who, as far as Brennan could tell, was jobless, homeless, and likely without a family, and he felt he had nothing to complain about. A bit of a lesson for the rest of us.

"You are Father Burke, if I am not mistaken. Do I have that right?"

"Yes, you do. Brennan Burke. I know I've seen you by the statue. And do you come in to our lunch program?"

"Well, not very often, Father, as much as I appreciate what you have to offer. At that time of day I like to be out on Spring Garden Road. That's when the lunchtime crowds are passing by. I enjoy that."

"I don't know your name," Brennan said. He put his hand out and the two shook.

"I am Ignatius Boyle."

"Well, my middle name is Xavier, so we have a couple of very illustrious Jesuits looking out for us."

"We do, indeed, Father. And they'd better be watching out for you this most unholy night."

"Oh?"

"This man Podgis has me concerned."

"What has you bothered about him, Ignatius?"

"He will try to trip you up."

"No doubt he will."

"He'll demand to know how we Christians can believe in something we can't see, can't touch, can't hear."

"It was ever thus."

"Yes, you're right. And this Podgis fellow is not the only one amongst us who is blind to the truth."

"No, he is not." Brennan's curiosity got the better of him then, and he asked, "Who else are you thinking of when you say that, Ignatius?"

"The young, Father. What kind of education are they getting in today's world? I confess that I did not go far in school myself. My own fault entirely, drinking and carrying on. But while the nuns had me, they managed to teach me reading and writing and 'rithmetic, as they say. Good English, world history, and of course the Catechism. And do you know what? The priests at St. Mary's University, the Jesuits who ran the place back in the day, they let me do a bit of studying there! They let me sit in on some classes. I was, and am, particularly fond of the great philosophers."

"It's wonderful to hear that, Ignatius. Who do you like in philosophy?"

"I'm a great fan of George Berkeley. An Irishman like us. Well, not exactly like us. A Protestant. But still. He was very concerned about abandoned children, was Berkeley, so that is a mark in his favour. His philosophy is easy to attack, I know, but I love him when he says there is 'an omnipresent eternal mind, which knows and comprehends all things, and exhibits them to our view.' I find that beautiful, don't you? I have always been grateful to the Jesuits for giving me so much. I wanted to be a priest, you know, Father, though I'm embarrassed to say so."

"Why embarrassed?"

"Kind of hard to see a priest in Ignatius Boyle as he stands before you today! But, well, I'm sort of a street missionary, I guess you could say. I have taken it upon myself to work with troubled youngsters, children who have lost their way. And no wonder they lose their way, without spiritual direction! I try to impart to them the truth, that they are in the hands — in the mind! — of a loving father. But they don't always listen to an old fellow like me! They listen to their friends, which is natural for kids, but sometimes their friends are the wrong crowd. Then there's trouble. And the boyfriends! I see it every day: sweet young girls throwing their lives away.

"But what am I doing?" There was a touch of humour in the deep blue eyes. "I'm preaching to the choir, so to speak! I must let you be on your way. I wish you the best of luck with that Godless man tonight!"

"Thank you, Ignatius. I'll be seeing you."

The man shambled away, back to the statue of St. Bernadette. An intriguing sort of fellow, without a cent to his name but a mind full of mystic idealism and love for those who were young and adrift. The words of Oscar Wilde came to Brennan's mind: "We are all in the gutter. But some of us are looking at the stars."

"That Podgis isn't fit to tie your shoes!" a short, wide woman shouted to Brennan from across the parking lot. "Give him hell, Father!"

"That's a hell of a way to talk to a priest, Ida!" another woman admonished her.

Well, however it went tonight on the talk show, Brennan knew he had a team of supporters cheering him on.

Monty

It was TV night again on Dresden Row, as Monty and Maura headed downstairs to watch the *Pike Podgis Show* on Wednesday night. Monty cracked open two beer, handed one to Maura, and they sat down side by side in front of the television.

"I've seen white-knuckled passengers on a plane, but never in a comfy chair in front of the tube," he said to her.

"I know, I know, but I just can't imagine it. Burke, of all people, on a freak show like this. Here it comes."

They were treated to the bang-crash-smash theme music, the hyped-up introduction of Pike Podgis as the fearless voice of truth, and something about tonight's guests going at each other's throats, the bloody battle between the God of religion and the god of science. Then Podgis's enormous mouth filled the screen.

"My guests this evening are Father Brennan Burke of St. Bernadette's church here in Halifax, site of the supposedly miraculous visions of the Virgin Mary, and Professor Robert Thornhill, who teaches sociology at Dalhousie University."

Burke was in his black clerical suit with Roman collar. Thornhill was trim and bespectacled with a close-cropped salt and pepper beard; he was dressed in a brown tweed sports jacket and dark green tie.

Podgis leaned towards the professor and thrust his head far into his personal space. "Professor Thornhill, what do you make of all this talk of visions and saints who supposedly do miracle cures?"

"Well, these claims, like the claims of religion generally, cannot be verified by science, so — "

"So. Science! Religion! In mortal combat!"

"No, not necessarily. It's just that science can only — "

Podgis butted in again. "Science geeks have been looking through telescopes and microscopes for donkey's years. It's now 1992 and not one of them's seen God. Am I right, Professor Thornhill?"

Podgis turned to Burke, who reared back as subtly as he could from the giant mouth that was close enough to kiss or devour him. "Way it is, Father. Sorry to tell you."

"It's not surprising that so many scientists are skeptical," Burke agreed. "From something as tiny as a bottom quark to the immensity of the universe with galaxies nine billion light years away from us — "

"Whoa! What are you talking about? Did you say 'bottom quark'? Sure you don't mean 'bottom *quirk*'? Talking dirty to us, Father? That's *next week's* show!"

The audience squealed.

"A quark is a subatomic particle, Mr. Podgis. One of the fundamental constituents of matter. As I was saying, nobody has seen God, or at least recognized Him, through a microscope or a telescope, because God is not a material part of the material universe. 'Heaven cannot hold Him, nor earth sustain.'"

"Well, I haven't picked up my Bible lately, but that verse sounds like a cop-out to me."

"Not the Bible. Poetry. By Christina Rossetti."

"Sounds like a babe. Gimme her phone number after the show. I'm a sensitive nineties kinda guy. I can write poetry. How about this? Roses are red, violets are blue, God don't exist, so I guess it's F you."

This was greeted by uncertain tittering from the audience.

"I guess it is," said Burke.

"Huh?" Podgis's eyes were glued to Burke. The TV man's face betrayed him just for an instant. A hunger for approval, a look of vulnerability. Then it was gone. "Guess what?"

"Guess it's 'F you.' I'd never have taken you for a moral philosopher, Mr. Podgis, but you're right." That needy look again on Podgis's face. "Your poem pretty well sums up where we would be in a Godless universe."

There were a couple of seconds of silence, then Podgis reverted to form. "All right, let's get back on topic. Father Burke. Science and religion. Engaged in eternal combat!"

"No. Science and religion are not opposed to one another. They operate in two different spheres, and they seek to explain two different aspects of reality. Science tells us about the behaviour of matter, about the workings of the universe, about the evolutionary process — "

"Whoa! Did you say evolution? What's your name again? Is it Burke or is it Darwin? Are you saying you believe in evolution?"

Burke looked at the man as if he was a simpleton. "Why would I not? That's how God's creatures came to be. Look at the fossil record. And it may be of interest to remind ourselves of the man whose theories filled a great gap in Darwin's work. Darwin had his theory of natural selection, but there was something missing."

"Oh yeah? Like what? A fossil of a big hairy baboon getting it on with one of the Dallas Cowgirls in the back of a pickup truck?" Podgis grinned. Wolf whistles and the stamping of feet signified the audience's approval of the image. "Is that it?"

There was a little smile on the lips of Robert Thornhill. He knew what was coming, whatever it was.

"What was missing," Burke said, "was an explanation of inheritance. How were traits passed down? Darwin didn't know, because he had not read the work of Gregor Mendel. Mendel had solved the problem in the mid-1800s but his work was not rediscovered until early this century."

"Yeah? So what did this Mendel guy do?" Podgis leaned towards his audience. "Even the name *Gregor Mendel* sounds like a brain. The guy in class who had all the answers, but never got the girl!" The audience giggled at that.

"Right on both counts, Mr. Podgis," Burke said. "Mendel was indeed a brain, a brilliant scientist who is now recognized as the father of genetics. He discovered the *gene*, although he did not give it that name. And he didn't get the girl because he was an Augustinian monk. A priest of the Catholic Church."

First they had heard of it in the audience by the sound of things.

Burke continued, "There are over thirty craters on the moon named after Jesuit scientists. And it was another Catholic priest — he was a mathematician and a scientist — who came up with the Big Bang theory before anybody else. He published a paper on it in 1931. Didn't call it the Big Bang. That was actually a sarcastic name given to it by a very prominent scientist who had not yet accepted it. It took a long time for the rest of the scientific world to catch up, to abandon the idea of a steady-state universe, to accept that there was a big bang nearly fourteen billion years ago, followed by the development of subatomic particles, then the elements and matter, and here we are today."

"He's right," Thornhill agreed with a smile, "we are stardust."

"Or, to put it less kindly," Burke said, "we are thermonuclear waste." This got a laugh from the audience. "Anyway, as I was saying, Monsignor Georges Lemaître of Belgium was way ahead of the pack on this. And much of his work was affirmed with the discovery of cosmic background radiation in the 1960s, which got two scientists the Nobel Prize in physics."

This too was news to Podgis's fans in the audience.

"Is he making it up about these priests?" Podgis demanded of Professor Thornhill.

"Of course not," Thornhill replied, "it's the gospel truth."

Burke looked directly into the camera for the first time and said, "If you want to see a bit of that cosmic microwave radiation for yourself, turn your television dial off the channel, find some 'static,' and those are microwaves still coming in."

"Jesus!" Maura squawked. "He's telling everybody to turn off the show!"

"That'll be the highlight of the evening for him."

But Burke had gamely returned to the debate. "We have a saying in the Church that truth cannot contradict truth. The Pope says theologians have a duty to keep themselves up to date with science. And, if necessary, to change their teaching."

Podgis made his eyes bulge in the direction of the audience and bellowed: "Who knew? Gotta wonder. Are these guys in bed with each other, or what? Or has somebody been paid off? Put a few thousand gold coins in the Vatican coffers and they'll say real nice things about science. Like that we all came from chimps. Even the Virgin Mary. The Virgin Monkey. Is that it?" This was rewarded with shrieking and the pounding of feet by the audience.

"What do you think of them apples, Professor Thornhill, the Church onside with the monkey gang?"

"I'm not surprised. Although there is resistance to the theory of evolution among some biblical fundamentalists, particularly in the U.S., which is lamentable, they are only one segment of the population of religious believers. Those are not the people I am interested in debating. It is much more important to engage those who — "

Podgis cut Thornhill off again and swung around to Burke, who again drew back from his leer.

"How do you know there's a God? Visions from the sky, or what?"

"Signs that have been thoroughly investigated are one way of knowing, yes. But we can use our reason. Aristotle teaches us that — "

"Sounds like you're taking us back to school, Padre. I don't know about you guys — " he jerked his head in the direction of the audience " — but this all sounds like too much work to me! Can you say it in thirty seconds before we go to commercial? I love commercial breaks. I got a personal itch and I get a chance to scratch myself raw during the break." Hoots from the audience. "Here's a question for you, Padre. If God is good — " Podgis made a big show of gouging at his crotch " — why did he create jock itch? Or maybe it's something worse. Thinking about the scrag I was with last night, maybe it's genital warts!"

"Imagine what Brennan — look at him!" Maura exclaimed.

Burke was out of his seat, leaning across Podgis, and offering his hand to Robert Thornhill. Thornhill looked at him uncertainly, took his hand, and shook it. "Rob," Burke said, "it's a shame we couldn't have had our discussion in an atmosphere of civility. Maybe another time." Then Burke took the microphone off his lapel, opened his fingers, let the mike drop to the floor, and walked out.

"*What!?*" Podgis bleated. "You cannot do this to me!" Anger flared in his face, followed by something that looked like panic.

The scene switched from host to audience. Some of the people watched Burke's exit with their mouths hanging open. Some stared straight ahead. Others looked embarrassed.

"Well!" Podgis's voice was heard again. "Looks like he's taking his marbles and going home. Whaddya say, folks? Sore loser?" A rhythmic clapping started up. The camera caught a man standing in the aisle, clapping his hands and trying to provoke a chant. "Loser! Loser!" A few in the audience took it up; others looked away.

The scene switched back to Podgis, who appeared to be enraged. He made a less-than-successful attempt at a grin and turned to Thornhill. "Looks like a knockout for you in the first round, Professor. Exit one sore loser!"

"I think not, Mr. Podgis. There's been no winner and no loser, because there's been no debate. Father Burke was evidently frustrated by — "

"No debate? Let's have one now. You guys out there. Who wants to get up here and debate miracles with Professor Thornhill? Who's gonna come up and get your face on national TV?" Podgis looked into the camera and said, "The war of words continues, right after these messages."

There was a break for commercials and then the camera zoomed in on Father Burke's replacement. The poor devil Podgis brought up to the stage would not have known where or when in history Christ was crucified, let alone what Aristotle taught or what a subatomic particle was. He identified himself as Del Snooks and wasted no time declaiming into the camera that we know God exists because the Bible tells us so, and if that is not good enough for some people they will find out on their deathbed when the fires of hell will be leaping at their feet. *Then* they'll be howling for a miracle.

Rob Thornhill looked as if he would have traded his tenured professorship, and perhaps his first-born child, for a miracle that would get him out of there, but good manners kept him in his seat. He offered a few half-hearted comments about what science looks for in terms of proof but did nothing to add to Del Snooks's self-immolation. That task fell to certain braying members of the audience who took up the argument for a Godless universe with about the same level of intelligence and effect as Snooks was able to muster for a loving creator.

"May I?" Monty picked up the remote and pointed it at the screen.

"Please do," Maura urged him, and the television blinked off.

"Well!" he said, at a loss for anything else to say.

Maura weighed the evidence. "I'd say the 'no' side has it. I was a believer while it was Burke and Thornhill, both of them bearers of the divine spark of intelligence and dignity. But once the show was turned over to Snooks and his antagonists from the audience, and Podgis egging them on . . . well, could any of them be the handiwork of an all-powerful, all-knowing, all-good God? As Burke said of our physical bodies, I say of these poor schmucks in their entirety: thermonuclear waste."

✝

Bruce MacKinnon's cartoon in the *Herald* the next day showed Podgis with a black eye, sprawled on the floor, but clinging to the leg of a departing man: "Baby, please don't go!" And early morning radio hosts and disc jockeys made Podgis the butt of their jokes. Judging from the expression on Podgis's face when Burke walked out on him, Monty figured he was not a man who would enjoy the role of laughingstock.

But the humour was short-lived. Monty heard the news on CBC Radio while driving to work that morning.

> "Halifax residents were shocked this morning to learn that a young woman was found dead on the property of St. Bernadette's church in downtown Halifax in the early hours of the morning. *And* that controversial television personality Perry 'Pike' Podgis has been taken into custody in connection with the death. Hugh Donaldson is on the scene. What can you tell us, Hugh?"

"Bill, all of Byrne Street, the church, choir school, and rectory, are cordoned off today, as police comb the area for evidence in the death of nineteen-year-old Jordyn Snider. Her body was found at the site where some people say the Virgin Mary has appeared in recent weeks. Jordyn's face will be familiar to people following the story of claimed apparitions at the statue of St. Bernadette. Well, now there is blood on the face of the saint, and the churchyard is a crime scene. And if all this was not enough to give people a jolt as they start their day, talk show guerrilla Pike Podgis is in custody and is expected to make an appearance in court this morning. Police won't confirm it, but sources tell CBC News that Podgis is going to be arraigned on a charge of murder.

"Podgis was in town to do a live show on the so-called miracles at the church. Bill, I don't know whether you caught the show last night, but Podgis hosted a debate between an atheist, Professor Rob Thornhill of Dalhousie University, and Father Brennan Burke, priest at St. Bernadette's. It was quite a scene. The cool, cerebral priest, the always-courteous Professor Thornhill, and Pike, the rabid controversialist. Twenty minutes into the show, Father Burke got up and walked out. An enraged Podgis invited a member of the audience to replace him, but it wasn't much of a debate after that. Pike Podgis was his usual inflammatory self. An autopsy will be held later today."

"Thank you, Hugh. We'll check in with you later on to see how things are developing. In other news . . ."

Monty was not interested in other news. A girl killed at St. Bernadette's, and Pike Podgis being questioned — possibly charged — in the murder. Instead of going to the office, he made a detour to St. Bernadette's.

As anticipated, the place had been overrun by police vehicles, television crews, yellow tape, crime scene investigators, and groups of onlookers outside the tape. Some of the pilgrims, preachers, and hawkers of miracle souvenirs were on hand as well, as was Monsignor Michael O'Flaherty. O'Flaherty, Monty knew, had just returned from the peace of a monastic retreat. From cloister to crime scene. It was said of O'Flaherty that, if he had not been called to the priesthood, he would have been a cop. An avid reader of detective fiction, he was occasionally tagged with the moniker Sergeant O'Flaherty. The monsignor was slight of build and white of hair. He spoke in a soft, lilting Irish voice. "Monty! Come round this way!"

Monty skirted the police tape and joined O'Flaherty at the door to the rectory.

"That man Podgis is in jail for the murder of a young girl. And it happened right here!"

"What have you heard, Michael?"

"Just that she was found here on the grounds, the life bled out of her."

"Who found her?"

"I don't know. Somebody called the police, but I don't know who. I was awakened in the middle of the night by the sirens. I got myself dressed, and the police arrived at the door."

"What did they say to you?"

"Oh, they were cagey at first. Said there'd been an incident in the churchyard. Asked me if I knew anything. I guess I had the look of innocence, because they proceeded to ask me whether I'd heard any noises, people about the place, and all that."

If anyone on the planet had the look of innocence, it was the mild, early seventies, sweet-faced Monsignor O'Flaherty. He still had that look, even after a close encounter with the Troubles in Ireland on a recent visit. Violence there, violence here in his own backyard. But Monty stayed focused on the present.

"Was the body still out there?"

"It must have been, but they took it away after doing their investigation of the scene. You can still see the blood on the face of our saint."

"Where's Brennan?"

"Up in his room preparing for his day at the schola. Go on up and see him."

Monty headed inside and took the stairs up to Brennan Burke's room, knocked on the door, and was invited in. Burke was at his desk with a musical score spread out before him, a pencil in his hand, a pair of half-glasses perched on his aquiline nose.

"Did you nab him?" Monty said to Burke.

"Didn't have to."

"Police question you?"

"Yeah."

"What did they want to know?"

"Where I went after walking off the set last night."

"Where'd you go?"

"Where do you think?"

"Midtown?"

"Yes, I stopped in for a couple of draft, then came home."

"Why did they want to know where you went? Are you a suspect?"

"I think I'm in the clear."

"So, what were they after?"

"Wanted to know whether I'd seen Podgis again after the show."

"Why would they think that?"

"Because I did."

"You did what?"

"See him after the show."

"*What?*"

"The gobshite tracked me down at the Midtown and — "

"How did he know to find you there?"

"He's an investigative reporter. Remember?"

"All right. So, what's this about him tracking you down?"

Burke waved a dismissive hand. "Wanted to continue the debate, I guess. Seemed a little perturbed that I left the program."

"I suspect that 'a little perturbed' is not in the typical range of emotions displayed by Podgis. More like frothing at the mouth, right?"

"Yeah, well . . ."

"Well, what?"

"Never mind that."

There was something Burke wasn't telling him, but Monty would get it out of him later. "So did you hear anything last night? Screams or anything like that from the churchyard?"

"No."

"What time did all this ruckus begin?"

"Around half-two in the morning, or just before. Police and

ambulance came roaring in. Then O'Flaherty was at my door, giving me the news."

"Well, there will be plenty of news before this is over. I'm off to court."

"Later."

Two uniformed police officers were standing at the entrance to Byrne Street, where it formed a T intersection with Morris. One officer Monty knew, Truman Beals. If you could picture Otis Redding in a regulation police academy haircut and uniform, that was Truman. And he had the voice too. Before joining the police force, he had done the occasional gig with Monty's blues band, Functus. Beals always prefaced these encounters with "Don't ask me to sing 'Dock of the Bay' again." And the band always agreed, then badgered him to do it anyway, and he always brought the house down with it, sounding uncannily like Redding himself. Of all the compliments Monty had received over his career as a bluesman, it was the one from Beals he treasured most: "Some of your tunes, not all, but some, if I close my eyes, you can almost pass for somebody who's not a blue-eyed little white boy."

They were still quite informal with each other. "Tru, what are you doing? This is an awful way to treat a visitor from Toronto, accusing him of murder. Until now nobody ever had an unkind word to say about Mr. Podgis."

"You talking about the same Podgis? All the unkind words said about him are words that would have my mama scrubbing my mouth out with oven cleaner if I said them. She'd spray the stuff in my mouth, keep it in overnight, and scour it out the next morning with a wire brush, if I said the kind of names that have been used to describe Pike Podgis in this town. And that's before we nailed him for murder."

"So, what's the connection between him and this poor little girl?" Beals shook his head. Either he didn't know yet, or the information was not for public release. "Sex crime?"

"The look of him, if there was sex involved, she would have killed *him*."

"Maybe she tried to."

"If she tried to, too bad she didn't succeed. She might have been awarded a medal, because he pissed so many people off. Looking back at recent shows he did, he would have made enemies out of hookers,

Holocaust survivors, priests, old folks in nursing homes, psychiatrists, cheerleaders, beauty contest losers, college boys, and people with worms in their guts."

"I'm sure you mean persons who host members of the parasite community."

"Yeah. I gotta watch my language or I'll never get to be community liaison person."

"Well, I'll let you go, Truman. You've got work to do."

Chapter 3

Monty

Monty's senior partner, Rowan Stratton, was waiting for him when he arrived at the law office. "Monty, you're on for Podgis."

Monty stood there, trying to absorb the news. The nationally known talk show host was now his client. It should not have come as a surprise, really. His firm, Stratton Sommers, was corporate counsel for the local affiliate of the television network, and Monty was the firm's one and only criminal lawyer. He knew all too well what Podgis was like as a public personality. What in God's name would he be like as a client?

"I don't know whether he's in cells at the courthouse yet," Stratton said, "or still with the police. I just got the call from Brett Bekkers." General manager of the TV station.

"I'll take care of it, Rowan, and fill you in later."

Monty hurried into his office, phoned the police station on Gottingen Street, and was given the information he needed. Podgis had been taken to the cells at the courthouse. Yes, he had spoken to a lawyer earlier that morning. Yes, he had exercised his right to remain silent. Well, not silent, but he had not given a confession to the murder.

Goal number one was to get to Podgis immediately, to make sure he did not exercise that infamous mouth and blow his case apart before he even made it to court for his first appearance. Monty left on foot for the old Victorian courthouse on Spring Garden Road, a one-minute sprint from his office at the corner of Barrington and Salter streets.

Defendants and hangers-on were gathered on the steps of the courthouse, smoking and grousing beneath the carved stone faces in the building's facade. Monty returned the greetings of people he knew outside and inside the courthouse but did not stop to chat. He went straight down the stairs to the cell area in the basement, rang the buzzer, and waited until the massive steel door was opened by one of the sheriffs, Donny MacEachern.

"Don, how's it going?"

"Not too bad, Monty. Never lonely down here."

"No, I'm sure."

"See the Jays last night?"

"Last few innings. Just in time to see the big catch by Devon White. But I had to watch Podgis first."

"Seeing him again today?"

"Yep. Just as soon as you can produce him for me."

MacEachern mouthed the words "lucky you," then, "Okay, go on in, and I'll deliver him to you."

Monty seated himself in one of the tiny meeting rooms for lawyers and clients, and it wasn't long before his client was brought in.

"I'm being railroaded!" Podgis bellowed in greeting.

He plunked himself down on the other side of the table. Podgis was a man who never looked elegant at the best of times. Today he looked like hell, in a garish green track suit, his hair sticking up and his jaw sticking out.

"Good morning, Mr. Podgis. I'm Montague Collins." He opened his briefcase and took out a pen and notepad.

"Did you hear me? I didn't do this. I'm being railroaded."

"You're just a patsy."

"You think this is funny? I don't know you from a hole in the wall, Collins. Brett Bekkers at ATV says your law firm is going to handle it, and that you're the best. You better be, or I want somebody else before this fucking day is out!"

"Settle down, Mr. Podgis. I'm on your side. First things first. Did you say anything to the police — I mean anything at all — about this incident?"

"Do you think I'm stupid? How could I confess to it if I didn't do it?"

"It wouldn't have to be a confession. It could be something you told them that you think would clear you, but in fact — "

"I didn't tell them squat. All I said was I didn't do it, they got the wrong guy, and I demanded to talk to my lawyer. They hooked me up with some guy who told me to keep my mouth shut, and I got to call Bekkers, and he said he'd be getting the station's lawyers to handle it, and that the station would put up bail for me. So get me out of here. This place is a nuthouse, crawling with lowlifes, and it smells like shit. When do I get bail?"

"We'll talk about that in a minute. Your time in here, as aggravating as it may be, is nothing compared to life in prison. So back to first things. Do not talk to anybody. The police obviously. And other inmates. Any one of them could be a jailhouse rat. An informer. The cops will tell you it will go easier for you if you come clean. Come on, clear your conscience; you know you want to. You're not like these other guys, these habitual criminals. You're a prominent man; you know you want to do the right thing. Spare the girl's family a long, drawn-out ordeal. This is the kind of thing the police will put to you to try to get a confession. Don't fall for it."

"I told you. I'm not stupid."

"And don't try to offer them another explanation of what happened, trying to extricate yourself from the murder charge. You never know what other information they have, which, combined with whatever you tell them, could be lethal for you."

"I know, I get it. There's nothing I could tell them about it because I didn't do it."

"They must think they have evidence if they're laying charges against a well-known individual like yourself. They know it will be a very public humiliation for them if they've screwed up. So they must think they have something."

"They have shit all. So set them straight and get me out of here. I mean out of here *now*."

Podgis was agitated, and Monty could smell the sweat oozing out of him. Monty assured his client he would schedule the bail hearing at the earliest opportunity after arraignment, but he stopped short of giving any kind of assurance about the result.

"Why do you think you were picked up for this killing?"

"I was in the wrong place at the wrong time."

"What do you mean? Where did they arrest you?"

"My hotel room. How come you don't know any of this?"

"Because I just got the word that I'm representing you, and I wanted to come down and reassure you that you have counsel, and reassure myself that you hadn't made any incriminating statements."

"Great. We're both reassured. Speaking for myself, I'm on top of the world."

"If the police didn't nab you at or near the scene of the killing, what do you think led them to your hotel room?"

"I have no idea!"

"They took your clothes. What were you wearing when they arrived at the hotel?"

"Duh — the clothes they took!"

"What clothing?"

"The stuff I had on that day."

"What time was this?"

"Three in the morning."

"And you were in street clothes?"

His eyes slid away. Then he said, "I fell asleep with my clothes and shoes on."

"Late night?"

No response.

"You changed into the track suit at the hotel while the police were there."

"Yeah."

"So. You say you didn't do it."

"I'm not just *saying* it. I didn't do it. This is nuts. Something is going on here; somebody is behind this, and I expect you to find out who it is."

"Tell me where you were last night."

"On national TV!"

"You weren't on TV all night. The show ends at ten. Where were you after that?"

"Not out icing young chicks, *capisce?*"

"Well, where? If you have an alibi, the sooner we give notice, the more credible the alibi will be."

"I was with a girl."

"A girl."

"You heard me."

"How old are you, Mr. Podgis?"

"Forty-six."

"How old was this girl?"

"Of age."

"So, would it be more accurate to say you were with a woman?"

"Whatever."

"You're being a bit nonchalant about this, aren't you? Considering she is your alibi for murder?"

"I don't like your attitude, Collins."

"My attitude wins cases, Podgis. Let's get back to you. Are you married?"

"Don't you read the entertainment news in the paper, Collins?"

"No."

"Well, since you don't know anything about me, maybe you should start."

"I'm starting here, today. Are you married?"

"Divorced. Long time ago."

"Are you in a relationship now?"

"I'm between dates."

"I see. What's the name of the person you say you were with last night?" Monty held his pen over his page, ready for the answer.

It took a while. "April."

Monty looked up at his client. "April?"

"Yeah, that's what she said. But I got the impression she was making it up."

"Why would she do that, do you suppose?"

"Stepping out on her boyfriend, maybe. I don't know."

"Okay. April what?"

"No idea."

"Well, where does she work? What does she do?"

"I haven't a clue."

"Come on, Podgis."

"I don't know, I'm telling you."

"She knows your name."

"Well, yeah!"

"So why didn't she introduce herself?"

"She was being coy. Just said, 'Call me April.' I mean, it didn't really matter. I wasn't going to go downtown and apply for a marriage licence."

Monty flipped his pen up in the air and didn't bother to catch it when it came down.

"What's your problem, Collins?"

"It's not my problem. It's your problem, Podgis. You've just given me the worst alibi in the world. Worse than no alibi at all. When someone says, 'I was alone in my room; nobody can vouch for me,' the jury thinks it's at least possible the guy's telling the truth. But saying you were with a woman and being unwilling, or unable, to identify her beyond a first name that is probably made up just comes off sounding like bullshit, doesn't it?"

"Fuck you, Collins! Get me somebody else!"

"Get yourself somebody else."

"I fucking intend to."

"Fine. I'll give you a bit of free advice before I go. Anybody who's any good will give your story just as rough a ride. And if he doesn't, if he or she goes along with the mystery woman as alibi story without nailing it down, and leaves it to the Crown to tear apart, you've lost your case before you even get to the courtroom door."

"All right, all right. If it takes a prick like you to get me out of this, I'll have to hold my nose and go along with it."

"That's better. Now, are you going to persist with this woman story or are we going to drop it and start all over again?"

The cogs were turning inside the reptilian skull. What to do? Did he think he could brazen this out, spin a credible tale about reclining in a lover's boudoir? Or was he going to find a way to back off? *You won't believe me anyway, so forget about it.*

"It's true."

Jesus Christ. He was going to bet the farm on it. Monty almost had to admire the chutzpah.

Almost but not quite. "Were you listening to me? This is not any better than no alibi at all."

"It'll have to do."

"This is a murder charge, Podgis. It carries a sentence of life in prison, with no chance of parole for twenty-five years. Would you care to rethink 'it'll have to do'?"

"What do you want me to do, make up a last name? And a social insurance number?"

"Why didn't you find out anything about her?"

"Because we didn't spend our time sharing our personal histories."

Swept away by a passion stronger than both of them. Monty sat there and tried to think of England, of hockey stats, of the hair-grease stains on the meeting room wall. Anything but Podgis and his choice of female companion cavorting in the buff.

"Well, we're going to have to find her."

"I'll try as soon as you get me out on bail."

"Where did you meet this person?"

"*This person* was in the audience for my show. She hung around after."

"Hung around for what reason?"

"What do you think?"

Monty restrained himself from replying.

"She wanted to get on TV, and . . ." Podgis said, then paused.

"And?"

"And the way to get on TV is to put out for Pike Podgis."

"An honourable calling, being a television personality."

"That's rich, coming from a lawyer!"

Monty did not deign to reply.

"Anyway, that's what happened. Take it or leave it."

"That's what I've been trying to get across to you. It would be better to leave it."

"This girl is my alibi. I'll find her once you get me out of this shit-hole. I'm not going down for this, Collins. I didn't do it."

"What age are we talking about here?"

Podgis's thick lips twisted into a smirk. "Young. But not so young that I'll be facing a stat rape charge after I beat the murder rap."

"If I can get you out on bail, you're going to find out where she is, and who she is. Then you're going to let me do the talking. Understand?"

"What *you* gotta understand is that I'm not going to stay behind

37

bars for something I didn't do. I don't want to hear *if* you get me out on bail. I want my hearing, I want it now, and I want it right. So when are we going to do that?"

"It won't be today. It will be in Supreme Court for a murder charge, not here. But looking ahead to that, you say Brett Bekkers has offered to put up bail for you?"

"Yeah."

"All right. Now tell me: where did this tender love scene take place?"

"I'll fill you in on all that when I track her down."

"Fill me in now."

There was a lot more information Monty needed, including whatever happened when Podgis tracked Brennan Burke down at the tavern after the broadcast. "Where did you go right after the show? Did 'April' accompany you for — "

"I'm getting sick here, Collins. I'm surrounded by scumbags. I have a headache that's just about splitting my skull in two. All I want to do is get out. They told me the arraignment would be at nine thirty. What time is it?"

"They always say that. It will be sometime today. Likely this morning. I'll see you up there. Now I'll go and talk to the Crown, see what they have."

"They don't have jack shit. I didn't do it."

"All right. See you upstairs for the arraignment. You won't enter a plea here. That will happen in Supreme Court, and that's when we'll set up a bail hearing. The onus will be on us to show that you should be released. As I say, it will take a few days to set up."

"So what happens to me till then?" His voice had gone up an octave and several decibels in volume.

"You'll be on remand out at the Halifax County Correctional Centre in Sackville."

Podgis ranted and raved about that, but there was nothing Monty could do. Procedure was procedure. He got up and knocked at the door. The sheriff came and led Podgis back to his cell. Then he returned and headed for the steel door. Monty had always been struck by the enormous key the sheriffs had for the door; if a child were to draw a picture of a jailhouse key, this would be it. Monty thanked Donny MacEachern and went upstairs to the main body of the courthouse.

His first stop was the Crown's office on the second floor. He was told Bill MacEwen was expected any minute, so he waited.

When MacEwen walked in, they exchanged greetings. Then MacEwen said, "Podgis."

"Right."

"Here's the Information."

That was the document formally stating the charge against the client. In this case, Sergeant Vern Doucette of the Halifax Police Department stated that he had reasonable grounds to believe, and did believe, that Perry Calvin Podgis, on or about the twenty-fourth day of September, 1992, at or near Halifax, in the Province of Nova Scotia, did commit first-degree murder on the person of Jordyn Jynette Snider, contrary to section 235(1) of the Criminal Code.

"What can you tell me about the arrest?"

"They picked him up at his hotel room at three o'clock, read him his rights, took him to the station, took his clothes and shoes." MacEwen paused, then, "Blood on the shoes."

Long years of practice enabled Monty to hear this without reacting. He waited for more.

"A witness saw him leaving the scene. Running from the scene, she said. Described his clothing, the clothing the police took."

This was going from bad to worse, but that was the usual trajectory of revelations in Monty's work.

"What time does your witness claim she saw my client?"

"Middle of the night. We don't have the exact time yet."

"And the time of death?"

"The body was discovered — "

"By whom?"

"Guy going home from work as a bartender, cutting through the churchyard around two fifteen. Police and ambulance got there in ten minutes. Medical examiner says she had been dead for an hour and a half, two hours."

"All right. Thanks, Bill."

Podgis was arraigned that afternoon in a courtroom packed to the rafters with reporters and onlookers. He was a very unhappy man, no doubt contemplating his immediate future, which would be spent on remand at the correctional centre with the general population of offenders until — unless — he was successful on his bail application.

The client looked even more spooked when Monty tipped him off about the Crown's evidence: that he had been spotted leaving the scene, and that the police had found blood on his shoes.

"If blood got on my shoes, it wasn't from killing her. It must have been splattered all over the place."

"All over the place where?"

"Where do you think? The churchyard."

"You were there?" Monty practically hissed at him. "You told me you had an alibi."

"I do, Collins. But look where my hotel is. The Halliburton on Morris Street. Less than a minute away from the church."

"Blood didn't fly from the statue of St. Bernadette down Byrne Street and across Morris! If so, it's as miraculous as the bullet that killed Kennedy."

"I'll explain it to you when you get me out."

"Don't hold your breath."

It took over a week before Podgis was granted a bail hearing in the Supreme Court on Upper Water Street. The Crown attorney argued forcefully against letting Podgis out, given that he was charged with murder, and the Crown had a great deal of case law on its side. MacEwen laid out the evidence of Podgis's guilt and argued that this pointed to a likelihood of conviction and therefore a reason for Podgis to flee the jurisdiction if released. But after a four-hour hearing, Monty succeeded in getting him out on a fifty-thousand-dollar recognizance with one surety, that being his employer, and a number of conditions: he was not to leave the jurisdiction, he was to surrender his passport, abide by an eight p.m. curfew, report to the police every Friday, and he was not to have any weapons in his possession.

The television cameras were waiting for the combative talk show host outside the courtroom, and he was true to form. He was being framed, there was a conspiracy against him, there were forces at work that were determined to remove him from the action, silence him for good, bring him down. But he was going to fight this thing. Nobody was going to stop Pike Podgis from getting to the truth. Wait and see. In the meantime, while these farcical charges were making their way through the system, the real killer was out there, and a poor girl's murder was going unsolved. Jordyn Snider's grieving family had his heartfelt sympathy, and he assured them he had not killed their daughter. Monty stayed well out of camera range and slipped away as soon as he had the chance.

†

On the Monday following the bail hearing, Monty arranged to meet his client at the television studio on Robie Street to watch the tape of the September 23 *Pike Podgis Show*, in the hope of spotting the alibi witness. The talk show was even more awful the second time around, but seeing Brennan Burke onstage was more fun this time because Monty could see him building up to a walkout. Summoned to discourse on the divine and the meaning of the universe, he looked instead as if he had been dropped into a steaming pile of excrement crawling with flies. Monty watched Podgis watching the show as the priest got up, dropped the microphone, and left the stage without another glance at his host. Next to him in the studio now, Podgis was livid all over again, his anger palpable.

But lawyer and client had another purpose for watching the detestable program, and that was to identify — or more likely, Monty thought, to select for the first time — the woman who could supposedly provide Podgis with his alibi. The camera panned the audience at regular intervals and whenever there was a particularly loud collective shriek or howl or stomping of hooves, but twenty-five minutes into the show, Monty was none the wiser as to the identity of the all-important alibi witness.

"Where is she, Podgis?"

"I dunno. I didn't see her till after the broadcast, so I haven't a clue where she was sitting."

Of course. The tape rolled on, Podgis stopping it every once in a while in an effort, or a feigned effort, to spot his beloved in the crowd.

"There!" He pointed at someone in a seat near the back of the studio audience, a head turned to the side, with only her white-blond hair and neck visible.

"That's the one, is it?"

"I think so."

"Keep rolling it. See if there's a better shot." But Monty was doubtful. In all likelihood, his client had already gone through the tape, found an unidentifiable blond he could christen "April," and reassured himself that there was no other image of her on the tape. A woman of mystery she was; a woman of mystery she would remain.

"Hold it!" Monty instructed him.

"What for?"

"Go back a bit."

"No, she's not there."

"But somebody else is. Go back and stop it."

Podgis rewound the tape. Reluctantly, Monty thought.

"There!" Monty said.

"What?"

"Jordyn Snider, right there in your audience."

Podgis made a show of peering at the image. "That's her?"

Monty looked at him. "Did you meet her? During, before, or after the show?"

"No! Of course not! I met that blond!"

"The police will find this interesting, to say the least. I assume they came by right after your arrest for a tape of the show. Unedited."

"They came by for all kinds of things. Fuck 'em."

"What kinds of things?"

"They took a tape. They cornered members of the staff here; listened to office tittle-tattle and petty gossip." Podgis said "petty gossip" with an intonation that suggested he was above that sort of thing, when in fact he had built much of his career on it. "They won't find anything."

"Except the murder victim in the room with you hours before her death."

"A studio audience is not a few people gathered in the living room. I don't know any of these people."

"Not even the blond you say you went off with after the lights went down, and before the blood started flying. Before you were spotted leaving the scene of the crime."

"I didn't just *say* I went off with her. And I wasn't leaving the scene of the crime. You really piss me off, Collins."

"Get used to it."

"Stay focused on the evidence here. I showed you my alibi witness. Now what?"

"You tell me."

"You're the lawyer. What are you going to do with this?"

"Oh, I don't know. Maybe run ads in the papers asking the woman who was banging Pike Podgis two weeks ago at the time of the murder to come forward in a blaze of publicity."

"Fuck you, Collins."

Things did not progress much beyond that on the question of the witness. Monty discussed with his client the next major proceeding, the preliminary inquiry. The purpose of the prelim was to determine whether there was enough evidence against the accused to send him to trial. It was something the accused could waive if he chose, but it provided the opportunity to get a good look at the Crown's case and its witnesses, to see the case the defence would have to meet. Podgis demanded that Monty get the hearing scheduled as soon as possible, so he could "get this over with." He did not seem to grasp that this might never be over, that this crime and its punishment could constitute the rest of his life. When Monty left, the alibi was still an open question.

Chapter 4

Brennan

Monsignor Michael O'Flaherty was a little too easygoing about the chaos in St. Bernadette's churchyard, in Father Brennan Burke's opinion. Brennan had succeeded in convincing Michael to clear the tents off the property and put an end to open fires, lowering the risk of the Church's liability for an accident or a conflagration. Michael had been quite happy to arrange accommodation for visiting pilgrims in local convents and hostels. But portable toilets were still on the site, and Brennan had to concede they were a necessary evil, but he made sure they were moved out of sight. Out of his sight, and that of the church and school. He would rather have a slash up against one of the storefronts on Spring Garden Road than resort to one of these public cesspits. But they were there for the duration, he knew.

More to the point, though, Brennan thought the monsignor should make a public statement that there was nothing whatsoever to the claimed sightings, and run the entire circus out of town. Instead, the affable O'Flaherty said he looked on it as a learning experience or, more properly, the opportunity for a bit of teaching about the Church's belief in the occasional — extremely rare — miraculous event. With this in mind, O'Flaherty had scheduled an information session, to be offered outside by the statue of St. Bernadette. He had the children at the choir school make up colourful posters advertising the late-afternoon event, and he was putting the finishing touches on his presentation. Brennan was to be there at Michael's side. Fair play to Michael; Brennan could hardly fault the pastor for wanting his curate along for moral support. But he had also dragooned Brennan into giving a lecture at a time to be announced. Brennan hoped and prayed that something would happen — a miraculous intervention, perhaps — between now and then to get him off the hook.

For now, though, the game was afoot. And Monty Collins was here for the show. They were going to the Athens for a bite to eat afterwards.

"I was hoping Brennan was going to prepare and deliver this lecture, Monty. But he got no farther than filling me in about the song."

"Song?"

"The 'Song of Bernadette.' Not to be confused with the movie of the same name. The Leonard Cohen song. And who was it, Brennan, the woman who wrote it with him?"

"What I heard," Brennan replied, "was that Jennifer Warnes, who sings it so beautifully, had originally been named Bernadette. But all the other children in the family had names beginning with J, and they badgered their parents to stick to that pattern. So the baby's name was changed to Jennifer, after Jennifer Jones, the actress who played Bernadette in the movie. Jennifer Warnes went to Catholic school and wrote an essay about Bernadette. Later, when she was touring with Cohen in France, near Lourdes, she mentioned her interest in Bernadette, and that was the genesis of the song."

"Lovely story, isn't it?" O'Flaherty remarked.

"Yes, it is," Monty agreed.

"But that's the extent of Brennan's contribution. Otherwise, he leaves it to an oul' fella to do all the work. Just when I should be gliding into retirement."

"I'll go out and tell the crowd you're in delicate health, Michael, not up to the task."

"Kind of you, Brennan, but the multitudes are restless. I can't bring myself to disappoint them."

"Disappoint them, Michael. Time they got used to it."

"You know the real reason he doesn't like this stuff, Monty."

"No, I don't understand. Father Burke is usually so co-operative."

"He's not able for it. Too squeamish! He can't bring himself to describe the condition of those who were cured, people with running sores and pus and all the unappetizing manifestations of bodily ailments. That's it, isn't it, Brennan? Fess up, now."

"Well, I . . ."

"You can't talk about some of these cures without making reference to purulent discharges and feces. Can't tell the stories of the illness, the cure, or the test results without getting your hands dirty, my lad."

Brennan made no attempt to hide his distaste. Nobody could ever accuse Brennan Burke of avoiding the pleasures of the body. But he, like other people who had never been sick a day in their lives, wasn't so hot when it came to its afflictions.

"Never mind him, though, Monty. What do you make of all this talk of miracles?"

"I have to confess to you, Mike, that I had never given it any thought before now. I'd hear the word Lourdes and it would go in one ear and out the other. I just assumed . . ."

"Yes? You assumed?"

"Well, that it was a bunch of pious claptrap. But that's without knowing one single solitary thing about it."

"Not exactly the scientific method."

"No, not at all."

"You're not alone. There are a whole lot of people who say they swear by the scientific method, then abandon the empirical method of inquiry when it comes to evaluating claims from, say, Lourdes. They don't read any of the case studies, any of the doctors' reports, and just dismiss it out of hand. They come to a conclusion based on no evidence and no observation.

"And of course there are the conspiracy buffs, who think it's all a gigantic fraud perpetrated by the Church and, presumably, by all those doctors. That would mean that a bunch of doctors, who don't believe in any of this, pretend they do, at the risk of being mocked and derided by their colleagues and having their reputations ruined for good. Why would they do that?"

"I couldn't tell you, Michael."

"Thousands of doctors have looked at thousands of cases over the past hundred and thirty or so years. The standards are extremely rigorous; that's why so many cures, even though medically inexplicable, don't make the final cut as miraculous according to the Church. Contrary to the idea that the Church wants to claim miracles left, right, and centre, it is in fact extremely cautious about these claims. Here we are in 1992, one hundred thirty-four years after St. Bernadette at Lourdes, and only sixty-five cures have been accepted as miraculous. And of course, most people are not cured and that can't be explained either! But it's time to get out there. Will you be joining us, Monty?"

"Wouldn't miss it."

"You might want to stick close to this fella," O'Flaherty said, pointing to Brennan, "in case he gets weak at the knees. It's de Rudder I'm going to be talking about."

"Ah. Maybe I'll have a shot of whiskey before I go, to give me strength."

But no drink was taken, and the three of them left the rectory for the churchyard. It was a spectacular October day, and the leaves were gold and vermillion. The statue of St. Bernadette of Lourdes was surrounded on three sides by evergreen trees. There was about six feet of lawn all around the sculpture, between it and the trees, leaving a sort of living grotto in which people could gather on their feet or on their knees. The statue of the kneeling saint rested on a granite base, so the whole thing was about five feet in height. It depicted the fourteen-year-old Bernadette gazing upwards with her hands together in prayer. The figure was done in white marble but the sculptor had managed to convey the rough fabric of the girl's dress and headscarf. Her round face was realistic, her expression one of awe and reverence. There was still a smear of blood on the saint's face, a vertical slash the width of a finger, as if the murder victim had reached out to grasp the statue while falling. Only the killer would know.

A crowd of up to two hundred people had gathered around and in front of the statue. Monsignor O'Flaherty introduced himself, made some preliminary remarks about Bernadette and her visions of the Virgin, then told the group he would describe one of the sixty-five officially approved miracle cures.

Brennan scanned the crowd. Many of the faces were familiar by now. He saw Befanee Tate, with a circle of admirers. And, was that the boyfriend? What was his name? Brennan had put the run to him on a previous occasion, on the suspicion that he had been soliciting money from regular visitors to the statue of Bernadette. Now there were hundreds of punters to prey upon. Brennan had not had the time or patience to determine what line the young miscreant was using to get people to pay up, but he had the impression it was more than simple panhandling. Whatever it was, it was not going to happen on the grounds of St. Bernadette's church, grounds filled with vulnerable, gullible people. There he was again. Tall, heavy-set, with a pockmarked face and thick dark hair that gave rise to the old word "pompadour." Was he trying to imitate the preachers on American television? Brennan would make a point of hustling him off the property after O'Flaherty had spoken but for now he tuned in to what his pastor was saying.

"This was the case of Pierre de Rudder. This man didn't actually go to Lourdes. He attended a Lourdes shrine in Belgium, so he certainly wasn't subject to any kind of mass hysteria or autosuggestion, the kind of effect critics of Lourdes try to evoke as an explanation of the cures. By the way, if such a phenomenon is at work, why isn't everyone cured? But this whole chimera of 'autosuggestion' is a non-starter anyway. As one of the presidents of the Lourdes Medical Bureau has pointed out, no kind of personal or collective suggestion could cause germs to neutralize each other, could fill in gaps in bones and tissue, rapidly form scars, or cause pus to be absorbed! And the Church refuses point-blank to consider any 'hysterical' or 'neurotic' cases; there has to be an organic, physical problem in the patient. One of the things that particularly astounds the doctors is that bones knit together, severed nerves are rejoined, skin wounds heal and form scar tissue — all of which, according to the laws of biology, take *time*. At Lourdes, they happen in minutes or hours.

"But I've gone off on a tangent. Back to Pierre de Rudder. He broke his leg in a fall. The fracture was so bad that, after the removal of some fragments, there was a gap of over an inch between the bones of his leg, and the lower part of the leg was no longer attached to the top; it swung back and forth in all directions. If that's not enough to make Father Burke weak at the knees, there is also the fact that over the years an abscess formed around the wound, a grotesque running sore that necessitated a change of dressings several times a day. There was nothing the doctors could do for him, and they recommended that the leg be amputated. But de Rudder refused. After suffering through this for eight years, he decided to make a pilgrimage to a statue of Our Lady of Lourdes near the city of Ghent. He took the train to Ghent, then boarded the bus to the shrine. The bus driver complained because the open sore was discharging so much blood and pus onto the seat! Are you still with us, Father?"

"Barely, Monsignor."

There was some soft laughter from those in the crowd who heard his reply.

"Good man. Anyway, Pierre de Rudder got to the shrine and prayed, but not for a cure. He asked Our Lady for the grace to be able to work and support his children, rather than have the family live on charity. Suddenly, he felt a change come over him. He got up and walked, without crutches. Within a few minutes at the shrine his leg bones reunited, his legs were of equal length, and he no longer had a limp. You'll be happy to hear, Father Burke, that the offensive wound had closed.

"De Rudder's doctor, an agnostic, refused to believe what he heard about the healing, so came to see it himself, and later wrote to the Medical Bureau that the cure had been complete and instantaneous, and was absolutely inexplicable. He could not explain how bone had somehow been created to fill in where he himself had removed the fragments. Twenty-eight doctors reviewed the case, and their work was supervised by both Catholics and non-believers. His cure was one of the few that made it through all the hoops to be declared miraculous."

This was met with prolonged applause, and then Michael resumed his spiel.

"There was another cure that I'm sure will make our man Father Burke a little pale on the telling of it. Sister Marie-Marguerite. She had a kidney condition that caused swelling and fluid in her legs. She had blisters that discharged serous fluid. Running sores again, in other words. She was cured, and I know you're wondering what happened to all that fluid. Aren't you, Father?"

"No. I can't say I am, Monsignor. I am content to hear that the

worthy sister was cured. So if there's nothing else you need me for . . ."
Brennan wanted to go to the edge of the crowd and make sure Befanee
Tate's boyfriend was not out there fleecing the weaker members of the
herd.

But his pastor had more to say. "I haven't quite finished with Sister
Marie-Marguerite."

"Ah."

"Her bandages fell off, because they were too big for her legs after
they diminished in size. One would have expected all that fluid to
pour out of the sores in her legs and onto the ground. Right, Father
Burke? But no, there wasn't a drop on the ground, and her linen was
dry and clean. The doctors had to concede that this was a 'material
impossibility,' yet it had happened.

"The case was so outstanding that it attracted the attention of a
prominent neurologist in Amsterdam, Dr. Koster, who reported it
to the Netherlands Psychiatric and Neurological Association in 1952.
Dr. Koster was a Jewish fellow, by the way, not a Catholic, and he
was very impressed with the scrupulous methods employed by the
Lourdes Medical Bureau.

"So, my dear brothers and sisters," O'Flaherty said, addressing the
crowd, "some of the incidents you hear about are well-founded. But
of course most are not. With that in mind, I urge you to think carefully about what you hear, use your common sense, and of course
continue your prayers. That's always good! God bless you, and we'll
see you next time."

The people applauded again, and O'Flaherty wrapped it up.
Brennan said to Monty, "Wait a second. I want to check on somebody out there."

"Who?"

"Just a little gouger who seems to be running a franchise of his
own."

"What do you mean?"

"Not important. Hold on."

Brennan walked briskly to the back of the crowd and looked
around, but the boyfriend of the visionary had vanished from sight.

"All right, let's be off," he said to Collins when he returned to the
statue.

"What's going on?"

50

"I think that one's boyfriend has been taking money off people in the crowd."

"What do you mean? Robbing them? Befanee's boyfriend?"

"Maybe not robbing them. Not at gunpoint or anything. Putting a good face on it, but I don't want it going on here."

"You'd better look into it, Brennan. You don't want Bef and company helping themselves in the guise of helping the poor on your turf."

"I'll take care of it."

"I too will have to embark on some boyfriend research for the Jordyn Snider case. This kind of killing has 'boyfriend' written all over it."

"True enough."

"There's something else I meant to ask you. When I saw you after the news broke about the murder, you mentioned seeing Podgis at the Midtown. What was that all about?"

"He showed up at the bar. Outside, when I was leaving. Started giving out to me about walking off his show."

"What did he say?"

"Just asked who I thought I was, walking out on him."

"And you responded."

"More or less just told him to get out of my way."

"More or less. What time was this?"

"It would have been around half-eleven."

"So he got out of your way eventually. Then what? You walked home?"

"Yeah."

"Did you see where he went?"

"I didn't look back at him. He said he had a date, so maybe he went to his hotel room to freshen up and make himself presentable for the lucky lady. But maybe things didn't go as planned, since he ended up killing — or *allegedly* killing — Jordyn Snider. I don't know how you can stomach the man as a client. A hateful creature like that. This must stretch your 'innocent till proven guilty' principles to the limit. But back to the Midtown confrontation, I paid him no more mind after I left."

"That's what he said? A date?"

"That's what he said."

"Anything more about that?"

"Not really."

"What do you mean 'not really'?"

"I didn't prod him for details."

"And you told this to the police."

"Yes."

"Have they contacted you again?"

"No."

"They will. They'll want you as a Crown witness for the preliminary inquiry and, if things go that far, for the trial."

"Crown witness! The British Crown."

"Well, even though the style of cause is *Regina v. Podgis*, it won't be Her Majesty sailing over on the Royal Yacht *Britannia* in a wig and gown to prosecute the case. She has people who do that sort of thing for her. You are familiar with our Crown prosecutor service, I believe."

Brennan was all too familiar with it, from his own time in the dock. But that was in the past. Now the tables were turned. He could imagine the reaction he would get from his Irish Republican relations in Dublin, if they got word that he might be an informer for the peelers, for the Crown! It did not bear thinking about.

He changed the subject and talked music with Collins until they got to the Athens for their dinner.

Monty

The Crown prosecutor would be busy trying to find out whatever he could about the accused, Pike Podgis. For his part, Monty had to find out whatever he could about the victim, Jordyn Snider. About the people in her life, about other possible suspects. Suspects he could dress up and parade before the jury, figuratively anyway, as people who might really have committed the murder, while poor Pike Podgis had to endure the slings and arrows of a miscarriage of justice. In the usual course of things, the first suspect in a killing of this kind was someone closely associated with the victim: husband, boyfriend, ex-boyfriend.

If there was one part of his job Monty detested, it was knocking on doors interviewing witnesses, or informants, or gossips, about a case. It was something he seldom had to do, but this time it could not be avoided. He had had a brief appointment with Podgis, told him what he was going to do, then hustled Podgis out of the office, so he could get to work. He had to learn more about Jordyn Snider and her circle of acquaintances. It sounded mercenary to put it this way, but the more questionable the background, the bigger the pool of other suspects.

Monty had put it off by starting with her teachers earlier in the day on Tuesday. But none of them seemed to know her well. She had moved to the Fairview area of Halifax just before high school. The principal of the school said the family had lived southwest of the city in Tantallon before that; if Monty did not get anywhere with her acquaintances from age fourteen to nineteen, he might go back to her time in Tantallon. But he hoped that would not be necessary. She had followed a patchwork program of studies in grades ten to twelve, with a few academic courses supplemented by offerings called Contemporary Life Issues and Diversity in Community. She graduated, but barely, with an average of fifty-four. Her highest mark was in Audiovisual Explorations, her lowest in Math Studies. That did not sound like real mathematics to Monty; did they just talk about math and not actually do it? She missed many, many days from school and did not spend much time in conversation with her teachers. She tended to sit in the back of the class when she was there, and fiddle with her hair and makeup. Her parents had never attended any of the parent-teacher nights or other school events, as far as anyone could recall.

Now, on a long street of rental properties in Fairview, just off the Halifax peninsula, Monty was introducing himself to Rhonda Hillier, in the apartment next to that of the Sniders in their building. But Rhonda was not all that forthcoming.

"I know you have a job to do, and you have to act for her killer, but — "

"I represent the person accused of the crime, but of course I believe the police arrested the wrong man. So anything I can learn about Jordyn might, I hope, lead to the real killer. The first place to look, of course, is boyfriends or old boyfriends."

"Oh, I wouldn't know anything about that. I just used to see her go in and out of the building. Didn't really know her."

"Did she seem happy the times you saw her? Or could you tell if anything was bothering her?"

"No, I wouldn't be able to tell one way or the other. Teenagers, you know! There's nothing I can help you with."

"Her family — "

"Hardly ever saw them. I have to go now. Sorry."

It was much the same at the other doors. Nobody had ever seen much of Jordyn or the members of her family. A couple of people mentioned that Jordyn's mother seemed nice, quiet, almost shy. There was an older sister, but she too seemed to come and go without connecting with the other residents of the building. The brother, Jason, was never there; he lived somewhere else.

Finally, at a little one-and-a-half-storey house across from the apartment block, he found someone willing to chat. Lorena Gouthro invited him in for tea and told him she had been living in the house since leaving Cape Breton in 1971, and still dreamed of going home. But here she was, still in Fairview, still missing New Waterford.

"So, Lorena, is there anything you can tell me about Jordyn, the people around her, anything that might help ensure we find who really killed her?"

"I used to be a little concerned about her."

"Oh? Why's that?"

"Nothing definite at all. It's just that I used to see her coming home very late at night. I don't mean night. It was morning, but it would be dark. I'm up at five in the mornings because of medication that I'm on; it conks me out early in the evening, and I wake up early in the morning. But I suppose I shouldn't make too much of the hours Jordyn would keep. She was a teenager, so late nights go with the territory. And I never saw her with a boyfriend, if that's what you'd like to know. I'm sure she dated; she was a very pretty girl. But I don't remember seeing her with a fellow here in the neighbourhood."

"Are you acquainted with the Sniders?"

"Dana, the mother. I see her once in a while at the Bluenose getting groceries, though I haven't seen her to speak to since the murder. I slipped a card under their door, but haven't had a chance to convey my sympathy in person. Poor Dana, she's a very nice person. Always friendly. A bit timid, but she always says hello, asks how I am, cautions me to watch out for the ice on winter days, that sort of thing."

"That's what other people have told me, how quiet Jordyn's mother is. Was, even before this tragedy. Was Jordyn a quiet girl, or . . . ?"

"Wouldn't have to be at her age. She could get out with her friends, blow off some steam, carry on with other young people. But of course I never saw her anywhere but here on the street."

"You said 'blow off steam.' Was there something going on, something that makes you think she might have had to blow off steam?"

"Oh, I have no idea, honestly. I really didn't know the girl. I was just thinking of the mother. It didn't look as if she got out much."

"How about Jordyn's father?"

"Stepfather. He wasn't the fellow that was here when they first moved in. I'll get a nod or a hello from him when I see him, but I've never had a conversation with him."

"Anything else? Can you tell me a bit more about these late homecomings?"

"Just that I'd see her walking home in the wee hours. Not with anybody, and that's why I worried a bit. A young girl alone on a dark street. Probably just coming home from a party. And before you ask, she didn't look as if she was drunk or on drugs. But when I think of it now, it was only on a few occasions. And it was years ago. Not recently at all."

"All right, Lorena. If you think of anything else, I'd appreciate it if you'd give me a call. Here's my card. And thanks for your time today."

"You're welcome, Montague."

†

Monty had not learned much of anything from his neighbourhood survey. There was a stepfather, a timid mother, the daughter walking alone late at night. One might mould those bits of information into a profile of sorts, but there were no concrete details that Monty could use. There were no names, specifically no boyfriends' names. So the next stop would be the police station. The police had their man, as least as they saw things, but they would have looked into the victim's background to see what might have led her to such a violent end. Monty hoped he might get something out of his police contact. If not, he would consider giving the assignment to a private investigator. But if he could tap into work that had already been done, he would begin there.

He picked up the phone and called the police station for Constable Truman Beals. He was out, so Monty left a message and heard back within the hour. They arranged to meet at the Tim Hortons on Spring Garden Road.

"Truman, how's it going?" Monty asked when they were seated with their coffee.

"Not too bad, Monty. You? Been blowing your harp at the Shag lately?"

"Oh, yeah. The usual. You should do a guest performance again sometime soon." Beals's guest appearances with Monty's blues band had become infrequent since Beals joined the cop shop. Too many "persons known to police" in the crowd at the Flying Stag, a.k.a. the Shag.

"I'll think it over. But in the meantime maybe Podgis will do a live show from there, little tribute to his lawyer after you get him off."

"Think I'll get him off?"

"Wouldn't be the first shit bird you got released from captivity."

"Thank you, Truman. That makes me feel really good about myself. I won't have to attend the self-esteem workshop this week."

"Damn. I won't be seeing you there? You're the only one in the whole group who shares with me. I feel a relapse coming on."

"You'll get over it. Couple of nights on the beat, everybody waving and smiling at their local coppers, you'll be your usual fulfilled, empowered self. But, to tide you over till then, here's a chance to help a member of the defence bar help his wrongfully accused client beat the rap. Think how good that will feel."

"I'm armed, white boy. Don't piss me off."

"Busy yourself with your coffee to cover the awkward moment while I try to figure out how to get this conversation to go where I want it to go."

Beals took a leisurely sip of his double-double. Monty did the same.

"All right," Beals said, "what are you after?"

"Jordyn Snider's love life."

"With Podgis, you mean? It didn't last."

"Not with Podgis. As far as I know, they never met."

"They met. It was nasty, brutish, and short. Like him."

"Well, I can't really expect you to be open-minded and inclusive about who else might have done this, Tru. But I know you would have looked into her background, to see how likely she would be to take up with Podgis on the spur of the moment. That would have involved her history with men. And that's what I'm looking for. Her boyfriends."

"Brandon the rapist, you mean? That who you're asking about?"

"Must be. What's the story? Was Jordyn the victim?"

"No. It was another, very young, girl."

"And the guy?"

"Brandon Toth, eighteen years old when this happened two years ago, convicted of sexual assault causing bodily harm. Got eight years."

"Whoa! Must have been bad."

"Oh, yeah."

"So he's still in the pen."

"He'll always be in. Soon as he gets out, he'll do it again. And back inside he goes."

"And this was Jordyn's beau."

"Till they broke up."

"I should hope they broke up. Having your boyfriend sent to jail for raping another girl is one of the leading causes of women ending relationships, according to the latest study in — "

"*He* dumped *her.*"

"Oh. Met somebody new in the showers in the penitentiary?"

"Who the fuck knows? Point is, he's behind bars in Dorchester. So you can't pin the murder on him."

"Yeah, yeah, I know. But maybe she had other suitors drawn from the same pool." *If so they would make very handy scapegoats in the defence of Pike Podgis.*

"I don't know whether she dipped into that pool more than once or not. But I do know Podgis did a show on that peculiar phenomenon."

"On what phenomenon?" Monty asked, trying to sound more casual than he felt.

"On girls who date bad boys. I don't mean guys with fast cars and a dime bag of weed in the glove compartment. I mean guys who have committed rape, aggravated assault, murder. Doesn't hurt their chances of scoring with some of the girls out there. Not a bit. The show was about the lengths these girls will go to in order to keep their psychopathic sweethearts happy. Whoa! Just when I thought I'd heard it all. Of course, Podgis also did a show on 'the things guys will do to get laid.' He'd know! Guy looks like that? What would he have to do to get lucky with a woman? Kill her, I guess."

Monty knew when it was better to keep silent and be thought a fool than to open his mouth and remove all doubt.

Beals smiled and made him an offer. "I'll dub you a copy of the tape of those shows. There are some other dandies on the tape too."

"That won't be necessary."

"Think nothing of it. I'll be happy to. Now, where were we before we got distracted by *Pike Podgis: His Life and Works*?"

"*Jordyn Snider: Her Life and Loves.*"

Beals looked as if he was thinking it over, then said, "Okay. We interviewed one guy she went out with."

"Who?"

"Drew MacLean."

"Did he give you an alibi?"

"He's definitely not a killer."

"So. No alibi."

"He doesn't need one. As I said, not a killer."

"You only see the good in people, Truman. Have you ever arrested anybody?"

"Have you ever had an innocent client?"

"On occasion."

"How about this occasion?"

"How can you look into the sweet face of Perry Calvin Podgis and ask such a question?"

Chapter 5

Brennan

If Brennan thought the appetite for miracles might miraculously disappear from his churchyard, a story in the Wednesday, October 7, edition of the *Herald* suggested otherwise. Miracle fever would not be extinguished any time soon.

New Miracle Claimed in Halifax

Pilgrims camped on the grounds of St. Bernadette's church in Halifax are claiming a new miracle. The church is the site of alleged apparitions of the Virgin Mary. It is also a murder scene, where 19-year-old Jordyn Snider was stabbed to death. But the crowds are still coming. And now, devotees say, a man has been given the miraculous gift of a second language, thanks to the intervention of the Blessed Virgin. Ignatius Boyle, a 56-year-old homeless man, is a well-known figure in front of the library on Spring Garden Road and at the St. Bernadette's statue where the Virgin is said to have appeared. Now Boyle, a unilingual anglophone, is speaking French. People who have known him for years say he has never spoken French before now. Boyle suffered a fall on Morris Street two weeks ago, and was rendered unconscious. He was taken to the Victoria General Hospital early on the morning of September 24 with undetermined head injuries. Befanee Tate, the young woman at the centre of the Mary sightings, says that when Boyle awoke from his coma three days ago, he began speaking to hospital staff in French. He has not spoken a word in English. According to Tate, one of the other pilgrims, a francophone woman from Moncton, New Brunswick, visited Boyle and was able to translate what he said. The New Brunswick woman said there was a religious component to his remarks. The hospital would not give out any information about Boyle's condition, but people have been gathering in the hospital parking lot and keeping a vigil beneath his window. One man said Boyle had acknowledged their presence with a wave and a sign of the cross.

Ignatius Boyle. Hard to forget that name. Brennan recalled meeting him before the infamous Podgis debate and remembered liking the fellow right away. What had Boyle told him? He had not finished school. Sounded as if he'd been on the drink as a young lad, but he had not said anything more than that in explanation of the way his life had turned out. He had been permitted to sit in on some philosophy classes at St. Mary's, thanks to a few sympathetic professors. Brennan was familiar with the philosophy department at the university; the courses were taught in English. There was also the mission Boyle had taken upon himself, to assist the street kids.

Now, what was this? He had been injured and had developed an ability he had never had before. Brennan read the article again. September 24. Did they have that right? That would have been the same early morning the young girl was killed.

There was a knock on his door, and he called, "Come in."

Michael O'Flaherty. "Morning, Brennan. Have you seen the paper?"

"I'm just after seeing it."

"One of us should go and see that poor man, Boyle."

"Certainly. I'll go. I met him a while back."

"Did you now? I've seen him around but, apart from saying hello, I've never met him. Did you notice the night they say he fell and hurt his head?"

"Yes. Same night as the murder. Well, the morning. And not far from here."

"You have to wonder."

"I'll see what I can find out. Though if he really is speaking only French, I won't get much out of him. You're not a French speaker yourself, Michael?"

"Sadly, no, apart from a few little phrases. Much of New Brunswick is French-speaking but not Saint John, where I grew up. I'll see if I can reach Father Cormier. No, wait, he's up in Moncton this week."

"No worries. I'll seek the advice of our friend Collins. He'll be curious about this, to say the least. He has some French but, if he's not up to the task, he'll know someone who is."

Brennan picked up the phone and punched in Collins's number at home. No answer after eight rings. Brennan tried his direct line at the office. Success.

"Hello."

"Monty."

"Yes."

"Have you read this morning's paper?"

"Mmm."

"Have you lost your ability to speak English? It's going around, they tell me."

"Right. Call you back." Click.

Brennan hung up the phone and shrugged.

"What is it?" Michael asked.

"Monty was being a bit odd. Wouldn't speak. But said he'd call me back."

"Maybe he was with a client."

"It's early but he must have been. Maybe seeing someone before court."

"All right, Brennan. I'll leave you to it."

Collins returned the priest's call ten minutes later. "Brennan, sorry about the earlier call."

"*Ego te absolvo*. What's going on?"

"Podgis was in here."

"Fortune smiles on you, my lad."

"Tell me about it."

"Anyway, what I was calling about was the story in the *Herald*. Have you — "

"Oh, yeah. I've seen it."

"Well?"

"Same date as the murder. I have to get in there. I'm hoping they'll let me in to take his statement if he's able."

"His statement."

"As you might imagine, Ignatius Boyle is a person of interest to me, if not to the police."

Of course. That's why Podgis had been in Collins's office so early in the day. Brennan had been thinking, to the extent that he had started to process the information at all, that Ignatius Boyle might have suffered violence at the hands of the same individual who had killed Jordyn Snider. And if that was Pike Podgis, so be it. But now Brennan saw things another way.

"You're going to try to pin this murder on poor Ignatius Boyle. That's what the early morning confab with Podgis was about."

"I'm not going to try to pin it on Boyle if he had nothing to do with it, Brennan. But you have to admit it's a curious set of facts. One of the 'seers' at the apparition site was murdered, and one of the regular pilgrims, Boyle, was found unconscious nearby on the same night."

"I notice you use the passive voice when you say the young one 'was murdered.' But then, what else are you going to say? As for Ignatius, he's not just a regular pilgrim. He was a regular visitor at the churchyard even before this. He's a familiar figure on the streets downtown as well."

"I know, Brennan. He was a client from time to time when I was with Legal Aid."

"For what?"

"I don't remember anything about it. I'd have to look it up."

"He's obviously had a hard life. This is probably not the first time he's been injured. So there's no obvious connection between the girl's murder and Ignatius being found on the street."

"Still, it's something I have to run down in building a defence for my client."

"How can you bear to be in the same room with Podgis?"

"Comes with the territory. But that's neither here nor there. The point is I want to get in there and talk to Boyle if I can."

"So do I."

"What for?"

"To offer a bit of comfort to the man, for one thing. And to see for myself whether he has acquired overnight the ability to speak a second language."

"A miracle."

"A bit early to be talking like that. But the news article said there has been a religious component to his conversation, so I'd like to know what that is all about."

"Well, let's meet at the VG and talk our way in to see him. Wear your collar."

"To help ease your way past the hospital personnel."

"You said it yourself: you want to comfort him."

"And in the process, help you defend Pike Podgis."

"Don't think of it that way, Brennan. Think of your duty to visit the sick."

"All right, all right. Now, do you have somebody who can act as an interpreter in case he really does speak only in French?"

"Monique LeBlanc, one of my law partners."

"Good. See you there in . . . ?"

"Half an hour."

✝

A speculative murmur arose among Ignatius Boyle's supporters gathered in the parking lot of the Victoria General Hospital as Brennan strode by. They obviously recognized him as the priest from St. Bernadette's. He nodded a greeting, but kept going. He did not know any more than they did about Boyle's rumoured acquisition of a second language. Monty Collins and Monique LeBlanc were waiting for him outside the entrance to the massive red-brick hospital. When he reached them, Monty introduced his partner to his priest.

"Father Burke," Monique said, "I have attended some of your

63

concerts. You are a wonderful musician. It's a pleasure to finally meet you."

"The pleasure is mine," he responded. As indeed it was. With big brown eyes and long blond hair, Monique LeBlanc was as pleasing to the eye as she was learned in the law.

"Monique is a native of New Brunswick," Monty told Brennan. "She hardly knew a word of English until she started university. And she is more than happy to act as our interpreter."

The party of three asked at the reception desk for Ignatius Boyle's room number, then proceeded to his room. Boyle lay in bed looking peaceful but tired. He opened his eyes when they entered but showed no sign of recognition.

Brennan took Boyle's right hand in his and held it gently. "Hello, Ignatius. Do you remember me?"

The patient looked at him blankly. Brennan glanced at Monique.

"Bonjour, Monsieur Boyle. Je m'appelle Monique LeBlanc, et je . . ."

That got his attention. Monique told him she would like to speak with him, and she requested his permission to tape the conversation. She drew out her little office Dictaphone and showed it to him. He made no protest, so the lawyers took that as consent, and Monique turned the device on. She started to speak to him again, but he began a soliloquy of his own: *"Notre siècle est fort bizarre . . ."*

The three visitors could all understand that much, and perhaps agree. Our times are indeed bizarre.

Monty signalled to Monique to prompt him again. She spoke to him in French, and they recorded his words: *". . . si par faiblesse je tombe quelquefois qu'aussitôt Votre divin regard purifie mon âme, consumant toutes mes imperfections, comme le feu qui transforme toute chose en lui-même . . ."* His voice trailed off and he smiled, then seemed to drift into sleep.

Monique played the tape back at low volume and listened to the words again. "I notice he uses the polite form of 'you,' that is, '*vous*,' but usually when we pray in French we say '*Tu*,' or 'Thou.' Anyway, what he said was: 'If through frailty I fall sometimes, may Your — or Thy — Divine glance purify my soul immediately, consuming every imperfection — like fire which transforms all things into itself.'"

Monty looked at Brennan, but Brennan simply did not know what to make of the man's intriguing remarks.

Ignatius remained silent for a few minutes, then resumed speaking: *"Toutes nos justices ont des taches à Vos yeux. Je veux donc me revêtir de Votre propre justice et recevoir de Votre amour la possession éternelle de Vous-même."*

Monique again replayed the taped remarks and translated them for her companions: "'All our justice is tarnished in Your sight. It is therefore my desire to be clothed with Your own justice and to receive from Your love the eternal possession of Yourself.'"

Even more intriguing: a discourse on justice, earthly and divine, though not the statement Monty came to get.

Monty looked to the priest in the group for enlightenment. "Would these be his own words or are they from a known prayer?"

"I wish I could tell you but I have no idea."

Ignatius did not respond to the discussion of his words, but looked at his visitors placidly and smiled.

Monty had a couple of questions for Monique: "How's his French?"

"Very good. There's some sophisticated grammar in there, and he has it right."

"What kind of French is he speaking? What accent does he have?"

She laughed. *"Nouvelle-Ecosse!"* Nova Scotian. It was his own voice, albeit in a language he had never spoken in his life before now.

†

The story made the paper again the following day.

COMPARED TO POLISH MYSTIC

Believers are comparing a homeless man in Halifax to a Polish mystic, following his sudden ability to speak French and discuss theological matters he would not normally understand. Ignatius Boyle, 56, is still under observation in the VG Hospital, after waking with a severe headache and language skills he never had in the past. Father Jerzy Zukrowski, priest at St. Catherine's church in Halifax, told this reporter that, if the statements he has heard about are in fact accurate translations of what Boyle said, the situation appears similar to that involving a Polish nun who claimed she had visions of Jesus Christ and the Virgin Mary in the period between the two world wars. Sister Faustina Kowalska "came from a very poor and humble background and she had only three years of schooling," Father Zukrowski explained, "yet she kept a record of her visions, writings which contained very sophisticated and subtle theological ideas. Ideas which were utterly original at the time. Her thoughts were so new that Faustina was suspected of heresy and her work was banned. But years later, the Church examined her writings and found that they contained no theological errors whatsoever. In fact, her idea of 'prevenient grace,' that is, that divine mercy can work on a person without any co-operation from the person's own soul, is now a dogma of Catholic theology. She was way ahead of her time theologically. A person with three years of education could not possibly have come up with this on her own, without divine intervention. Maybe we have a similar case here in Halifax, with Ignatius Boyle." Father Zukrowski cautioned, however, that he himself does not understand French and can only rely on what others have told him about Boyle's pronouncements. The Catholic Church is in the process of considering Sister Faustina for sainthood. "I think she's on the fast track, with Wojtyla (Pope John Paul, from Poland) in the driver's seat," Father Zukrowski said, smiling and holding up his right hand with his fingers crossed. "Maybe if the next Pope's name is O'Malley, Mr. Boyle will have a shot at sainthood too!"

Monty

"If he's a saint, I'm the Easter bunny. Some old bum gets knocked on the head and now instead of bandages he's wearing a halo." Pike Podgis was leaning across Monty's desk, delivering his verdict on the question of the sainthood of Ignatius Boyle. "Now what can we find out about this guy that will help our case?"

"We won't necessarily find out anything that will be of use to us."

"I got a better idea, Collins. We find out everything we can about him and we *make* some of it good for our case. Maybe I should be the lawyer here."

"Many have suffered from the same delusion. Perhaps you should do a show on self-represented litigants and how they fare in the courtroom. And in life in general."

"Okay, okay, so represent me. You can't believe it's a coincidence that this Boyle guy got knocked out the same night and only a few feet away from where the Snider girl was killed."

"It is a striking fact. But it could still be pure coincidence. Ignatius Boyle has been living on the streets for years. Street people frequently meet with violence. But of course we will be looking into it. I'll check into his background, any criminal or psychiatric history he might have."

"Good. Don't let me hold you up." Podgis heaved himself out of the chair and went to the door. He turned to say, "And when you get the dirt, I want to hear about it. Call me." With that, he was gone.

Of course, notwithstanding the casual attitude he had displayed in front of Podgis, Monty was very interested in the timing and location of Ignatius Boyle's misfortune. And he would be doubly interested if whatever happened had resulted in blood in the street near his client's hotel. Monty in fact had every intention of digging into Boyle's background. He did what he had intended to do before being interrupted by Podgis: started some paperwork to obtain information from the hospital about Boyle's admission, and then picked up the phone to call a former colleague at Nova Scotia Legal Aid.

"Bob Mahoney, please. Tell him it's Monty Collins. Is that Cindy?"

"Yes, it's me. How are you, Monty?"

"Great. You?"

"Can't complain. But then, who'd listen if I did? Hold on, I'll get him for you."

A couple of seconds later, Bob Mahoney was on the line. "Hey, Monty, how's it going?"

"The usual craziness."

"You've got a high-profile client, I see."

"Oh yeah."

Mahoney laughed. Monty knew his former colleague could predict exactly what it would be like to represent the abrasive TV man.

"So, what can I do you for?"

"I'm interested in one of my old clients."

"Let me guess. Ignatius Boyle."

"You can be the next psychic on the *Pike Podgis Show* once I get him off."

"Yeah, but for now I'll keep my day job. So what are you looking for?"

"My files for Ignatius. I represented him on a couple of things years ago, but I can't remember what they were. Nothing too outrageous, I don't think, or I wouldn't have forgotten."

"Let me retrieve the files and call you back."

"Great, Bob. Thanks."

Mahoney was on the phone half an hour later with the information. "You had him for a bunch of minor offences in the early 1980s: public drunkenness a couple of times, creating a disturbance, and common assault in 1984."

"Tell me about the assault."

"It was a fight. Three of them were brought in. They got into a tussle over a pack of smokes that one of them had. Nobody was seriously hurt. They all got probation. Then we had him again after you'd been long gone, in 1989. Indecent exposure."

"That doesn't sound like Ignatius."

"No, I didn't think so. Give me a minute to read through the file." Monty waited, thinking of new possibilities concerning Ignatius Boyle if he had a record as a sex offender.

"Here we go," said Mahoney. "A couple of young girls met him on Hollis Street. Not a stitch on him. He started talking to them, and they ran away and called the police."

"Was he, uh, doing anything when the girls approached? Enjoying his own company, so to speak?"

"Could have been. The girls said he had his hand between his legs, but we don't have any more details than that."

"I see."

"His story was that somebody had stolen his clothes. Who knows? He was piss drunk at the time."

"What did he get for that?"

"Again, probation. It was on the low end of the scale, and he had no record of similar offences. In the end, Boyle has never done any jail time."

"That's it for the sex offences?"

"That's it for our files on him, anyway. And I don't imagine he's ever been able to afford a private lawyer. So I'd say that's it. And now he's a saint."

"He wouldn't be the first saint to walk around bare naked. Didn't St. Francis of Assisi throw away all his clothes at some point?"

"I don't know about you, Monty, but we didn't learn that in Catechism class. All the holy men and women were appropriately dressed and decently covered up when the nuns taught me."

"It must have been a rogue nun who let slip the word about St. Francis in the buff. But that's interesting news about Ignatius."

It was with great relief that Monty sank into oblivion that night. Before taking refuge in sleep he had descended far beneath the realms of saints Ignatius and Francis of Assisi. Constable Truman Beals, true to his word, had delivered to Monty's office a copy of a tape containing several episodes of the *Pike Podgis Show*. Monty had zapped through the first few shows, one on ugly and dangerous insects that had allegedly been crossbred by chemical companies known collectively as Big Pesticide and were now amongst us and out of control, and a program in which a leering Podgis told viewers about the items men were buying out of vending machines in certain parts of the Far East, including used panties supposedly worn by schoolgirls. Monty did not even want to think about this or what it said about the men who constituted the market for such items. Next was a show about parents who were in crisis over whether to give up their dangerous pet dogs or snakes in order to regain custody of their kids from Children's Aid. That dilemma was not unknown to Monty's client base; he hit fast-forward. He also skipped over the plight of aging porn stars trying to make a comeback on the nursing home circuit and some of the embarrassing injuries that resulted. Monty didn't hit the play button, or the hard liquor, until "Things Guys Will Do to Get Lucky." Monty recalled with some unease Truman's remark about the lengths to which Podgis himself might go for some success in the crib. The broadcast was a tedious litany of bad disguises, bad hair, and comically phoney French and Italian accents; impostor physicians in soiled white coats and sex therapists with smarmy smiles; and one guy who had invested in a brand-new Cadillac and made the rounds of the bars and modelling agencies in Toronto with cheesy photos and business cards claiming he was a "hospitality agent" for the actor Michael Landon, not realizing Landon had died two weeks before the first payment was due on the Caddie. The show ended with the line "And, of course, rape." Statistics on sex offences in Canada and the U.S.A. scrolled over the screen, and Monty hit fast forward again, until he came to "What Girls Will Do For Guys." It opened with a collage of news clips showing nasty or ratty-looking guys heading in or out of court, each with an entourage of females in his wake.

By the time it was over, Monty had witnessed the story of a woman who had left her husband and houseful of children to marry a psychopathic killer who was in prison for life; a girl who had delivered her younger sister, drugged and undressed, to her boyfriend for his own pleasure; a woman who had tried to hire a hit man to kill her daughter after the daughter blew the whistle on the father of the family for sexually abusing her; and a woman who had murdered her daughter because the woman's boyfriend didn't want the little girl around. And Podgis hadn't made any of this up; these were real cases from the police blotters and the Canadian courts. As his head hit the pillow, Monty prayed that the booze or the mercy of God would save him from nightmares about the human depravity he had just witnessed, courtesy of his client.

Chapter 6

Monty

"How's my case coming along?" It was Podgis, on the phone to Monty at the office Friday morning.

"It's coming. I don't just sit around and ignore my murder cases, Podgis."

"Oh yeah? Well, *I'm* doing a lot of sitting around because I don't have the money to do anything else. I gotta pay rent on a shitty apartment over here in Dartmouth. Can't afford to stay in downtown Halifax. I've only been here a week since my bail hearing, but it feels like a year. Had to take the cheapest place I could find because I'm paying a mortgage on a new condo in Toronto."

"I know, I know. But be thankful for a couple of things. You're out on bail. It could easily have been otherwise. And your employer has you on paid leave till you 'put all this behind you.' You're in luck there."

"It's not luck, Collins. It's principle. You remember it, don't you? Maybe you don't. A man is innocent until proven guilty. So get out there and make sure I'm not found guilty. Through your slackness. I'll ask you again: what's happening with my case?"

"I've been knocking on doors searching for men in Jordyn Snider's life, but I haven't come up with anything we can use. At least not yet. And I haven't received all the disclosure I need from the Crown, but that will come. Blood test results, for instance." No response from Podgis. "How about your alibi witness? Miss April. Any luck tracking her down?"

"Not yet. You know how it is. One-night stands."

"But you told me she wants to get herself on television. How is she going to do that if she doesn't call you? That would be true under the best of circumstances: 'Gotta call Pike, see if he can get me a spot on TV.' But now, her hopes of fame are really dim. If Pike does federal time, April gets no screen time. Right? So why hasn't she called to help you beat the rap?"

"She's scared, you moron. Scared of getting involved in all this."

"Did she tell you that? Did she contact you?"

"No, but even an idiot could figure out why."

"Maybe you should have treated her a little better, Pike. If only you had known she would hold the rest of your life in her hands, you'd have asked for her address so you could send roses."

"The only reason I'm putting up with you, Collins, and taking all this crap off you, is because I assume you'll be just as much of a fucking asshole to the cops and the Crown witnesses who are going to get up and lie about me so they can bring me down."

What kind of an ego thinks the whole world is out to bring him down? But Monty tried to bring things down to earth.

"You still haven't told me where this tryst took place."

"In her car."

"Her car."

"You heard me."

"You were staying at the Halliburton House. Beautiful hotel."

"Yeah. Nice little spot. Really close to the church and all the bullshit going on there. That's why I picked it."

"So why didn't you take your girlfriend to your hotel room? Order in room service? You know, class the evening up a bit for her."

"I didn't want her in my hotel room."

"Why ever not?"

"Might have been hard to get rid of her, if she was on my turf."

Monty tried to imagine a gorgeous young blond in diaphanous

apparel clinging to the squat form of Pike Podgis as he tried manfully to manoeuvre her out the door. The picture did not quite come into focus.

"You're a cad and a bounder, Podgis."

"Fuck off, Collins."

"All right. Let's get back to the car."

It had to be a car, Monty figured. Podgis could hardly claim to have been at the woman's apartment, then turn around and say he had no idea who she was beyond the sobriquet "April." And he could not assert with a straight face that they had shared their love while lying in the grass somewhere in Halifax on the night of September 23 when the temperature was an unseasonably chilly four degrees Celsius. So he had little choice but to say they were in a car.

"Did you take note of the licence number by any chance?"

"I said I was porking her, not arresting her."

"Not, perhaps, a love that will be immortalized by poets down through the ages."

"You know why people get murdered, Collins?"

"Why don't you tell me?"

"I don't know from experience. But I can sympathize with the motives. And one of those motives would be 'This guy really, really pisses me off.' Combine that with 'Kill all the lawyers' and you've got a lethal mix. Am I right?"

"I would advise you not to give voice to your motive theory if you take the stand in your own defence. Not that I would advise you to testify. God forbid. Now, let's get back to your defence. What kind of car was it?"

A little shitbox, Monty predicted. He'd heard it all before.

"Some little shitbox. I don't know what it was. I don't know cars."

"What colour was it?"

Dark.

"Dark. Black, grey, I don't know. It was nighttime."

"Time. Let's talk about that. You were with a woman. You didn't invite her to your place; she didn't invite you to hers. She knows who you are; you don't know who she is. You were bunched up together in her little car. It strikes me that this affair probably didn't last too long. Not a lot of soul-baring conversation before or after. Am I right?"

No answer.

"What was the time frame? What time did you get together, and what time did you say *au revoir*?"

"Eleven thirty or so. We were together for a couple of hours."

"Long time, for the encounter you've described."

If he lived to be a hundred and five, Monty would never put a client on the stand to tell a tale like this. He formed an image of Pike Podgis in the witness box spinning this yarn and then being cross-examined by the Crown prosecutor. What would he look like up there, trying to keep this tissue of lies together? Might as well find out now, and put paid to any illusions on his client's part that he would be able to tough it out in a court of law.

"Here's what we're going to do, Podgis."

"What?"

"You're going to walk me through the whole thing, starting with where you met the woman who would one day become your alibi witness."

"I'll try to ignore your bad attitude, Collins, but I may not be able to."

"Try. Now give me your story."

"I met her at the studio. I told you that."

"Then where did you go?"

"I didn't stick with her then. I made plans to meet up with her later."

"Where did you go before then?"

"Went downtown for a while."

"What for?"

"Nothing. Nothing to do with this. Just kil — whiling away the time till we could meet."

"Why? What was she doing before then?"

"After the show, she had to put in some time with a group of girls she had promised to meet, fill them in about the program, eat some chicken wings, whatever."

"Tell me where you went downtown."

"Walked around."

"Where?"

"Why do I suspect you already know that, Collins?"

"Your confrontation with Brennan Burke outside the Midtown

Tavern didn't take up a lot of your unaccounted-for time on murder night. Though you could start by telling me about that."

"Nothing to tell. I wanted to head downtown, maybe have a drink or two. I had heard it around town that Burke's a lush. Spends a lot of time at the Midtown, so I decided to stop by there."

"Burke is not a lush."

"If you say so."

"He likes a drink from time to time, as a lot of us do."

"Like I said, so I heard."

"What happened?"

"He came out of the bar with a glow on, and I saw him and told him what I thought of him leaving in the middle of my show after he had agreed to participate."

"This was a nice, polite disagreement, was it?"

"I told him what I thought of him."

"What was his response?"

"He was an asshole. I don't see what you get out of hanging around with a prick like him."

"Okay. Where did you finally meet up with April?"

"The waterfront."

"Why the waterfront?"

"She said she liked it down there."

"Whereabouts on the waterfront?"

"Down at the end of Salter Street."

"All right. You've told me. Now you're going to show me. I'll see you on the waterfront one hour from now." Click.

†

Predictably, Podgis kept him waiting. Monty had walked down Salter from his office and was standing at the water's edge, watching a navy frigate move silently past him in the fog on its way out to sea. Still no client, so he walked out on the wharf. The ferry was steaming across from Dartmouth, and something on the deck had attracted a flock of crying seagulls. Finally, he turned and saw his client lumbering towards him from the parking lot. He was encased in a sheepskin-lined bomber jacket with lots of wool trim and a matching hat with the front flipped up. There are many reasons men need wives, Monty reflected, but kept it to himself.

"What are you doing way out there?" Podgis bellowed. "Me and her weren't out on the wharf."

Monty joined him and said, "All right. How did you get here that night?"

"Walked."

"Why didn't she pick you up?"

"She was coming from Clayton Park or someplace. I was downtown. It was easier for me to walk down the hill and meet her here."

"Why here?"

"I told you, she liked it here."

"Liked it here for what?"

"The view, I guess. The harbour. We didn't discuss the beauty of the water and the boats."

"What did you discuss?"

Podgis looked at him with what was almost a leer. It was all Monty could do not to turn away.

"Where exactly did she park?"

Podgis flapped his hand at the lot in general.

"And you walked to the car and got in?"

"Yeah."

"Front or back seat?"

His client looked at him as if he had asked something too indelicate to merit a response.

"Were there other people on the waterfront?"

"I didn't see anybody."

That much was true, since he almost certainly had not been here.

"Now let's get back to the timing. I can't escape the notion that the love scene at which you have hinted would not have taken a couple of hours to consummate."

"Have you gotten punched out much in your life, Collins? I'm not a violent guy usually. I've never killed anybody. Not Jordyn Snider. Not anybody else either. But I feel like beating the shit out of you right here and now. Because you fucking deserve it. You and all the other snotty little rich kids who grow up to be lawyers and sneer at everybody else."

It had been a long, long time since anybody had called Monty a snotty little rich kid. And, given the fact that Podgis had built a career out of sneering at people, Monty could not bring up any feelings of guilt about taking the mickey out of his client.

"Attacking me would be yet another bad idea on your part, Pike. One, it would look very bad for you when you got arrested again. And two, I'd fight back and beat the shit out of *you*. Now let's get back to how I can help you beat the murder charge. We were talking about timing. Without being overly crass, tell me what you and this woman did on the night in question for, what? Two hours?"

"We had some drinks."

"I see. Where did you drink?"

"The car."

"The car again! You wouldn't even take her to a bar and buy her a drink?"

"She had a bottle in the car."

"Bottle of what?"

"Tequila."

Of course.

"So we got into that."

"Glasses?"

"She had a pack of styrofoam cups."

"Not the best date you ever had, I take it?"

"Shows how much you know, pretty boy. Parts of that night *were* the best date I ever had. And I've had my share of good dates. The advantage of being a single man. What this chick lacked in crystal stemware she made up in other areas. As skilled as a French courtesan in some ways."

"Maybe she's been servicing the NATO fleet. That would account for her affinity for the waterfront. Did she charge you?"

"Are we finished here?"

"No, we're not. The two hours, were they all spent here in this spot in the car?"

"Yeah."

"Then what?"

"Then I vamoosed back to the hotel."

"All right. Let's go."

"Go where?"

"We're going to retrace the route you took to the Halliburton."

Podgis headed up to Lower Water Street and turned left. Monty followed and stayed a few paces behind, even though it meant walking at an uncomfortably slow pace. Better than having to make any more conversation with his client. Podgis turned right on Bishop Street and went left almost immediately, cutting between two beautifully restored wooden apartment houses and on into the St. Bernadette's churchyard. Naturally. This would be his explanation for the blood on his shoes. Monty had little doubt that the test results would show it was Jordyn Snider's blood.

Byrne Street was a cul-de-sac that opened onto Morris at the south end but stopped well short of Bishop at the north end. The rectory and church were on the east side of Byrne. The churchyard was a large rectangle of grass with a few stands of shrubs and trees in back of the church and rectory. The statue of St. Bernadette, in its grotto of evergreens, was just behind the two buildings.

As soon as Podgis reached the edge of the churchyard, Monty called to him to stop. He caught up with his client and said, "Is this exactly where you entered the yard?"

"Yeah."

"All right. Carry on."

They started walking again, diagonally across the yard. On their left were the spruce and pine trees partially enclosing the statue. Monty knew from the Crown's evidence that Jordyn Snider's body had been found in the grass between the statue and the trees, out of sight of the back windows of the rectory and the church. Now Monty and the man accused of the murder skirted the outer side of the trees on their way through the yard. A few of the Marian tourists stood around in the fog, making desultory conversation.

Again, Monty asked his client to stop. "What did you see when you walked through here?"

"Nothing. No people."

"No dead girl lying on the ground."

"I didn't see any dead girl. I was just walking home, minding my own business."

"Is this where you were in relation to the trees?"

"Yeah, right here. So where was the girl's body found?"

"On the other side of the trees. In between them and the statue. Out of view."

"Okay."

"So the closest you would have been to the murder scene was twelve to fifteen feet. Yet you had blood on your shoes."

"Yeah, which must mean I walked through blood."

"Which must mean, if Jordyn's body was not here, it was moved from here after she shed some blood."

There was also the streak of blood on the face of the statue. It was possible that it had been the killer and not the victim who reached out to the face of the saint, but Monty had no way of knowing.

"So that's what we're hoping, that the body had been moved. That's what I'll be looking for in the evidence from the police investigation and the medical examiner's report. If there is no evidence the body was moved, we cannot explain away the blood." The client was uncharacteristically silent. "Right?"

"Yeah. Right. Obviously. I didn't see any body, and I didn't see any blood. But it got on my shoes. So it was here, and she wasn't. No matter what their evidence shows."

"Their evidence will be evidence of the facts. We had better hope it is in our favour."

"It will be."

"You sound very confident."

"I am. I was here."

"Yes. You were."

Monty paused and looked around, then ahead towards Byrne Street.

"The police of course know you were here because they have a witness who says she saw you running from the scene. Running down Byrne Street and out onto Morris."

"I wasn't *running from the scene.* I was walking fast because I was cold. After being in an overheated car with an overheated young female, I nearly froze my ass off when I got out. So I was gum-booting it across the church property to get to my hotel."

They started moving again, making their way around the pilgrims and oddballs occupying the site. One man was walking around in circles carrying a foam rubber tablet with the Ten Commandments on it; every time he stopped by someone, he pointed at the tablet and thundered, "Thou shalt not kill!"

The accused killer and his lawyer ignored him, and Monty stopped when they had reached the corner of Byrne and Morris.

"All right. Now what I'm going to do is run an ad in the *Herald* and the *Daily News*, and anywhere else I can think to run it, looking for a young blond woman who . . . well, I won't say 'was with Pike Podgis.' I'll say 'was in a small, dark car parked on the Halifax waterfront in the late night or early morning hours of September twenty-third to twenty-fourth.' I'll ask her to come forward to assist in a matter of great urgency. And I'll give my office phone number. Do you think that will bring results?"

Podgis looked miserable. Monty almost felt sorry for him.

"I don't know," Podgis said.

"Should I use the name April?"

"Why? If she sees the ad, she'll know it's her anyway."

"If we use the name April and that is her real name, or if she goes by that name for some purposes, that increases the chances that some-body else will recognize who we are looking for and call April about it. Or call us. Right?"

"Yeah," Podgis said without enthusiasm. "Right."

Monty stood there and looked at his client, who took to staring defiantly into Monty's eyes. Monty replayed the whole saga in his head, then said, "Mr. Podgis, I told you when this all began that a bad alibi is worse than no alibi. And your story just may be the worst alibi story I have ever heard."

The client turned on his heel and stomped away.

The worst alibi story? Almost, but not quite. Monty had heard worse in his twenty-plus years in the courtroom: for example, the young boyfriend and girlfriend who both claimed to have been in their respective doctors' offices, being diagnosed with cancer on the same day, and therefore were nowhere near the murder scene at the given time. But the story spun out by Podgis, if not the very worst, was highly implausible and smacked of desperation. He should have claimed he was in his hotel room alone. Reading, working, watching television. Nobody saw or heard him; still, nobody could prove he wasn't in there. Once he committed himself to this unlikely tale of romance by the sea, with a person he could not identify, he was forced to pile on one unlikely fabrication after another. No identifi-able address, no bed, no grassy field, so a car. Again, unidentifiable. Then he had to place the car somewhere. And he had to account for those two hours in the car, after their passion was sated. And, finally, he had to explain why he was at or very near the murder scene when the body would still have been warm, only to emerge with blood on his shoes.

It was so bad, especially coming from someone who had the capacity to know better, that Monty was almost ready to give it the tiniest benefit of the doubt. There were countless real-life stories, tales of blunders and stupid decisions and screw-ups, even bizarre coincidences, that were almost unbelievable and yet were true. Could this be one of those instances? As obnoxious and crude as he was, Podgis was not without intelligence. He had enjoyed a long and successful career, at least on his terms, in television. Before becoming a talk show host, he had been an investigative reporter. Innocent or guilty, he could have made up something far better than this to stave off a murder conviction. Monty also had to acknowledge some of the idiotic things he himself had done, and scrapes he had got into, when he was young and trying to get laid. Podgis was a lot older than that and should have been wiser, but nobody would call him a handsome or a charming man. Were these the lengths he would go to for a night of female companionship? Was it possible that this ridiculous story was true?

✝

Ridiculous or not, Monty dutifully wrote out his "Cynically Seeking April" ad and took it to his secretary, Tina, with instructions to submit it to the newspapers.

Then he returned to his table and opened the file. The first item on his checklist was the question of whether or not Jordyn Snider had been moved during the attack — whether the struggle with her killer had taken place all in one spot or whether it had begun outside the stand of trees and ended on the inside next to the statue. In the alternative, had her body been moved after death? He hoped he could find this documented one way or the other in the records generated so far in the case. If he had to ask, that would alert the prosecution to one of the key elements of his defence. He wanted to postpone that as long as possible.

He knew he had not registered anything about movement of the body, but that did not mean there was no reference to it. He may have glossed over it, though it was unlikely, or it may have been there between the lines and he had not drawn the inference. The Crown had delivered only scanty information so far, but the rest would come. The defence was entitled to full disclosure of the Crown's evidence by law. And the real presentation of the evidence, with witnesses on the stand and the chance to examine those witnesses, would come with the preliminary hearing in three months' time. For now, he had the statements from the officers who responded to the call and from the arresting officers, the "will-say" statements from the woman who had seen Podgis leaving the scene and the man who had discovered the body. Monty also had the autopsy report.

The autopsy showed without doubt that Jordyn Snider died from loss of blood from two stab wounds to the chest, one directly to the heart. There was a third, superficial, knife wound to the side of her neck. The murder weapon had been removed and not yet found. She had sustained a blow to her face. There were no cuts on her hands, no traces of blood or minute pieces of skin under her fingernails, for the simple reason that it had been an unusually cold night and she had been wearing gloves. There was blood on her gloves, but there were no tissue samples to compare with those taken from the suspect.

Monty glanced over the "will-say" statement by Ward Sanford, who had found the body while walking across the churchyard at two fifteen in the morning on his way home from work as a bartender downtown. Jordyn was lying face up and it was obvious there were no signs of life; he stayed several feet away and did not touch her before making a dash for the nearest pay phone and calling the police. The other witness statement was from Betty Isenor, who was at home in the big wooden apartment building at the corner of Morris and Hollis streets, when she was awakened by noise outside her window. She described seeing Pike Podgis, whom she recognized on sight from his television show, running from St. Bernadette's churchyard, down Byrne Street, and up Morris to his hotel. She said Podgis kept looking behind and around him. Although she had not yet known a crime had been committed, something in Podgis's manner frightened her, and she stayed out of sight behind her curtains. She went back to bed but was awakened again soon afterwards by the sirens of the police vehicles and ambulance converging on the church property.

She dressed quickly and went out to find one of the police officers; she told the cop what she had seen.

The arresting officers described finding Podgis in his room at the Halliburton House Inn on Morris Street, which was located minutes away from St. Bernadette's. They read him his rights as soon as he answered their knock on his door, but Podgis had not availed himself of the right to remain silent. When had he ever? He had been vocal in his denial of involvement in the killing. But the police had their witness statement and his clothing, which matched what the witness described and which he was still wearing when they arrived. And they had blood on his shoes.

There was nothing in the record about the victim being moved. That may have been because the question never arose, because she had been attacked and killed in the spot where she was found. But at least there was nothing definitive to preclude making the argument. And there was nothing to say one way or the other whether blood had been spattered for any distance beyond the scene of the killing.

Chapter 7

Monty

Monty had nearly forgotten that Befanee Tate had another claim to fame besides her status as a visionary. But on the first Monday of November his secretary, Tina, gave him the rundown of the week ahead and reminded him that he had scheduled a discovery examination in Tate's wrongful-dismissal suit against the church. Discovery was the opportunity for each party to question the other on oath before trial. He would question Befanee Tate; at some point later her lawyer would question Monsignor O'Flaherty and Father Burke. The fact that discovery was proceeding so expeditiously was an indication of how simple — and, from Monty's perspective, how frivolous — the lawsuit was. Monty considered the whole thing a waste of time and a waste of the church's money. Tate should have taken the month's pay she had been offered. Instead, she apparently hoped to milk the claim for all she could get, including damages for mental anguish. Not a chance.

He made a call to St. Bernadette's to let the priests know that the discovery was on but they were not obligated to attend. Burke was out but O'Flaherty was there, so Monty filled him in. The monsignor, however, had something else on his mind.

"You'll never guess who's coming here, Monty."

"Who?"

"A man from the Vatican!"

"Oh? What's the occasion?"

"He's coming to conduct an investigation into the sightings!"

"No! They're taking this seriously? I have to say I'm a little surprised."

"That makes two of us. These matters are normally investigated by the local bishop first, before any Vatican involvement, but I haven't heard a word about Bishop Cronin looking into it."

"Maybe he's hiding in his office with the phone off the hook."

"Could be."

"So what will happen now?"

"The Church has very elaborate procedures to evaluate claims of this nature, Monty. The man coming from Rome today is an expert. He will carefully consider all the facts and make his report to headquarters, so to speak, and then we'll have our answer."

"What do you know about the fellow who's coming?"

"I don't know his name. All I know is that he is with the Congregation for the Causes of Saints. That's the office that looks into events like this one. He's going to be our guest, or so I would assume, and I'm looking forward to assisting him in his inquiries. I'm going to be out when he's scheduled to arrive, but Brennan will be greeting him and making him feel at home. Which is good in case his English is not up to snuff. Brennan speaks Italian, as you know. Though I wouldn't be surprised if the two of them will be conducting their meetings in Latin!"

"So what do you make of this whole thing yourself, Michael?"

"Personally, I think — or I did think — it highly unlikely that this is a genuine apparition. But I'm not the expert from Rome. And it's often been the case that the people chosen to receive these visitations seem to be the least likely people to be chosen for divine favour. And maybe that's the point. To humble the rest of us!"

"Maybe so. And nobody can judge it if nobody else can see it. Or hear the messages."

"Well, of course that is one of the biggest problems with these things. Even if there is a genuine revelation, the person tries to describe it in his or her own terms. So you end up with layers of subjective interpretation, human interpretation, which you always have to treat with caution. You'd be familiar with this: an eyewitness to a crime gives evidence of what he thinks he must have seen, what he assumes must have happened. Ain't necessarily so."

"You can say that again, Mike."

"That's why St. Bernadette is so highly regarded by the Church's experts. She didn't embroider her account with any interpretations of her own. When the local monsignor asked her, 'Do you expect me to believe you saw the Virgin Mary?' she told him she wasn't there to make him believe; she was there to report what she had seen. And of course when she dug in the ground where she had been instructed to and found the spring of water, well, that was a physical fact. The spring was there and has been, since 1858."

"You're not holding your breath for the finding of a miraculous spring of water in this case, I take it, Michael."

"I expect to be drinking from the kitchen tap well into the foreseeable future, Monty."

"How long do you expect the man from Rome to be in town?"

"Could be quite a while. It's a painstaking process. I've read volumes of material in some of these investigations in the past. It could take days. Maybe weeks. I sent out a press release first thing this morning."

When Monty got off the phone, Tina came in with an envelope. The Crown had just delivered the blood-test results from the lab. Monty did not so much as blink when he read that the blood on his client's shoes matched that of the murder victim. He had never thought otherwise. Nor had Podgis, judging by his subdued reaction when Monty called him with the results.

Brennan

Brennan heard a car pull up outside the parish house, and he walked over to the window. He recognized a young priest from St. Mary's Basilica at the wheel, in conversation with someone in the passenger seat. The passenger emerged a couple of seconds later, a carry-on bag draped over his left arm. He was wearing a well-cut black overcoat and a fedora. The Vatican's man. Brennan decided to get out there and welcome him before he was spotted by the housekeeper, Mrs. Kelly. Greeting the visitor himself would save time and a lot of pointless blather.

He opened the door, and a clump of reporters and two television crews appeared as if out of nowhere. They called out to him.

"Father Burke, are you going to introduce your investigator?"

"Could you give us a statement, Fathers?"

"Buongiorno, Padre! Una statement, *per favore?"*

Brennan ignored them, as did the man from Rome. Brennan ushered his guest inside.

"Welcome to Nova Scotia, Father," Brennan said, extending his hand.

The priest from Rome was around Brennan's age, maybe a little older, mid-fifties, with a red-tinged face and bright blue eyes that radiated intelligence. He shook Brennan's hand and said, "Thank you. It's my first time here. Lovely place."

Brennan laughed. "You didn't grow up in the streets of Rome, Father."

"Nor did you. Maybe we kicked a football at each other in Dublin back in the day."

"Could be."

"Donal O'Sullivan. Glasnevin."

"Brennan Burke. Mountjoy Street, and then Rathmines."

"There you go."

"Come in, Donal. How was your flight?"

"Long."

They entered the rectory and went into the priests' office. O'Sullivan unbuttoned his coat, removed his fedora, and placed it on the desk.

He looked around the office and said, "Who's this Tate girl, Brennan?"

"Former secretary here in the parochial house. We had to let her go after four months. Not up to the job."

"Not a friendly parting, then."

"She's suing us."

"Is she now."

O'Sullivan's eyes scanned the small office and came to rest on

O'Flaherty's film poster of Jennifer Jones in the old classic *The Song of Bernadette*. He said, "Lovely girl, Jennifer Jones."

"Yes."

"Won the Oscar for her portrayal of the saint, if I'm not mistaken."

"She did. O'Flaherty is quite talkative on the subject."

"I see. So, Brennan" — he picked up his fedora from the desk — "where do you drink?"

"Let's go. Out the back way."

Monty

The discovery examination in the Tate wrongful dismissal suit got underway on Thursday, November 5. The parties had provided each other with the documents they would be relying on, bound and separated by numbered tabs. Tate's lawyer had requested, and Monty had agreed, that there would be no questions about the claimed sightings of the Virgin Mary. Monty would not need that to make the plaintiff's case fall apart.

So, on Thursday afternoon, Befanee Tate and her lawyer, Louise Underhill, were seated at the table in the boardroom of Stratton Sommers with a court reporter on hand to record and transcribe Tate's sworn testimony. After going through the basic identifying information, Monty wasted no time in getting to the subject of Tate's employment.

"For the record here, what date did you start work at St. Bernadette's?"

"May the fourth."

"Of this year."

"Yeah."

"How did you come to be working in the office at St. Bernadette's?"

"They had an ad in the paper for a secretary."

"So what did you do? Send in an application form? A resume of your qualifications?"

"No, I just, like, showed up and asked for the job."

"Who did you talk to?"

"Monsignor. He's the older guy there."

"Monsignor O'Flaherty?"

"Yeah."

"Tell us about that."

"He invited me in and asked me if I wanted a cup of tea, but I was too nervous about what I was going to say, so I said 'No, thank you' about the tea. And then he asked me some questions."

"What kind of questions?"

"About what school I went to and what jobs I did."

"Did you have any secretarial experience?"

"Not . . . well, sort of."

"How do you mean?"

"I did filing and stuff at my other job."

"Which was where?"

"Nova Sun Glow."

"What's that?"

"A tanning salon."

"I see. What all did you do there?"

"I was an attendant, and I brought the people into the tanning rooms, and I cleaned them."

"Cleaned the . . ."

"Rooms and the equipment. But sometimes I also typed some stuff. And put papers in the files."

"So you told all this to Monsignor O'Flaherty?"

"Yeah."

"And what did he say?"

"He said there was a bunch of other people trying out for the job, but I had a good chance too. He was going to let me know."

"Did anyone else interview you at the church office, besides Monsignor O'Flaherty?"

"No."

"Did you meet Father Burke when you were applying for the job?"

She made a face that suggested she might have been quite happy never to have met him. "No. He was away somewheres."

"And had you been hired by the time he came back?"

"Yeah, I was there."

"Was it your job to greet visitors to the rectory? Were you a receptionist as well as a secretary?"

"No, I never saw anybody. They had people go into the living room."

That would explain why Monty had caught only rare glimpses

89

of her when visiting the priests at the rectory; he had been in the living room, the kitchen, and the priests' rooms but never, as far as he remembered, in the office.

"Who did you do most of your work for, Monsignor O'Flaherty or Father Burke?"

"At first it was Monsignor. *He* was really nice."

"And later?"

"Burke too."

"Anyone else?"

"When they went to Ireland for most of the summer, it was Father Drohan. That was the guy that filled in."

"That would have been early July to mid-August?"

"Yeah. It was good then."

"Good because?"

"I didn't have Burke lording it over me."

"How did he do that?"

"He would bark questions at me. 'Where were you yesterday?' And I'd tell him I was sick. And he'd say, like, 'What was the matter with you?' And I'd say it was personal. Then he'd order me to tell him what I was doing all morning, or who I was on the phone with. And he'd be like, 'Nobody has to be called on the phone here. So stay off the phone and get those letters done.' And there was one day when I told him I couldn't type for a long time. I had to take breaks. And he just said, 'Do your job,' and walked out. That's the way he'd talk to me. And he never called me by my name."

"What did he call you?"

"Miss Tate."

"But that is your name . . ."

"He never called me Befanee."

"Ms. Tate. I'm going to show you a letter. Please turn to the plaintiff's list of documents, tab five. Do you have it?"

"Yeah."

"We'll mark it Exhibit One. Do you remember this letter?"

"Yeah, I guess so."

"Please take the time to read it over again." She bent over it, her lips moving along with the words. "Does anything strike you about that letter?"

"What do you mean?"

"Do you see anything wrong in it?"

"Like what?"

"Any words spelt wrong?"

"I don't know. I don't think so. Except that name. The singer. I just guessed."

"You guessed that was how the opera singer's name was spelt?"

"He dictated it. So, like, how was I supposed to know how to spell her name?"

"Who dictated it?"

"Father Burke."

"He didn't tell you how to spell it?"

"He told me to look it up."

"And did you?"

"I didn't know where."

"Uh-huh."

"I couldn't look it up because I didn't know how to spell it."

"I see. Why didn't you just ask him?"

"Because he left. So I just guessed at it."

"Right. And you don't see any other mistakes?"

Silence

"Spelling? Punctuation?"

"What's wrong with it?"

If English was her first language, Befanee, like so many others these days, was not even unilingual.

But, for the record, he had better check.

"What is your first language, Ms. Tate?"

"First language? I only know, like, one."

No, you don't.

"What is your education level?"

"Um, high?"

"How far did you go in school? What grade did you attain?"

"You mean, like, pass?"

"Yes."

"Grade twelve."

"You graduated from high school?"

"Of course!"

"Did you take any English courses in high school?"

"Yeah. We had to."

"How about before that? In elementary school or junior high?"

"Yeah."

"How did you find the English courses you took in school?"

"They were easy."

In Monty's opinion, it was time for the ministers of education from all across the continent to be in the witness seat somewhere, to be grilled about the easy English courses that allowed people to graduate from high school sounding like Befanee Tate.

"Do you have any post-secondary education or training? Any college program or course?"

"I took business at community college. Or I started to, but I didn't need it, because I got the job at Nova Sun Glow."

"All right. So you would occasionally prepare letters for Father Burke."

"Yeah. Like I said, he was away when I started in the office. New York or somewheres. When he came back it was really hard to work because he didn't write things out for me like Monsignor O'Flaherty did. Father Burke just dictated it all out loud, and I was supposed to figure out how to spell everything! Then he'd blame *me* if it was wrong."

"So, returning to the letter to the opera singer, Kiri Te Kanawa. You sent it off like that? The way we see it here?"

"Yeah. I had the address, so I knew she'd get it anyway."

"All right. Would you turn to tab eight of your list of documents? Tell us what that is."

"It's photocopies of my day timer. My schedule."

"We'll mark it Exhibit Two. You used this at the office?"

"Yeah, to remind myself if I had to go somewheres or what I had to do. Like send the receipts out for the big school."

"What do you mean by that?"

"People come from all over the world for the adult choir school. Priests and stuff. They pay money and we send them a receipt."

"What other kinds of notes did you make to yourself?"

"If I was getting my hair done, I'd put the hair appointment in my book. Or if I was meeting friends for lunch the next week, I'd write in the time and place."

"Okay, now let's look at page fifty-six of the list, one of the pages in your day book. What's written there?"

"It's just an initial."

"What initial?"

"S."

"And what does S stand for?"

"Sick."

"Meaning you were sick that day?"

"Yeah."

"Could you flip through your book there and count up the S entries for me?"

"Uh, okay."

She went through the pages, counting under her breath. She had to restart a couple of times but in the end she found twenty-seven entries.

"And you worked there for four months, which came to eighty-five work days in all?"

"I don't know."

"So, twenty-seven out of eighty-five. That's almost a third of your time. One or two sick days every week."

"No, I was there more than that."

"Perhaps so. Let's look again." Monty made a show of turning the pages. "What was your last day in the office at St. Bernadette's?"

Her eyes darted to her counsel, but Underhill's face was without expression.

"Never mind your lawyer, Ms. Tate. You have to answer the questions yourself. What was your last day on the job?"

"I don't remember."

"Would it refresh your memory if I showed you the termination letter at tab one of your list?"

"August twenty-eighth."

"You were let go on that date."

She answered in a voice barely audible. "Yeah."

"And yet you had a sick day marked for Friday, September eleventh?"

No reply.

"Ms. Tate? A sick day entered in your book in advance? Could you go ahead to Friday, September eighteenth? Another S there? And ahead again to Monday the twenty-first?"

Still no response.

"How do you account for those entries?"

Silence and squirming.

"Ms. Tate? Did you plan ahead to take so-called sick days?"

She did not supply an answer, but Monty did not need one. He let her experience the discomfort for a couple of minutes, then resumed his questioning.

"Did Monsignor O'Flaherty ever criticize or make any complaint about your work?"

"No! He was really nice. Not picky, picky, picky."

"Did Father Burke ever criticize you for anything, other than the spelling and punctuation errors in your correspondence? And all your . . . sick time?"

Her expression was that of a child of ten. "He was mean! He's not a very good priest!"

"Oh? Why do you say that?"

"He growled at Gary!"

"Who is Gary?"

"My fiancé."

"What happened with him?"

"He would come and pick me up after work or, like, at lunchtime. And Father Burke was rude to him!"

"In what way?"

"He would say he had to leave."

"Where was Gary, that Father Burke told him to leave? Was he waiting in the doorway?"

"He was, like, with me."

"In the office?"

"Yeah."

"So what would Father Burke say to Gary?"

"He'd say, 'Get out of the office.'"

"I know you can't put yourself in Father Burke's mind — " God knows " — but what was your impression of why he said that? What do you think he objected to?"

"He thought Gary was looking at stuff on the computer. But he wasn't."

"He wasn't at the computer?"

"Well, he just used to sit at it when I was doing other stuff."

"Did he use the computer?"

"Not to spy on the church's stuff, or the money records, just to . . . he likes computers."

"I see. So that's what Father Burke took issue with."

"And he thought Gary was looking through the file cabinets. But he wasn't! He was just leaning on them, and if they were open that wasn't Gary's fault."

"That would be your responsibility, wouldn't it? Keeping the filing cabinets closed and the records private?"

"I was busy! And anyway, that's not all of what he did. One time Gary was outside, and he swore at him! Burke did."

"Is that right? What did he say?"

"It's too rude to say it here."

"Say it anyway. We don't mind."

She looked to her lawyer again, and received a slight nod.

"He said to Gary, 'Get the fuck out of my churchyard or I'll boot your arse from here to the fucking harbour.' It was unbelievable, a priest talking like that! I was so upset! I told Monsignor, and he tried to cover it up by saying people in Ireland use the F word a lot and it's not as bad as here. But that didn't make me feel any better."

She had informed on Burke to O'Flaherty; it was a wonder she still had her kneecaps. Aloud, he asked her when this last incident had happened. The open conflict between Burke and the boyfriend was news to Monty.

"It was after."

"After what?"

"After I stopped working there."

"So that incident does not form part of this lawsuit."

"It should!"

"Those are all my questions, Ms. Tate. Thank you."

The fact that the plaintiff's lawyer was in no hurry to examine Monty's clients till some date to be agreed on in the future told him what the lawyer thought of Tate's case; Monty could expect an offer to settle before too long. There was no case, and the church's offer of one month's salary was more than she would ever get from a court.

†

95

Monty dropped in on Brennan Burke that evening to fill him in on the proceedings.

"Well?" Burke asked, when Monty had made himself comfortable in one of Burke's chairs. "How did it go?"

"It went as expected. I wouldn't lose any sleep over it if I were you."

"I haven't been. What did she say?"

"She said you never called her Befanee."

"Nobody should call anyone Befanee. Sounds like baby talk for Bethany, which I assume it is. The parents couldn't spell it, or pronounce it properly. *Befanee, did you type that fing for me yet? It has to be done by Fursday, for the Feology Conference, on the Summa Feologiae. Ah, thuck it!*"

"I have to say I was a little surprised at the letter you sent out to Kiri Te Kanawa." Burke's lips pressed in on each other. "First of all, what's the story on her? I know she's coming to the Cohn, and I'm hoping to get tickets. But, Brennan, this letter. Hardly up to the standard I'd expect of you . . ."

"Never mind it."

Burke looked as if he were going to be sick. Monty knew he was a great admirer of the brilliant New Zealand soprano, and his admiration encompassed more than her work.

"I'd as lief be picked up by the Blessed Mother, levitated from the churchyard, carried through the skies, dropped over New York City, and left impaled on the Empire State Building, as to imagine Kiri Te Kanawa receiving such an abomination in the mail. With my name on it. Now fuck off about it."

Time to let up on him. "What was Tate's boyfriend doing in the office?"

"Reading files and financial records on our computer and in our cabinets. And some notes I made in connection with my ministry to the inmates at the correctional centre. No doubt recognized a name or two. One time I caught him looking at the tallies of our Sunday collections."

"No wonder you were mean to him."

"Mean to him. That little gurrier. I put the run to him."

"What happened later on? She says you told him to get the fuck off the property."

"He was taking money off people at the statue. People devoted to St. Bernadette. I told you that before."

"Right. You did. So it obviously didn't end when Befanee lost her job."

"I'm sure it intensified after the claimed apparitions, to make up for the lost family income."

"Tell me what else you know about this."

"He had a scheme going. He was approaching people in the churchyard, offering some kind of service or favour; I don't know what it was. I threatened to do him grievous bodily harm if I ever saw him at it again."

"What kind of scam was it?"

"I don't know and I don't care. I've been keeping an eye out for him. Which I imagine he has copped on to, because he's never there when I am. Yet I have spoken to people, and they've said he's pestered them for money. What a pair. So, back to the point, what is going to happen with the lawsuit?"

"Nothing. They'll settle it. They should have taken the offer in the first place. Now we cut it down, and they'll have to take it as is. But Befanee may be on her way to a more exalted status than ex-employee of the parish of St. Bernadette. Right?"

"What?"

"The Church is taking this seriously. I could scarcely believe my ears when Michael O'Flaherty told me about the expert from Rome, someone from the investigation arm of the Vatican. Michael says these investigations are rigorous and take a long time to complete. That's the last thing I expected in a case like this one. So, what's the story on this priest from Rome?"

"He's taking part in a conference in Ontario. Decided to stop in here."

"What is he, some kind of psychic detective?"

"Hardly."

"Well, what kind of investigation does he do? How detailed is it? O'Flaherty suggested that it would be quite elaborate and could go on for a while."

"It's over and done with."

"What?"

"He did his investigation, and he's already left town."

"You're joking."

"No."

"Well, what did he find out?"

"What's there to find out, Montague?"

"He must have interviewed Befanee Tate, for one thing, considered the statement she made on television, examined the site, and — "

"Why in the hell would he do any of that?"

"What else would he do? Is there some kind of ritual he would perform at the site?"

"No rituals. He came into the office. Asked about the Tate girl. I told him she's suing us for wrongful dismissal. He saw the poster of the movie about St. Bernadette across from the secretary's desk, and noted the fact that the actress achieved great fame and an Academy Award. And that was it. All he said was 'Where do you drink?'"

"Drink? Does that mean he's . . ."

"He's *what*, Mr. *Collins*?"

"Um, not a native Roman?"

"Donal O'Sullivan, from Dublin."

"I see."

"We went out, had a few scoops, talked hurling and football, enjoyed some laughs, caught up on the news from Rome, and he flew out this morning."

"So this 'investigation,' instead of taking days or even weeks, took only — "

"Seconds."

Brennan

The following day, just after morning Mass, Brennan was in the kitchen having a glass of orange juice when he heard a knock on the door. The priests' housekeeper, Mrs. Kelly, came bustling in and said she would get it. She was back half a minute later with a heightened sense of alarm, over and above her usual case of the janglers, and announced, "It's the police, Father!"

"All right. I'll go see them."

"There's just the one. And he asked for you."

"All the more reason for me to go see him."

"What does he want?"

"I don't know yet. I'll go see him."

He left her fretting in the kitchen. Never in his life had he seen a person so permanently fretful and nervous as Mrs. Kelly. It was all he could do to maintain his shallow reserve of patience in her presence.

He went to the door, and there was a police officer who looked familiar, beyond the fact that he looked like the reincarnation of the soul singer Otis Redding. Brennan had seen this cop before, maybe the morning of the murder.

"Father Brennan Burke?" the cop asked.

"Yes. What can I do for you?"

"I'm Truman Beals. We haven't met."

Brennan put out his hand, and they shook.

"I've got something for you."

"Oh?"

"A subpoena requiring you to testify at the preliminary hearing of the Podgis murder case, on Monday, the fourth of January, at the courthouse on Spring Garden Road."

"Right." Brennan took the document from the officer's hand. "I knew this day would probably come. Still, it could be worse."

"How's that?"

"I could have been called to testify *for* the fucker."

Beals looked startled for an instant, then laughed. "I hear you, brother. Father, I mean. Well, I'll be off to spread more joy."

"That's the spirit. See you in court, Truman."

"See you there."

The officer left, and Brennan returned to the kitchen to finish his juice. Mrs. Kelly was bent over the table reading the *Daily News*.

"Have you seen this, Father? You're in the paper!"

"No, I haven't seen it."

"Well, here. Look. It's about the miracles they say happened outside the hospital."

"Is there anyone left in this city who's not playing host to the Virgin Mary or performing miracles and magic tricks?"

"Father!" The housekeeper looked at him with shock and disapproval, her usual attitude towards him. She had disapproved of him the day he arrived to start up the choir school and to replace the sainted Father Shea who had moved on to another parish, and Brennan had not found his way into her good graces yet. Never would, it seemed. Not that he made an effort. Mrs. Kelly's prissiness and nervous manner around him were minor irritations; he had other things to occupy his mind.

"Here, Father, you read it. I've already seen it." She went off to her duties elsewhere in the house, and Brennan read the news article.

He knew what it was about because he had been interviewed. More claimed miracles, this time supposedly performed by poor Ignatius Boyle after being released from hospital. He had largely recovered from his injury and had regained his ability to speak English. Brennan liked Boyle, and his heart went out to the man for the life he had endured and for his current difficulties. And Brennan was intrigued by Boyle's sudden ability to speak excellent French and discuss theological matters in that language. But nothing could persuade him to speculate in public about whether Boyle's newfound abilities were miraculous. That went double for the latest claims about the man. If he, Brennan, had the power and might and authority to do so, he would issue an index of words that would hereafter be forbidden to Catholics. Top of the list would be the word "miracle." He looked at the news article.

"Ignatius Cured Us": Women in Vigil Outside VG Hospital

A woman from Hammonds Plains says she has been cured of a longstanding condition as the result of touching the hand of Ignatius Boyle. Boyle is the man who was found unconscious on Morris Street on September 24 and who woke up in the Victoria General Hospital speaking French for the first time in his life. Muriel Chisholm, 45, says she has always had a stammer. Something about Boyle's story drew her to the parking lot of the VG where supporters of Boyle gathered after his admission to hospital. When Boyle was released, on October 11, he met with the group, thanked them, prayed with them, and shook hands with several of the people before going to the homeless shelter where he has spent much of his adult life. Chisholm said from the moment Boyle touched her hand, she was able to speak fluently without a trace of a stutter. The problem has not recurred.

Another woman, from Eastern Passage, tells a similar story. Agnes Dempsey, 68, says she shook hands with Boyle and prayed with him. From that moment, she says, a longstanding anxiety disorder and related phobias ceased to trouble her.

Father Brennan Burke was quick to dismiss the claim of a miracle. "The Church does not accept claimed cures of nervous disorders as miraculous. Unless it's something physical, we do not even consider it," he said. But Monsignor Michael O'Flaherty said there is no reason to discount the women's claims entirely. "Even if there is no connection with Mr. Boyle, perhaps their prayers to God and their faith in Him gave them the strength to overcome their troubles by themselves. I will keep them in my prayers and hope that they maintain their recovery." Muriel Chisholm was untroubled by the disagreement. Agnes Dempsey nodded her agreement when Chisholm declared, "I know Ignatius cured me. There is no doubt in my mind. It was a miracle, and Ignatius Boyle is a living saint."

Chapter 8

Monty

The preliminary hearing for Pike Podgis got underway on Monday, January 4, 1993, in the courthouse on Spring Garden Road. Judge Ivan Thomas, a white-haired veteran of the Nova Scotia Provincial Court, would hear the case put forward by the Crown and decide whether there was enough evidence to send Podgis to trial on a charge of murder. In the usual course of things, Monty did not call any evidence for the defence at a preliminary hearing. There was no point showing his hand to the Crown with respect to the case he would be presenting on behalf of his client. But this time he had one witness to call. Otherwise, all he wanted to do was hear and evaluate the Crown's evidence; he might do a bit of cross-examination if he could make that evidence a little weaker, or clarify a point or two for use in the future.

Another departure from the norm was his client's insistence that the media be allowed to publish the evidence called at the prelim. Usually, the defence lawyer would apply for a publication ban, so that the evidence against the accused would not be out there tainting potential jurors for the trial down the road. If the defence applied, the judge was required to grant the ban. If the Crown applied, it was up to the judge to grant it or not. Pike Podgis, in his role as crusader for truth and freedom of expression, had instructed Monty to make a stand for the free circulation of information. Monty suggested to Podgis that he might regret it, but Podgis was having none of it. Monty had tipped off the Crown prosecutor, Bill MacEwen, in advance; after looking at his opponent wondering where the trap was, MacEwen said he had no interest in a ban himself and would not apply for it.

MacEwen presented his first group of witnesses: the police officers who first arrived at the crime scene, the arresting officers, the detectives who conducted the investigation, and the medical examiner who performed the autopsy on Jordyn Snider. A number of items were entered as exhibits, including Podgis's heavy, brown, gum-soled, blood-tainted shoes and the lab report showing that it was Jordyn Snider's blood on the shoes.

The facts were as Monty had read them in the file: the body was discovered at around two fifteen in the morning, lying face up near the statue. The Crown's theory was that the struggle between victim and killer had taken place very close to the statue of St. Bernadette, and that Jordyn had at one point reached out to the statue, presumably to try to hold herself upright. There was a smear of blood on the face of the saint, and this had come from the victim's gloved hand.

Monty had a few questions for Constable Truman Beals. "Constable, did you conclude that the victim had been killed where she was found, as opposed to having been transported from another location?"

"Yes, it was apparent from the scene — the blood distribution and everything — that the struggle had happened right at that spot."

"A lot of blood around the area?"

"There was some on her body, yes, but not a wide distribution."

The cop knew exactly what Monty was up to with that question, trying to find a way to claim Podgis had got blood on his shoes from walking through the grounds some distance from the body. Monty had one more question for Beals and then he would get off the subject. "From your experience investigating murders, Constable, stabbings in particular, would you expect the killer to have a lot of blood on his clothing?"

Beals was not going to give any more than he had to on this one. "It all depends on the circumstances. I've seen perpetrators' clothes with a lot of blood, but I've also seen them without. You just never know."

The medical examiner, Doctor Andrea Mertens, gave the cause of death as cardiac tamponade. She explained that the heart was enclosed in the pericardial sac, and that the killer's knife penetrated the sac and the aortic root, where the aorta met the heart. As soon as the aortic root was pierced, blood would have rushed in and filled the pericardial sac. This would have compressed the heart and caused it to stop beating. The victim would have been incapacitated almost immediately. There was another wound to the chest, non-fatal, and a laceration to the side of the neck. The Crown got the doctor to confirm that the murder had been committed in the place where the body was found.

Then, to close off another avenue for the defence, Bill MacEwen asked about blood. "Doctor Mertens, you have testified that one of the two wounds sustained by Ms. Snider was to her heart. Would this cause blood to pump out and travel, so to speak, some distance? Onto the clothing of a person standing close to the victim?"

"Not necessarily. There would have been a great deal of internal bleeding. But with a wound like this, caused by a very sharp object, the skin and muscle tissues would have retracted when the knife was withdrawn, and this would have prevented a lot of external bleeding. The wound to the neck would have bled some, but there would have been no spurting of blood."

The next witnesses were two receptionists at the Halliburton House Inn. One testified that Podgis had left the hotel around seven thirty, and she wished him good luck with his show that night. The other said he saw Podgis come in around one thirty in the morning. There was no conversation between him and Podgis.

After that came Ward Sanford, who had discovered the body when he walked through the churchyard on his way from work as a bartender. He testified to the facts set out in his statement, with one addition.

MacEwen asked him, "How close did you get to the body?"

"I went over to the point where I was about three, three and a half feet away. Then I took off and called the police."

"So you may have been as close as three feet?"

"That's right."

"Did you have any blood on your shoes?"

"No."

"How do you know?"

"I was wearing grey and white sneakers. I went back and waited near the scene for the police to arrive. Once I saw the precautions they were taking to avoid contaminating the crime scene, I began to worry that I might have done that myself. Or I might have got blood on myself. I looked everything over, my clothes, my sneakers. No blood. The police checked me out too, I guess to eliminate me as a suspect and to see what my sneaker treads were like. If they found my tread marks and they knew I wasn't the killer, they'd be looking for other kinds of footprints. They didn't find any blood either."

"Thank you, Mr. Sanford."

Thank you indeed. The witness was a godsend for the Crown. And bad news for Podgis, who claimed to have been much farther away and yet managed to get blood on his shoes.

Sanford was followed by Betty Isenor, a middle-aged woman who lived in the big grey wooden apartment house on the corner of Morris Street and Hollis. The nineteenth-century building was a landmark, with a great wraparound veranda and a rumoured history as a brothel at one point in its life. Now it provided rental accommodation for people of modest means who wanted to live downtown. On the morning of September 24, Betty Isenor had been awakened by noise, got up, and looked out her window, and saw Pike Podgis running from the churchyard. She pretty well stuck to her original statement, except to add that Podgis had been looking "wildly" behind and around him as he ran.

There were a couple of points Monty wanted to make with her on cross.

"Ms. Isenor, what time was it when you say you were awakened by noise?"

"I don't know. I didn't look at the clock."

"Where is your clock, in relation to your bed?"

"It's on my bedside table but I didn't turn the light on, so I didn't see what time it said."

"Is it a digital clock or the older kind?"

"Older, regular kind."

So no LED light to show up in the dark.

"What was it that woke you up? What did you hear?"

"Footsteps and someone yelling."

Someone yelling? This was the first Monty had heard of any yelling. And by the look on Bill MacEwen's face, it was news to the Crown as well. If Podgis was running alone, who would he have been yelling at? Monty was about to break the old courtroom rule: never ask a question if you don't already know the answer. But he could not pass up the chance that this might help him.

"Tell us about that, Ms. Isenor. What did the voice sound like? What was it saying?"

"I couldn't make out any words. This was when I was still mostly asleep. I just heard loud voices and footsteps and they woke me up."

The witness had Monty's full attention, and that of Bill MacEwen as well.

"You heard more than one voice then, did you?"

She looked to the prosecutor, whose face offered nothing in the way of assistance.

"Ms. Isenor?" Monty prompted her.

"I'm not sure. I thought maybe it was more than one voice. But it couldn't have been, because when I looked out there was only one person. Him." She pointed to Podgis.

"Where exactly was Mr. Podgis when you first saw him out your window?"

"Coming out of Byrne Street onto Morris."

"What floor do you live on, Ms. Isenor?"

"Third."

"Do you have a view of St. Bernadette's church from that height?"

"Yes, I do."

"So the instant that you first saw Mr. Podgis, where was he in relation to the church?"

"He was a little way past the church, almost to the corner with Morris."

"Quite a distance from your window in terms of being able to hear footsteps. Would you agree?"

"I heard them, and I saw him."

"But when you first heard the sound of feet, you were still in bed.

That's what woke you up. So at that point, Mr. Podgis would have been even farther away."

Bill MacEwen got to his feet. "Mr. Collins seems to be giving evidence, perhaps even opinion evidence, Your Honour."

"Do you have a question for the witness, Mr. Collins?"

"Yes, I do, Your Honour. Ms. Isenor, on reflection now, do you think it must have been footsteps sounding before you saw Mr. Podgis approaching the corner? Do you think that whoever was yelling might also be responsible for the footsteps?"

"I don't know. He's the only person I saw."

"Because the other person or persons had already gone by the time you were fully awake and at the window?"

Again, she looked to the prosecutor for guidance, but he could not help her.

"Let me ask you this. You said voices in the plural. Did you hear two or more different voices?"

"Well, I just thought I'd heard voices or a voice. I was very sleepy at the time. Drifting in and out of sleep."

"Yes, I understand. When you looked out and saw Mr. Podgis, could you tell if his mouth was moving, as if he was speaking?"

"I don't remember seeing that."

"Were the voices you heard men's voices?"

The witness suddenly looked as if she was in way over her head.

"Ms. Isenor?"

It took her a while. Monty waited. "Maybe a man and a woman."

Well. This changed the water on the beans, as Monty's mother-in-law was fond of saying. It was not going to get any better than that. The witness could not have heard Podgis and the murder victim's voices, if in fact they had been together. The distance between the apartment building and the back of the churchyard was too great. Of course what she heard may just have been a guy and a girl passing by late at night or early in the morning. This was an area of the city where a great many university students lived. But Monty would make as much of it at trial as he could: other people in the area of the crime scene at the same time as Podgis. He thanked the witness and sat down.

Bill MacEwen got up to examine her on redirect. "Ms. Isenor, you did not see anyone else in the area of Byrne and Morris streets when you got up, correct?"

"That's right."

"Just Mr. Podgis, running from the church area and looking wildly about him. Is that right?"

"Yes, he's the only person I saw. And something about him scared me!"

"Thank you."

Monty leaned over to his client. "Are you sure you don't want a publication ban?"

"No! I've been stuck with them as a journalist. I'm not going to hide behind the curtains now that I'm the one being persecuted."

The Crown's next witness was a familiar one. Bill MacEwen called him to the stand and the court clerk swore him in.

"Would you state your full name for the court, please."

"Brennan Xavier Burke."

"And you are a priest?"

"That's right."

"Where do you work, Father?"

"St. Bernadette's, the church and choir school."

"How long have you been there?"

"Since 1989."

"And before that, where did you live?"

"New York. Before that, Dublin. Rome for a while. A couple of other places."

"How long have you been a priest?"

"Over twenty-five years."

"All right. Thank you, Father. Now, can you tell us where you were on the night of September twenty-third?"

"For the early part of the evening, I was at the Atlantic Television studio on Robie Street."

"And what were you doing there?"

"I was a guest on the *Pike Podgis Show*."

"How did you come to be on the show?"

"As a priest I have a duty of obedience to my bishop."

There was laughter in the courtroom at that.

"And on this occasion?"

"The bishop gave me my orders: go on the show."

Laughter again.

"Are you telling us you did not want to appear on the program?"

"That's correct."

"Why not?"

Monty rose to object. "Your Honour, with respect, I do not see how Father Burke's feelings about the program are relevant to the question before us today."

"Mr. MacEwen?"

"Your Honour, Father Burke's reluctance to go on the show, and the events that unfolded during the show, are relevant to the conversation we are putting in evidence, a conversation that occurred sometime after the conclusion of the broadcast."

"I'll allow it. Go ahead, Mr. MacEwen."

"Father Burke, I was asking you about your enthusiasm, or lack of enthusiasm, about appearing on Mr. Podgis's TV show. Could you tell us a bit about that?"

"Last thing in the world I wanted to do. I don't like talk shows, which, from my experience of hearing them on the radio — I'd never seen the TV version — involve a lot of shouting and rudeness and lack of depth with respect to whatever is the topic of the day. I saw no value in participating."

"But Archbishop Cronin thought differently? He thought it was a worthwhile endeavour?"

"He told me it would be mud wrestling." Bursts of laughter greeted his remark. "But if religion and the faith were being debated, we should put someone forward to explain our position. So of course I deferred to a higher power and turned up for the event."

"Who else was on the show?"

"Professor Rob Thornhill of Dalhousie University. He teaches sociology. And Pod — Mr. Podgis was the host."

"You were to debate Professor Thornhill, was that the idea?"

"Yes, Rob would speak from the point of view of a non-believer, and I would argue in favour of belief."

"Belief in God."

"Yes."

"Tell us how it went."

"Dennis Cronin was right. It had all the dignity of a mud-wrestling match. That was no fault of Rob Thornhill, who is one of the most pleasant and mannerly people I know. It was Podgis and his vulgar remarks, and his pandering to the audience and really, it seemed, the lowest common denominator in — "

"Your Honour!" Monty exclaimed. "This characterizing of Mr. Podgis in such a way is uncalled for and not at all helpful in this proceeding. I would ask the court to admonish the witness to stick to the facts, and to comport himself with the dignity he seems to demand of others."

Monty was getting the death stare from Burke's coal-black eyes. He affected not to notice.

"Mr. MacEwen?" the judge asked. "Is this a bit of editorializing by the witness? Are we straying a bit from the facts here?"

"Your Honour, the atmosphere on the set of the show is relevant to what occurred later. But Father Burke, perhaps you could just let us know what happened, and not spend as much time on your own characterization of Mr. Podgis's style of performance."

No reply from Burke.

"So. Father Burke. What happened on the show?"

"Mr. Podgis asked a couple of questions about religion and science, and I gave my answers, imparting some facts and history that seemed to have been hitherto unknown to Podgis and his audience. But I was constantly interrupted by crass and puerile remarks directed at me or at the audience. When asked what reasonable arguments one can make for belief, I began to lay the groundwork for my answer but again was interrupted by crude comments and gestures."

"And what happened then?"

"I decided I'd had quite enough, and I got up and left."

"You walked off the set?"

"Right."

"Did you notice any reaction from Mr. Podgis as a result of that?"

"No. I didn't give him another look."

Bill MacEwen took a few seconds to review his notes, then resumed his examination.

"What did you do after that, Father Burke?"

"I drove home to the parish house."

"And?"

"Stayed there for a few minutes, took off my collar, and put on casual clothes, then went out again."

"Where did you go?"

"Midtown."

"The Midtown Tavern on Grafton Street."

"Right."

"And what went on there?"

"I enjoyed a beer and talked to a few people there, and then I left."

"What happened when you left?"

"I started to walk down Grafton Street and I was accosted by Mr. Podgis."

"What time was this?"

"Around half-eleven."

"Eleven thirty?"

"Yes."

"Now, what do you mean, accosted?"

"He lurched towards me on the sidewalk and started roaring into my face."

"What was he saying?"

"He was blathering on about the show, and who was I to walk off the *Pike Podgis Show* when he got dozens of appeals every week from people who were dying to appear on the program. I tried to step around him and get on my way, but he tried to block me."

"How did you react to his attempt to block you?"

"I suggested that he let me pass."

That was not the version of events Monty had heard, but he would get to that in time.

"Was anything else said at that point?"

"Words were exchanged."

"Tell us about that."

"I may have said something to the effect that if he didn't get out of my way, I would make him consubstantial with the pavement beneath our feet."

"Consubstantial meaning . . ."

"One in substance with the pavement, as in I'd pound him into it and then walk over him to get away."

Muted laughter and a stern look from the Crown.

"Did you have any intention of carrying out that . . . course of action, or was it just a manner of speaking?"

"If I'd intended to carry it out, I'd have done it. Flattened him. I didn't."

"Your Honour!" Monty protested again. "This witness has admitted to threatening Mr. Podgis with physical harm. I submit that his evidence against my client should therefore be — "

"You'll have time for submissions later on, Mr. Collins. Mr. MacEwen, proceed with your witness."

"What occurred after that, Father Burke?"

"Podgis told me to get along home. He didn't have any more time to waste on me because he had a date. He was going off to meet a woman somewhere."

"Those were his words, that he was going to meet a woman?"

"He didn't say 'woman.' He referred to her as a young bit of stuff or something like that."

"Is there anything else you can tell us about the conversation or the encounter with Mr. Podgis?"

"No, that's about it. I left him there and walked back to St. Bernadette's."

Monty was about to rise to cross-examine the witness when Podgis leaned over and bleated, "Tear that fucking bastard apart!" Monty was taken aback by the viciousness in his client's voice and the look of sheer hatred on his face. If there was anyone who could dish it out — on national TV — but not take it, it was Pike Podgis. Might be rethinking the publication ban about now.

Monty spoke into his ear. "Take it easy, Podgis. He had to testify to what happened. He was subpoenaed by the Crown. This is the way it works, when you get yourself charged with murder. Now compose yourself as if none of this bothers you in the least, because you know you're innocent, and let's do our jobs here."

He got up then, and addressed the witness. His closest friend, when they were not facing each other in a courtroom.

"Father Burke, you told us you went to the rectory before going to the Midtown. You were only there for a few minutes. Why did you go there?"

"To change my clothes."

"Why did you do that?"

"To take off my work clothes before heading out."

"To take off your collar?"

"That's part of taking off my work clothes."

"Is there any particular reason you didn't want to wear your white collar to the tavern?"

"Your Honour, how is this relevant?" the Crown asked.

"I'll move on, Your Honour," Monty conceded; he could have added *now that I've tried to suggest Burke was off for a night of heavy boozing and did not want to be seen in the collar of a priest of the Church.*

"How did you get from the rectory to the Midtown?"

"I walked."

"Didn't take your car."

No reply. He had already answered. Burke could be a man of few words when he chose to be.

"How long were you in the Midtown?"

"Hour and a half, two hours."

"I take it that, if you were in the Midtown, you were drinking?"

Burke gave Monty a look that said he knew the Pope was Catholic, and Monty should too.

"Answer the question, please, Father."

"The one doesn't necessarily follow from the other. One could go to the Midtown to talk with friends, watch a game on the screen, and drink ginger ale. But in my case, yes, I had something to drink."

"And what were you drinking?"

As if Monty didn't know, from more than two years of drinking at the Midtown with Burke.

"Draft beer."

"How many did you have?"

"Not many."

"You don't know how many draft you had?"

"I knew at the time how many draft I had. But the number was not outstanding enough to remain in the forefront of my mind."

"Nothing unusual about drinking a lot at the tavern? Is that what you're saying, Father?"

"No, it is not. Not what I'm saying."

"How often do you go to the Midtown?"

MacEwen was on his feet. "Your Honour, how often Father Burke goes to the Midtown or any other restaurant or bar is not relevant here. What is relevant is what Father Burke heard and saw of Mr. Podgis on the evening of September twenty-third."

"Mr. Collins, unless you can show that this witness's past behaviour is relevant, I would ask that you stick to the events of twenty-three September."

"Yes, Your Honour. Father Burke, you say you walked home after drinking at the bar, and you went to bed. Correct?"

"Correct."

"What did you do before you went to bed?"

"What do you mean?"

"Well, did you head up to bed as soon as you got to the rectory?"

"Am I missing something here?"

"I'll ask the questions, Father."

"So ask one that makes sense, Mr. Collins."

Judge Thomas looked from witness to lawyer with a questioning expression but did not speak. Monty knew he'd be hearing about this at the next Collins-Burke session at the Midtown. If there was a next session. But this was his job. It was rarely a pleasant one, for him, the client, or the opposing witness.

"Did you stop and chat with anyone else at the rectory before hitting the sack?"

"I had a few words with Michael O'Flaherty."

"That's Monsignor O'Flaherty, the pastor at St. Bernadette's?"

"Yes."

"Tell us about the conversation."

"Mike had missed me when I went home briefly after the television show, so he waited up to talk to me about it. He'd been watching the show. Saw me leave the set."

Monty could picture the scene. Michael would be bubbling over, wanting to talk about the drama of the TV studio walk-out.

"Yes?"

"He was quite appalled, I have to say."

"At your walking off?"

"No, at the low level of programming. The nasty, tawdry drivel that is fed into people's homes even when the topic is as lofty and sacred as the existence of the Divine and the meaning of human life."

"So you chatted about this. Over a late-night snack maybe? A cup of tea?"

"The occasion called for something stronger."

"So what did you have?"

"One glass of whiskey."

"I see. Big glass, little glass? What?"

Burke gave him the evil eye again. "A couple of ounces."

"You went to sleep after that, did you, Father?"

"I did."

"What time did you wake up, do you recall?"

"It was around half-two. I heard the sirens."

"Before that, had you heard anything? Sounds from the churchyard?"

"Not a thing."

"No screams or sounds of a struggle?"

Burke did not reply. He had already delivered himself of the response and did not deign to elaborate.

"So it took the sound of sirens to rouse you from sleep, and you only had one glass of whiskey before bed? Could it have been the amount you drank at the Midtown that accounted for you sleeping through the attack on Jordyn Snider in your backyard?"

Burke's eyes bored into him. Finally he said, "The fact that I did not hear the murder implicates me in something, is that what you're suggesting?"

"As I said, Father, I'm asking the questions here. But to give you the courtesy of a response, let me explain. It occurred to me that if you had consumed a significant amount of alcohol at the Midtown just before meeting Mr. Podgis on the sidewalk, your recollection of what he said and how he said it may be less than accurate."

Bill MacEwen was on his feet. "Your Honour, Mr. Collins is not a witness. I would respectfully ask that he not give evidence but limit himself to his proper role, asking questions, not testifying on behalf of his client."

"Mr. Collins?"

"I apologize, Your Honour. No more questions for this witness."

Burke was excused, and directed one more damning look at Monty before he left the courtroom.

The Crown's next witness was Al Baker, a sound engineer who went to Grafton Street after working a show at the Metro Centre the night of September 23. He had arranged to meet a pal outside the tavern at eleven thirty and was waiting on the sidewalk when he saw two men arguing fifteen feet or so from the Midtown's door.

"I didn't catch on who he was at the time, but I know now it was Podgis. He was hollering right into the other guy, the taller guy's, face. The tall guy was just standing there looking down at him as if he was thinking, 'Who is this asshole?' And Podgis was crapping all over the tall guy, going on and on. The tall guy got off a few good lines. I couldn't tell you now what they said to each other at that point. But it was obvious that Podgis was just wasting his time, because he was outclassed in every way by the taller guy."

"So, what happened then, Mr. Baker?"

"After this went on for a bit longer, Podgis said he had better things to do than hang around, because he had a girl he was going to meet. Or he called her something, a piece of tail or something. I don't recall exactly. And he made this gross motion with his hands, like, you know . . ."

"Like what, Mr. Baker?"

"Well . . ." He looked at Judge Thomas uncertainly, and the judge nodded at him to go ahead.

"He made a circle of his forefinger and thumb, and then moved a finger from his other hand in and out. You know . . . and then stuck his tongue in and out of his mouth. It wasn't pretty, let me tell you."

"Yes, all right, go on."

"The tall guy made a face, the kind of face you'd make if you found a bug in your salad." Monty could picture it all too well; he had seen the same look of distaste on Burke's face many a time. "And he said something to Podgis like 'Maybe she'll get lucky tonight. If the stars and planets are aligned just right, maybe a meteorite will come to earth and crash in front of her door, or she'll be abducted by aliens, and won't be able to get out to meet you.' Something like that."

There was muffled laughter in the courtroom. Pike's face was like a thundercloud.

"So then Podgis said, 'Eat your heart out, Burke.' That was the tall guy's name. 'Eat your heart out, because I can have a woman whenever I like and you can't. Nah nah nah *nah* nah. Like a little kid! Unbelievable. But he got zung right back."

"Excuse me, Mr. Baker? Did you say 'zung'?"

"Yeah. Yes. Sorry, I meant Burke got him with a zinger, because he started singing that George Thorogood song, 'Bad to the Bone.' You know, the one where the guy brags about how bad he is and how he has all the women after him. Well, Burke sang him a few lines from the song. Even had the stutter on the 'bad.' Bit of air guitar happening. It was priceless." Baker started laughing, enjoying the scene all over again.

This was the first Monty had heard of Burke — the Reverend Father Burke — doing a bad-ass Thorogood song outside the Midtown. It was all Monty could do to keep a straight face at the defence table.

"How did Mr. Podgis react to that bit of . . . to hearing that song?"

"I thought his head was going to blow up."

"I see. Angry, was he?"

"Objection, Your Honour," Monty said, rising from his seat. "Leading."

"I withdraw the question, Your Honour. Please continue, Mr. Baker."

"All I could think was that any woman I know, like my wife, would have gone for the taller guy, Burke, over this TV clown. I don't go for guys; don't get me wrong. But anybody could see that Burke was the tall, dark, handsome type the women look at, you know? And he had a good voice too. Sounded smart. Unlike Podgis quacking away. The boys in the studio must have to do some serious adjustment before that grating voice goes out over the air."

Monty did not look at Podgis; he could almost feel the steam coming out of his ears.

Baker paused for a second, then said, "I thought Burke maybe had something wrong with him that he couldn't . . . you know, Podgis saying he couldn't have a woman. Maybe he had a war wound or something — pissed off the IRA and got hurt — I don't know. He turned so his face was in the light, and I could see he had a little bit of a downturn in one of his eyelids as if he'd been in a fight."

Monty did not care to be reminded of that eye injury, given that he was the cause of it when, at the low point of his marital woes, he had lashed out at Burke in a moment of drunken anger. But he did not want to think about that now.

The witness said, "Or I thought maybe it was just that he was married, and couldn't go out cruising. But I get it now. He's a priest. I didn't know that at the time; he didn't have a collar on."

"Did Mr. Podgis say anything more about this woman he was going to meet?"

"I don't know. My buddy arrived and we took off."

"Nothing more for this witness, Your Honour."

"Mr. Collins?"

Monty got up. This would not take long; there was nothing to be gained by giving the witness more time to paint Podgis as an obnoxious loser. But there was one point that could stand to be reinforced. "Mr. Baker. Your evidence is that Mr. Podgis was very open about the date that he had planned."

"Oh, yeah, for sure."

"He didn't try to hide the fact."

"No way."

"Thank you. I have nothing else, Your Honour."

That was the Crown's last witness. Now it was time for the sole witness for the defence. Jurgen Leitner was an emergency room doctor at the Victoria General Hospital.

"Doctor Leitner, you saw a man named Ignatius Boyle when he arrived at the emergency room at the Victoria General on the morning of September twenty-fourth, correct?"

"That's right."

"What time was he admitted?"

"One eighteen."

"Could you tell us what you observed about Mr. Boyle?"

"He was unconscious. There was swelling in the back of his head."

"Did you form an opinion as to what had happened to him?"

"I thought he had fallen."

"Did you consider any other possibilities?"

"Sure. We had seen Mr. Boyle in the ER in the past. We knew he was a person who had a hard life. Occasionally he came in with an injury and we treated him."

"What sort of injuries had he suffered in the past?"

"Facial abrasions, lacerations, bruising."

"Do you remember how these injuries came about?"

"The information we had was that he had been beaten up."

"Would you have any way of knowing 'who started it,' so to speak?"

"Only what he told us, that this or that fellow in the street had attacked him. They were definitely injuries that could have come from a fight."

"Fights that could have been instigated by others, or by him."

"Either way, we looked after his injuries. Those incidents were quite a while ago; I don't have the details."

"I understand. Coming back to his admission on the morning of twenty-four September, what were your observations of Mr. Boyle? He was unconscious with swelling in the back of his head. Anything else?"

"We checked him over, of course. No other injuries."

Monty picked up a copy of the ER record. "It says here, doctor, that there was blood on Mr. Boyle's face."

"Yes, a bit on his face. His forehead and right cheek."

"Was it his own blood?"

"No."

"How do you know that? Did you run tests on it?"

"No, we didn't."

"So how did you know it was not his own?"

"Because he was not bleeding. He had no open wounds anywhere."

"So it was someone else's blood." Monty stated the obvious and let it hang in the air for a moment, then went on, "What did you do about the blood?"

"I'm not sure what you mean."

"You didn't test it."

"No."

"What did you do?"

"Nothing. We just cleaned him up."

"Wiped the blood off."

The doctor hesitated for a second, then said, "Yes."

"And the cloth or whatever you used to wipe the blood, where would that be now?"

"Long gone."

"Did you have any contact with the police at all?"

"Well, no."

"Even though this man was found unconscious and had someone else's blood on him?"

"This did not come to us by way of an emergency call. He was not brought in by ambulance, so the police would not have been notified, at least as far as I would know."

"How did he come to be in the emergency room?"

"He was carried in by some young fellows. They told us they were on their way back to St. Mary's U after a party. They were walking on Morris Street and saw the man lying there. They said they knew him, or at least had seen him before, on Spring Garden Road, around the library and the basilica. At first they thought he was just asleep. Or, you know, passed out. They tried to rouse him because they were concerned; it was cold and he was not wearing a coat. But they couldn't wake him. They didn't know what had happened to cause his fall. They hailed a taxi, placed Mr. Boyle in the car with them, and brought him to the ER. Good Samaritans."

Monty had in fact already spoken to the St. Mary's students and knew they had nothing to add.

"This blood. How did it look?"

"What do you mean?"

"Was it smeared around, or . . ."

"Not smeared. It was more like spots of blood."

"Thank you, Doctor Leitner."

It was late in the day, but judge and counsel agreed to keep going and wrap things up. The Crown's argument was short and swift, because the burden on the Crown at a preliminary hearing is not nearly as onerous as it is at trial, where guilt has to be proved beyond a reasonable doubt. At this stage, all MacEwen had to do was convince the judge that there was evidence upon which a jury, acting reasonably and properly instructed, could convict the accused. Monty did what he could with what he had: there was no known connection between Podgis and the victim; there were other people in the area at the same time; the shoes Podgis was wearing had soft soles, and would not have made enough noise to have awakened Betty Isenor; there was another man near the scene with blood on him. But just before six o'clock, as expected, Judge Thomas committed Podgis to stand trial for the murder. Fortunately for Podgis, his bail provisions were left in place, and he would be free pending the trial. Free to rant and rail at his lawyer and the media about his wrongful committal to trial for a murder he did not commit.

Monty listened with half an ear and assured him that this outcome had been expected, almost inevitable, and they would get to work planning the trial. He started to skirt around the edge of the media pack.

"Where are you going?" his client demanded.

"It's six o'clock and I'd normally say that's the end of my workday but I have some other files to catch up on before I go home."

"Well, call me tonight. I want to go over this disaster with you and see what went wrong."

"I told you all along that this would happen. There is almost always a committal for trial. And I won't be able to call till tomorrow. I have a gig tonight."

"Yeah, right, go out and live it up. Never mind what's happening to your clients."

"I won't be living it up, Podgis. It's a blues band. There will be a room full of my present and former clients crying in their beer at the Shag."

"The Shag! What's that?"

"Its real name is the Flying Stag. Regulars call it the Flying Shag. Now I have to get going. I'll call you tomorrow."

Podgis moved towards the assembled reporters and cameras with the shuffling gait of a man shackled and walking to his execution.

Chapter 9

Monty

The blues gig was scheduled to get underway at ten o'clock and would wail on into the wee hours. After clearing away some tasks at his office and scoffing down some leftover pizza at home, Monty got himself cleaned up and dressed down for the night at the Shag, a smoky dive in a suburban strip mall, flanked by a pawnshop and a quick-cash outfit. Monty's band Functus had been playing the blues there from time to time for nearly twenty-five years. He decided to take a jaunt over to St. Bernadette's to give Burke the news first-hand about the committal for trial and to invite him along to the gig. The priest had enjoyed sessions with Functus in the past, and Monty hoped this might smooth things over after the cross-examination, if indeed any smoothing was necessary. Burke knew this was part of the job of a trial lawyer, Crown or defence, but nobody would pretend it was pleasant being on the receiving end. Burke had been there before, during his own trial, and had endured a shellacking by the Crown. That time Monty had been on his side. Now Monty was "on the side" of Perry Calvin Pike Podgis, and Burke's opinion of that individual was plain to see. And obviously, the feeling was mutual. Monty had felt the heat of his client's animosity towards Burke when they were all in the courtroom together. Perhaps an evening of music would have a mellowing effect.

When Monty got to the rectory, Michael O'Flaherty informed him that Burke was taking part in a philosophy seminar at St. Mary's University, McNally building. The talk had begun at seven o'clock. O'Flaherty was sure Monty would be welcome to sit in, even as a latecomer. It would make a nice contrast, an hour or so of metaphysical speculation before a night of booze and blues at one of the city's seediest guzzling dens.

It was after eight by the time he got to the university. It was a mild, overcast evening, damp with a feeling of impending rain. When he arrived at the big greystone building named for Archbishop John McNally, he saw a cluster of people outside the walls. Smoke break? Yes, there was Burke, just putting the flame to a cigarette in his mouth. A younger man sucked on a pipe, and a woman stood with her hands in her pockets, rocking back and forth on her heels. There was someone in a dark-coloured rain jacket with the hood up, standing apart from the group, leaning against the building. It was either a smallish guy or a big girl. A guy, judging from the cut of the jeans and the oversized sneakers. He seemed to be tuned in to the professors and their chat. Must be a student, looking for all the enlightenment he could get.

Burke blew out a plume of smoke and continued whatever he had been saying: ". . . but he maintained a fundamental duality between the world and consciousness, the two not linked by objective causality but by the *intentionality* of consciousness. So, approaching the question from that perspective . . ."

Monty heard the sound of giggling and turned to his right. Two young girls were approaching, dressed in what looked like exercise outfits: one had on skin-tight pink leggings, green slouchy socks and sneakers, and a neon green nylon jacket. Her hair was held back in what Monty's daughter, Normie, called a scrunchy. This too was green. The other girl had on the same kind of rig, but all the colours were the reverse of her friend's. Belying the exercise motif was the carefully applied makeup on their faces. They appeared to be of high-school age, cutting through the university property or perhaps attending an event there.

The one with pink legs said to her companion, "She's like *whoa!* And I'm like *excuse me? Hello!* And she's like *no way!* And I'm like *way!*"

They looked at each other, their mouths hanging open, then shook their heads in tandem and moved on, their vocabularies exhausted.

The man with the pipe addressed Burke: "What were you saying, Professor Burke?"

"I was *like*, the two are linked by, *like*, the intentionality of consciousness, in the thought of Husserl."

The woman in the group called out, "Girls! Would you like to sit in on a free lecture?"

The young ones looked at each other; their mouths fell open even further in alarm.

"We, like, have to . . ." Pink Legs began, but her voice trailed to a halt. Perhaps there was nothing in the world they had to do.

"We're doing a bit of a survey here," the professor ad libbed.

"Okay," Green Legs said warily. "A survey about, like . . ."

"Who was Socrates? Can you tell me?"

The two looked to each other again, then Pink Legs said, "He was famous."

"Right. Famous for what?"

She thought for a moment, then said, "Famous but not, like, in a good way."

"No? How so?"

"He . . . went to jail!"

The professor nodded her encouragement. "Good. How do you know that?"

"'Cause there's this book."

"Have you read it?"

"Well, not me but I, like, heard of it. 'Cause they were going to talk about it on TV when I was clicking through. Some kind of trial he was in. But it was, like, PBS."

Burke looked at her. "Do you know what he went to trial for?"

She stared into his eyes, then looked down and took in his collar. She had it. "For killing Jesus on the cross!"

Burke's head dropped and he slumped as if the last breath had gone out of *him* on the cross.

The girls looked at him, then turned and tripped away down the walk. "Well, *excuse me!*" they exclaimed in unison.

Monty caught Burke's eye then. Burke raised his cigarette in greeting.

"Did you feel like Socrates on trial today, Brennan?"

"I do not feel the need to relive my moments in the court of justice."

It was not clear whether he really was perturbed about his time on the stand or this was just his usual sardonic way of addressing a subject he deemed unworthy of consideration. Either way, Monty thought it wise to deliver the verdict and leave it at that.

"Perhaps it won't displease you to learn that the judge committed Mr. Podgis for trial on the murder charge."

"I should bloody well hope so."

"Well, there you have it. I just wanted to deliver the news in person."

"I won't ask how he's taking it, because I don't give a flying — "

"Break's over, ladies and gentlemen," someone called from the door of McNally. "Time to resume."

"I'll come in and hear the rest of the talk."

"Sure."

"Then, afterwards, we're playing at the Shag. Go home, ditch your collar, put on something scruffy, and meet me at the bar. We'll go on a toot."

"As long as I don't have to testify about it afterwards in some tawdry proceeding. And," Burke added, "as long as you remember you're singing with the choir tomorrow morning. Latin Mass."

"I know, I know," Monty claimed. He was a charter member of the St. Bernadette's Choir of Men and Boys. But, with all the other things going on, his choirboy duties had slipped his mind.

The lecturers went inside and took their places at the head table. Monty found a seat at the back of the room. There was a sizeable crowd, for such an obscure topic. Well, obscure perhaps to the public, but not to the cognoscenti gathered here. For all his technical knowledge of the subject, Burke did not seem all that keen on the phenomenological school of philosophy and was much more interested in critiquing something called transcendental Thomism, which was apparently an attempt to reconcile Aristotle and Thomas Aquinas with Immanuel Kant. Whatever it was, Burke wasn't buying it. Monty's mind drifted towards the upcoming gig. Would he open with Muddy Waters or T-Bone Walker? Harp or vocals? When the seminar was over, Burke joined Monty at the back of the room.

Monty complimented him on the session. "That was, like, totally awesome. Especially that dude Gilson's *The Unity of Philosophical Experience*. Is there, like, a movie version? A video game?"

"Those two girls, and thousands like them, have provided me with an inspiration, Monty."

"Should I even ask what they have inspired in you, Father?"

"Given that there are so very many young people today who can play with gadgets and spend hours racking up points on video games, but do not know when Socrates lived or where, when the Second World War took place or who won it, where to put an apostrophe, or how to speak with a vocabulary of more than fourteen words, I feel compelled to address that unfortunate development in whatever way I can. I know kids have the same native intelligence they have always had, so I am left to wonder who's at fault for today's sad state of affairs. Television? If it's television, I have no intention of taking my message to that medium again. But if students are being ill-served by their schools, let that not be said of my choir school. I am going to reach back to the days of the classical education and initiate a course in rhetoric at St. Bernadette's. Your daughter, who speaks like someone well beyond her years, will excel in the program. I shall get to work on it right away."

"Not really right away, though. Blues night first."

"Right. Come with me while I get changed, then we can grab a cab."

"Good thinking." The Flying Stag was located off the peninsula in the suburbs. If the past was any indication, neither Burke nor Monty would be fit to have care and control of a motor vehicle when the session was over.

They drove to St. Bernadette's in their respective vehicles, parked, and emerged just in time to be drenched by the rain that had been threatening all day. They ran for the shelter of the rectory. Burke went up to his room to wash and change, and came down in a pair of faded jeans and a white T-shirt that depicted a group of monks around a musical score in Gregorian chant notation. Monty asked him what it was but then started to sing the notes, and exclaimed, "Hey, it's the guitar riff from 'Smoke on the Water.' Deep Purple. Cool."

Burke carried an old, soft leather jacket over his right arm and had a pack of smokes in his left hand. Ready to roll. They were just about out the door when Michael O'Flaherty called down to them from the top of the stairs. "Come up and watch this!"

126

They climbed the stairs and went into O'Flaherty's room. The television was on, and there was Pike Podgis in a studio, giving an interview about his legal troubles and giving out to the police for focusing their investigation on him.

"What are the police doing about finding the real killer of Jordyn Snider? Nothing. Because they've got me. Why me? Oh, they say they have enough 'evidence' to send me to trial. Well, let me tell you, when the time comes, I'll be able to explain away their 'evidence' and show that somebody else committed this heinous crime. Don't you think it's rather convenient that they found 'evidence' against me? Think about it. I'm sure a lot of your viewers caught the show I did last spring exposing sloppy and sometimes downright crooked practices on the part of the police in order to frame somebody for a crime. They gotta get somebody for these things, right? So, hey, let's pick on the unpopular guy, the guy who went public with their long history of mistakes and planting evidence. The guy who's not afraid to stand up and tell the truth about the powers that be. I tell it like it is. And I make enemies in the process. I've been a target all during my career! There's been times I've needed to hire a bodyguard. And now they think they have me on the ropes. No way. Pike Podgis doesn't go down without a fight."

"Insufferable," Brennan muttered.

Egotistical and paranoid as well, Monty said to himself. But that was no surprise.

"So if they won't find the real killer, I will. There were some strange things happening the night Jordyn Snider's life was taken from her. For instance, not far from the crime scene there was a man lying unconscious with blood on him! Have the police found it curious that this happened at the same time another person was found with blood all around her nearby? Guess not. Make no mistake: my own personal investigation — not the cops' — uncovered the fact that there was indeed blood on this man."

"His own investigation, my arse!" Monty exclaimed. "It was *my* work that brought that to light."

Burke gave Monty a pitying look.

Podgis was still wound up. "And I brought that out at the prelim. It's right there in the emergency room records at the VG Hospital. Does this bother the mighty Halifax Police Department? Nah. Why should it, when they've got Pike Podgis in their sights? Well, I have news for you, boys in blue: I'm going to expose your sloppy practices once again, where it really counts, when a man's life and freedom are put on trial in court! You wait!"

Monty was incensed. Burke looked at him and laughed. "Get used to it. That blithering eejit is your life now."

"My life now is the blues. Let's go."

†

Functus opened the first set with "Stormy Monday." Monty alternated between lead vocals and harmonica as always, and alternated between performing and quaffing ale from a steady supply brought to the stage by the waiters.

There was a good-sized crowd, and a few people were dancing. That didn't always happen on blues night, but he decided to go with it and vary the tempo and the set list to do a few danceable numbers over the course of the evening. He concluded the second set with B.B. King's "The Thrill Is Gone." He saw a fairly young woman who was not all that steady on her pins approaching Burke at his table, where he was sitting with three other guys, all smoking, all half in the bag. Monty recognized them as frequent flyers at the Shag but only knew one by name, Mel. Burke was in the process of lighting up a smoke when the woman reached him. He shook his head but smiled at her, and she teetered back to her place. A middle-aged man got up then and lurched in her direction; they stumbled around the dance floor till the last note faded away.

The piece ended with enthusiastic applause, and Monty sat down with the band; his beer supply was redirected for the duration of the break. Burke raised a glass to him in salute from his place at the next table. There was a steady flow of barroom chat between the two tables until it was time for the third set.

What was going on over in the corner by the door? Monty noticed a lone drinker who appeared to have a tape recorder on his table. Couldn't be. Monty had never seen anyone come in and record the band's performance. Time to go back onstage. He would check into the situation later.

He was feeling no pain at all by this time, though "no pain" might not be the best way to approach the blues. That was easily remedied. Don't call it "no pain." Call it "wasted" and then it was perfectly appropriate. His gaze came to rest on one young lady who had been giving him the eye all night, unless that was just his booze-fuelled imagination at work. Possibly. But he didn't think so. She was a fine-looking girl, with soft brown hair and big dark eyes. He thought he remembered her from other performances here. But time to concentrate on the tunes.

He had half the room up dancing, and the young one with the dark eyes got up and danced by herself in front of the stage. A couple of women tried to get Burke onto the dance floor, but he smiled and shook his head, holding up his glass as if to say "I'm spending the evening with this" or maybe, to use one of Burke's frequent expressions, "I'm legless with drink." But Monty decided to make him an offer he couldn't refuse so, after a rousing version of Wilson Pickett's "Land of a Thousand Dances," he announced, "Here's a nice, slow number that everyone can dance to. Even my pal Brennan here. He prefers the classics, so let's give him Schubert, as interpreted by Deodato. With a name like that, the guy has to be a saint."

Burke, being a good sport, gave the eye to one of the women who had asked him earlier, and they waltzed together to Deodato's instrumental "Ave Maria." He gently pried her arms off him at the end of the piece.

The band got back to more traditional blues fare after that. They wound up with Jimmy Reed's "Cold and Lonesome" and a long harp solo by Monty on James Cotton's "Slow Blues."

The performance earned applause, the thumping of tables, and some drunken shouts of approval. The other band members had been joined by their wives and girlfriends, and the one female member by her husband. Monty felt a pang of regret that Maura was not with him as she would have been in happier times, but he tried to put it aside. Last thing he needed with so much alcohol on board was to get maudlin. One of the guys had left Burke's table so Monty seated himself there, and they all engaged in small talk about sports, cars, cops, aggravation at the unemployment insurance office, the usual. Burke made the occasional comment and enjoyed his whiskey.

At another table were two women Monty had seen before. They spent a lot of time in this bar, and he knew why. They didn't call the place the Flying Shag for nothing. He nodded to them and they gave him a little wave.

Monty's back was to the bar, and he faced the front door. He took a glance in that direction, towards the table in the corner by the door and, at that moment, caught the lone stranger eyeing him before the guy could look away. It struck him then that the guy looked familiar; he had seen him somewhere. Monty was about to get up and have a word with him in case he really was recording the band. The members of Functus would not welcome that kind of private initiative. Pirate recordings of Functus? The music market in North America would go into a tailspin.

But Burke said something then, and Monty turned to him. There was a burst of loud conversation nearby and the banging of a tray of glasses, and Monty missed whatever was said. When the priest got up and pointed to the back of the room past the bar, Monty realized he must have been asking the fellow next to him, Mel, where the washroom was. After all his visits to the Flying Stag, Burke would have been aware that the toilets were beyond the bar somewhere. But now that Monty thought of it, he had never known Burke to use the public facilities anywhere. Not even at the Midtown, where he spent several hours a night several times a month. Typical of the fastidious priest. Well, here at the Shag there were several doors, and it would not do to enter the wrong one.

Burke was holding the bottom of his white T-shirt, and Monty could see there was brown liquid spilt on it. Who but Burke would feel compelled to go and wash off a stain in a place like the Flying Stag?

"Brennan," Monty said to him as he passed by, "you'll see three doors. Make sure you go past — "

"Yeah, yeah, I know it's back there somewhere. I'll find it." He continued on his way.

Monty leaned across the table to Mel. "Did you fill him in?"

Mel broke into a grin. "He's a big boy. He'll have to learn his way around."

"You didn't warn him about . . . the Honeymoon Suite?"

No response except a wider grin.

Monty noticed that one of the two women regulars had got up from her table and headed down past the bar. Monty ordered another beer and waited for Burke's return.

Less than two minutes later Monty heard, "We could go some-where else, if you don't like the . . . room there."

The woman's voice came from the area of the bar counter, behind Monty. He heard Burke clear his throat, and Monty turned around to watch. The woman was tripping along in Burke's wake. His T-shirt was still stained. He had his left hand out in a gesture that said, "Leave it. Never mind."

"Honey, you were digging it. I *know* you were."

The hand made a slashing movement. It said, "Shut up."

The guys at the table exchanged glances and snickered. They buried their faces in their glasses as Burke sat down. He lifted his own glass and drained it.

Mel leaned over and said to Monty, "That one over there's got her eye on you. You got it made in the shade, Monto. Come on," he said to his buddy at the table, "let's let the lovebirds get together." The two of them got up and made ready to leave. "You already got yours," Mel said to Burke.

"I did not!" Burke exclaimed.

"Any requests?" Monty asked Burke when the others had gone. "How about 'Third Rate Romance'?"

"Fuck off."

Monty then heard Mel saying to the dark-eyed beauty, "He asked me to ask you to join him." And the next thing Monty knew, she was sitting next to him, beaming.

"Hi," was all he said.

"Hi. You were really good up there. I've heard you here before, but I was too shy to say anything."

"Well, I'm glad you spoke up this time." Monty could hear the slight slurring of his voice. He was well over his customary limit.

She leaned towards him and gave him a view down the front of her shirt. "Maybe you could get the other guys to sing, and then me and you could dance together."

"That's tempting," he said, "but I don't think they'd appreciate it if I slacked off for the last set."

She leaned farther in and put her arms around him, putting her lips to his and giving him a deep and prolonged kiss. He responded to her, and thought, *Yes! This is going to happen. Lay off the booze, do the last set, then off to her place, and . . . in like Flynn.* Just like old times playing the bars when he was single.

But he wasn't single. He had spent the last two years trying to resume his married life with Maura, his family life with the kids. Despite the overwhelming temptation to seize this opportunity, he could end up blowing his chances forever. Starting something with this person, this fan, would not be a good idea. Having a one-night stand and avoiding her ever after would be caddish behaviour on his part. He pulled away and shook his head. "No," he said. "I'm half-cut here, and I shouldn't be doing this."

"It's okay. I want you to."

"I'm married." He didn't even want to think about the repercussions if, after all they had been through, Maura were to learn of him getting it on with someone she would call a groupie. She would banish him to hell for all eternity. What he wanted to do was finish the set and take a cab to Maura's. And be with her and stay with her. But she would blast him for being so pie-eyed. He wouldn't go tonight. He'd go when he was fresh and sober.

"You don't look married," Dark Eyes said. "I thought you were single, or divorced."

"No."

"I'm leaving."

"No need of that. Stay around and listen to the music. I'll do a song for you. What would you like to hear?"

"No! I'm leaving!" She got up and marched to the door and out into the night.

He looked across at Burke, whose expression was unreadable behind a pall of smoke. Monty got up and signalled to the band that they should start getting ready for their last set. Before heading to the stage, he sat in the chair next to Burke's.

"Quite a night, Father."

"You lost a friend there, Collins."

"Yep. Not much of a night for me in the romance department. But you, now, that's a different story. Spent some time in the Honeymoon Suite, I noticed. I can't help but contrast that with the way I saw you earlier tonight, in the lecture hall. From the Reverend Doctor Burke, scaling the heights of metaphysical speculation, to a guy in a dirty shirt getting his rocks off with a twenty-dollar hooker in the toilet of the Flying Shag."

"I didn't get anything, you bollocks! I was standing there at the

132

sink and the next thing I know this one is on her knees in front me with her hands . . . I put a stop to it."

"You've never used the can here before?"

"No. And I didn't use it tonight either; I tried to wash a stain off my shirt."

"I guess I never told you about the services available to those who enter door number one. The girls see a guy go in there, and it's assumed he's looking for company. Paid company. It's all part of the charming ambience here at the Shag."

"You've enjoyed those services yourself, have you?"

Monty wasn't about to answer that. If he had ever been in there — and he made no admission to that effect — it would have been as a callow youth, a drunken young arsehole who had not yet been granted the hand of Miss Maura MacNeil in marriage.

"The place is filthy!" Burke griped. "The sink is dirty. The urinals are sewers. The floor is dirty and pissy, and your feet stick to it. I have to feel sorry for those poor girls working in conditions like that."

"If not for the dirt and the stench, though, if this opportunity had arisen, say, after the Shag's semi-annual refit, toilet flush, and hosing down, would your priestly vows have been maintained?"

"Yeah. They would. Now don't you have a job to do before we fall into a taxi for home?"

"I guess this means we'll wrap things up after my last set, eh?"

"I'd say so."

The band played on through one last, abbreviated, set. Just as Monty was about to announce the final number, he looked down the room and saw the guy with the recorder putting his jacket on. It was the dark rain jacket Monty had noticed outside the lecture hall at St. Mary's. He remembered then where he had seen the guy before. The television studio. He and Podgis had been having a word when Monty arrived to watch the replay of the show. This amateur spy was a reporter, working with Podgis, and he had seen and recorded all the night's sordid events. Starring the defence lawyer and the Crown witness, out boozing and womanizing together.

"Hold on for a second," he instructed the band, and leapt down from the platform. Burke was giving him a questioning look, and Monty gestured towards the reporter. When he got to Burke, he said, "That's a reporter. He's working with Podgis. We'll put him out of service."

Monty saw the implications cut instantly through Burke's inebriated state. No doubt the priest pictured himself, and his brief sojourn in the Honeymoon Suite, as a news item the following day, just as Monty pictured Maura hearing the news about his own short-lived encounter. Burke got up so fast his chair tipped over with a clatter. He and Monty reached the reporter just before he could make his escape. Burke stepped in front of him and blocked his exit. The fellow was short and skinny with pointy facial features. He glared up at Burke and demanded, "What do you think you're doing?"

"I was going to ask you the same thing."

"The answer is none of your business."

"It's my business if you are in here recording the band," Monty said.

"I didn't come to record the band."

"Oh, yeah? What did you come for?"

"I got what I came for, and now I'm leaving. So get out of my way."

"You're not going anywhere with that." Monty pointed to the tape recorder. He made a grab for it and wrenched it out of the reporter's hands.

"Give me that! This is theft! I'm calling the police!"

"Go ahead, you little weasel. That tape is not going to exist by the time they get here."

Monty opened the recorder and removed the cassette, then began pulling the tape out with his fingers. Burke reached towards the guy and grabbed something. A notebook.

"You can't do that! That's my own private property."

"To be used to violate the privacy of how many people? And for whose benefit?"

Burke read from the pages of the notebook: "Collins blues at Stag tonight. Burke lecture at SMU. Burke flirting with teen bimbos. Collins at SMU." He looked at the reporter. "Flirting with bimbos? How did you come up with that one?"

"Those two outside the lecture hall."

"You mean the two he was mocking outside the lecture hall?" Monty asked. "You don't have a very good grasp of human behaviour if you couldn't even get that right. I wouldn't trust you to report the facts of any event accurately, pal. We'll take these off your hands," he said, referring to the notebook and tape. "Save you from embarrassing yourself."

"It won't be me who's embarrassed when this night makes the news," the guy insisted.

Who was Podgis out to get? His own lawyer? Did that make any sense? Or Burke, the Crown witness who had testified against him at the prelim, and who would testify again at the trial? The witness whose testimony made Podgis look boorish and pathetic, and positively swinish in relation to women.

"Beat it," Burke ordered him. "And don't be slandering people when you know they haven't done anything wrong."

"What's the matter, Father? Are you a little sensitive about your adventure with a hooker in the bathroom?"

"Nothing happened. Nothing could have happened in that short a time. Maybe your sexual encounters are finished in less than ninety seconds but not mine."

"You're not supposed to have any of those encounters."

"And tonight I didn't. I speak from memory. Have you any of those memories yourself?"

"Fuck you. Do you expect me to believe nothing went on in there?"

"Ask her yourself. She'll tell you."

"She'll say or do whatever you pay her to say or do. That's what a prostitute does."

"Speak for yourself. And if you think she'll say whatever she's paid to say, pay her more. Then see what she says."

Monty had to shut this down before things got any worse. Burke looked ready to pound the guy to a pulp. So Monty did something he could not remember ever doing before, something he despised when he saw it done by others: he used a version of "Do you know who I am?" This situation called for desperate measures.

"Your boss, Brett Bekkers, is a very good friend of my boss, Rowan Stratton. And Rowan is a very good friend of mine and of Father Burke's. When Rowan hears about this, you can be sure he'll put in a call to Bekkers. And Bekkers will not be impressed with your dirty work on behalf of Pike Podgis. If you don't want your career to be over by high noon, you'd better be on your way. Here's your recorder minus the bootleg tape."

Monty handed the machine back to the reporter, who looked up into the implacable gaze of Brennan Burke and obviously decided to cut his losses. He left without another word. And without his notebook.

How low was his client willing to stoop, Monty wondered, to get back at those who crossed him? He returned to the stage to close things down with the band's slow and sloppy version of "Shame, Shame, Shame."

Brennan

Morning dawned painfully for Brennan. There was a reason he had set his alarm clock for eight o'clock; what was it? Mass. Of course. He was doing the old Latin Mass with the boys' and men's choir. Right. His eyelids felt like sandbags. He let them close and he rolled over in bed and fell unconscious. But the alarm rang again, jolting him from sleep. How much had he had to drink last night? Where? O God, he remembered, he had been in the jacks at the Flying Shag. He could smell it all over again. And wasn't there . . . yes, yes, he was with a hooker. But he hadn't brought her along; she had appeared unbidden and . . . nothing happened in the end. *O my God, I am heartily sorry for having offended Thee.* . . . He threw the covers off and bolted for the shower.

After he was scrubbed clean and shining, with his mouth tasting of mint and his smoke-infused clothing from the night before in his laundry basket, he dressed in his clerical black and went down to the kitchen. He found a croissant and a bottle of orange juice, and sat down at the table for his breakfast. The *Chronicle Herald* was there and, once again, there was a story about Pike Podgis. Another memory assailed him from the night before. Some little minion of Podgis had been in the bar, watching and recording the goings-on. Brennan thought that, between the two of them, he and Monty had put the fear of God into him. Monty had destroyed the tape, and Brennan, the notebook. But the horrid Podgis was an inescapable part of Brennan's life now, he realized, because he would have to testify against the man at the trial whenever that would be. Was the episode last night Podgis's revenge for the evidence Brennan had given, or was Podgis trying to intimidate him out of testifying again? Well, it was not going to work. Brennan was not in the least intimidated by the likes of Podgis; in fact, he only wished he had more evidence to use against him to make sure he got convicted and sent away for good. Brennan picked up the paper, which offered more of the same.

"Saint" a Possible Suspect in Girl's Death: Podgis

He's been called a saint and a mystery to the medical profession. Now he's being talked about as a possible suspect in the murder of 19-year-old Jordyn Snider, who died of stab wounds in the early hours of September 24 on the grounds of St. Bernadette's church. Her body was found near the site where some people claim the Virgin Mary has appeared. Pike Podgis, the controversial TV personality who has been committed to stand trial for Jordyn's murder, issued a statement last evening referring to a man who was found unconscious not far from the murder scene. Podgis said the man had blood on him when he was found, a fact that came out at the preliminary hearing. Although Podgis did not name the man, it was clear that the reference was to Ignatius Boyle. Boyle, a 56-year-old homeless man, is the person whose sudden ability to speak French has drawn comparisons with a revered Polish mystic. Supporters of Boyle claim he is a saint whose ability to speak a new language is not the only miracle he has performed. Two women have come forward with claims that they were cured of illness by Ignatius Boyle.

In his statement, Pike Podgis accused the Halifax Police Department of ignoring the fact that Boyle was found near the murder scene with blood on him because the police have focused their investigation solely on the talk show host, who has criticized various police departments of "sloppy" investigative work in recent years in his broadcasts. Podgis levelled his charges during an interview with ATV News, the affiliate of CTV, which airs the *Pike Podgis Show*. Podgis's lawyer, Monty Collins, was unavailable for comment but his law partner, Rowan Stratton, distanced himself from any allegations against Boyle: "There have been no charges against any other person in connection with this offence. If there are other possible suspects, we will of course look into them. In any event, Mr. Podgis will fight the charge against him, he will have a fair trial, and we are confident that he will prevail."

People who know Ignatius Boyle say he was a frequent visitor to the statue of St. Bernadette even before the claimed apparitions brought hundreds of pilgrims to the site. Residents of the First Day men's shelter say Boyle sometimes bunked down at the shelter, but on many nights he slept in makeshift quarters in the same area of the city as St. Bernadette's church. Supporters of Boyle maintained a vigil outside the hospital until he was released on October 11. One of those supporters told this newspaper that Boyle is nothing but a convenient scapegoat. "Let's hope these nasty rumours do not turn into something worse, like false charges of murder. Ignatius Boyle is a saint. God knows he is innocent."

Of course he is innocent, Brennan said to himself. Or, at least, let us hope so. He got up from the table, decided to brush his teeth again, and started for the stairs. He met Mrs. Kelly coming down. She gave him a look of churchy disapproval and said, "Late night, Father?" He ignored her, went on to perform his ablutions, and then headed over to his church to vest for Mass. He wondered whether Monty Collins would remember and be able for his liturgical obligations this morning.

Monty

"Where the hell have you been, Collins?" Pike Podgis bellowed from his seat in reception as Monty arrived at Stratton Sommers to begin his workday.

"I've been at morning Mass, Pike," he replied, and winked at the receptionist, Darlene, on the way to his office with his client in tow.

"Bloody likely!"

He had indeed been at Mass, and had been surprised and impressed, not for the first time, at how Father Burke was able to recover from a hard night of drinking and carrying on to fulfill his role as a stand-in for Jesus Christ at the sacrificial altar. When

Monty knelt at the communion rail with the other members of the choir, Father Burke looked fresh-faced and clear-eyed, and gave the appearance of one who had never been troubled by a minute's lost sleep, let alone a hard night in a sleazy blues bar. The priest held the host before Monty and every other communicant, saying without a trace of a slur, *"Corpus Domini nostri Jesu Christi custodiat animam tuam in vitam aeternam. Amen."* The splendid neo-Gothic church with the sunlight streaming through the coloured glass of the windows, the ancient tones of the chant, and the magnificent harmonies of the Renaissance motets lifted Monty from his workaday cares and his hangover, and he had felt as if he were suspended between heaven and earth.

The presence of Podgis, bug-eyed and sweating in his fur-lined bomber jacket, slammed him down onto the hard ground of earth once again.

"How may I help you today?"

"You could start by being in your office during normal business hours, so when I come all the way over here on a bus from Dartmouth, I don't have to wait around till you saunter in."

"Well, here I am."

They sat in the office, and Monty offered Podgis a cup of coffee. This did nothing to soften his client's belligerence.

"Yeah, coffee. Now when are you going to start taking my case seriously?"

Monty picked up the phone and asked Darlene to bring in two cups of coffee. When he and Podgis had each enjoyed their first sip, Monty said, "Of course I'm taking your case seriously. I don't know why you think otherwise."

"First of all, you blow it at the prelim."

"We've been over that. We didn't blow it. What's your next point?"

"You sit there as cool, calm, and collected, as bored, as if this was some petty shoplifting by a little greaseball whose name you can't remember. That's not what this is, Collins."

"Your point?"

"My point is that this is the biggest fucking case of your career. This is so big there will be book deals, maybe even a movie! That's if you stop dicking around and do a good job. If you don't, I'll be your worst nightmare!"

"Get over yourself, Podgis."

"How dare you talk to me like that!"

"Be serious. And tell me this. Why did you have some little gopher follow me to my gig last night?"

"I don't know what you're talking about."

"Yes, you do. If I hear or see one word on the news about my evening or anyone else's evening of relaxation at the blues bar, you and that little shithead are going to regret it. Your cub reporter is going to regret it because Brett Bekkers will get an earful about his amateur antics, and that will be the end of his TV career. You are going to regret it because I, as an officer of the court, will feel compelled to reveal to the police and the Crown that I saw what you attempted to do to a Crown witness. And that constitutes an obstruction of justice. It's theoretically possible that you did not kill Jordyn Snider, but I saw the obstruction offence with my own two eyes. By the way, it carries a sentence of up to ten years in prison."

He had him. Monty could actually see the colour draining from his client's pugnacious face. Podgis evidently realized that he had crossed the line and pissed his lawyer off to the point where he would turn his own client in.

Monty drove the point home. "You play hardball with me, I play hardball with you. Now, what's it going to be? No more of the kind of activity I saw last night?"

"Okay, I hear you."

"Call him. Let me hear you say it."

"Are you serious?"

"I'm going to make sure this goes away. Get him on the phone."

Podgis was seething, but he picked up the phone and found his man. "That work you were doing. The, uh, backgrounder on some of the people involved in my case. Job's over. Don't need you anymore. Ever. What? Did I hear you right? You're telling me what is a crap assignment and what isn't? Dream on. They won't want you over there. Oh yeah? Don't come to me looking for a reference!"

Well, that was that.

Monty moved on to his next point. "Your interview only served to emphasize our reliance on Ignatius Boyle as an alternative suspect. As a result, the prosecutors will be looking for a way to clear Boyle, eliminating him as an effective defence for us. So, no more interviews with the media. If anyone gives interviews, it will be me. And that is unlikely. Agreed?"

"Whatever."

✝

Monty put the talk show bigmouth out of his mind for the rest of the workday. He made a call to Maura at lunchtime to see if she might be interested in going out for dinner, but she already had plans for a girls' night out. She would be dropping their daughter, Normie, off at a birthday party, and their son Tommy Douglas had been tapped to babysit his baby brother, Dominic. Dominic was a bone of contention, given the fact that he was conceived when Maura and Monty were on the outs, and Maura was seeing someone else. The someone else was an Italian named Giacomo, and Monty assumed he was Dominic's father. The baby had his dark Mediterranean looks. In the early stages, Monty could not imagine the day when he would accept another man's child into his family. Never mind that he too had enjoyed the company of the opposite sex during the long separation, so Maura was no more "guilty" than Monty himself, and never mind that the pregnancy was, to say the least, unplanned and unexpected. He had still been unable to accept it. The situation was not made any easier by times they had all spent together with Father Brennan Burke, and the baby in the group looked more like Burke than like his mother's husband. Not that Monty believed there had ever been a coupling between his wife and his best friend, and he went weak in the knees whenever he tried to imagine what Maura would do to him if she could read that unworthy thought in his mind. But there had been the occasional glance from others that Monty found acutely embarrassing. He knew, however, that it was long past time to get over all that. The baby was nearly a year and a half old now. Monty wanted to develop a solid relationship with Dominic, a delightful child, and that was starting to happen more and more in recent months.

Father Burke had read the Riot Act to Monty and Maura when they were in Ireland together the previous summer. An exhausted Burke, following a night on the streets assisting a troubled homeless young boy, had taken Monty and Maura aside in the sacristy of a

Dublin church and, without any of his usual irony or sardonic comments, pleaded with them to put their differences behind them. Life was too short to let their troubles keep them apart any longer. He had been particularly forceful about the need for Dominic to have a father present in his life. And Monty could not disagree. He felt the same way. And he was becoming more attached to the little boy with every passing week.

Here was a chance to spend some time with him alone. He called Maura again, and offered to look after the baby himself, letting Tommy Douglas off the hook if he had other things to do. So that was the plan.

Maura was all dressed up and ready to go when Monty arrived at the family home on Dresden Row. Normie was in a scarlet-red party dress, which set off her auburn curls. She held a brightly wrapped present in her hand.

"Whose birthday?"

"Megan's, from school."

"How old is Megan? Eighteen now?"

"No! She's ten, Daddy. She's *my* friend, not Tommy's! You're making jokes again."

"Oh, right. Have a good time, dolly."

"Yeah, it's going to be really fun."

Monty turned to Maura. "You have to see this." He pulled a piece of paper from his pocket.

"What is it?" his daughter asked.

"Copy of a letter full of mistakes — the kind I know you would never make, Normie — and it was written to an opera singer named Kiri Te Kanawa."

He put the letter on the coffee table, and his wife and daughter bent their heads to read it, Normie squinting at the lines.

"Where are your glasses, sweetheart?" Monty asked.

"I'll get them before I go to the party. Promise. I can read this without them."

Under the letterhead of the Schola Cantorum Sancta Bernadetta, there was an address in New Zealand, and the document read:

Keeree The Canowa

Dear Ms. The Canowa,

I note with interest you are shedjuled visit to Halifax on 6 February 1993. I have long been an admirer of you're work, but I shall for the time being restrane myself from lodding you're talents and acomplishments, and perseed to the purpose of my letter. I am the Director of a Choir school for children here in Halifax, and of the Schola Cantorum Sancta Bernadetta as well. (I inclose a Brosherr describing the Schola.) I intend to arrange for members of both School's to attend you're matinay Performance at the Rebecka Cone Auditorium. And I am wondering weather you might be so kind as to except our invitation to drop by the School and recieve a little tribbute from our Student's. I would be happy to make all the arraignment's for the visit — transpertation, refreshments and so on. I can be reached anytime at the above Address and phone number. I thank you for considdering my request, and irregardless of your decision, I look forward to hearing you at the Cone.

Sincerely,
Brennan Burke

"*Ir*regardless? Perseed? Every second word spelt wrong. Apostrophes in all the wrong places." Maura looked up. "Who typed this thing?"

"Befanee Tate. It's in our list of documents for the wrongful-dismissal case. Unfortunately, the only thing she got right was the address, because Brennan handed it to her. Then he dictated the letter and went on his way. This is the result."

"Brennan must be wild."

"I thought he was going to have to be put on life support when I brought up the subject after the discovery exam. The only woman he thinks more of than Kiri Te Kanawa is the Blessed Virgin Mary."

"What will Kiri think of him when she gets this?"

"You might not want to mention it to him. Could send him over the edge."

"I can imagine. Well, it's time we were off, eh, Miss Normie?"

The ladies said their goodbyes then and headed out for the evening, and Monty turned his attention to the baby, Dominic, who was sitting on the dining room floor playing with a train set. He was a handsome little boy with black hair and dark eyes that sparkled when Monty walked into the room. He remembered the feeling he had when Tommy Douglas and Normie would kick up their feet and look positively joyful to see their dad. He had the same feeling right now, and he picked Dominic up and swung him around, bringing out gales of laughter from the little fellow. Then they sat on the floor together and staged multiple train wrecks to the boyish delight of both of them. Dominic gabbed away, using his ever-increasing vocabulary of nouns, verbs, and exclamation points.

When it was bedtime, Monty got him cleaned up and changed, and picked out a story book to read. But Dominic had other ideas. He toddled into his closet and began rooting for something; Monty had no idea what.

"Come on, buddy, time to get into bed and have your story. What are you doing in there?"

Dominic began pulling toys off a shelf in the closet and trying to hide them behind his back. He looked up at Monty with his big brown eyes. Monty could almost see the mischief in those eyes.

"What are you up to, you little sneak?"

"Neek, neek!" The little boy clapped his hands together and laughed as if the word "sneak" was the funniest thing he had ever heard. At that age, it might have been.

"Wait till you hear what else is in store for you with the English language, Dominic. Do you know what everybody says about guys like you after you've done all your *sneaking* around?" He gave the baby a gentle poke in the belly. Giggles again. "They say you *snuck* around."

There were peals of laughter, the little face suffused with joy. How simple things were at that age, how uncomplicated the bliss.

"Yeah, Dominic, everybody's gonna *snarl* and *snipe* and *snap* at you because you *snuck* around pulling all your toys out when you're supposed to be *snug* in your bed."

Monty wagged his finger like the old schoolmarm of days gone by and pointed to the bed. Dominic ran in the opposite direction, back to his closet, and began banging on the door with the palms of both hands, then turned to Monty with an evil grin.

"Don't get *snarky* with me, you little *snoop*. You know you're not allowed to be *snooping* in there."

The door opened, and Maura walked in.

"You're back already!"

"Mama!"

"What's going on in here, boys?"

Monty put his finger to his lips and mouthed an exaggerated *no* at the baby. "Don't tell!" Dominic looked at his mother, laughing, then looked away.

"Nothing going on here. Just having a discussion about the vagaries of the English language before putting this little *sneak* down for a *snooze*."

That set him off again.

"All right, then. You'd better get on with it. I'll come back in and give him his good-night kiss. *If* he's good."

"Oh, he's a good boy. Aren't you, Dominic? There's nothing *snide* or *sneaky* about this little guy. Let's get you into that bed now."

Maura quietly slipped out the door, and Monty picked the child up, lifted him high in the air, and wiggled him. Dominic went into a fit of laughter again, and his mother called from the hallway. "He'll never settle down if you get him all wound up."

"You heard your mother. Wipe that grin off your face and *snuggle* down in your blankets."

Monty got him under the blankets and kissed his forehead, then said good night and started to tiptoe from the room.

"Dada! Dada!"

Monty turned to see Dominic with his arms outstretched to him. Nothing in the world could have made him resist. He went back to the child, sat on the side of the bed, and held him in a long embrace till he heard the soft, even breathing of sleep, and left the room.

Chapter 10

Brennan

Brennan was assigned to yard duty on Thursday. He had promised Monsignor O'Flaherty he would materialize before the multitudes and talk about miracles. It was the last thing he wanted to do, and he had succeeded in avoiding it up to now, but O'Flaherty had him down for January 7. The day had arrived, and here he was. At least he didn't have to discuss the miraculous healing of diseased organs and running sores.

It was cold and there was the occasional snowflake, but there was a crowd of around seventy-five people outside, kneeling at the statue or milling around the grounds or standing in line at the gaudy souvenir stands. There was now a laminated photograph of Ignatius Boyle affixed to a light pole. Brennan walked over to the statue of St. Bernadette and announced that he would be giving a short talk for anyone who was interested in the timely subject of miracles. The people gathered around him.

"The most outstanding theophany — divine intervention — of the modern era occurred in southern Europe in 1917. At Fatima in Portugal. There had been a coup d'état in 1910, and the new government was anticlerical and hostile to the Church. Seminaries were shut down, Church property was seized by the state, it was forbidden to wear a cassock, religious orders were driven out of the country, and religious education in schools was forbidden. Like Ireland in the penal times. Anyway, this was the backdrop to the miracle of 1917.

"Three young shepherds said that they had a vision of the Virgin Mary, that she appeared to them regularly at the same spot on the thirteenth day of every month. The three were Lucia dos Santos, who was ten when this happened, and her cousins Francisco and Jacinta Marto. He was nine; she was seven. The kids claimed that Mary had told them a secret, and they were not to reveal it to anyone else. Lucia's mother repeatedly called her a liar, scolded and beat her to get her to admit she had made it up. Lucia wouldn't back down. A ten-year-old girl, with her mother against her. Then the authorities got into the act. The government wanted the superstitious peasants shut down. And they wanted to know about this 'secret' the apparition had imparted to the children. Why this interest in the secret, if the apparition didn't exist? But anyway. The police rounded up the children, brought them to jail, and shoved them into a cell with some of the local ne'er-do-wells. The kids had a bit of fun there at first. One of the prisoners played the harmonica, and another danced with Jacinta. But the frolicking was short-lived. The children were taken out of the cell and brought before the senior administrator, who demanded to . know the secret the lady had imparted to them. The children refused to tell. The man threatened to boil them in oil."

"Oh come on! That's laying it on a bit too thick, isn't?" someone called from the crowd.

"Look it up," Brennan responded. "That threat didn't get them anywhere, so they took Jacinta away and left the other two with the administrator. A guard returned sometime after that and told Lucia and Francisco that Jacinta had been put in the oil and cooked. The two little kids believed it, and believed they were next. But still they wouldn't tell. Then Francisco was taken to be 'boiled,' leaving Lucia by herself with the boss. In the face of what she believed was certain death, she refused to reveal the secret. The authorities had to admit defeat; the three were eventually released.

"I make no comment on the secrets of Fatima," Brennan said, "or on the timing of what were very political messages recounted much later by Lucia. But I have no doubt whatsoever about the miracle of the sun. This was a miracle announced three months in advance. 'It's happening at noon on the thirteenth of October at Cova da Iria. Be there.'

"At least fifty thousand people witnessed the event. That's the estimate given by Avelino de Almeida, who was there to report on the event for his paper, the liberal, anticlerical *O Seculo*. The paper had been mocking the claims all along, and Almeida expected that nothing would happen. Most historians say there were seventy thousand people there.

"Of course there were the usual claims that this was a situation of mass hypnosis or religious fever. Well, if so, it affected the antireligious press as well as the supposedly gullible peasants, because they all saw it at the same time. As did a devout socialist who had gone to debunk the whole thing, but instead ended up in a state of shock in a hospital for three days afterwards. It was also seen by many who could not have been part of any kind of group hypnosis, people miles away from the site.

"So here's what happened. The seventy thousand people, rich and poor, educated and simple, pious and skeptical, trooped to the site. It was bucketing rain the night before, and the ground turned to muck. Everyone's clothing was soaked through. But the people stuck it out, determined to see the promised miracle. The three children were brought by their very nervous parents. Twelve noon came, and nothing happened. People waited. Nothing. The children's families were terrified that, if nothing happened, the crowd would turn on the kids and tear them apart.

"Then just around one thirty — which, by the way, was solar noon in Portugal at that time of year — the rain stopped abruptly and the sky cleared. The sun appeared as a clear-edged disc. A scientist present, Dr. Almeida Garrett, described it in unscientific terms as looking like a gaming table. It kept its heat and light but you could look directly at it without hurting your eyes, without damaging the retina. The *O Seculo* reporter, Avelino de Almeida, likened it to a silver disc. Then it began to turn on itself at a dizzying speed, throwing out light in all the colours of the rainbow. All those brilliant colours were reflected in the faces of the people, their clothing, and the earth itself. This went on for some time, then the object seemed to detach itself from the firmament. It turned blood red and came hurtling towards the ground. People were terror-stricken. But it veered away.

"The previously skeptical journalist, Almeida, described it this way." Brennan reached into his pocket for a photocopy of the news clipping. "'Before the dazzled eyes of the people, whose attitude transported us to biblical times, and who, dumb-founded, heads uncovered, contemplated the blue of the sky, the sun trembled, it made strange and abrupt movements, outside of all cosmic laws, "the sun danced," according to the typical expression of the peasants . . .'

"He took photos of the crowd with their faces upturned. Once people got their breath back, they noticed that their clothing was completely dry. It had dried in seconds.

"When, as expected, Almeida was attacked for reporting such a thing, he responded: 'I saw . . . I saw . . . I saw . . . Miracle, as the people shouted? Natural phenomenon, as the experts say? For the moment, that does not concern me, I am only saying what I saw. . . . The rest is a matter for Science and the Church.'

"Was it really the sun?" Burke asked. "Apparently not. The Greenwich Observatory did not record anything out of whack. But it was a celestial display of some kind. Almeida, quite rightly, left open the question of whether this was a natural phenomenon. But how often do we have a never-before-seen natural phenomenon, appearing on schedule as announced by three peasant children after a conversation they claim was with the Virgin Mary?

"A well-attested event, in that case. But all of us should be a bit like Avelino de Ameida when we hear reports of supposedly miraculous events or appearances. Be skeptical, check it out, weigh the evidence pro and con, and then describe the findings without embellishment."

A number of people asked questions, and Brennan did his best to answer them. Some of course were unanswerable. But he had another mission now that he was among the pilgrims. He surveyed the crowd looking for suspicious behaviour on the part of the visionary's boy-friend. Was he out there, taking money off the deluded and the desperate? Brennan would take a stroll through the grounds. In the absence of the boyfriend — Gary was his name, Brennan remembered — he decided to seek out a familiar face or two in the crowd and ask whether there had been anyone taking up a collection recently.

His first few inquiries were met with a tentative "no" that did not quite convince him. Had some of these people been taken in, and were they embarrassed to admit it? Or was it more straightforward than that: nobody had been tapped. But an elderly woman in a brown wool coat and hat overheard the conversations and came up to him. She said she had given money to a young man a few days ago. What did he look like? The description matched Gary. No surprise there.

"How did he get the money from you?"

"He asked me."

"What did he say?"

"He told me that in eighty percent of appearances by the Virgin, her message had included instructions to be good to the poor and homeless."

Gary and Befanee's attempt at sophistication, Brennan assumed. They knew better than to claim that the BVM *always* demanded a shakedown. Somebody could check on that. But if a person looked into an apparition story and found no reference to money, well, that would be one of the twenty percent in which filthy lucre was not mentioned.

"He used the word 'homeless'?" Brennan asked.

The woman looked confused. "Well, I think he did. That's the way I remember it."

"Please go on. I'm sorry for the interruption."

"Oh, that's quite all right, Father. That's all there was to it. This young man felt called to do what he was doing. And he said not to worry, that he was not stealing it for himself, because he didn't need it. He said he was just here at the church while on a break from his work as an assistant manager. And he told me to watch him, and I would see that he was indeed giving the money to poor homeless people. So I did watch, and he gave money to a couple of poor souls who were just lying on the ground, ill or perhaps even drunk or on drugs."

"I see."

"I of course was worried that they were in cahoots with him, pretending to be poor but really his buddies in disguise."

"And you don't think that was the case?"

"I could be wrong, but I don't think so. One of the fellows got up and hit him! And really hit him, I mean. There was a fight, and it wasn't staged, let me tell you. It didn't last long, but it was the real thing."

Maybe it was, thought Brennan. Maybe part of Gary's performance was to go up to "real people" in the crowd, the poor and disadvantaged who were always attracted to this type of spectacle, and hold money out to them. Or hold pieces of paper out. Or perhaps even give them part of the take to cement the cover story into place, should anyone go around asking. The fellow who hit him might have been ticked at the miserly sum and been angling for more. Who knew?

Was this robbery or fraud, or just panhandling? Should Brennan be calling the police? He could not quite bring himself to do it; the Burkes were not police informers. He would deal with this petty crime figure in his own way.

He thanked the woman, urged her to hang on to her money and to consider carefully what she thought was going on in the churchyard.

"Do you believe this is really the Blessed Virgin, Father?"

He hesitated for a few seconds, then said, "No."

She took a moment to think it over. "That's too bad. I'd like to think she is really with us."

"She may indeed be with us, but not physically and not as reported by Befanee Tate."

"Or by the murdered girl, Jordyn. Do you think that's why she got killed, Father?"

"What do you mean?"

"Killed for her religious beliefs."

"By Podgis?"

"Well, he certainly is anti-religious. I heard him mock the Blessed Mother on that show of his."

"I don't think Podgis would kill over a religious disagreement. I'd say the antics around this place would be more likely to offend a deeply religious person than someone who dismisses it all out of hand."

"So you're saying it was a person of faith who killed her, for her statements about the Virgin?"

"No, no, I was just speaking off the cuff. I don't think that at all. I think she was murdered for some other reason. Known now only to the killer."

"And to God."

"And to God."

†

151

Brennan left her then because he had another duty to perform. For the next couple of weeks he would be spending more time than usual in the confession box, not as a penitent but as a replacement for Father Bernie Drohan, who had gone on a retreat. He walked into the church, brushed the snowflakes off his hair and clothing, genuflected deeply, and made the sign of the cross. Then he went up to the confession box, replaced the "Fr. Drohan" name plate with his own for the evening, and entered the booth. He donned the purple stole he kept in the box and closed the door. He knew he could expect the usual litany of minor, barely sinful transgressions, the occasional report of serious misbehaviour, and the rambling life histories of the lonely. For most of the penitents, he felt the sacrament was necessary and valued.

"Bless me Father, for I have sinned. It has been, well, a shameful number of years since my last confession."

The voice was soft, raspy, but vaguely familiar. Brennan looked through the screen but could make out nothing but the silhouette of a hooded jacket.

The man fell silent.

"Yes?" Brennan prompted him.

"Well, it's about that girl, Father." Silence again.

"Girl?"

"That poor young girl who was found dead in your backyard."

Brennan felt all his senses going on alert. "Yes? What about her?"

"I keep thinking about her."

The last thing Brennan wanted to hear was the role sin played in this man's thinking about the murdered girl. But, again, the silence compelled him to prod the man to get on with it.

"What sins do you wish to confess?"

"My thoughts about her."

"What kind of thoughts?" His voice was sharper than he intended.

"I . . . I imagine what she might have gone through."

This time it was the priest who was silent.

"Maybe she was . . . violated. By this guy Podgis. Or whoever else did it. Father? Are you there?"

"I am."

"The kind of guy who would smash a young woman in the face and drive a knife into her . . . a man like that is a monster."

An all too common kind of monster, Brennan thought: another in an infinite succession of corrupt, evil, fallen human beings.

"Wouldn't you agree, Father?"

"I am here to take your confession."

"I'm just saying a guy like that gets a young girl on the ground. What's he gonna do, you know what I mean? She's right there for him."

"What is your point? If you are not here to confess your sins, but to commit more of them, get out of here and come back when you've examined your conscience and are remorseful about whatever sins you have committed. Until then there is no point in your being here."

"I'm sorry, Father. Please forgive me."

There was something about the man's grating speech; it sounded as if he was disguising his voice. Well, it wasn't the first time that had happened. "Please get to the point."

"This TV asshole, Podgis. Excuse my French, Father. But Podgis. Do you think he really did it?"

"Do you?" What was going on here?

"Oh, I wouldn't know one way or the other."

"Why are you bringing this up?"

"I'm just wondering what kind of a sicko he is. They let him have his television show all these years, he's famous across the country, and it turns out the guy is really a killer. If he is."

"Did you yourself have something to do with this girl's death?" Brennan made an effort not to raise his voice. "Is that what you're trying to say?"

"No! I didn't have anything to do with it! How can you say that?"

"Because there is something distinctly wrong with your so-called confession here today and, if you had something to do with this murder, I urge you to turn yourself in."

"Because *you* can't. You're not allowed to." A priest could be excommunicated for breaching the seal of the confessional, which this fellow well knew. "But I told you. It wasn't me."

"Then either get on with it, or leave the confessional. There are other people waiting."

"You're a guy yourself, Father."

Brennan didn't bother to reply.

"You must have thought about it too."

Again, Brennan kept his silence. But he wasn't going to be able to maintain his patience much longer.

"You read the news about a young, hot-looking female lying there, helpless. And if you're anything like me, you're forming a picture in your mind of what the guy might have done to her. What you'd have done yourself. Or what you'd like to do. And it's a sin. Because it gives you a big — "

"Get out of this confessional! Get out of here now, before I get up and throw you out. If you know anything about this crime, take yourself off to the police station right now."

The man made a noisy departure. A child's voice said, "Bless me Father . . ." and the priest decided to stay put rather than cause a scene in the church, in front of this child and whoever else might be in the nave. Whoever had whispered those sick thoughts into his ear must surely have had nothing to do with the crime. The killer wouldn't dare come in here. And the police had Podgis for it, with the victim's blood on his shoes, and a witness who saw him leaving the scene. This man in the confessional was just a sick, twisted pervert who . . . Brennan shook his head and tuned in to the little fellow confessing his theft of a tub of chocolate ripple ice cream from the school lunchroom refrigerator.

He granted absolution, but the boy did not leave. "Uh, what's my penance, Father?"

"Ah. Right. Next time they're giving out ice cream, take the plain vanilla. And only one scoop. That sound about right?"

"Yes, Father. Um . . ."

"Yes?"

"So I don't have to say any prayers?"

"I assume you'd be saying prayers anyway. Part of your regular interior life. Right?"

"Uh, sure, yeah. Yes, Father."

"And you'd never commit the sin of lying in the confessional."

"No!"

"All right. Off with you then."

"Yes, Father."

Chapter 11

Monty

Monty attended a discovery examination on Friday morning with a client who was a snow-removal contractor. He had been named as a third party in a lawsuit by a woman who had slipped and fallen in the icy parking lot of a shopping centre. After that, Monty had an appointment with a private investigator he employed from time to time on his cases. Moody Walker was a retired police detective who had gone into business for himself after leaving the department. He had been on the opposing side all during his police career, but he was a good investigator and worked as hard for the defence as he did for anybody else who retained him.

The former sergeant arrived at eleven thirty, and Monty welcomed him into his office. Moody had short bristly grey and white hair and penetrating brown eyes. You would make him for a cop anywhere on the planet.

"How's it going, Moody?"

"Everything is copacetic."

"I'm hoping you can do something for me." Walker waited for the assignment. He was not a man for small talk. "As you know, I'm representing Pike Podgis for the murder of Jordyn Snider."

"Oh, yeah. I know."

"You're not a fan?"

"When I walk out of here, is he my client as well as yours?"

"I'm hoping so."

"Then for the duration of the contract, I'm his biggest fan. Can't wait till his show is on the air again, and I can sit there with a jumbo bag of Cheezies taking it all in."

"Thanks, Moody. What I need is a canvass of the residential buildings on Morris and Hollis streets. At least near the intersection of those two streets. The woman who says she saw Podgis leaving the murder scene the morning of September twenty-fourth also admitted at the prelim that she had heard voices. Plural. One of them may have been a woman's. And it sounded as if these voices woke her up before she became aware of Podgis. He had soft-soled shoes on, and was alone. So my thinking is that she heard somebody else's footsteps going by. And these voices. I'd like to know whether anybody else heard something that morning."

"Sounds pretty straightforward. I'll get on it first thing tomorrow. Anybody who is out, I'll go back and check in the afternoon or evening till I catch them at home."

"Perfect. Thank you."

"Good. You'll hear from me as soon as I have something."

†

"What are you doing for my case, Collins?"

It was Podgis shouting down the phone at him twenty minutes after Moody Walker left on his assignment.

"I am examining all the evidence disclosed by the Crown and figuring out where we can attack it. Lining up witnesses to interview and possibly call to testify at trial. Waiting for your alibi witness to have an attack of conscience — *oh, baby, I can't let them take you away from me forever; I'll call your lawyer and offer to take the stand and tell the world you were with me that night* — only she hasn't called. Hasn't called me, at any rate. You?"

"You really piss me off, Collins. When this is all over, I'm gonna do a show, more like a series of shows, about smartass lawyers who don't give a fuck about their clients and just string them along and take their money."

"It's already been done. And the fact that I piss you off does not mean I am not working hard on your defence. Does not mean I will not do a stellar job in trying to get you off. I know what I'm doing, Podgis. I've been doing it for over twenty years."

"What you've been doing for over twenty years is defending guilty people."

"And frequently getting them acquitted. Or getting them very good deals in sentencing."

"Yeah, there you go. Sentencing. Guilty. But let me tell you this again, Collins. I'm not one of your guilty clients. I am innocent. In case you don't recognize it, that's a seven-letter word that means I didn't do it."

"Eight."

"What?"

"Eight letters."

"How much are you going to soak me for the math and spelling lesson?"

"It's all part of the package."

"Now let me get back to the point. Why aren't you out there in front of the cameras, arranging interviews with CTV and CBC and the papers, telling them about this miscarriage of justice? One more wrongfully accused man in this country, one more man about to lose his whole life locked up for a murder he didn't commit. Not news anymore?"

"I don't work the press, Podgis. I work the justice system."

"Well, then, work it. Get out there and investigate. Like me. I shouldn't have to do all the work here. Somebody else did this. There's a killer on the loose, and an innocent man facing trial."

"Do you know why you are facing trial, Podgis? Because you were observed running from the murder scene in the early hours of the morning, and Jordyn Snider's blood was on your shoes."

"We've been over this a million times, Collins. Is your memory going? I was not running from the scene. I was hurrying to my hotel room in the cold. I walked near the scene, but I did not see the girl lying there. Either her blood was sprayed a long distance out, or she was moved."

"She wasn't moved. That was established at the prelim, by the police and the medical examiner."

"And you believe them."

"Yes, I believe them."

"You've been a lawyer how long, and it's never occurred to you they're lying?"

"Why would the medical examiner be lying?"

"Ah-*ha*. I notice you don't ask that about the cops. So I assume you're familiar with their tendency to lie and say whatever they have to in order to get their man. And the man they want to get this time, *desperately*, is Pike Podgis."

"Why are they out to get you, Podgis?"

"You know fucking well why. I told you before. I've exposed their lies and their shoddy investigative practices on my show over and over again. I'm on their most-wanted list. It was a fantasy come true for them when they found out I had been near the murder scene, thanks to that old crone that flew across the street to rat me out for walking on Byrne Street in the middle of the night. But she blew it. She revealed that she had heard voices that night. That's what woke her up. As you made clear on cross-examination — I'll give you credit for that much — whatever woke her up was long over by the time she hauled her skinny ass out of bed and saw me on the street. She saw me alone, not yelling at somebody else. She admitted that one of the voices was female. So, somebody else was out there. She knows it, the police know it. And nobody's doing a goddamn thing about it. Because they want Pike Podgis to go down for this. Well, I intend to find out who else was out there that night, even if you won't. If I have to be my own detective, so be it. Won't be the first time I investigated a case. Too bad this time it's my own ass on the line."

Of course, Podgis was not the only one intrigued by the fact that somebody else was out there. More than one person, perhaps a man and a woman.

"I have a private investigator working on the case."

That stopped him.

"Are you there, Podgis?"

"Yeah, I'm here. I'm just stunned to find out you're actually doing something. Who's this private dick?"

"He's a retired police sergeant by the name of Moody Walker. And he's good."

"He better be. What's he doing for me?"

"He's checking out the neighbourhood around Morris and Hollis streets to find out if anyone else heard those voices."

"Glad to hear it."

He didn't sound all that glad to hear it. But Monty was not about to use up any of his time wondering what would constitute glad tidings in the life of Pike Podgis.

"Let me know as soon as you get anything," his client said. "I'm paying the bills here."

The news about Walker, though, was not enough for Podgis. He wound himself up again. "And another point you made at the prelim, about the blood . . . the cops were lying about that too. They knew perfectly well that whoever did this would have been splattered with blood. They took my clothes and they know they weren't bloody, except for the shoes from that walk through the grounds. So they pretend some killers never get any blood on them. Yeah, right. Well, guess what? We all know there was a guy with blood on him that night, only a hop, skip, and a jump from the murder scene. *Saint* Ignatius Boyle."

Ignatius Boyle was still the most obvious alternative to plant in the minds of a future jury; there was no question that the location and timing of his head injury and bloodied face were a curious coincidence, to say the least. But Monty's concern was that, if he found out what had really happened to Boyle, it might be more damaging than helpful to his case.

Podgis was still railing against the local saint. "Half those saints were wacky anyway, right?"

"Holy, Podgis, they were holy. They weren't out killing young women."

"This one was, by the look of things."

"Not necessarily. He may have been another victim. Or a witness, knocked out of contention by the killer."

"The killer would have killed him, not left him there to wake up."

"He very nearly didn't wake up. He was in a coma for a week and a half. Killer may have thought he was dead, and couldn't take the chance of being seen standing over the body checking for a pulse. We just don't know. Or, at least I don't."

"I've had enough of you right now, Collins. Why don't you take an hour or so off from billable time and drop in to the law school? See if they're giving a course called Representing the Innocent Client 101. You do that, and I'll go find the real killer, so I can get this over with and get on with my life. Goodbye."

†

Monty had in fact been planning to do another bit of probing on behalf of Podgis but, when the ill-mannered lout had lit into him yet again, it took away any incentive Monty might have had to reassure him. Now that he was off the phone, Monty proceeded with the task he had set himself, to ask a few questions about Ignatius Boyle. This would not reflect well on Monty or his client, so he intended to stick to people he knew, rather than wander all around the city asking questions of anyone who would likely have come into contact with Boyle. He had two places in mind, the First Day shelter for homeless men and the public library on Spring Garden Road.

Simone Deveaux was the house director at First Day. Monty had worked with her from time to time when he was with Nova Scotia Legal Aid. She welcomed him into the shelter, a large wooden building a few blocks from the downtown core on Barrington Street. Several dozen men were gathered in the television room, and Monty recognized many of them from the streets and the courts. Simone wore a tweed blazer over a pair of jeans, and her white hair was pulled back. She brought him into the kitchen and placed a cup of tea on the table in front of him. Monty explained the situation: Ignatius Boyle found unconscious near the murder scene with blood on his face. None of this was news to Simone, who had been following the story, including the claims of miracles associated with Boyle.

"As you can imagine," he said, "I can't ignore the fact that Ignatius was found there. But I realize there may be no connection at all between him and what happened in the churchyard."

"I understand. Sometimes Ignatius bunks down outdoors, as you may know; he has a favourite spot behind an old house on Hollis Street. Where he was found that night was not far from that 'other home.' So we don't have him here every night."

"Why is that? Why does he go out on the street when he has a nice, warm bed in here and a roof over his head?"

"I'm not sure, Monty. We always make it clear he is welcome. And he loves to come in for his showers and his meals. But I think he's disturbed by some of the other guys here. The graphic stories, the language. It can be a little strong, a little offensive. Sometimes it gets to be too much for Ignatius, and he goes off on his own."

"What's your understanding of why he's, well, why he's homeless?"

"Severe alcohol dependence, is all I know. He told me he started drinking at a very young age, never finished school, lost a few jobs, a long downward spiral. It ran in his family, he said. It's a real shame, because he is a very intelligent person. Any chance he gets, he sits down and reads, and not just drivel. He once told me he had wanted to become a priest or a teacher. I have to say I have never seen him drunk myself. For what it's worth, Monty, my take on Ignatius is that he would more likely be a victim of violence than a perpetrator. I have not seen any signs of violence or hostility in him any time he's been with us at First Day. He is quiet and kind and considerate. And he's quick to try and help the other men here if he can, especially the younger ones. I've never seen him work any miracles, but I would describe him as a spiritual person."

"Ever hear him speak French?"

"No. I have a French name so sometimes the fellows here will say *bonjour* or *merci*. I don't remember even that from Ignatius."

"All right. Thanks, Simone, I appreciate it."

"Any time."

Next stop was the library. The lawn in front of the 1950s greystone building and the low stone wall along the sidewalk were gathering places for people downtown, and Ignatius Boyle was one of the regulars sitting on the wall. He would greet friends and acquaintances as they passed by, and would occasionally issue a recommendation for this or that event at one of the nearby churches. Monty went inside and met with a senior administrator of the library, a woman he had known since his undergraduate days. Emma Sparks was slim, dark-skinned, and elegant. Like Monty, she was an opera buff, and they discussed the production of *Traviata* they had heard recently on CBC Radio.

Emma then said, "After I spoke to you on the phone, Monty, I conducted a bit of an inquiry around the place. Discreetly, of course.

All I can tell you is that I would see Ignatius sitting on the wall outside, and we would say a friendly hello and that was it. So I asked a few other people here. Sarah Fulton has something to tell you. She's in the reference section, and it's fairly quiet up there right now. Why don't you go up and see her."

"I will. Thanks, Emma."

Sarah Fulton was short and a bit on the heavy side, and she appeared a little anxious when she saw Monty approaching. She took him into a room behind the public area, where they could speak privately.

"I didn't know what to do with this information, so I'm glad you stopped in. I'll pass it along to you, and you can do whatever you see fit."

Monty waited.

Sarah hesitated, then said, "I saw Ignatius Boyle with Jordyn Snider."

What? All Monty said was, "Oh, is that right?"

"Yes. It was a few years ago. I've tried to remember when, but I can't. It didn't really stand out at the time."

"Was this outside the library or somewhere else?"

"Out front, but they got into a vehicle together." This was getting worse by the minute, for Boyle. Better for Monty and his client.

"Actually, no," Sarah corrected herself. "She was already in the van, but she got out to let him in. Let me start again. I was working here one night, and I had just gone out and was standing on the front steps. I looked towards the street and saw that a van had pulled up. One of the doors opened. The sliding door on the rear passenger side. So the light went on and I saw several young people inside. Teenaged kids. Ignatius was standing there saying something to them, and the next thing I saw was a girl getting out. It was Jordyn. I didn't know her name at the time, but I recognized her from her pictures after the murder. She got out of the van, and Ignatius got in. She went back in herself. The door closed and they pulled away."

"What was Ignatius Boyle doing in a van full of teenagers?"

"I couldn't tell you. But whatever it was, I'd say it didn't go all that well, because the next time I saw Ignatius and Jordyn together — not together, but her passing by on the sidewalk and him sitting on the wall — I could tell she wanted nothing to do with him. He seemed to be trying to talk to her, and she made a face as if to say 'Leave me alone, you creep!' and she moved away from him and then took off at a clip. Apart from that, I have no idea what happened. If they ever crossed paths before or after that, I didn't see it. I'm here every day and I see him frequently, but those were the only times I noticed Jordyn."

Monty thanked Sarah and left the library, trying to figure out what this stunning new information meant, what it told him about Ignatius Boyle, and how he could use it in his defence of Pike Podgis.

Brennan

Brennan headed over to the church for confessions on Monday evening, following a weekend he had managed to devote to prayer and music. It was a cold, crisp January night, with a bit of snow on the ground and the moon bright in the sky. He was almost smiling as he walked. The choir school children had done a stellar job singing Mozart's beautiful motet "Laudate Dominum." Normie Collins had requested it for a "sick friend," someone down with "consumption," to hear her tell it. Well, regardless of the reason, he was happy to add the piece to the choir's repertoire. He would bring in the men and older boys for the lower parts. The music was running through his head. Nothing better.

"Bless me, Father, for I have sinned."

This was the fourth person to enter the confessional, and it was that rasping, hissing, disguised voice again. The nasty piece of work who had wanted to talk about the murdered girl. Brennan steeled himself for another encounter.

"I can't get her out of my mind, Father. Jordyn. Have you seen the pictures of her in the paper? On TV? I mean the pictures before she was a stiff. Or maybe you saw her in the churchyard when she was still moving and breathing."

"What do you want?"

"I want forgiveness, Father. Absolution. I want to be a better man than the weak, lustful sinner that I am. I want to stop thinking about her! The long pale legs, the finely turned ankles. The high-necked but always — did you notice? — tight sweaters she would wear. And did you see her that time she had the hot pink miniskirt on? You guys probably spent a whole lot of time looking at her out the window of the rectory, right? Are those little skirts back in style, or was she just flaunting that firm little ass and, as they say, lookin' for it — "

"I don't want to hear another word of this selfish and twisted talk. About a young girl who was murdered. You are here for reasons unbefitting a Catholic in his church, making a mockery of the sacraments. If you need treatment for your problems, I can give you the name of a counsellor or a psychiatrist. If you have committed a crime, if you have some responsibility for the death of this young woman, again I urge you to turn yourself in. If you're just here for shock value, get the hell out of here. I do not want to hear you. If you ever feel remorse for your sinful behaviour or your thoughts, come back in and confess properly. Preferably to another priest. Get out."

"Let's cut the crap, Brennan. You know what I'm here to confess."

He had dropped the disguise. The voice belonged to Podgis. When Brennan looked through the screen the hood was down, the silhouette of the head visible.

"Father? You there?"

Brennan did not reply. His mind was racing.

"Yeah, you're there. I didn't hear you stumbling out of the box, trying to run away from your responsibilities. So let's get on with it."

"You're not a Catholic, Perry Calvin Podgis."

"Oh, I beg to differ. I was baptized a Catholic by my dear old dad before he left for parts unknown. My mother was a Presbyterian. Then she turned Holy Roller. Took me to a few different Protestant churches when I was small. Then my stepfather came along. He wasn't much for church. So my mother went along with that, and I didn't have all the benefits of a religious upbringing. Thank God. If He exists. I have no idea. I don't pretend to know. Unlike some. But He might exist. So I'm here, to cover my ass just in case. Where were we?"

"What are you really here for, Podgis?"

"I want to get it off my conscience."

"Is it troubling your conscience at all?"

"Yeah, yeah, sure it is. Why else would I be here?"

"I can't begin to fathom your motives, so I won't even try."

"I want to confess to this mortal sin I've committed, before I go to trial and plead my innocence!"

"You feel remorse for it, do you, Podgis?"

"I do, Father."

"I see. Why don't you just plead guilty, if you're so remorseful? Try a bit of plea bargaining. Try for a reduced sentence. Say you were driven mad by this girl's rejection of your advances. Take your punishment like a man. Gather lots of material for a series of television shows about the prison and its inmates to use when you get out."

"Would you?"

"Would I what?"

"Plead guilty to murder?"

"I'm not the one who killed a person and then proceeded to enjoy all kinds of hateful, perverted conversations about it."

"I know, I know. I feel bad about it. I just feel compelled to relive the whole thing. Fantasize about it. About her. You understand."

"No. I don't."

"I figure I'll be too distracted when I'm on trial. I won't have time to think about her. Maybe that's why I'm so obsessed now, so keen on bringing up the images. And feeding off them. Gives me something to do when I'm alone in my room. I figure I won't get lucky too often as an accused murderer, so I mostly avoid the pickup joints."

Brennan had to stifle the urge to question how often the stunted, ferocious-looking creature would ever get lucky at the best of times; that was hardly an appropriate question for a priest to ask while performing the holy sacraments.

"But maybe I'm wrong, Brennan. Ever hear of Ted Bundy?"

Of course he had heard of the sadistic psychopath who had killed more than thirty young women in the United States. He didn't reply.

"You've heard of him, right? Some of the things he did to those girls! Did kinky things to them, beat their heads in, bit them, strangled them, you name it. And guess what? He had a fan club. Girls sitting in the front row of the courtroom, giggling when he turned and smiled at them. Broads from all over the world writing to him. Making phone calls, trying to reach him. To tell him they loved him. Go figure, eh? Maybe I should plead guilty after all. Build up a following. I did a show about that phenomenon. That and other cases like it. Did you happen to catch it?"

Brennan remained silent, wondering what to do about the appalling man, how to get him to either turn himself in or shut up once and for all. What was he getting out of this sacrilegious confession?

"Brennan, are you listening? I am a man in crisis, and I don't feel I have your attention."

"Is that what this is all about, Podgis? Attention? Haven't you received enough of that already? With more on the way?"

"I don't like your attitude, Burke. I never did. But you're my man now, my priest."

"No. I am not."

"Yeah, you are. You're my confessor."

"So confess and move on."

"I think you need some spiritual guidance, Father. You do not strike me as a holy and forgiving man of God."

"You don't believe in God."

"Hey! I don't know one way or the other, so I gotta hedge my bets. Who was the guy, that that was his philosophy about God? Thornhill mentioned him after you walked off the show. Ever hear of him?"

Blaise Pascal. Pascal's wager. He didn't bother to enlighten Podgis.

"No reply? That can only mean one thing. You want me to do the talking. Okay. I got lots to talk about, lots to confess. I bet you get tired of the predictable confessions of the little old church lady who promised her dying friend she'd pray for her every day and then forgot, and the friend croaked and it's the church lady's fault as if she holds people's lives in her claw-like hands, or — "

"Go away."

"No, I'm not going anywhere until you hear this. It's a tragedy about Jordyn Snider. Dying at the point of a bloody knife driven into her tender flesh. But I've already confessed to that, so I'll move on. Old news and stale headlines don't sell. So how about this? Ever hear about Jeanie Ballantine?"

Brennan had heard. A horrific murder. The girl's body was found but they never caught the killer. The girl's mother suffered a nervous breakdown and was confined to a psychiatric hospital.

"Father, I asked you a question. Did you ever hear about Jeanie Ballantine?"

"No."

"Well, let me give you the short version. Eighteen years old, missing for over a month. Happened in Toronto but the family was from here. Oh, the pleas of that family. Please, please just bring our little girl back. We won't ask any questions. They wouldn't have wanted her back if they'd known what she looked like at the end of her short life. She had been abducted, subjected to repeated sexual attacks and beatings, and was finally stabbed to death. Police never solved it."

Why was this vile man taking it upon himself to discuss the fate of the young girl in Toronto?

"If you're talking to them, Brennan, the police I mean, you might help them out by telling them that the carpet knife they found under Jeanie's body — which, by the way, was never made public — was left there on purpose. It wasn't accidentally left behind at the scene by a careless, incompetent murderer. This guy isn't stupid.

"Don't go out of your way," Podgis said, his tone now pleasant and conversational. "I'm just saying if you happen to be talking to the police, you could pass that helpful tip on to them. Oh, wait. Sorry. You can't talk to them, can you? You can't reveal anything you hear in this box. I guess it's just our little secret, Bren."

Brennan's heart was pounding, his thoughts running wild. Was Podgis guilty of yet another murder? Had he stalked the country leaving the bodies of young women in his wake? It was unbearable. And the fact that this malevolent individual knew he could slip into the confessional and boast about it in the secure knowledge that everything he said, and every bit of information arising out of it, was protected from disclosure forever, was an outrage in itself. Monty had told Brennan about a similar situation in the law. Prosecutors could not use any information that came out of an illegal search. Fruit of the poison tree, or something like that. Priests were stuck with the same prohibitions.

"If you have one speck of humanity in you, Podgis, if there is any part of you that is the crusader for truth you claim to be, if you committed these crimes, turn yourself in and get help. Go now and talk to — "

"I'm all talked out for today, Brennan. Oh, will you look at the time? Am I forgiven or what?"

"Podgis, you and I are going to meet outside the bounds of confession. It's the only way to — "

"Nope. See ya, Padre."

With a swiftness Brennan would not have thought possible of the awkward man, he was up and out of the confession box. Brennan had to fight an almost irresistible urge to get up and go after him, and throttle the life out of him unless he agreed to confess to the police every word he had confessed to Father Burke. But he could hear other people in the church, others waiting their turn for confession. He would put the Podgis situation in the back of his mind. For now. Later he would try to suss out how to bring this abominable man to justice.

Chapter 12

Monty

Monty was in the office Tuesday morning preparing his arguments for the Court of Appeal on a hopeless narcotics-importing case that had been part of his life for two years. He did his best to concentrate on it, but a portion of his mind was replaying the conversation with Sarah Fulton at the library. Ignatius Boyle had gone off in a van with Jordyn Snider and some other people her age. What happened on that outing? Whatever it was, Jordyn had shrunk away from him when he tried to speak to her on Spring Garden Road.

Monty had just returned his attention to the drug case when his secretary buzzed him to say Sergeant Walker was there to see him.

"Good. Send him in."

The retired cop came in, took a seat, slapped a file down on the desk, and said, "I got one hit."

"Great, Moody. What did you find?"

"One resident who heard something that night. Same apartment building as Betty Isenor, but on the Hollis Street side, not the front on Morris. I interviewed every man, woman, and child I could find in that area, and nobody else heard a thing."

"Well, it was late at night, or early in the morning. No real surprise there. But you did find one."

"Yeah, Richard Campbell. Sixty-two years old, resident of the building for eight years. That morning he was asleep till he heard voices outside. A guy and a girl."

"Really! There was a female voice. Could the witness make out what the people were saying?"

"He said it sounded like a lovers' tiff. Those were his words. All he could make out from the guy was 'please' and her saying 'no' over and over again. Then they were quiet. Our witness didn't get out of bed, or look at a clock. Just went back to sleep. I don't know what good this is going to do you, Collins."

"Well, it tells us there were other people out there. And this guy was not Podgis. Because we know Podgis was coming from the churchyard, not Hollis Street, and he was alone."

"We also know the victim was lying in the churchyard with a knife wound in her chest by the time Betty Isenor saw Podgis. And if you think you can fudge the timing . . ."

"I know, I know. It had already happened. When Podgis came through, he already had the blood on his shoes."

"And this Campbell is on the Hollis Street side of the building. So that must have been where the voices were coming from that woke him up. Morris Street would be better. I don't know how this helps you."

"I'll think of a way."

"Gotta admire that about you, Collins. You don't give up, even when anybody else would pack it in."

"Thanks, Moody. Leave your account with my secretary, and we'll take care of it right away."

"Will do."

Walker left, and Monty sat there, saying over and over to himself, as if to a jury: "There was somebody else out there." He tried to come up with a scenario whereby a guy and a girl arguing on Hollis Street the same morning of the murder could be used in the defence of his client, who was seen running from the Byrne Street crime scene on bloody feet.

✝

169

The Nova Scotia Court of Appeal reserved its decision the next day in the narcotics-importing case. There were two men and one woman convicted in the scheme, which involved drug dealers in a chain from Medellín, Colombia, to Yarmouth, Nova Scotia. Monty represented the woman, who was the mother of a child now in foster care so, regardless of her guilt, he wanted to get her out of prison. There was not much hope of overturning the guilty verdict, but he had given it his best shot. The two co-accused had their own lawyers, as was always the case when criminal conspirators were arrested and began trying to pin the blame on one another. Monty was well acquainted with the other two lawyers and, after they had duly excoriated each other's clients before the judges, they gathered outside the courtroom for a gab unrelated to the case. One of them, Jamie McVicar, had been at law school with Monty, and they had remained friends.

When it was clear the gathering was about to break up, McVicar looked at Monty and signalled with his eyes to the anteroom between the now-vacant courtroom and the lobby. Monty gave a nearly imperceptible nod and, when their other colleague had gone, Monty and Jamie stepped into the anteroom.

Jamie said, "Between the two of us, nobody else."

"Sure."

"There's something you should know about a client of yours, something I should not be telling you."

"It won't go beyond here." Monty pointed to himself. "No matter what it is." He steeled himself for whatever it was.

"Podgis was in to see us." In to Jamie's firm. "About filing a malicious prosecution suit against the Crown and the police."

"No! A little premature, isn't it? He can't sue till it's over and he's found to be innocent. An innocent man who was prosecuted with malice."

"Tell me about it. We told *him* that it's not going to happen. I wouldn't be involved with him personally, even if it did go ahead. Which it won't. But the main thing I want to tip you off about is: he wants to sue you for negligence, incompetent representation, and not having his best interests in mind."

"What horseshit! I may well get him off. Doesn't he think he should wait before seeing whether I turn out to be a bum or I save his ass?"

"I know, Monty. You and I know that. Even if you don't get him off, you'll have given him the best defence he could get anywhere. There's something seriously wrong with the guy. This is some kind of campaign he's on, presumably for the publicity. He wants to portray himself as a martyr and a champion of truth who's being hounded and persecuted. And everybody's in on it, including his own lawyer."

"Unbelievable. Makes me want to chuck it all and go work at Tim's making doughnuts for a living."

"I hear ya. The other thing is . . ."

"There's more?"

"He intends to start an action against Father Burke too."

"Jesus Christ."

"Moses, wasn't it? Thou shalt not bear false witness against thy neighbour."

"Podgis is spouting the Bible now?"

"When it suits him."

"Well, he's not entitled to sue a witness for his testimony in court. We all know that."

"Yeah, even Podgis knows it. He knows court testimony is privileged. So he's pretending Burke slandered him by whatever he said in the presence of third parties outside the Midtown Tavern that night, and that Podgis's reputation has been harmed as a result."

"Oh, for Christ's sake. His reputation is so bad already you'd almost say he's defamation-proof."

"I know, I know. He's really got it in for Burke. Walking off the show like that. And, from what I hear about the prelim, Burke's evidence made Podgis look ridiculous."

"Burke didn't make him look ridiculous. Podgis made himself look ridiculous. Burke just described it in court, the encounter between the two of them outside the bar. With a few onlookers present. If he sues, even more people will hear about it, which will sully his reputation even more. All it was, was a bit of badinage in response to Podgis being an arsehole."

"Wish I'd heard Burke singing 'Bad to the Bone' in the guy's face!"

"You and me both."

"Seems Podgis doesn't react well to being shown up. Doesn't take humiliation in his stride the way the rest of us learn to do."

"Tell him to grow up and get over it."

"I suspect he doesn't get over anything. It all goes back to the schoolyard, Monty. I'm sure we can imagine him as a younger version of himself and how others reacted to him back then."

"Yeah, it's all too easy to imagine."

"Anyway, we obviously told him none of these turkeys will get off the ground. And, knowing that, we could not represent him. But some recent law grad, or someone with lower standards than yours or mine, Monty, will take the case. I just wanted to fill you in, to show you how his mind is working. Obviously, I shouldn't be telling you, but we put the run to him, and frankly I don't give a damn whether I shouldn't be telling you."

"And you didn't. We didn't have this conversation. That being said, thanks, Jamie. I owe you."

"Nah. Least I could do."

✝

Knowing what might be facing Brennan Burke in the future in the form of a frivolous but annoying lawsuit, Monty felt a twinge of guilt calling upon him to assist with the defence of his client. But he already had plans to see Burke that evening. Dinner at Maura's place, the family home on Dresden Row. Monty would be off the clock, but he planned to slip in a bit of work if the opportunity arose.

"Scots wha' hae wi' Wallace fled," Burke said when he walked in and spotted Monty's daughter, Normie. It was a joke he had started with her one evening when she was reciting the Burns poem as part of a project on the Scottish part of her heritage. Burke's slander, and his over-the-top Scottish brogue, never failed to get a rise out of the little girl.

"Wallace didn't *flee*, Father, and neither did the Scots who fought with him. That's what the poem says: they stayed and fought with him. It was bad in the medieval days. The poem says, 'with Wallace *bled*!'"

"Oh, I'm sorry, pet. I misunderstood."

"That's okay. You can't understand Scottish talk because you're Irish."

"That must be it. Speaking of Scots, where is your big brother tonight? He's named after another Scotchman of renown, if I'm not mistaken this time around."

"You're right this time. Except it's not *Scotchman*. It's *Scotsman*. Tom is named after Tommy Douglas, who gave us free doctors' care, so we don't become poor if we get sick or have a baby. He came to Canada from Scotland when he was little and went to live out west."

"Right, right. And your Tommy Douglas is out for the evening, is he?"

"He's out with Lexie. She may be buying a car! She's going to try and get a red one, and I'll be the first person to get a ride in it except for Tommy!"

"That will be grand."

They all had dinner, and then Normie took the baby, Dominic, upstairs to entertain him before bedtime. Monty, Maura, and Burke shared a bottle of red, but there was no serious drinking.

"How are things at the carnival, Father?" Maura asked. "Have you been doing your regular shift at the Bernie Bears souvenir stand?"

"If you get up in the morning and read that the Bernie Bears stand and the stand selling lurid glow-in-the-dark pulsating sacred hearts and all the rest of the korny kiosks of katholic kitsch have been razed by a purifying flame, you will know who struck the match."

"Oh, Father, where's your entrepreneurial spirit? Why aren't you out there at the Knights of Columbus barbecue, flipping Befanee burgers?"

"Flip *this*."

"Is that what you said to the one in the Honeymoon Suite, Father?" Monty inquired.

Maura looked at Burke. "What's this?"

Burke gave Monty a black look, and Monty took the opportunity to get off that subject and back to Befanee Tate.

"Speaking of Befanee, I've been meaning to ask you about her boyfriend. Gary, is it?"

"You're asking me about him why? So I can assist in the defence of the killer of Jordyn Snider?"

"The man wrongly accused of the murder, I'm sure you meant to say, Brennan."

"That clown!" Maura exclaimed. "I'd like to see him behind bars even if he didn't commit the murder."

"He is not just a clown, MacNeil," Burke replied. "He is evil."

Monty was surprised at the vehemence of the assertion, and said of his client, "He is a clown, Brennan. A buffoon, a nuisance. That doesn't mean he's a killer or that he's evil. He's pathetic."

"He's more than that. He's not just a poor, sad bastard. There is evil there."

Monty looked at Burke. There had been times when the priest seemed to be able to feel evil coming off someone, but perhaps many of us were like that. Monty had read accounts in the law reports of victims who had had encounters with true psychopaths, and sometimes the victims claimed they could sense evil in the perpetrators. Could see it in their eyes. But Monty did not get that feeling from Podgis. That did not mean it was not there; it could be obscured by the man's customary bluster.

"Monty," Maura said, "just among the three of us here, do you really think there is any doubt — any reasonable doubt — that Podgis killed Jordyn Snider?"

He decided to give a forthright answer. "I think he probably did it, but there is room for doubt. My job as we all know is to expand that doubt enough to get an acquittal."

"How probable is 'probably'?"

"Highly probable. But I have to tell you he flatly denies it."

Burke looked at him as if to say, as he often did, "Are yeh *well*, Montague?"

"He says he has an alibi, and I've been trying to check it out."

"Been trying, eh, Monty?" Maura asked. "I notice you didn't say, 'And it checks out.'"

"Hey, I could solve this tomorrow, nail down the alibi, and get the charges dropped, but I have to milk the case for all the billable hours I can get."

His wife did not even bother to respond. She knew him better than that; if he had evidence exonerating a client, he would present it immediately. Money was not a big motivating factor for him.

Instead, she asked, "What was the motive? There's no evidence that he had ever met her."

Monty did not reveal the fact that Jordyn had been in the studio audience for the Podgis show. No doubt the police and the Crown knew that, but it had not come up at the prelim. They might be holding it to make an impact at trial.

All he said was, "Sex would be the most likely motive. You've seen her. A killing like this is most often a sex crime, and that's the case even if there was no actual sexual assault. Failure to score sexually commonly leads to violence, as I'm sure we all know. I'm just speculating that this was likely the situation, if indeed he killed her."

"Daddy! Come up and see my farm!" Normie called from her bedroom.

"Coming right up, dolly!"

Good. He could enjoy his daughter's company for a few minutes and put off his unpopular request for more assistance with his defence of Podgis. He climbed the stairs to Normie's room, where she and little brother Dominic were playing with the toy farm she got for Christmas. She had it set up on her windowsill where her dolls used to be. Now Monty saw a menagerie of animals ranging from horses to barn cats to species not native to the continent, like lions and a rhinoceros.

"Hey, gang," he said on arrival. He bent down and hugged his daughter, ruffling her auburn curls.

"Hi, Daddy!"

"Dada! Kitty! Walk!" Dominic picked up a cat and pushed it along the floor, making it walk, then patted its head and said, "Good!"

"Daddy, he learned a new word. Watch this. Wait."

Normie scrabbled around under her bed. Monty had never been under there, but he understood that it contained the store of all his daughter's earthly goods. She drew out a piece of white paper and began making creases in it. Dominic watched the process in great anticipation. When she finished her work, she had produced a paper airplane, and Dominic reached out to grab it. "Plane! Plane!"

"See? He can say it now." She lowered her voice. "He can't fly it very well yet. But maybe it's my fault because of how I made it."

"I'm sure it's pilot error and not a manufacturing defect, sweetheart."

"But we won't blame him. He's too little."

"Absolutely. Here, let's give him a ride."

Monty picked the little boy up around the waist. "You make his wings, Normie."

"Okay!"

She took his arms and gently stretched them out and slightly back in delta formation, for all the aerodynamic advantage she could produce. Monty flew Dominic around the room, to the accompaniment of jet noise coming from his daughter. The little guy was ecstatic and kept saying, "Plane! Plane!"

When Monty put him down, he begged for more and was given a couple more flights before being grounded for the night.

Monty kissed his daughter and gave her another hug. He did the same with Dominic, and Dominic put his arms around Monty's neck and clung to him. Monty didn't rush away. When the baby finally let go, he gave Monty a beatific smile, then got back to work. He looked from the paper airplane to the farm animals, and Normie offered the only solution possible. The farm would acquire its own airstrip for bringing in more creatures from afar. Monty left them to it.

"How are things up there?" Maura asked when he returned.

"Couldn't be better."

Maura smiled and said no more.

"Now, Brennan," Monty reminded him, "you were going to give me some information on this Gary."

"Was I now."

"What's his last name, and what do you think he's been up to at the church? I'll want a word with him."

"Well, no harm, I suppose, unless you manage to pin the murder on him. He's a ne'er-do-well, and a petty grifter, but I don't imagine he'll stand up for long as your alternative suspect. You've already got poor Ignatius Boyle — street philosopher, linguistic miracle man, and missionary to disadvantaged kids — in that particular frame."

"Speaking again of sex crimes," Monty said.

"What?" Burke demanded. "What's Ignatius got to do with sex crimes?"

"He's got a record."

"No doubt, for trespassing or public drunkenness."

"Worse."

"Oh, God help us. What is it?"

"Indecent exposure."

Burke gave a weary sigh. "Tell me."

Maura did not look any happier than Burke as they awaited the news.

"Exposed himself to two young girls on the street a few years ago. That's all I know."

"No!" Maura exclaimed.

"I don't want to believe it."

"He was convicted, Brennan."

"Well, it's a big step from there to murder."

"For sure. But it's not a big step from a minor sexual offence to a more serious one. Maybe it escalated to something worse, maybe not. If so, he never got caught. What were you saying about Boyle and kids? Brennan?"

"Nothing. He's kind to them. That's all."

Nobody spoke until Burke said, "Any more joy to spread this evening, Collins?"

He spared them the story he had heard about Boyle in the van filled with teenage kids, one of them the murder victim, Jordyn Snider. He would be keeping that to himself until he knew what it meant and what use to make of it.

"Nope. Your turn. What can you tell me about Gary?"

"His last name is Hebb, and he was hustling people for money in the churchyard. Claiming it was for the homeless, for charity, whatever else he came up with. I've never managed to catch him at it. He always disappears when I'm around. But why are you interested in him?"

"I told you before. A murder like this has 'boyfriend' written all over it."

"Well, then," Burke said, "you wouldn't be looking at Befanee's boyfriend; you'd be looking at Jordyn's."

"You said a mouthful there."

"What do you mean?"

"I'm already working that angle."

"What do you want with Befanee's beloved?" Maura asked.

"If he considers Befanee his meal ticket and the churchyard his turf for making money, he might not have appreciated Jordyn muscling in on the action."

"How did she muscle in? I know we saw her on television."

"Remember how she and Bef tried to outdo each other in that news clip? Who knows what went on when the TV lights went off?"

"When the TV lights were off, Befanee and Jordyn were probably off too. Getting on TV could have been the whole *raison d'être* for the two of them."

"Could very well have been. All the more reason to check out Gary. Big TV careers at stake for the girls, hanger-on or even management status for the boys. Even if it was only in their own minds, that's where motive resides."

Brennan

The following morning found Brennan Burke in the unaccustomed role of media researcher. Specifically, he was in the library at St. Mary's University going through crime stories generated by the news media in Toronto for the past ten months. He knew in advance that he would probably find nothing and that, even if he did find something, he would not be able to do anything with it. He taught an evening course in philosophy at the university, and he knew one of the professors in the criminology department, Fiona O'Regan. He had called upon her to see how he could find and examine the media reports for the ten-month period. He did not let on that he was interested only in coverage of the murder of eighteen-year-old Jeanie Ballantine. His interest in the Ballantine case had arisen from what he had heard in the confessional, from Podgis, and therefore he could not breathe a word about it. Fiona had been curious, but circumspect, and gathered the information for him, providing him with a television and video player in addition to microfilms of the newspaper stories for the given range of dates.

Brennan ignored all but the material relating to Jeanie Ballantine and did his best to ignore much of that. The sadistic attack on the lovely young girl was unbearable to contemplate, and he did not want to read the details except as they might pertain to a carpet knife found under the body, as disclosed by Podgis. He also wanted to see any stories done by Podgis himself. It took the better part of a day to go through all the newspaper articles and half the television reports. It was a dismal process. He felt soiled even by reading about the case second-hand at a distance of eight hundred miles.

He gave it up for the day, having received no enlightenment, and decided to finish the search if possible the next day. So, as soon as the library opened on Friday, he was at it again. Nothing about the knife found under the body, but a couple of articles hinted that there were elements of the crime, the injuries, and the scene that had not been made public. Brennan knew as well as anyone that this was typical of a crime investigation: the police would keep certain facts to themselves in order to test the credibility of witnesses who might come forward with real or bogus information.

He had saved to the last Pike Podgis's stories on the murder case. This was not saving the best for the last, but putting off the most distasteful task until it could no longer be avoided. Not having followed the television mouthpiece's career, Brennan had not been aware that he continued to file the occasional news report in addition to his work on his own weekly program. Brennan's research confirmed what he would have predicted: that Podgis's return to news reporting was limited to the most salacious or disturbing major news stories. Lurid murders, other violent crimes, sex scandals, misdeeds committed by politicians or other well-known people. Scanning his reports on the Ballantine case bore this out; Podgis's face on the screen was distorted with outrage and excitement about the horrible details of the case, the dreadful injuries and indignities visited upon the poor, dear little girl who had been attacked and slain.

Brennan came upon a series of interviews Podgis had done with the girl's parents. One took place in the family's kitchen, with Podgis leaning across the table, holding the mother's hand as she wept about her daughter. The woman was shaking; her lips trembled, and tears streamed from her eyes. The camera switched from her agonized face to that of a sympathetic Podgis. "Just let it all out, Cheryl. We all feel your pain." As much pain as Brennan felt watching this, he knew that nothing could approach the pain of a mother or father whose child might be enduring unspeakable horrors in some unknown location. The father could be seen standing stoically in the background. In another clip, Podgis stood side by side with the distraught parents on the lawn of their large suburban home, again before the girl's body had been found, as they begged the abductor to return their beloved child to them. They said they would do anything the perpetrator asked, anything, to get her back. Podgis's face filled the screen, and he seemed to be blinking away tears as he echoed the parents' plea: "Whoever you are, wherever you are, if you see this broadcast, please please bring Jeanie home." His voice cracked on the last word. The stories after that were about the finding of her body, the cause of death, and the absence of any useful leads to a suspect.

If Podgis had had anything to do with the abduction and murder of Jeanie Ballantine, Brennan did not know what on earth he was going to do. The confessional seal was sacrosanct, no matter how horrific the confession. Podgis could keep on scuttling around in the shadows; what could Brennan do to bring the ugly truth into the light?

Monty

Monty made a couple of reconnaissance missions to the statue of St. Bernadette hoping to catch sight of Gary Hebb mooching off the well-meaning pilgrims in the churchyard. If Monty struck out three times, he would find Hebb's home address and track him down there. Sure enough, no luck the third time. He decided to seek out Brennan Burke or Michael O'Flaherty at the rectory to see if they had any information other than the bare minimum Burke had already provided.

Only O'Flaherty was in residence on Saturday morning, so Monty settled in for a chat with him.

"I know his name is Gary Hebb. He lives out in some place called Beaver Bank. I'm not sure where that is, but I remember hearing from Befanee that he lived a ways out of the city. That fellow has me very concerned, I have to say, Monty. I believe he is out there taking money from poor, unsuspecting people who are here for the most honourable, if misguided, reasons. One of the pilgrims told me Hebb claimed Befanee has been receiving private revelations and that the Virgin made references to individual people in the crowd. And that those who contributed most to charity would be the most likely to be graced with a personal revelation!"

"Close it down, Michael. This isn't doing anyone any good. The longer the people are out there, the more of these scams will be perpetrated on them. And call the police on this Gary. He's defrauding people. On your property."

"Oh, Monty, I've been thinking the same thing, that I should call the police. But Brennan said he would take care of it. That makes me a little nervous; I'm not sure what he has in mind."

Burke would probably threaten to pound this Gary into the churchyard and bury him there.

"Brennan's not one for bringing in the cops. It goes against his family tradition. As you well know."

"You're right on the money there, Monty."

Monty and Michael O'Flaherty had both been in Ireland and had met some of the Burkes over there; whether it was Irish Republican subversion or shady dealings of a less political nature, the Burkes had a long history of avoiding the authorities.

"But, Michael, this is a matter for the police, not for Brennan's own brand of intimidation. So give them a call. But before you do, let me at this boyfriend."

O'Flaherty looked alarmed. "What do you have in mind, Monty?"

"Nothing violent, Mike, I assure you. I want to talk to him about the murder case."

"Do you think he might know something?"

"He might. Or he might have had his own motive for getting rid of Jordyn."

"Good heavens!"

"It's highly unlikely, but it's a loose end I have to tie up for my defence of you-know-who."

"That man. I don't know where you get the patience to deal with some of the people you have to represent, Monty."

"It's part of my job, but that doesn't mean it's not aggravating at times."

"I'm sure. Well, as I say, he's a Hebb from Beaver Bank."

"Thanks, Mike. See you later."

Monty found Hebb Sunday afternoon, living in a trailer in the Beaver Bank area north of the city. He knocked, and heard a voice telling him to come in. There was no sign of Befanee, or of a woman's touch in the decor or in the refuse in the tiny kitchen. The place stunk of dog and of grease. Kentucky Fried Chicken boxes were stacked on top of the garbage can. Bargain-of-the-week booze bottles filled one corner, and an ashtray filled with butts teetered on the arm of a La-Z-Boy chair in front of a humongous, new-looking TV set. Monty perched on the edge of a folding metal chair facing a couch where Hebb sat with a massive, brutal-looking dog at his side. The visionary's chosen one was big and heavy with lank, dark hair. Like the dog.

He looked around, looked at Monty, and said, "I'm busy."

"I'm sure you are, so let's make this quick."

Monty spied some library books on a packing crate beside the couch. The top one was titled *Marian Sightings: The Catholic Tourist's Guide*.

"Been doing a bit of devotional reading, Gary?"

"What do you want?"

"I'm a lawyer, and one of my clients from time to time is the Catholic Church in Halifax." That was not the client Monty was billing for this research trip, but he would get into that later. "What do you expect to gain from your girlfriend's claimed visions?"

"She really sees things. She's always been like that."

"You mean she has seen the Virgin Mary before this?"

"Not Mary, but other stuff. Predictions, psychic dreams. She wants to write a book about her dreams. I'm trying to find her a publisher."

Monty did not take him up on that, but asked, "What's in it for you?"

"What do you mean? She's my girlfriend. I help her out."

"By taking money off people in the churchyard."

"I can sue you for saying that."

"No, you can't. What do you tell the people, that you're collecting for charity?"

"The Virgin Mary said in her messages to Bef to support the poor. Just 'cause you're not poor I guess that's why you're crapping on what we're trying to do."

"What are you trying to do, Gary?"

"I know a lot of poor people, homeless guys. I try to help them out. What's wrong with that?"

"What's wrong is if you're taking people's money and not giving it to the poor but spending it on yourself."

"Fuck you."

"New TV, Gary?"

"Fuck off. I paid for it myself."

"I'm sure you did. Where did the money come from?"

"I got a job. I don't just sit around and collect pogey, like . . ."

"Like who, Gary? Poor people?"

"What's your problem?"

"Where do you work?"

"I'm on layoff right now, but I'll be called back."

"Called back where?"

"Earl's Excavation and Demolition."

"What do they excavate?"

"Nothing now. That's why I'm on layoff."

"What do you know about Jordyn Snider?"

"Why are you asking about her?"

"She got killed. Why wouldn't there be questions about her? But the point here is that I'm the lawyer for the guy charged with her death."

"You represent Pike Podgis! That's pretty cool. Maybe you'll get on his program. Great show. The old Pikester. He tells it like it is."

"I doubt I'll be invited on the show. But about Jordyn . . ."

"I don't know nothing about it."

"Where were you the night of September twenty-third and the morning of the twenty-fourth?"

"What the fuck is this? I didn't have nothing to do with that."

"I don't know, Gary. If you were somewhere else, why not just say so? Seems to me Jordyn might have presented a bit of unwelcome competition to Befanee and Gary Enterprises."

"She moved right in on Bef. But I didn't have nothing to do with her death. I was here all night."

"With whom?"

"Befanee."

"Tell me more about Jordyn. When did she come on the scene?"

"One day she just showed up and started hanging around, all dressed up and with her hair done. Then she came again another day when the TV reporters were coming to do another story about it all. And Jordyn kept pushing herself in front of Bef, talking to the people there. She even brought flowers to give out. And she talked about bringing a bunch of little kids next time because she said the Virgin Mary likes kids, and wanted to see them there. She was a fuckin' faker."

"And Befanee's not."

Silence.

"Did you know Jordyn before she showed up at the statue?"

"No."

"Did Befanee know her?"

"She never seen her before in her life. What a bitch."

"What? Who? Jordyn?"

"Yeah. You're not supposed to crap on the dead but it's true. She was a little bitch."

"Tell me about her."

"Befanee told her to get out of her way. The TV cameras were coming for her, not for Jordyn. And Jordyn started shitting all over Bef, saying she was too short and her face was too fat, and the cameras would pick up acne scars, and her hair was too thin and stringy, and her makeup looked like a kid had put it on and it made her look like a clown, and she would never make it on TV and would never make it as a model. Everybody would laugh at her. And Bef was all upset and told Jordyn that she was just jealous because of all the attention Bef was getting, and that she was going to be on TV a lot from now on, and Jordyn could just get lost and eat her heart out. But Jordyn didn't back off. And then the TV truck pulled up, and Jordyn said she would get some people to hurt Befanee, hurt her really bad and mess her up. And Bef was scared shitless because she believed Jordyn would do it. She was dead serious. Jordyn was. Then the TV cameras were on, and Bef was on, and then Jordyn shoved her way on camera. Bef was really scared of her after that. But then she got killed."

"Problem solved."

"I didn't do it. I'll take a lie detector test!"

"You weren't the only one whose interests were threatened by Jordyn."

"What do you mean? Hey! You don't mean Befanee had something to do with this! That's fuckin' sick, man. Befanee couldn't hurt anybody. She never did nothing violent in her life. And she was with me that night. Ask anybody."

"But who would know, if it was just the two of you here by yourselves?"

"Maybe somebody seen us, somebody from one of the other trailers." He brooded on the problem for a while, then said, "Hey, I just remembered. The guy three places down was having a party and it got out of hand, and I went over and told him off, and told him to turn the music down and keep his buddies inside and quiet. It was late that night. You can go ask him!"

"I will. But that doesn't prove Befanee was here."

"Well, she was."

"All right, Gary. Do you think that other guy is at home right now?"

"Yeah, he's always there. He sleeps all day, parties all night. He's in there." Gary pointed three trailers down.

"Here's what we're going to do. You come outside and stand where I can see you. So I know you're not on the phone to your alibi witness, telling him what to say."

"I wouldn't do nothing like that."

"And I'll ask him about that night. Let's go."

They went outside, and Gary stood in front of the trailer by the door.

"One more thing, Gary. If you ever turn up at St. Bernadette's and ask for money again, the priests there will have you arrested. Now stay here where I can see you."

"All right, all right."

Monty walked down to the party trailer, which looked the part, with piles of bottles and cases of empties all around the battered exterior. He knocked at the door and waited. Nearly a full minute passed before someone answered. A bleary-eyed man wrapped in a bedsheet stood at the door blinking. "Whaddaya want?"

Monty explained that he was trying to find out what certain individuals were doing the night of September twenty-third and twenty-fourth, when Jordyn Snider was killed. He asked whether anyone had come to his trailer, perhaps to complain about noise. The man stared at him through bloodshot eyes and made an obvious, and strained, effort to think back to that night. Then he had it. "Yeah, I remember that night! Or the next morning, because somebody stole my fuckin' copy of the *Daily News*. I heard there was a murder, and wanted to read about it in the paper, and some asshole stole it. But then I got it back from the guy, and the story wasn't in anyway because it happened too late for the paper to have it. That was when that Jordyn girl was stabbed."

"Right. Do you remember anything about the night before? Were you here?"

"What the fuck are you talking about? I didn't even know her. Yeah, I was here. I had some people over. And I can prove it. Go ask the asshole who lives in that place." The man pointed to Gary Hebb's trailer, where Gary still stood by the entrance. "Yeah, look at him standing there, the nosy bastard. Some people got nothing better to do than whine at their neighbours. He came over in the middle of the night and started ragging on me and my friends about a bit of music we had on. It wasn't even loud. He was the only one to complain, not even the old geezer who lives next door. Maybe he's too deaf to hear it, I don't know."

"So that man, Gary, came here that same night to complain."

"Yeah. He's always doing stuff like that. I think she puts him up to it."

"Who?"

"The Virgin Befanee. Maybe messages from God's mother are what keeps her awake, not my parties. She had her face in the window that night, watching every step he made, making sure he came over and butted in."

"All right. I won't keep you any longer. Thanks for your help."

"Yeah, any time. Just feel free to wake me up."

Monty walked back to Gary Hebb. "Looks as if you're in the clear. The guy gave you your alibi, and he doesn't like you much. Befanee's off the hook too."

And Monty had heard something new about the murder victim. There was a nasty streak running through the personality of Jordyn Snider.

Chapter 13

Monty

Just after lunch on Tuesday, the receptionist at Stratton Sommers put through a call. "Somebody on the line for you, Monty. If she gave a name, I couldn't make it out."

"Thanks, Darlene. I'll take it. Hello?"

"Hello? Mr. Collins?"

It was a timid voice; Monty could barely hear her. There was noise in the background, and he missed whatever else she said.

"Could you say that again?"

"I'm, uh . . ." The woman cleared her throat and spoke with a bit more volume. "I'm here to see Perry."

"Perry?"

"You know, Pike."

Could this be April? The alibi woman really existed?

"Okay," was all Monty said.

"Yeah, I'm, uh, his wife." *His wife?* "Well, we're divorced, but . . ."

That's right, Monty remembered. Podgis told him he was divorced. "I see. You're Mr. Podgis's wife, or ex-wife, and you're here . . . where are you?"

187

"I'm at his place. Well, his building. He's not home, so I can't get into the apartment. One of his neighbours is letting me use her phone."

"Did Pike say what time he'd be home?"

"No, not exactly. He doesn't . . . well, he gave me his address and phone number, but he doesn't exactly know about me coming."

Oh.

"I took the train all the way here from Toronto."

"How long did that take you? Day and a half?"

"Yeah. It was a long ride. I'm pooped."

"I can imagine."

"So, he's not here, and you're the only other number I have. I mean, the only other person whose name I know, because of all the publicity. Well, I guess I could have called the TV station, but . . . Anyway, if you hear from him, will you tell him I'm here?"

"Problem is, I have no idea when I'll hear from him, and you're stuck there with your bags and no place to settle in. Tell you what. You go to the lobby of the building, and I'll swing by and get you. If Pike comes home in the meantime, great. If not, we'll figure something out."

"Oh, no, don't do that, Mr. Collins. I'll just wait."

"See you in twenty minutes. Oh, what's your name?"

"Phyllis."

"All right, Phyllis. Call me Monty. See you in a bit."

But before leaving for Dartmouth, Monty made a call. He saw an advantage in getting to Podgis's ex-wife before Podgis did. With any client, especially one of this sort, Monty was always leery about what might come out of the woodwork and rear its ugly head at trial; best to hear it sooner rather than later. The former Mrs. Podgis could be a gold mine of information about his client, information Podgis himself would never divulge. But the talk might flow more freely if there was another woman in the group. He would shanghai Maura into taking a trip across the water.

His hopes were dashed, however, when he and Maura pulled up outside the five-storey yellow-brick building Podgis was renting while awaiting trial. The place was rundown and shabby, and the glass doors were so dingy and abraded that Maura had to hop out of the car and enter the building to see whether anyone waited in the lobby. Nobody there.

"Shit," Monty muttered when she returned to the car. "If she's not waiting there, it probably means he's home, and they're both in the apartment."

"Easy enough to find out. What's the apartment number?"

"Twenty-four."

"Let's go up."

"The Podgises at home. Can't quite picture it."

"You will soon enough."

So Monty drove to the far end of the parking lot, where the visitors' spots were, and locked up and walked back to the building with Maura. They went inside and up to the second floor, knocked on the door, and waited. Knocked again. They heard someone shuffling to the door. Podgis in bedroom slippers?

"Who is it?" Podgis barked.

Monty considered several options — Jehovah's Witnesses, Avon lady, Royal Canadian Mounted Police, Girls to Go — but just said, "Monty."

This was met by silence, then a belligerent, "Whaddya want?"

"Double date."

"Fuck off." His words sounded slurred.

"Open up, Podgis. We didn't come all the way over here for nothing."

"Who's *we?*"

Then Monty heard Phyllis's voice. "Perry, that's your lawyer! Let him in!"

The door opened, and Monty was looking into the blotched red face, and breathing in the boozy fumes, of an obviously drunken Pike Podgis, still in his winter jacket. "I don't need you here, Collins. If I want to pay for your time, I'll choose the time. Got that?"

"Perry! Don't be so rude to Monty."

Phyllis Podgis, if she still went by that name, was a short, very thin woman with badly dyed brown hair in long, wavy layers and thick curly bangs cascading over her forehead — the hairstyle of a country singer on a downward slide. Tiny pale eyes were set in a small, weak-looking face. A set of glaringly white teeth, although perfectly straight, looked incongruously large in the little mouth and were obviously false. She gave the newcomers a bright smile.

Monty felt an overwhelming urge to put his arms around her and shield her from the cruelties the world would surely visit upon a woman who looked like this.

"Please come in."

Podgis turned to her. "This isn't your house to invite people in."

"He just got home now," she said to Monty and Maura. "From a bar! He doesn't hold his liquor well. He never did."

Podgis glared daggers at her, but she did her best to ignore him. "Now, have a seat. I cleared some of his junk off the sofa."

"Okay, thank you. Phyllis, this is my wife, Maura. Maura, I don't believe you and Pike Podgis have been introduced."

"I heard you didn't have a wife anymore," Podgis said in greeting.

Maura gave him a look that would have shrivelled several of his vital organs if he had caught it, then turned from him to Phyllis and greeted her warmly.

"Can I get you something?" Phyllis asked.

"There's nothing to get them," Podgis snarled, "and they're not staying."

"Nothing, thanks," Maura replied, as if Podgis had not spoken.

"I brought a few things for him that he'll like. You know, make it more homey for him being stuck here in this place by himself."

"I'm always by myself," he declared. "What do you think? All of a sudden I need a nanny looking after me?"

"Here." She reached into her bag. "I brought you a couple of pictures to put on your desk."

"What?"

"Your family, Perry. And me. To remind you people are rooting for you. You'll beat this charge. We all know it." She placed a frame containing two photographs on a table Podgis was using as a desk.

"Get that off there."

She put her hand over the double frame. "No man is an island, Perry."

"For Christ's sake." He looked over at Monty and Maura. And Monty saw something that looked like desperation in his eyes.

"This is our wedding picture." Phyllis was all but dwarfed by a big white lacy dress and veil, but her homely little face was beaming in the direction of her groom. Podgis, looking much the same as now but a bit less blocky, was decked out in a beige tuxedo with brown piping along the lapels, and a shirt with frills all down the front. Monty had long been of the opinion that photographic evidence of 1970s weddings should be put to flame and burned until only fine ash remained. The groom in this picture was half turned away from the bride, his eyes looking elsewhere.

"And here's Perry with his family." Phyllis pointed to a group of four. "That's him as a teenager. He looks exactly the same, doesn't he?"

He did. His mouth was closed awkwardly, presumably to hide the bristly teeth, but otherwise it was the same old Podgis in miniature. His sister looked remarkably like him. An older brother, tall, blond, and fairly handsome, towered over the other two even though he was leaning on a goalie stick. He faced the photographer with a rakish grin. Beside him was a frail-looking woman who appeared to be wearing a blond wig. She smiled stiffly at the camera.

"That's his mother on the end. And his sister and brother."

"He's not my fucking brother!" Podgis bellowed from the kitchen. Monty heard the clinking of ice cubes and the sloshing of liquid into a glass.

"Yes, he is, Perry. He's your half-brother. That makes him your brother. And my brother-in-law. Arnie played junior hockey in Ontario!"

"He played like shit. And kept selling his equipment for money to party with. And *she* kept replacing it."

"Now, Perry, you know that only happened the one time."

"Twice."

"Okay, twice. But he made it up to your mother later. Paid her back, with interest."

"Yeah, fifteen years later."

"Well, he had other expenses. Once his little girl came along."

"His little girl didn't just come along, Phyllis. He was banging every little hockey ho on the Ontario junior circuit. I wonder how many other bundles of joy came along that we never heard about."

"That's not very kind, Perry. If he had other kids, he would be supporting them too. But he doesn't. He just has Cherry Dawn. She's a cutie. And really popular!"

"She was Arnie the goalkeeper's daughter, but many a shot got past her crease."

"Shut up, Perry! That's enough of that kind of talk."

Phyllis turned to her guests. "Brothers! Isn't it always the way? And there's no excuse."

"Fuck off about it, for Christ's sake!"

"Arnie was so good to Perry. When Arnie got a job at the Chrysler Dodge dealership, and Perry finally got his first job in radio, which didn't pay very well, Arnie offered the money to fix Perry's — "

"I told you to shut the fuck up!" Podgis came barrelling out of the kitchen with a nearly empty glass in one hand and a bottle of tequila in the other. As he entered the living room, he tripped and fell to his knees, smashing the glass and bottle, and letting out a roar of anger and frustration. He stumbled to his feet, batting the shards of glass from his clothing.

Phyllis left the photos and went into the kitchen. "Where do you keep your broom and dustpan, Perry?"

"Not your mess, Phyl," Maura couldn't help but say. But the woman could be heard opening drawers and cupboards.

Monty thought Podgis was going to blow a blood vessel, so great was his outrage and embarrassment.

"Look what you made me do! I gotta go out and replace this now. Pay a cab to the fucking liquor store and back. I knew I should have rented a car!"

"You wouldn't be able to drive it, Podgis."

"Well, you're here, Collins. Why don't you make yourself useful for once and give me a drive instead of sitting here and prying into my personal life?"

"I don't think you need any more to drink right now, Podgis. Why don't you go into your room and sleep it off?"

"Oh, you're an alcohol counsellor now, are you? Gonna bill me for that too? My AA partner. Yeah, I suppose you're used to that role. Since your best buddy is a boozehound."

"He is not a boozehound. He is not a lush. He does not need any assistance from me. He can hold his liquor. Not everybody can."

"Get the fuck out."

"I think we've worn out our welcome, my dear," Monty said to Maura. "Perhaps it's time to make a graceful exit." He made a show of looking at his watch. "Oh, will you look at the time? We really should hit the road."

Maura got up, and they headed for the door, but not before catching a beseeching look on the face of Phyllis Podgis.

"Phyllis, would you like to come with us?" Maura suggested. "Maybe there are things you need at the grocery store?"

Phyllis made a grab for the lifeline offered to her. "Yes! I should pick up a few things!"

But Podgis was having none of it. "You're not going anywhere! Sit down and let them get the hell out of here, so they can get on with telling all their lawyer friends at the Thirsty Duck this oh-so-amusing tale about his latest client."

"I don't want to stay when you're like this, Perry," his ex-wife said. "You didn't even want me here. Now you won't let me go."

"Yeah, well, you're here now, so stay put."

"She's coming with us, Podgis," Monty said. "We'll check in later to see how you're doing, and play it by ear after that."

Phyllis put some things into her handbag and walked to the door, studiously avoiding the eyes of her former husband. But he had drawn a bead on her back and moved towards her. He grabbed her arm, and she tensed. As did Monty and Maura. But all he did was lean towards his ex and whisper in her ear. Something about "blabbing to *them*." Monty pried Podgis's fingers off Phyllis and ushered her out the door. Maura followed, no doubt after directing another killer look behind her.

On the way down the corridor, Maura turned to Phyllis and asked gently, "What's the story, Phyllis? How long have you been divorced?"

"Ten years. And we were separated for quite a while before that."

"So why put yourself through this now?"

"You don't understand Perry. And how could you? You just met him in the middle of this bad business, so you're not seeing him at his best."

Monty stifled a reply. If, for instance, Podgis's television show was him at his best, what was there that any sensible person would want to see?

"Don't pay him any mind when he's like that."

In Monty's experience, Podgis was always like that.

But the pugnacious broadcaster had a defender in his ex-wife. "He doesn't mean it when he talks to me that ornery way. He knows I'm here to support him. He always thinks he's a tough guy who doesn't need anybody. So when he acts like this, I just let it all run off my back."

"Maybe you shouldn't, Phyllis," Maura advised her in a voice tight with unexpressed anger.

"If you still feel so attached to him, Phyllis," Monty asked when they were downstairs in the lobby, "why did you get a divorce?"

"Oh, that was his idea, not mine. He thought he needed a wife who was more . . ." Everyone present knew what he thought he needed. But his long-suffering ex spelled it out anyway. "I guess I didn't look the part of a television wife! I don't hold with all this makeup and fancy clothes and a new hairdo every week. Well, he got what he wanted. A TV-type wife, someone who ran for Miss Mississauga. And guess what?"

Her companions preferred not to guess.

"She flew the coop as soon as she got her TV career launched. Bye-bye, Pike Podgis; I don't need you anymore."

Podgis had not specified that there were two divorces in his past. But then again, Monty had not asked for numbers.

"You don't have any children, do you, Phyllis? Pike never mentioned any."

"He wouldn't. Outright refused. He sneaked off and got his tubes tied, or whatever they do to men."

They left the building and went out to the parking lot.

"Where are his brother and sister now?" Maura asked. "Is his mother still alive?"

"His mother's dead, and his sister's out west somewhere. Nobody ever hears from her. And his brother, half-brother, well, Perry won't have anything to do with him."

"Why not?"

"It's because Perry always felt that his mother liked Arnie better. And you know what? He's right. His mother had some bad relationships with men after Perry's father left the family. And then she met Arnie's dad, and they had Arnie, and — "

"Arnie came after Perry?" Monty asked. "I thought Arnie was older."

"No, no, Arnie is Perry's little brother. Well, not little. He was bigger than Perry, and more . . . well, their mother sure had her favourite. She didn't have much money but whenever she did, she spent it on Arnie and his hockey. Perry's right about that. Perry wanted her to get braces for his teeth but she never had the thousand dollars they would have cost. But when Arnie needed hockey gear, well, I don't know, she found the money for that. But to hear Perry tell it, Arnie was a, pardon my French, but, an A-hole. Except he wasn't! He was so good to Perry when he got out working. He even said he would pay to fix Perry's teeth. But Perry was so weird about it. Didn't even thank Arnie. Told him to take his money and shove it you-know-where."

"But Perry started making money himself. Why didn't he ever fix his teeth?"

Phyllis shook her head. "He was working in TV before he had enough to pay for it. I don't know; he's weird about things like that. When Arnie offered, Perry said something like, 'What do you think I am, a girl?' As if only girls get braces on their teeth, or care what they look like!"

Something struck Monty then about the teeth. Podgis had brazened it out all his life with the mouthful of spiky, crooked teeth. Then he had an offer from his brother — younger brother, at that — who must have been making more money, to fix the unsightly problem. Not hard to imagine Podgis bristling at that. Then, by the time he himself had a decent income, by the time he was on television, he no doubt had a reputation as a scary-looking, tough-talking guy who didn't give a shit what people thought of his appearance. Even if he, Podgis, really did. The mouth was part of his aggressive persona. It may have been too late to make the admission that his teeth looked like hell and he cared enough to pretty himself up.

Monty remembered an old saying: "Sometimes you have to be cruel to be kind." Here, in a way, was a reverse situation: being kind could be cruel. Particularly if the "kindness" was coming from a favoured, much more fortunate, younger brother. Not for the first time, Monty was taken aback at what a simple creature the human being could be. The same old forces — envy, humiliation, the favoured and the ill-favoured, bullying and bravado — produced the same old effects, formed the same personalities, generation after generation. Monty remembered Jamie McVicar's take on Podgis: "It all goes back to the schoolyard, Monty."

Monty and the two women arrived at the car and were about to get in when they were hailed by the aggressive, scary-looking guy himself. Podgis was galumphing towards them in the parking lot, with something on his mind.

"What kind of stuff are you blabbing to these two? Get back in the apartment!"

"Men!" Phyllis said with mock exasperation. "They're all the same!"

"How would you know? I'm the only one you ever had."

"You think so, eh Perry? Well, you're wrong. I had another boy-friend after you left."

"Yeah, I can imagine what — " He stopped, and his face flamed red.

It was a drunken slip. He had revealed himself, and it was an excru-ciating moment. What he meant was clear to everyone there: the only man Phyllis could get would be second rate. Like him. It wasn't hard to read the flip side of the page, that *she* was all *he* could get. At least in his pre-TV days. And he held her in contempt as a result, a varia-tion on "I would never join a club that would have someone like me as a member."

In the end, Phyllis decided to stay with him, for reasons Monty could not fathom. He and Maura got in the car and drove to Halifax. Maura sat fuming all the way home.

Chapter 14

Brennan

Tuesday was choir night, the weekly rehearsal of the St. Bernadette's Choir of Men and Boys, and Brennan was looking forward to it as always, particularly as they were going to do the Vivaldi *Gloria*, a piece that had the power to fill him with *gaudium quod est immensum*, immense joy. *If* properly performed, which it would be with his choir. This week they were preparing for a special morning Mass Brennan had initiated for the choir school students and their families. The Mass was held twice during every school year, at the beginning of the September term and again in late January. It was the traditional Latin Mass that Brennan preferred, for its dignity, reverence, and splendid liturgy. Confessions first though, till seven o'clock.

A young girl came in and confessed to shoplifting makeup, an older woman admitted to anger with her in-laws, and a man told him a long and complicated tale of stock fraud. Brennan did not even try to follow the story of securities, short-selling, derivatives, and a whole lot of other words Brennan could not have defined to save his life. He had no idea what the fellow was on about, except that he had defrauded some people out of large sums of money. He was in the process of making restitution, or so he claimed, and Brennan grilled him to try to determine whether he was truly repentant. It seemed he was. Brennan handed out a heavier-than-usual penance, requiring a period of service to the poor in addition to regular prayers. There were a few more people with negligible sins after that, and then a lull. He thought he might be finished for the night, but he heard someone else come in.

"Ignatius Boyle hangs around here, right? The churchyard here?"

It was the voice of a fairly young woman, not a voice he recognized.

"Yes, he does," Brennan answered.

"And you went to visit him in the hospital. I heard that."

"That's right."

"Are you a friend of his?"

He was not about to deny the man. "Yes, I am."

"So you should know this."

"Tell me."

"Ignatius Boyle bought me for a pack of smokes."

O God of mercy and compassion, what now?

"Are you there? Father?"

"Yes. Yes, I'm here."

"I'm in here because you know him. And you can't repeat whatever I say, so it's not going to end up on the news."

"True." His confessional had become a witness box for those who wanted to testify in the shadows.

"I have a better life now. I have a little girl, and I don't want her to know the things I used to do."

"Anything you tell me stays in here."

"My mother's life was nothing but a series of men. They came and went. Most of them were in and out of prison. The only reason the others weren't inside is because they never got caught." She spoke in a flat voice as if reciting what time the buses came and went. "Maybe you can imagine what kind of a life that was for me. Or maybe you can't. But one thing you can guess is that I was desperate to get out. All I wanted to do was get away from there. So you'd think I wouldn't quit school in grade ten. Or even if I did, I would try to get a good job and make something of my life. You wouldn't think I'd get into drugs and start hooking. But that's what I did, became a hooker when I was fifteen. I figured I could use that kind of life, not really fall into it, just use it to earn money to lift myself up. I bet a lot of people start out thinking that, and they never rise above it. The same kind of life I was trying to escape from; how did I end up following the same stupid pattern for my own life? I don't know.

"But, about Ignatius Boyle. There was him and some other guys like him standing around on Brunswick Street when I was walking by. A bunch of drunks and bums. And they started hollering at me, being gross. One of them knew my name. I don't think I ever did him or anything like that, but he knew who I was. He came over and grabbed a hold of me and I was trying to fight him off me. He was really drunk. That's when Ignatius Boyle moved in on me, and said he wanted me for himself."

First it was Pike Podgis unmasking his evil persona in Brennan's confessional. Now somebody was going to strip away any illusions Brennan still maintained about Ignatius Boyle. He stayed silent, and the girl continued.

"Ignatius came up and started telling the other guy off, saying I should go with him, Ignatius, and the other guy should buzz off. Then Ignatius pulled out a pack of cigarettes from his shirt pocket and said the other guy could have them, in exchange for me. So the guy grabbed the pack of smokes and took off. So that's how Ignatius got me."

She was quiet so long Brennan finally prompted her. "What happened then?" He didn't want to know, but there was nothing to be gained by putting off the inevitable.

"He kind of grasped me by the arm and started walking me away from the other guys. Stopped when we got to St. Patrick's church, and he took me in there. There was nobody else inside. That was the first time I had ever gone in there. It looks like pictures of churches they have in Europe, with all the colourful paintings and stained glass and all that. I thought, does he expect me to do him in here?"

Brennan fervently hoped not.

"But he started working on me to give up hooking, to stop taking drugs before I got myself addicted. He gave me the name of a social worker who could help me. He said I was — " she stopped and cleared her throat " — I was too precious and my life was too important to throw away. I was a lovely girl, and it wasn't too late for me at all. If I didn't want to end up on the streets like him, I should go see the worker first thing the next morning. I could think about training for a job. Someday I could have kids. And all that. Normal stuff, but to me it might never have happened. It was Ignatius Boyle who started me on the right track. Because it wasn't just talk. He seemed to pass over to me some kind of power. Strength or something, to change my life.

"I got a job. I won't tell you where in case you go in there and see me. I'm only working part time right now, so I can be with my baby. I even baptized her in that same beautiful church. But I haven't really started to go to church myself. Oh, shit. Oh, I'm sorry! Am I in trouble for saying that?"

"No, you're grand. I'm so relieved to hear that your story turned out all right, and that Ignatius didn't hurt you, that a little bit of un-churchy language isn't going to do either of us any harm at all. But what's wrong?"

"It's just that, if I don't go to church and this isn't a real confession, maybe you can tell people what I said. About the way I was, and what I did."

"I'm not going to tell a soul. You have my word."

"Yeah, well, I just wanted to tell you about Ignatius, and what he did for me. When I got pregnant, I told him if it was a boy, I'd name him Ignatius. And he laughed and said, 'You don't want to do that. Call him John! Or Patrick, after the church and the saint.' It's a girl, so I called her Patricia."

"Lovely. How old is she?"

"Almost two. And me and my boyfriend are getting married. He's a really good guy. Not mean or violent, and he has a good job."

"That's wonderful, sweetheart. I'm very happy that things are working out. God bless you."

"Thanks. Thank you for listening to me. And stick up for Ignatius. They're trying to connect him with that murder. But he wouldn't hurt anybody. If there really are saints, Ignatius is a saint!"

Brennan was very moved by what the young one told him about Ignatius. What a relief. A life that could have been utterly lost and wasted, saved by the love and wisdom of Ignatius Boyle.

How much love and wisdom had Boyle himself enjoyed during his lifetime? Not much, Brennan had to assume. A person deprived of love and guidance, of stability and nurturing — how could such a person have so much to give a young girl like the one Brennan had just encountered? More often, surely, deprivation caused such damage to the personality that only harm and devastation could result, harm to the self and to others. How exceptional was a man like Ignatius Boyle?

Nobody else came into the confession box. Brennan peered out and saw that there was no one in the church. Time to go. He looked at his watch. Twenty to seven. Better stay to the appointed time, just in case. A couple of minutes later, he heard someone enter the booth, and fall heavily to his knees.

The fellow delivered himself of a loud, world-weary sigh. "Where to begin, Father?"

"I don't want to hear from you, Podgis. Your place is in a cell, not in a confessional. We both know it. Turn yourself in."

"But what would become of me, Brennan? Don't you care about the lives of your flock? Can you see what life would be like for poor ole Pike in prison? Homemade liquor, drugs to mask the boredom and the despair, the lonely hours with smuggled porn? I don't know the rules in prison. I'll have to ask Monty. Oh, wait, no, can't ask Monty. He believes in my innocence. So I'll ask you. What do you think? Would they let me bring in my own collection of dirty pictures? Is there a special jailhouse rule if they are pictures of my own victims? Victim, I mean. Did I say victims? This whole ordeal of facing a life sentence is making me a bundle of nerves. Anyway, my picture collection. Jordyn posing before her death, and then posed by her killer afterwards. *My* little Jordyn. Tell you what. If I can't bring my photos with me, I'll leave them in an envelope for my parish priest, Father Burke. The priest who was sleeping in a house overlooking the murder scene. Too bad you missed it. Slept through it, I guess. Passed out, from what I gather. What a night it was, Brennan. For me, and for her. Poor kid. Maybe you could have saved her, if you had heard her begging for her life. But I'm sure you're not losing any sleep over it. Then or now."

Brennan was on the verge of losing it with the twisted, malicious, evil man on the other side of the screen. But he willed himself to keep it together until he could come up with a way to bring Podgis out in the open with his admission of guilt.

All Brennan said was, "You are a very sick, very deranged individual.

You should throw yourself on the mercy of the courts, take your punishment, and maybe get some treatment."

"Nah, I'm not really going to jail. Monty's going to get me off. I'm going to walk away from this, and Jordy's misfortune will remain forever unsolved."

"Get out of here, Podgis. If you ever do have a moment of remorse, confess it. And plead yourself guilty. Spare the girl's family the agony of a trial."

"I know, I know. You're right, Father. That poor family. The mother, particularly. Did you see her on the news? She lost it. Every time. Poor thing."

"Well?"

"I really would like to spare them, now that you mention it."

"Good. Do so. Go now, speak to your lawyer and get it arranged."

"Your good friend, Monty. Not so friendly now, maybe. I hope I haven't spoiled things between you."

Brennan took a few deep breaths and restrained himself.

"But I hear you. I should do the right thing for the family's sake. I know something about that first-hand. Remember we were chatting about little Jeanie Ballantine the other day? Eighteen years old, missing for nearly six weeks, the parents frantic. I was covering the story, doing my very best to find leads to where that poor little girl was being hidden. Her family came to rely on me, knew that if any reporter could uncover the real story it was me."

What was he on about now? Revelling in the prurient details of a killing one minute, the victim's champion the next.

"Seeing the family like that, terrified for their daughter. Facing at last a parent's worst fear. And of course fearing the worst. Knowing how unlikely it would be that little Jeanie would be coming home safe and sound. Grieving already. The mother in such pain. The dad really tried to hold it together, but the mother just couldn't handle it. One time I interviewed her on her front lawn. She started to talk about Jeanie, then she just doubled right over with the pain. Couldn't even stand. What a shame. I watched the video when it aired on the suppertime news. Mrs. Ballantine pleaded for witnesses to come forward. There is nothing as powerful, as painful to see, as a mother's grief for her child. It makes you cry just looking at her. Or a wife grieving for a dead husband. Think back to 1963.

Jacqueline Kennedy at JFK's funeral. All in black, her beautiful face veiled. The iconic image of a grieving woman. And then there's Mrs. Ballantine. The pale, blotchy skin, the freckles standing out like zits, the red-rimmed eyes. And the sniffling. Her nose was running, on suppertime TV. Eeeuuw. I've seen Jackie Kennedy, Mrs. B., and you're no Jackie Kennedy!"

Brennan bolted from his seat, yanked open the door of the left-hand confession booth, and pulled Podgis from the kneeler. He grabbed the front of his jacket in both his fists and shoved him against the wall of the church. Podgis looked up at him, his expression one of fear mixed with something else, something beyond the man's natural complement of malice and spite. Exhilaration? Triumph?

"Temper, temper, Father. Have patience. Is not anger one of the seven deadly sins? Is not patience a virtue?"

"Shut your filthy mouth, you psychopath!"

"Me? A psychopath? What are you talking about? I come to my priest to confess my sins, like what I just told you, that I didn't declare all my speaking fees on my income tax return. Sure I've always felt guilty about it, but 'psychopath'? And the time I shouted out in anger to the driver who cut me off. I shouldn't have done that, but not a big sin. And hardly a major crime."

"What are you on about now?"

"Are you getting a little senile, Father? Have you forgotten already what I confessed in there? What do you think I said? Maybe your hearing is starting to go? That would be bad for a musician, a choirboy like yourself."

"Get the hell out of here before I commit murder myself, you loathsome object."

"Murder? Who said anything about murder? You must be delusional, Father. Driven mad perhaps by the image of that young girl with her legs sprawled open in your churchyard, her body still — "

Brennan seized him by the front of his jacket, whipped him around, and got him in a chokehold, squeezing Podgis's neck between his forearm and his bicep. Podgis's arms flailed, and he tried to scream but it came out as a squeak. Brennan pulled him out of the nave to the vestibule of the church. Brennan then backed up against the door and pushed it open. As soon as the door opened, the priest heard voices coming from the parking lot. A couple of the lads early for choir. They'd hang about outside till the last minute, if past experience was any guide. Brennan slammed the door shut, released his captive, and shoved him against the door.

Podgis turned around, his hands caressing his neck, his eyes bulging. "You nearly fucking killed me! I couldn't breathe!"

"You don't deserve to breathe."

"You're a fucking stone-cold killer, Burke. I can see it in your eyes. Like your old man, I guess. Surprised? I had my people look into your background when I found out you were going to give evidence against me in court. I told them, dig up some dirt. See if we can discredit the witness. Collins was too easy on you at the preliminary. He better come down harder on you at the trial or I'll fire his ass and find somebody who will. Now we have this. Your unprovoked attack on me, based on whatever hallucinations you're suffering from about my character. It's no accident you're like this, though, is it? I wonder if we can get your family roots on the record. Declan Burke, gunned down at a family wedding. Barely survived. Him and the rest of the Burkes are a bunch of fucking Irish terrorists, and you're obviously made of the same shit as them."

Brennan grabbed him by the throat and lifted him off the ground. He saw genuine fear in Podgis's eyes. "Don't you ever utter my father's name again. Don't you ever boast to me about the depraved crimes you've committed against innocent people. Don't you *ever* mock a grieving mother in my presence or anywhere on this planet again. And don't ever set foot in my church. I do not want to see your hateful, spiteful face again until I see you in court. Just before they pack you off to a lifetime in prison. Where you'll meet the fate you so famously deserve."

The man squirmed and lifted his leg to deliver a well-placed kick, but Brennan saw it coming and backed off, leaving Podgis to slump to the floor. He got up and stuck his face into Brennan's. "Yeah, you'll see me in court, Burke. Then you'll see me on the courthouse steps waving to my cheering fans after I beat the rap. 'Cause there's no way Pike Podgis is going down for this! Your buddy Collins is gonna get me off. I'm gonna walk. That's what you're gonna see. There won't be enough Paddy whiskey in the world to drown out the sight of me walking away."

Brennan held his clenched fists down by his sides, forcing himself not to use them on the skinful of evil who stood before him against the door of his church.

Podgis turned and opened the door, peered outside. "All those little choirboys singing like angels. Should I stand up at the front of the church and tell them and their mummies and daddies just how far you really are from being a choirboy? That you're a violent street brawler like the rest of your bog Irish family?"

"Get out of here. Do not go near my students or their families. Do not even look at them. Do not loiter on these grounds. If you're not gone in thirty seconds, I'll have you arrested. If they can't find something to arrest you for, I'll make something up. Go back to whatever hole you're living in and examine your conscience. But we both know you don't have one. So instead, sit there and contemplate what it's going to be like when I, and all the other witnesses, present an overwhelming case against you and see you dragged away in handcuffs to a place where nobody is going to show you the mercy I showed you here tonight. I didn't kill you. Somebody else will. Guaranteed. And no mother will grieve the loss of you."

Once he was sure the reptilian creature was off the property, Brennan sprinted up to the sacristy, went in and washed his hands and face. He only wished he had time for a shower. But he did what he could. He took a towel and brushed his clerical suit in case there was a lingering trace of Podgis's foul person upon him.

Most of the boys were in place in the choir loft by the time he finished. He was walking towards the stairs to join them when Monty Collins came into the church.

"Evening, Father."

"Mr. Collins."

Collins peered at him in the dim light. "Everything all right with you? You look a little tense."

Brennan waved him off and headed up the stairs. Shuffling, whispering, and bursts of adolescent laughter halted abruptly when he arrived and faced his choristers.

"Ian."

"Yes, Father?"

"You've passed out the music?"

"Yes. The Vivaldi *Gloria* and Mozart's 'Laudate Dominum.'"

"Good. Run in there and get the Pergolesi *Stabat Mater* as well."

"Okay." Ian McAllister got up and headed for the steeple room where the music was kept in file cabinets.

"The rest of us will bow our heads." Brennan began the opening prayer with the sign of the cross: *In nomine Patris et Filii et Spiritus Sancti. Amen. Confiteor Deo omnipotenti . . ."*

He saw Monty looking at him. Wondering, no doubt, why he was opening the choir practice with a penitential prayer, a general confession of sin, instead of the usual prayer to St. Cecilia, patron saint of church musicians.

". . . peccavi nimis cogitatione, verbo et opere, mea culpa, mea culpa, mea maxima culpa." I have sinned exceedingly in thought, word and deed, through my fault, through my fault, through my most grievous fault.

When he finished, Richard Robertson spoke up. "How come we said that prayer, Father? It's all about sin, right?"

"It's all about sin. You said it, Richard. The sins of all of us. Sometimes it's well to remind ourselves of that."

Ian was back with the Pergolesi, and he passed the books around.

"Stabat Mater. What does it mean, lads?"

They looked from one to the other wondering whether to chance it. Monty would certainly know. Perhaps some of the other adults. But, wisely, they left these little lessons for the boys.

"It's something about a mother," Ian said.

"That's right. *Stabat Mater dolorosa iuxta crucem lacrimosa.* The sorrowful mother, the grieving mother, was standing by the cross weeping."

Again, a curious look from Collins. Brennan ignored it and proceeded to sing them the melody line of the gorgeous, haunting piece.

Monty

Instead of heading straight to the office on Wednesday morning, Monty drove to Byrne Street, entered the church, and climbed the stairs to the choir loft, where he would join the other members of the St. Bernadette's Choir of Men and Boys for the twice-yearly choir school Mass. Not that the choir school students, including his daughter, Normie, attended Mass only twice a year. No indeed. Frequent Mass attendance was part of life at Father Burke's choir school. But this was the special liturgical event for the students and their families, and everybody knew it was not to be skipped. Woe to anyone who misseth this Mass, woe in the form of the displeasure of the Reverend Doctor Father Burke; it would be better for that man, woman, girl, or boy if he or she had never been born. The choirs, that is, the school choir and the men and boys, would be singing some exquisitely beautiful motets by Palestrina and Victoria and, apparently, Pergolesi. Monty surveyed the nave from his perch in the choir loft. The church was packed with the mothers, fathers, sisters, brothers, and teachers of the students.

The choristers got to their feet as Father Burke walked up the aisle behind six altar boys carrying candles. Burke was, as always, a striking figure in his immaculate green vestments. He wore a black biretta on his head and carried the chalice covered by the chalice veil. Priest and choir sang the ancient chant together as the Mass proceeded. Whenever Burke was saying Mass, he deputized Frank Stanton, a member of the men and boys' choir and an accomplished musician in his own right, to direct the singers. The fact that Stanton still had this job after a year said it all about how good he was as a stand-in conductor. Not a note was out of place. At the Offertory, the choir sang Palestrina's *Adoramus Te Christe*, and Monty's thoughts turned to the inexcusable and sometimes evil acts he heard about every day of his working life, the appalling things human beings did to one another. And he wondered, when they came to the phrase *redemisti mundum*, thou hast redeemed the world, whether the world could ever truly be redeemed. Monty also wondered how Father Burke was able to perform so beautifully, whether he had slept the sleep of the angels or had been out carousing till the wee hours. Something had been bothering the priest last night at rehearsal. Monty had not had a chance to speak to him after practice. Had Burke gone to the Midtown to anaesthetize himself from whatever had set him off? No way to tell.

The time came to switch from Latin to English for the sermon. Burke never spoke for more than ten minutes, usually less, and never talked down to the congregation. Whether or not they understood some of the arcane terminology he used, or the ethereal ideas he floated before them, he accorded them the respect of treating them like equals, though few in the crowd would have attained anything close to the level of education he himself had achieved. And he never thundered at people about worldly vices; his homilies tended to be lessons in theology. Today the subject was St. Paul's matchless hymn to love, in his first letter to the Corinthians: "Faith, hope, love abide, these three, but the greatest of these is love." Father Burke was only about two minutes into his talk when a baby at the back of the church set up a wail. He kept on speaking, and the baby kept on crying. Monty leaned over the choir rail and watched the scene from above. He could see the baby's mother, red-faced and flustered, desperately trying to calm the infant, who appeared to be around four months old. Two pre-school children flanked the mother.

Suddenly, Father Burke stopped speaking, stepped away from the pulpit, and started walking from the sanctuary and down the centre aisle. Monty could see the sudden tension in the postures of the children and the mother. He could hardly believe his eyes. How cranky was Burke today? How sore was his head? Had he had such a hard night that he would interrupt his sermon and march down the aisle to confront a family with a crying child? All heads turned as he passed them on the way by. Everybody in the church was watching as he drew even with the mother and baby. The mum looked up at him, a mortified expression on her face. The brother and sister watched the priest with wide, apprehensive eyes. Monty saw Burke lean over, say something to the mother, and remove the baby from her care. He then proceeded up the aisle towards the altar with the squalling infant in his arms. All heads turned to the front and followed his progress. He returned to the pulpit and faced the congregation.

"This," he said, turning his face to the baby, "this is what it's all about. This is where love, unconditional love, begins. A mother's love for her child. A father's love." He bent over the baby and kissed its forehead, spoke words nobody else could hear, and the baby calmed down, made a little cooing sound, and lay contentedly in the priest's arms. "How can anyone look at this beautiful face and not be filled with love?"

There wasn't a sound in the church except for his voice. Everyone stared at him, rapt with attention.

"When anyone does anything to hurt another human being, when anyone takes another person's life, this is who they are hurting, this is who they are killing. This is the life that is destroyed. Every one of us starts life as a helpless child like this. Any time we are tempted to

mistreat a person, to lash out, to do a person harm verbally or physically or any other way, we must stop and think, that this is how we
all began, this is who we all are. Everyone is precious in the eyes of
God and everyone should be precious to each and every one of us. If
we can't see the face of Christ in every person, and I admit it is difficult with some, then we should do our best at least to see the face
of the child."

Monty took a quick look at his fellow choristers. To a man, to a
boy, they had their eyes fixed on Father Burke. They were stunned
into silence and immobility.

Brennan

If ever there was a night that called for a trip to the Midtown with
Monty Collins, it was the night after the third confession of Pike
Podgis. Brennan had seen Monty at the choir school Mass, but he had
to avoid a night of drinking with Monty when he was in this frame
of mind, a mind consumed with seeing Monty's client go down in
flames for his crimes. And he could not go and unwind with a drink
chez MacNeil for the same reason. Turning up on the doorstep of
Monty's wife was out of the question. All because Monty was stuck
representing the odious Podgis. Brennan thought of a couple of other
fellows he might go drinking with, but figured he would be lousy
company for them.

So he holed up by himself in his room at the parish house, with
a quart of John Jameson and the music of the Mozart *Requiem*. The
dark, brilliant music washed over him. But it was wasted on him, lost
as he was in his bottle of Jameson and his black thoughts about Pike
Podgis. He knew he should confess yesterday's violent outburst and
the nearly overwhelming temptation to pound the man to a bloody
pulp. But he could not confess it. Not yet. For the same reason he
could not have granted absolution to Podgis: no remorse. He drank
and brooded, drank and brooded. Podgis had brutally murdered a
young girl, a young girl who had once been a dear little baby like
the one at Mass, and then Podgis had brutally gloated about it in the
confessional. He virtually confessed to killing young Jeanie Ballantine
as well, the girl who had moved from Halifax to Toronto with her
family. And the sexual innuendoes: did they reflect his true impulses,

or were they just meant to goad Brennan into some kind of response? Why would Podgis do that? But, then, why come to Brennan's confessional at all? What was he up to? He had made cruel, callous remarks about the girl's grieving mother. And he was convinced he was going to walk. The foul creature seemed confident that he would escape punishment for the Jordyn Snider murder. On what grounds? Was there some way he thought he could pin this on someone else? What had he found, or made up? How could he explain away the victim's blood on his shoes, or the fact that he had been spotted leaving the scene? How could he get out from under the weight of that evidence? What was going on?

Brennan reached for the bottle again. Two ounces left. Infinite and loving God of all creation, had he downed a whole quart of Jameson sitting here stewing about Podgis? Was the man worth the price of a bottle? He poured the last two ounces into his glass, drained it, and banged the glass down on his table. He was going to deal with this. He just didn't know how. A priest was bound by the seal of the confessional. Brennan was so utterly committed to his sacramental duty that, even in an extreme situation like this, he would not reveal what he had learned. He was not an agent of the state, and rightly so. But he could not just sit and do nothing. He had to find out whatever it was that Podgis knew, or whatever it was that Podgis had manufactured, to make him so cocky about his chances of acquittal. Was it something he and Monty were working on together, or was Podgis digging around on his own? Whatever it was, if Brennan could find it, perhaps he could counter it, neutralize it, make it go away. Maybe he could spook Podgis into making a mistake and convicting himself by his own actions. Brennan had one and only one goal in this: to see Podgis go away and spend twenty-five years in the purgatory of prison before being cast into the outer darkness for all eternity. Brennan just hoped he could send the man to hell without risking excommunication himself.

He had to get into Podgis's flat. Podgis had rented a place when he was released on bail, and Brennan had a good idea where it was. He would get the address and . . . then what? He couldn't very well follow the man into his apartment and search the place with Podgis sitting there on his arse watching him. Unless Brennan beat him unconscious, which was a fairly tempting idea. But no, he had to be practical, if pouring a quart of whiskey down his throat and plotting a break-in could be termed practical. How in the hell could he break into the place? Smash the door in, and be arrested himself? Podgis was on a curfew, so that reduced the hours in which a break-in could be done. And, again, how would he get in? He gave a moment's thought to calling up certain relations of his in Ireland, people who had occasionally crossed the line into illicit behaviour in the past: "Howareyeh? Good, good, the blessings of God on you and all belonging to you. Oh, while I have you here, could you instruct me in how to pick a lock?" No. And he could hardly call upon Monty Collins to introduce him to one of his criminal clients for assistance in breaking in to the home of his current client . . .

Wait a minute. Monty wasn't the only person with a stable of criminal acquaintances. What about all the fellows Brennan had met and counselled in his ministry at the Correctional Centre? Who was out? Who could be persuaded to do a little undercover work for kindly Father Burke, the prison chaplain? Who had finely honed burglary skills? Who could be trusted?

Monty

Monty had not given up the idea that there might, just might, be someone out there who could be set up as the straw man, the alternative to Pike Podgis as the likely killer of Jordyn Snider. Ignatius Boyle was looking good for the role, with his conviction for indecent exposure and the fact that he knew the victim. Knew her, went off with her in a van full of kids, and then was spurned by her in the aftermath. But it would not hurt to have another guy on standby.

He nearly lost his resolve when he answered a call from Phyllis Podgis, thanking him and Maura for their kindness to her and informing Monty that she would be boarding the train back to Toronto. She said she could not be with Podgis when he was "like this." But, in the same breath, she pleaded with Monty not to judge her former spouse too harshly. "He puts on a front to hide his . . . When he's unhappy, he tries to hide it." Monty did not ask when the man had ever been happy, and under what circumstances. Obviously the goodwill of a woman who, however inexplicably, truly cared for him, and had travelled a long distance by train to support him, had done nothing to pierce his armour-plated hide. Monty wished Phyllis well, and they said goodbye.

He dialled Maura's number to give her the update but there was no answer; he left a message with the details of Phyllis's call.

He turned then to the notes he had made following his conversation at Tim Hortons with Constable Truman Beals. Right. Drew MacLean, an old boyfriend of Jordyn's. He was listed in the phone book with an address in Bedford, and when he answered Monty's call, he said he would be willing to talk about Jordyn. He was coming downtown Thursday evening, to meet friends for a movie at the Oxford. So he and Monty decided to get together across the street at the Spartan restaurant before that, at six o'clock.

Monty arrived a few minutes early, engaged in his regular banter with the owners about their rivals at the Athens restaurant, then sat at a booth and waited for Drew. He too got there ahead of the appointed time, and Monty stood to greet him. Drew MacLean was of medium height, slim with short brown hair and wire-rimmed glasses.

"Have a seat, Drew. Are you going to eat? I thought I might as well have supper here."

"Well, I don't know . . ."

"It's on me. Order whatever you like."

"Okay. I am a little hungry. Better to eat now than fill up with popcorn at the movie."

"Right."

Monty ordered the moussaka, Drew the souvlaki, and then they sat in silence, Monty wondering how to begin. He could hardly tell the young fellow he was looking for a boyfriend to cast in the role of a likely suspect to deflect guilt away from his client. But he had another angle worked out.

"As I explained on the phone, Drew, I'm representing the man accused of killing Jordyn."

"Podgis."

"Yes. And, as you might expect, we say Podgis did not even know Jordyn, so what would they have been doing together at that time of night? What I'm hoping to do is talk with some of the people Jordyn knew. To see how likely it would be that she would go off with a man she didn't know, or barely knew, if you see what I mean. But before we get to that, what about you? What do you do?"

"I'm taking my science degree at Dalhousie."

"How's it going for you?"

"Great. A lot of work but I love it."

"Glad to hear it. Are you going with anyone these days, or . . ."

"I've just started dating a girl in my class at Dal."

"All right. So, could you go back a few years and tell me how you met Jordyn and how long you went out together?"

"We went together for two years in high school, on and off. Grades ten and eleven."

"You both attended Halifax West?"

"Yes. She lived in Fairview and I lived in Clayton Park."

"What was she like?"

"Maybe you're asking the wrong guy."

"But you went with her for two years!"

"Two years in which I loved her and dreamed of marrying her when we were older. It took me a while to realize I didn't know her. At all."

Drew was calm and matter-of-fact, but there was an element of bitterness that he could not quite hide.

"Tell me what you mean."

"This should tell you something. It should have told *me* something, but you know how it is. Young and foolish, and not too clued in about the ways of the world when you're a guy in grade ten. I made a big elaborate plan to take her out skating on the frog pond. Do you know where that is?"

"Yeah, out on Purcell's Cove Road."

"I love to skate outdoors, and I figured she would too. I didn't have my driver's licence yet, but my dad said he'd drive us out there, and come back and get us later. And my mum would make a picnic with hot chocolate in Thermos bottles. And put everything in a special container. And she was going to lend me one of the quilts she made, so we could huddle under it if we got cold before Dad came back. And I went out and bought black and white film for my camera, because I love those old-fashioned pictures. I figured Jordyn would like pictures of herself skating. And then we'd come back and watch a movie at my place."

"How did it go?"

"It didn't. She laughed at me and made fun of me about it. 'Go in the car with your *dad*? Because you can't drive? Are you crazy? What kind of a date is that? And your mum is making us hot chocolate, like we're little kids or something? I'd never live it down! And we have to hang around outside in the cold? Wow! Big date!' She went on and on. It was painful!"

"It's painful even hearing about it, Drew. It sounded like a wonderful day you had planned for her. Why did you ever go near her again?"

"I figured it was me that was wrong. I didn't know what girls liked. I was a loser. So I should smarten up and think of more grown-up things to do on a date. I spent the next day at school kind of following her around like a puppy. And I saw her giggling and whispering about something with a couple of her friends. Which could have been anything, so I didn't think much of it till Cole Pilcher came strutting down the corridor with his hangers-on. This guy was bad news. Everybody knew it. And he said something really rude, really gross, to Jordyn. And instead of looking offended or even scared, she laughed and looked at her friends, and this set off another bout of the giggles. Even as naive as I was then, I caught on that she liked this guy. He was notorious! He had a juvenile record, he'd got at least one girl pregnant, and he treated girls like shit, and blabbed about everything he did with them.

"But then Jordyn was all sweet and lovey-dovey with me later, so we started going out steadily. Till she dumped me for another jerk. I forget his name. She went with him for a while. But he stood her up for our high school dance, so she went with her girlfriends and saw Cole Pilcher there with a girl from another school. Jordyn caused a big scene, screaming and crying and shoving the new girl out of the way. Then Cole grabbed her by the arm, dragged her out of the gym and outside. I didn't see any of this, but I heard about it from friends who saw her after. She had a bruise on her neck and a cut lip. Didn't call the police, though. Spent all her time on the phone begging Cole to come back to her. He told her to get lost, but she persisted."

"I see."

"So you're probably wondering how Jordyn and I ended up back together again!"

"Well . . ."

"She showed up at my house one night and said she wanted to

214

talk. So we went out for a walk, and she said she was sorry about the way she had been acting. Those other guys were nothing to her, just an experiment. She felt she had grown up a lot as a result of this bad period in her life, and she now knew those fellows for what they were. And it all made her appreciate me more than ever. That I was the type of guy any girl would be lucky to have. And all that. So we started going out again. And things were fine for quite a while. Then I heard rumours that she had been seeing Brandon Toth. He ended up in prison because he raped a girl! But even before he did that, anyone with eyes could see there was something wrong with him."

The tape of the Pike Podgis show about women who date violent men flashed through Monty's mind like a fast-forward perp walk of murder suspects. Though at this distance in time, the probability that one of Jordyn's cast of perps decided to kill her was admittedly low. Still, it opened up a new window on Jordyn as victim.

"Well, that was enough for me," Drew said. "I broke up with Jordyn once and for all. About time, eh? She made a big drama out of it even though she didn't care a fig about me. It was all so pathetic, on my part as well as hers."

"Drew, somebody told me that Jordyn was acquainted with Ignatius Boyle. You know who I mean?"

It was clear from Drew's reaction that this was unexpected. "The homeless guy they're calling a saint. Got knocked out and started speaking French. How would he have known Jordyn?"

"I don't know, just something I heard."

"You're not saying he . . . no. I've seen him hanging around on Spring Garden Road. Jordyn loved to shop, so she'd be downtown quite a bit. She might have seen him on the street. But she would have ignored him. Having a kind word for the poor and homeless would not have been Jordyn's style. So it wouldn't make any sense for someone to say she knew him. As far as I'm aware, anyway."

"Maybe my information is wrong."

"Or maybe I'm wrong. I don't have a very good record when it comes to Jordyn."

Monty would not have been doing his job if he didn't ask the next question: "Where were you on the night of September twenty-third?"

He expected Drew to be offended, but he laughed. "If I didn't kill her back in grade eleven when I gave a shit, I sure didn't kill her last fall. She was bad news, but she was old news. I should feel at least some sorrow about the fact that she was murdered. I know I should. But I don't. I can't help it. I can believe she pissed off the wrong kind of guy. Maybe even Podgis! Though that's not what you want to hear. But honestly, if you ask me whether she would have taken up with him all of a sudden, late at night, I couldn't say no. Especially if there was TV involved. Maybe he told her he'd get her on his show. That would have been enough. Her dream in life was to become a model or a TV star. She never did anything about it, as far as I know. Her main course of study seemed to be noting every detail of what other girls wore, or how they did their makeup or their hair, and making snarky remarks about them and constantly trying to outdo them. Apart from that, and sending photos of herself to God-knows-what modelling agency or TV show, she didn't do much to pursue her ambitions. But I didn't follow her career after high school. Podgis? That would be pretty low. But she'd been in worse company in her day."

"Did you tell the police about these other guys?"

Drew hesitated, then said, "No."

"How come?"

"Because I was afraid they might think I was jealous about all the times she cheated on me. They might try to pin the murder on me."

The poor lamb, Monty thought; *I'm more likely than the police to try to do that.*

Chapter 15

Brennan

On Monday, January 25, 1993, Nick Stockall and Brennan Burke, dressed in hooded jackets, jeans, sneakers, and leather gloves, loitered in the late-afternoon shadows outside the apartment building in Dartmouth where Pike Podgis had taken up residence until his legal difficulties were resolved one way or the other. It had taken Brennan a few days to set up, but here he was at Podgis's apartment building, about to break in; he was about to create another crime scene. The building had seen better days. Presumably. Some windows were taped up or supplemented by sheets of plastic, and the grounds were littered with candy wrappers and cigarette butts. Podgis had told an interviewer that he had just bought a new luxury condo in Toronto and was now forced to make monthly payments for lodgings in Nova Scotia. Monty Collins had given voice to the suspicion that Podgis for some reason actually wanted a downmarket living experience. For journalistic reasons perhaps. Or maybe to enhance his reputation as the victim of a miscarriage of justice. Well, if so, he had found what he was looking for in this place.

Stockall was a convicted housebreaker Brennan had met in his prison ministry; he was small and wiry, with a ratty-looking moustache and small, close-set eyes. He was nerved up, bouncing up and down on his toes, anxious for some action. Or maybe in need of a fix. Brennan tried to picture what he himself must look like, skulking around on someone else's private property with his young sidekick. He did not want to think about whether he looked more sinister than idiotic, or the other way around, and he had to overcome the temptation to bolt and abandon the whole ill-conceived mission. The consequences of being caught like this were unimaginable. He was breaking the law and crossing an ethical barrier in conscripting young Stockall as his accomplice.

"Nick, you have my word that if this goes awry . . ."

"If it what?"

"If this plan goes south, I'll take full responsibility. Your name won't escape my lips no matter what happens. This is important, and I can't see any other way to make sure this guy goes down for the girl's murder. You understand."

"I don't give a fuck about Podgis. I say we stick it to him. I'd like to see him try to kill a *guy*. No way. So he kills a girl. She probably told him to go fuck himself. Put him in Dorchester; he starts running his mouth up there, he won't last a week."

"Thanks, Nick. I appreciate your help." Brennan peered at the building. "He should be going out soon. I know he has an appointment." With his lawyer. Monty had mentioned a Monday afternoon appointment.

Brennan looked about him and wondered whether he and Stockall should be doing something. Throwing a ball around would hardly do the trick, given that it would call attention to them rather than make them blend in. But maybe they should light up cigarettes, anything to look half normal. Wait! There he was. Podgis was leaving the building just as a taxi pulled up. He must have been watching for it from inside. When the car pulled away, Brennan said, "All right. Let's go."

There was no security, and the door to the lobby of the building was not locked during the day. Brennan had done some research and reconnaissance the day before, feeling as foolish then as he did now. He approached the building in what he hoped was a casual manner, with Stockall at his side. They headed for the stairs in preference to the elevator and nearly walked over an elderly woman in their hurry to get on the steps and out of sight. Brennan excused himself, natural manners kicking in where silence would have been advised. The woman looked up at him, frowning. Was there something in his voice that made him an object of suspicion? Someone out of place here? What was he thinking? Everything about his appearance and that of his co-conspirator was suspect. He tried to put it out of his mind as he got to the staircase and took the steps two at a time to reach his destination. The sooner this was over, the better.

Podgis's apartment was number twenty-four, halfway down the corridor. Brennan looked around from under his hood and was strongly tempted to take it off. A gentleman removes his hat upon going indoors. He could not remember the reason, but it had been drilled into him since childhood. But a man about to break into the dwelling place of another was no gentleman. They drew up in front of the door, and once again Brennan had to wrestle down the temptation to run and abandon the whole crazy scheme.

But Stockall was already working the lock with some sort of pick and was jiggling it around. Brennan heard a creak of the floor and whipped around in the direction of the sound. Nothing. Why was he so fearful here, when he had never shown fear in the face of threats from rough characters in the streets of Dublin, New York, or Rome? He had been a scrapper when necessary in his younger years, and even in later life he was not easily intimidated. Then he got it. It wasn't fear at all; it was shame. Because he was doing something wrong, not just illegal but wrong. Breaking into another man's home. Wait, though; he was doing wrong in order to accomplish a greater good. He listened to himself and didn't like it; that kind of reasoning had been used to justify everything from state terror to . . . He shut down the lecture on moral philosophy and put his mind to the task at hand, right or wrong. He had a major threshold to cross, from law-abiding citizen and — Christ! He wasn't a citizen of this country. If he got caught, would he be deported? What had he been thinking, out of his mind with drink and plotting this criminal enterprise?

Brennan could not go through with it. "Nick," he said *sotto voce*, "forget about it. This is a wacky idea, and it's too — "

"Hey!" Brennan heard a shout coming from the staircase, and he willed himself to stay calm. He looked around — he could not stop himself — and saw a couple of young fellows bounding down the stairs. He turned his head away. One of the guys must have shouted to his companion. They were gone.

"We're in." Stockall pushed open the apartment door and started into the room. Brennan grabbed his elbow and pulled him back. "Nick, thank you. Your work is done. Go on now. As far as we know, nobody has seen you here. Keep it that way. Don't mess up your probation. I'll take things from here."

"Come on, Brennan, let me at this place. That motherfucker deserves it."

"He does. But the last thing you need is another conviction on your record. Right? Walk away. And thanks."

Stockall was reluctant, but he backed out of the doorway. "Okay, okay. Take it easy, Brennan, but take it. Whatever it is, man, get it. And you ever need to bust in anywhere again, you give me a call. *Capisce?*"

"*Capisco.* Now get going before you get spotted here."

Stockall walked swiftly away, took the stairs, and vanished from sight.

Brennan slipped into Pike Podgis's apartment, quietly closed and locked the door behind him, and looked around. The small living room was painted in what Brennan's mother would have called a "bilious green." Dusty brown curtains hung at the windows. Some of the hooks were missing, so the curtains sagged in the middle. The air was fetid, and Brennan had the impression the windows were never open. There was a brown and pinkish flower-patterned couch and matching chair, and a lounge chair in place before the enormous television that dominated the room. There was a new-looking video player beneath it. Brennan flipped through Podgis's small collection of videos. His interests appeared to lie with crusading foreign correspondents, action heroes, and young people in peril from everything from nasty schoolmates to chainsaw-wielding Texans. He opened the cases to see if the tapes were the real thing instead of . . . what? Home movies? Amateur porn? Nothing appeared to be out of order except the man's taste in entertainment.

One of the teen movie cases was empty; that must have been his current interest. But Brennan was not about to turn on the machine; no telling how much noise would come out of it, or what might alert Podgis to the fact that someone had used his equipment. So Brennan contented himself with reading the description of *Everything's Wrong with Evie*.

It was petite, brown-haired Evie Henshaw's first day at the big high school in town. She put on the nice new dress her mom had bought her at Wal-Mart, applied a little bit of makeup, not too much, smiled at herself nervously in the mirror, kissed mom goodbye, and before she knew it she was standing in front of her locker at Styx Valley High. And that's when it all started to go wrong. Very wrong. Because, according to popular girl Breagh-Lee Verdell, the queen bee of the A-list clique at school, Everything's Wrong with Evie: her face, her hair, her clothes, her mom and dad. Everything. The In Girls start to pick on Evie like wild animals on a helpless kitten. Evie goes home every night and cries herself to sleep. Until she meets Willie "Wolf" Wollmer, a personal trainer, and they start pumping iron together. And planning Evie's Revenge. Nothing will ever be the same at Styx Valley High! Rated R for nudity and violence.

Brennan was revolted, both by the tawdriness of the subject matter and by the thought of a grown man watching such a thing. But he could hardly claim to be surprised, knowing what he knew about Podgis.

A shout in the corridor made Brennan jump and nearly drop the video case. Someone was running in the hallway. Footsteps were approaching the apartment. He held his breath and tried to figure out what he would say if Podgis came through the door.

The footsteps kept going past, and silence descended again. Brennan resumed his search.

There was a big pile of clippings about the murder case and about Podgis himself. Again, no surprise. He had saved photos of himself facing a phalanx of microphones and vowing to get to the bottom of the false and malicious charges against him. He had always been a crusader for truth, as much as that got under the skin of certain people and the powers that be, and they were out to get him now. He would never rest until the real killer was found, and if his crusade had to be conducted in a prison cell, so be it. It would take more than a miscarriage of justice to stop Pike Podgis. The sort of blather you'd expect.

The flat had a tiny galley kitchen. Brennan didn't think he'd find much of interest there, but that's where he headed next, for no other reason than to eliminate it from consideration. He opened the fridge, the cupboards and drawers. Nothing but a few dishes and utensils. In the sink were plates with egg yolk congealed on them, mugs with a film of milk turned sour. The less said the better about the bathroom. Brennan held his nose and cast his eye across the scummy tub and basin, the unspeakable toilet. The soap had hairs stuck to it. An oxymoron in one word; if soap be filthy, can it still be called soap? Giving thanks for the fact he was wearing gloves, he opened the medicine cabinet and examined the contents. A cup contained a toothbrush with the bristles curled outward, little gobs of dark matter stuck to them. You'd think a person could change his toothbrush once in a while and rinse it off. But that was neither here nor there. Brennan wasn't there to find evidence to prosecute Podgis for his gross personal hygiene. One visit to the apartment would be sufficient to make such a case. But this was murder, and he soldiered on. No narcotics on the shelf, no bags of white powder.

The bedroom was cramped and stuffy, the bed unmade, the sheets dingy, an oily stain on the pillow. Brennan regarded it all with revulsion. Podgis's squat. Squat, squalor. What was it with the sound of "squa" in English that so perfectly described the squalid? *Lo squalo*. The shark, in Italian. Podgis should be so lucky as to be compared with the ever-gliding predator who ruled the seas. A pike: what had Brennan heard about that? He couldn't remember, but it wasn't edifying; he knew that much. Nothing of the glamour of a shark. He snapped his attention back to the squat he was in and resumed his investigation. At the bottom of the bed was a suitcase with clothing spilling out of it. Brennan was loath to paw through it but he stifled his squeamishness and rummaged through the clothes. He wondered how detectives could stomach this part of the job. There was nothing in the suitcase that he would recognize as being relevant to the murder case. Same with the bureau drawers. Nothing but clothes. And a package of condoms, unopened. They'd be more use in Podgis's back pocket, Brennan figured, where at least somebody might see the outline and think he had need of them. There was a desk made out of something that was meant to look like wood, but didn't. There was nothing of interest on the top of it or in the drawers. What Brennan thought he would find, and didn't, were notes made by Podgis about the murder charge. Maybe he worked on his case elsewhere. The television building? He did not seem the sort of person to leave it all up to his lawyer. Did he type notes into a computer at the newsroom? If so, whatever he had found and noted would be off limits to Brennan; he certainly couldn't jimmy the lock and break in there.

Only the closet was left to explore. He heard a heavy step in the corridor, and a muffled voice. Was Brennan fated to be the comic figure cowering in the closet when the homeowner (or the husband) came home unexpectedly? Not hearing anything more, he pulled the closet door open and looked inside. There were a few jackets and pairs of pants on hangers. The shoulders of the jackets were sprinkled with dandruff. Revolting. Even so, he had no choice but to touch the garments with his gloved hands. He searched the pockets, found nothing but a couple of crumpled receipts and a few coins. Nothing on the floor but a pair of out-sized track shoes and a gaudy pair of very shiny cowboy boots.

There did not appear to be anything on the top shelf but he reached up and slid his gloved hand along it just in case. There was something. He made a sweep of the entire shelf and brought forward whatever was there. Folded pieces of paper. More receipts. For restaurants, bars, taxis. What was this? A scrap of paper with various times scribbled on it, and the word "Yukon." And "Mon–Fri, 4:30." Another paper was wrapped around something. Brennan unfolded it and found a Polaroid photograph, the kind that came straight out of the camera, so you didn't have to take it somewhere to have it developed. It had been damaged by something, possibly water. It was rippled and discoloured on one side. Brennan took it to the window for a better look. Oh, God. A naked girl or woman, back view, shown from her thighs up to her head. She was slim and had long dark hair. She was lying on top of a man. One of his flanks was visible, and it was clear that he, too, was naked. Most of his face was covered by hers, except for his right eye and cheek. His hair was dishevelled and grey. Brennan stared at the picture, then rewrapped it and put everything back the way it had been. He gave the apartment a final glance; as far as he could tell, it looked exactly as it had looked before he searched it. The door seemed to close and lock properly. He peered around like the shifty, guilty intruder he was and left the building.

Brennan felt sick to his stomach. He knew the man in the photograph. Ignatius Boyle.

Monty

Monty was in his office going over a trial transcript for an appeal hearing later in the week when his secretary, Tina, poked her ingeniously coiffed head in his door.

"Monty, there's a gentleman here to see you. Jason MacDonald. He doesn't have an appointment."

"I'll see him. Send him in."

A man in his early twenties appeared at the door, and Monty invited him in with a gesture towards one of the two chairs on the other side of the desk. The man had long black hair dragged back into a ponytail and a tattoo of a tarantula crawling up his left hand. He turned and closed the door, then sat down and looked at Monty without speaking.

"Mr. MacDonald? Monty Collins. What can I do for you?"

"It's not MacDonald."

"Oh? My secretary gave me the name Jason MacDonald."

"Yeah. Sorry about that. It's Jason Snider."

It took a second for Monty to register the name. He sat forward in his chair. "You mean you're — "

"Yeah, Jordyn's brother."

"I see. How can I help you?"

"I heard you been out looking for information."

"Well, yes, part of the job."

"I've got something for you." He reached inside his jacket. Monty tensed and considered his options for movement if the murder victim's brother were to pull out a gun.

But it was a manila envelope, which he placed on the desk and pushed towards Monty. "This is something you should see."

Monty picked up the envelope and drew out the contents. A bunch of papers held together by a butterfly clip. Each page had been cut or torn along the top and the bottom.

"Go ahead. Read a couple. I got time."

Baby,

You have to be strong. We both do, till I can get out
and we can be together. Because it was meant to be.
You and me. There's a whole lot of people out there
that will do anything in their power to keep us apart.
Any chance they have, they'll put me down. Try to
turn you against me. Saying this one or that one was
an "innocent victim." That's just words. Innocent victims are people who don't deserve what happened to
them. Like getting run over by a bus or by some idiot
who got his licence out of a corn flakes box. People who
deserve what they get, who ask for it and act like whores
and finally somebody gives them what they want and
then all of a sudden they're "no, no, no," people like
that are not "innocent victims." So don't listen to all
these lies and negative stuff they're saying. Because you
know how I feel. I would never "hurt" you, because you
would never "hurt" me. And you know that everything
that happened was meant to be. Because it brought
you to me!! So you be my good little girl and don't do
anything to make my life in here any harder than it is.
Remember: you're not the only one who's alone. I'm
alone. In a cell. All night and most of the day. So it's
only fair that you're alone too. Yes? But don't worry.
We'll be together. No matter what they try to do to
keep us apart!!

Monty looked up at Jason. "Brandon Toth, I presume? The old
boyfriend in prison?"
"Nope."
"How do you know?" Jason looked down at his hands and focused
all his attention on tracing the tarantula tattoo with the index finger
of his right hand. "Jason?"
"Toth gave her the heave-ho. She supported him when he went on
trial for . . . well, you seem to know about it. She was there for him,

225

in court every day, and then when he got sent to Dorchester, she was writing him and trying to call all the time, and he told her to get lost. Pathetic, eh? It's not like he could get anybody else in there, but he ditched her anyway."

Pathetic indeed. Toth would rather have nobody, no letters, than have Jordyn Snider. But Jordyn had apparently rebounded from the loss; she had found love again, with another violent freak.

"Who is it then?"

Jason merely shrugged.

Monty flipped the pages and picked out another of the letters.

Fate brought us together! I wanted to punish that so-called "reporter" who did the TV stories about me. "Reporter = one who reports the facts." Not one who lies and twists the truth to get her face on TV, or to sell papers to all those nobodies out there who don't have a clue, little worms who crawl their whole lives in the dirt and don't see anything better, and they're right, there won't be anything better because they are small men who will never stand out from the herd. So they read about the people who do things, the actors of the world. "Actor = one who acts, gets things done." They read about *me*. You know what? They say I did these things, that I'm a criminal, that I deserve to be locked up. But that's what they *have to* think. Because they don't want me out there. I walk the earth my own way. And they can't stand that. So they have to put me down. But they read about me, every word. They love it. Deep down. You know why? Because they want to *be me*!

It's the same in here. But don't worry your little head over *the incident*. No matter what you hear, I was not involved, except to the point where I did what I had to do to protect myself. The riot was caused by *rioters*. The mob mentality. That's why they know it wasn't me, even though they can't admit it, and they have to punish everyone. I didn't touch the guard, not until he came at me. Asshole had it in for me, and this was his big chance with all the craziness going on. It was him or me. Take your pick! But he's out of the hospital and on the job again, this time with a little more respect for yours truly. So don't worry. This won't hold me back. We will be together!! You stay true to me, I know you will, and I'll keep my nose clean in here even if it means putting up with idiots and not dishing out the punishment they deserve, because you have to play their game to get out. So I'll play their little games, or that's what they'll think I'm doing. But not really because I'll be playing to win. And I will win. I shall be released and you shall be mine!

"Do you know what institution this guy is in? Whether he's still inside?"

"Somewhere in the Maritimes because in one of the letters he bugs her to come visit, and says it would only be a few hours on the road there and back. But we dunno any more than that."

"We?"

"My mother found the letters squirreled away in her stuff."

"In whose stuff? Your sister's?"

"Yeah. In her room."

"Were the tops and bottoms of the letters cut off when your mother found them?"

"Yeah. Mum didn't cut them off. Jordyn must'a. So's nobody would see who they were from."

"Have the police seen them?"

"No."

"Why not?"

"Why do you think?"

"Well, they could be a very serious lead in the case, so — "

"My mother thinks the case is solved."

"And you don't?"

"I dunno, one way or the other. If this Podgis asshole did it, he deserves to swing for it. Yeah, yeah, I know. We don't do that in this country. Somebody else could do it though. I'd put the rope around his neck myself. If it was him, and they lock him up for life, I hope they find him hanging from the bars in his cell."

"But?"

"But if it wasn't him, he'll get off. Or even if they nail him anyway at the trial, the guy who really killed her will still be out there, laughing in all our faces. So when I got a hold of these love letters I started to think maybe it's this guy. This psycho, whoever he is. 'Cause there's no dates on these letters, so we don't know when the guy was inside. He may be out by now. And he sure sounded hot to see her. I wanna make sure all the bases are covered."

"All the more reason why your mother should have taken them to the police."

"Would you?"

"What? Take them — "

"I mean, if that was your kid. If Jordyn was your kid, would you want anybody seeing that shit? Looking like some psycho's bitch? Starting to write to a guy she saw on TV for some really bad crimes? A guy who did all this damage to other people, and she's all over him? If that was your kid and she was dead, and this would trash the memory of her in front of everybody, would you show the letters around?"

He had a point. But not if it meant obscuring the search for the real killer. Monty said to Jason, "Right. But then, why haven't you brought the letters to the police yourself? Why give them to me?"

"Bit of history with me and the HPD."

"You've had some involvement with the police."

"Yeah. Anything coming from me, they're not going to believe."

"They'd think you made these up?"

"I dunno."

"But you didn't?"

"No way, man. What kind of a sicko do you think I am, writing this fucking shit about my own sister?"

"All right. I understand." And he did. Monty believed Jason when he said he had not composed them himself.

"You know I'll have to show them to the police. I will *want* to show them to the police."

"I know. You'll use them to try to get Podgis off. But I don't give a shit about Podgis one way or the other. If he did it, I hope he gets nailed. Even if he is your client. But if it's somebody else, I don't want the guy slipping through the cracks."

"Okay then, Jason. Thank you for bringing them in. These are the originals, I take it?"

228

"Yeah, they're the real thing."

"Good. Have they been handled much?"

Snider reddened. "Well, yeah, I read them. And I know my mother did."

"All right. I had to check."

"Okay, I'm going to take off. I hope you find this scumbag. And if he's still inside, well, we'll know it wasn't him. But if he's out . . ."

"Exactly. Thank you, Jason."

"Yeah, okay."

He got up and left the room.

If he's out, the case is wide open.

Brennan

Ignatius Boyle was seated on a wooden bench that someone — not the church — had recently placed by the statue of St. Bernadette. It was the evening after the day Brennan wished he could forget, January 25, 1993, the day he had broken into Podgis's apartment and found the photo of Boyle and the murdered girl. Brennan had no idea what to make of Ignatius Boyle now. He had tried to dismiss the man's criminal record, the indecency charge, from his mind, and that had been easier to do when he heard the young girl in the confessional, urging him to stand by Boyle because he had rescued her from a life on the streets. But then Brennan had seen photographic evidence of Boyle lying naked with a teenage girl. And it didn't require any stretch of the imagination to conclude that the girl was Jordyn Snider. Not when the photo was in the possession of the man charged with killing her. Not when the man charged with killing her had boasted, in Brennan's confessional, about photographs of the victim.

Beside Boyle on the seat was a scuffed, dog-eared Roman missal with a number of holy cards sticking out at various pages. Boyle was intent on a pack of cigarettes in his hands. A close look revealed that the cigarettes inside were half-smoked butts. He picked one out, looked it over, then replaced it in the pack. Picked up another, examined it, and reconsidered the first one. Brennan wondered whether the butts were his own, or whether he had scooped them up off the street. He tried to reconcile this with the other things he knew about Boyle, that he was a very articulate man, that he had wanted to become a priest, that he had sat in on courses at the university and had fallen in love with the idealist philosophy of Berkeley. Brennan sat down beside him, pulled out his own pack of smokes, and offered one to Boyle. It was as if he had offered him the chalice of the new and eternal covenant.

"Thank you, Father. Bless you!"

"You're welcome, Ignatius. How are you doing these days?"

"Can't complain, can't complain."

"Ignatius, the way you live, without a home . . . I can't help but ask you. How did things end up this way?"

"Do you know what I did, Father? I ruined every chance God gave me. I hit the bottle when I was a boy, and I just gave in to it."

"Was drink a problem in your family?"

"It was, Father. Both my parents, God rest them. Gone now, of course. But I make no excuses for myself. I didn't do my school work after grade nine, really, and then the kinds of jobs I'd get, I'd think I was too good for them. Me with a grade nine education, thinking I was above it all! But I thought I was smart because I always did a lot of reading. So I didn't take well to the kinds of work I had to do, and that would start me boozing again, and it went on and on. And there's also . . ."

"Also?"

"Ignatius of Loyola was a Spanish knight, born to a noble family. He cut a fine figure in the sixteenth century. But he gave it all up, his dreams of military glory and romance. He gave away his fine clothing and dressed like a poor man. All to serve God and help others. I was not born to nobility, but my parents named me Ignatius. Was I perhaps meant to live a humble life, to be close to those who are suffering? Or am I just a lazy man who drank his life away?" He shook his head. "I don't know."

Brennan didn't know either. But what he did know was that people who had risen far above Ignatius Boyle in terms of education and opportunity had taken to drink or drugs and had lost it all, ending up on the skids just as Ignatius had done.

This was getting them nowhere, however, so Brennan homed in on the problem at hand.

"That was an awful thump on the head you had."

"Oh, it was, yes, it was." Ignatius rubbed the back of his head. "But God was with me. He decided my time hasn't come yet, so here I am."

"Good. I'm glad you're out and about again. What do you remember about that night, Ignatius? The night you hurt your head."

He gave Brennan a wary look. "I don't remember a thing."

"You don't remember how you fell?"

"Nope."

"Any idea whether you were alone before you were injured?"

"Oh, yes, alone for sure."

"So how long before your fall can you remember, if you know what I mean? You know you were alone. What part of that night are you remembering?"

Boyle made himself busy with his cigarette. Held it sideways in front of his face, examined the burning tip as if he had never seen one before.

"Ignatius?"

"I was just walking along Morris Street by myself."

"And then?"

"And then I don't remember."

"What about before that? What were you doing earlier?"

He gave an elaborate shrug. "Nothing stands out for me about that night."

"Were you with anyone?"

"Nobody."

"Did you come here to the statue?"

"I don't think so."

"But you often come here."

"Yes."

"It would be unusual for someone to fall backwards, wouldn't you think? Unless a person had a stroke or a heart attack or something like that. But I believe they gave you a clean bill of health when they released you from the hospital, didn't they? No heart problems or anything?"

"Liver."

"What's that?"

"The liver is one of our most vital organs. Its functions include detoxification and — "

"Oh, I know, sorry. I just meant what did you mean about your liver?"

"They told me to stay off the booze. But I'm already off it. Haven't had a drink since . . ." He swallowed and looked away, peering into the distance as if something had attracted his attention. But there was nothing.

"Since?"

"Eh?"

"You haven't had a drink since when?"

"Oh, a few years ago. I'm not sure. But I'm off the stuff."

"That's good."

"Do you drink, Father?"

"I do. More than I should."

"It's not good for you."

"No, you're right. I should cut down on it."

Then he thought of the other unanswered question about Ignatius Boyle. Time to work in a little bit of Catholic detective work. "Ignatius, were you a French speaker at any time in your life before your injury?"

Boyle shook his head. "We weren't French. We were Irish. My grandparents came over from there."

"Where do you think your sudden ability to speak French came from? We're told it was excellent French, and there was a very sophisticated theological aspect to your conversation."

"I have no idea, Father. I couldn't believe it when people talked about it afterwards. I can tell you this much, though. I'm no saint! Not even close! If God gave me the gift of a new language for a while, I give thanks to Him for that and every other gift He has bestowed on me throughout my life."

Brennan felt a rush of love for the man, thanking God for blessings when in fact he had endured a life of deprivation and hardship. It struck Brennan that there was perhaps something holy about him after all.

"Ignatius, did you always live with your family?"

"Always did. I was always with my mother and my big sister, aside from a time when I was in the hospital when I was really little. I was sick but I don't remember anything about it. They say if you drink too much, your memory goes. It kills off your brain cells."

"You're right. We would all do well to bear that in mind. And you say you're off the stuff now."

"I'll never put a drop to my lips again."

"Good for you. How did you come to that decision?"

Boyle's eyes shifted away. "Nothing. It was just . . . I decided."

He must have reached a crisis point, Brennan thought. Well, that's what they say. You have to reach rock bottom before you can truly motivate yourself.

"But you were asking about my family," Boyle said. "My mother kept us with her. It wasn't easy for her; she had a hard life. I don't know how she managed. She's long gone now, but I keep her in my prayers every day." He lifted the prayer book and showed it to Brennan.

"That's good, Ignatius. I think you are a very kind and very devout man."

"Thank you, Father."

"Now I want to get back to the night of September twenty-third."

"There's nothing I can tell you!"

"Did someone push you down that night, Ignatius?"

"I don't know!"

"Is there someone you don't get along with? You were in a fight maybe?"

"Father, I told you I don't remember!"

"There was blood on you, but you weren't cut. Where do you think it came from?"

"I didn't do anything!" His voice rose in panic.

"You know there was a young girl murdered that night." The man stared at Brennan, his eyes huge. "Do you know anything about her death, Ignatius?"

"No! How could I? What would I know about it?"

Brennan stayed quiet for a minute or so. Boyle tamped out his cigarette, and Brennan gave him another. He lit it for him, let him enjoy the first drag, and then asked, "Did you know Jordyn Snider?"

"No!" Again the large-eyed stare. He kept his eyes on Brennan's without a blink. "Why would I know her, a young girl like that? Why are you saying these things, Father?"

"Ignatius, I saw a photograph." Boyle reacted as if he had been kicked in the gut. "There was a young girl in it, and a man — "

"I don't know what you're talking about!" Boyle screamed, and launched himself off the bench. Brennan was surprised at how fast the man could run. Ignatius stumbled over something on the ground and turned back. "You were so nice to me and now you're talking like this! You must be crazy, a priest saying this stuff! You should get some professional help!"

Brennan sagged backwards with his head on the back of the bench and gazed at the stars. If he had been hoping he was wrong in identifying Ignatius Boyle as the man in the Polaroid photo, all hope had just died. The photo wasn't news to Boyle. And another thing struck Brennan about the encounter: when he had asked Boyle what he knew about the young girl's death, Boyle said he didn't know anything about it. He did not say what any other man, woman, or child in the city of Halifax would have said, that the talk show host Pike Podgis had killed her.

Chapter 16

Monty

Clients kept Monty busy till late in the afternoon on Wednesday but, when he was finally alone in his office, he returned to the letters delivered by Jason Snider, making notes of anything that might provide a clue to the writer's identity. He would turn the papers over to the police, but not just yet. He had to decide how useful they were to his client, before releasing them and allowing them to make their way through the system. These were hardly the love letters of Lord Byron, but Monty ploughed on. The unknown scribe had promised that Jordyn would be his someday soon. She would be his, but only if she played her cards right.

> What the fuck is this???? Am I seeing what I think I'm seeing??? You dressed up like a coke whore? You've got on shorts that are all the way into the crack of your ass, they're so fucking tight, and your top is oh so conveniently falling off while you bend over and smirk at whoever is taking the picture. And oh yeah, by the way, who took the picture??? Who are you smirking at???

I have to believe you did this as a joke, because you obviously can't *do sexy*. That's something girls have to learn, and I'm the professor at the head of the class, baby. You're going to do sexy in a way you cannot even imagine, when you're united with me for life. Being with me has changed the life of many, many a woman before you! It will change yours too. You better believe it. So I'm going to let it pass. This time. As the stupid joke of a little brat. But a word of advice, babe: don't wear red and black! Those colours look like shit on you. Your skin's too white; it looks like fish. You look sick, like some old maid or something. How old are you? Were you lying about that? Get into a tanning bed and make yourself back into the pretty girl you showed me with your first picture. And next picture, you get it taken in front of a mirror so I can see who's holding the camera. Got that? I've got your letters here telling me you love me and you're mine for life, and then I see this. I better not find out you picked up some loser when you were out there dressed like a ho. And believe me, I'll find out. Suddenly I don't feel like writing anymore tonight. Thanks to you.

P.S. You said you would get your brother's car, so get it. I'll say it again in case you didn't hear me the first time. In case you're planning on breaking your promise to me. Get-the-CAR-and-get-here!! All I'm asking is a few hours out of your precious life. I can't wait forever.

Yes, pal, you can wait forever. You're the one doing time on the inside with nowhere else to go. "Can't wait forever" is supposed to be her line, Monty thought. But was the guy still inside? How old were these letters? Had he come to claim his bride? Was this a case of, as the headlines often read, expressing the obvious, *Love Affair Turned Sour Before Murder*?

Monty picked up the phone and called a fellow lawyer who worked with prisoners and parolees, and she gave him the name of someone she knew in the Correctional Service of Canada. Harold Lowther.

Monty called, got Lowther's answering machine, and left a message asking him to return the call. Monty needed a break. He wanted a drink. He thought of calling Burke but, if he let his hair down with his regular drinking buddy, he might blurt out something about the letters. He might not be able to help it, being just one of the lowly herd of worms despised by the lofty writer of letters from the lockup.

Monty tried to process what he had read. The guy had demanded that Jordyn come to visit, by car, and he said it would only take a few hours. That suggested, as Jason had said, an institution in the Maritimes. The inmate could be in Springhill, medium security, in Nova Scotia. Or Dorchester, again medium security, just on the other side of the provincial border in New Brunswick. A lot of bad actors in those places. Or he might be in maximum security in Renous. Again, New Brunswick. Some very bad actors in there. Renous was farther away but all of them were within reasonable driving distance of Halifax. This guy's troubles had made the television news, and the reporter was a woman, but that hardly set the case apart. His threat that he would know if Jordyn took up with another loser could mean he was from the Halifax area, but Monty could not put too much stock in that. This type would claim to be in the know, claim to have a network of informers, claim nobody could fool *him*, even if he did not know a soul within five hundred miles of the place. The most promising clue was the reference to a riot and an injured guard. Not a unique occurrence, but it would narrow things down.

In the meantime, Monty packed up his briefcase and made a decision not to go out to his place on the Northwest Arm, but to stop in and see the family downtown. He was greeted at the door by Normie, who waved a pair of concert tickets in his face.

"What are those for, Normie?"

"Daddy! How could you forget? The whole choir school is going to the Cohn Auditorium to see Kiri Te Kanawa. And the big guys' choir is going too. Mum organized getting the tickets for us all. But everybody paid for their own, except the kids who couldn't afford it, and the school paid for theirs. It's an afternoon matinee on Saturday, the sixth of February."

Monty was keen on the concert but, with all the other things occupying his mind, he had not realized it was coming up so soon. Good. "This will be a great concert, Normie. Maybe it will be you up on that stage someday, if you keep singing your scales and doing your homework for choir school."

"Do you think so?"

"Why not?"

"That would be so great!"

"Where are your brothers today? Out in the bars?"

"Daddy! Dominic's too little for doing that. He's playing in his room. I was playing with him till I saw your car outside. And Tommy, well, maybe *he's* in a bar somewhere, drinking beer."

"I certainly hope not. Now, why don't you go back upstairs and keep Dominic company?"

"Okay."

Once Normie had gone upstairs, Monty greeted Maura, sat down across from her in the living room, and said, "Hope remains alive for my wrongfully accused murder client."

"Oh? Have you taken on a new case?"

"No, same old case."

"Then you'll have to pardon me for doing exactly what I wrongfully accuse others of doing: not listening. Because I thought you said 'wrongfully accused' in relation to your current murder client, but that would be Pike Podgis, which doesn't make any sense. So start again. I'm all ears."

"There may be another suspect in play."

"I see. Another suspect in addition to poor old Ignatius Boyle?"

"Ignatius Boyle, the sex offender." Ignatius Boyle, known to the victim in years past, whatever happened there.

"I know, I know. I thought, at best, he's a saint and a miracle worker. At worst, a harmless wino. Now he's a sex criminal."

"Just the indecency charge. Walking around starkers and maybe exposing himself to a couple of girls years ago. That's it as far as I know. But you never really know with these things. What else might he have done without getting caught? But that's not who I'm talking about."

"Who, then? Another poor, disadvantaged man of no fixed address who can't possibly come up with an alibi for one o'clock in the morning because nobody can say whether that was him asleep on the sidewalk in downtown Halifax, or just his pile of damp and mouldy rags?"

"This guy has a fixed address. Very fixed. If he was home, everybody would know it. And if he wasn't, that would be a matter of public record."

"A non-paying guest of the Crowbar Hotel."

"Right. I just don't know who, or what institution. Nova Scotia or New Brunswick."

"Well! It's just piling right up for old Pike, eh? Sounds as if the charges will be dropped before sundown, and he can go on his slimy way back to Toronto."

"It needs work, I admit. But I have letters from a prison inmate to Jordyn Snider."

"You already knew that. She had a boyfriend who went to prison."

"This is a different guy."

Maura sighed. "Tell me."

"Her brother came in to see me."

"The vic's brother."

"Yeah. Jordyn's brother, Jason. Came in and gave me the letters. Told me his mother had found them hidden in the girl's room."

"So, do the police have them?"

"Not yet. They will, obviously."

"Okay. Go on."

"All identifying information has been removed from the letters."

"Removed by whom?"

"Jason says by his sister. When the mother came upon them, the tops and bottoms of the papers had been cut off."

"So the mother sent Jason to deliver them to you? Does she really think Podgis didn't do it? She heard all the evidence at the prelim; your guy's shoes were spattered with Jordyn's blood!"

"If the mother had her way, the letters would have stayed buried. As Jason said to me, if that was my child, would I trash her memory by revealing these letters? But Jason wants to make sure we get the right guy. If it's Podgis, Jason will happily lynch him. But, if it's somebody else, he'll want to save the rope for that guy."

"So, how bad are these letters, that the mother would keep them under wraps rather than explore all possible suspects?"

"See for yourself." He opened his briefcase, withdrew the envelope full of papers, and handed them over.

Maura read a few of the pages, the expression on her face darkening

239

as she descended into the netherworld of the man of letters. "Listen to this." She read aloud:

When you say you'll do 'anything' for me, do you have any idea what you're signing up for, baby girl? Do you even have a clue? I think not. Let me give you a bit of an education, baby. There's two kinds of people in this world. Those who have power and those who do not. Only a moron would believe that everybody can achieve power. Because then there would be nobody to have power over, so that would mean no power. Right? We discussed this. Best thing you can do, if you're not one of the powerful, is to form an alliance with someone who is. That person will protect you, keep you away from the bottom feeders of this world. In return, you give loyalty. Complete loyalty. And love. You love me. I love you, in a different way, but in a way you're going to love and beg for more of. Like all the women who came before you, and I changed their lives forever. Before we found each other. You'll fear me, but that's only natural when you look into the face of power! Oh, yeah, you'll see. When our time comes. But I expect something in return. You saw the word above. Loyalty. If you're mine, you're mine. Not anybody else's. That includes, not just other guys. (From what you say, the only guys you've ever known are a bunch of losers.) But not just guys. Loyalty includes not listening to a bunch of weak-kneed nervous Nelly women who want to close you in, put limits on the heights of what you can experience in this world with me. They're jealous of what we have. They're losers.

"I can't read any more of this trash." Maura threw the letters in the general direction of Monty's briefcase. "Who is this egomaniac? All the women begging for him! What's the song you said Brennan sang to Podgis that night at the Midtown, taking the mickey out of him?"

"'Bad to the Bone.' Devastating to the female population. What Podgis would like to be. Maybe this guy's the real thing."

"And you think Podgis isn't?"

"I don't know what to think. His ex-wife showed up to support him. Surely she would not have gone out of her way like that if she saw him as a lady killer, in either sense of the term."

"She wouldn't be the first, would she?"

"I know, I know. What am I saying? It happens all the time."

"And remember, Monty, you left me a phone message saying Phyllis took off the next day and went back to Toronto. That doesn't speak well of old Pike."

"But our visit to his apartment, hearing her tales of his family and his upbringing, didn't that make you feel a little bit sorry for him?"

"I felt sorry for *her*. He should have been kissing that poor woman's feet, not treating her like shit. If that's how he behaves towards a woman who cares about him, imagine what he might do to someone who brushed him off, or made a snide remark."

Monty could imagine. And he remembered something else about the encounter with Podgis and his ex. It almost seemed as if Podgis held her in contempt precisely *because* she cared for him. Was he contemptuous of any woman who would take up with a guy like him? Monty decided not to pursue that line of thought with Maura.

"Back to this guy." He pointed to the letter written to Jordyn Snider.

"What's his connection with Jordyn?" Maura asked.

"I have no idea. That's what I have to track down. Find out who he is, where he is, whether he's still inside, or whether he could have been in Halifax on the night of September twenty-third."

"So we don't know whether this is somebody she knew from here, or . . ."

"As far as I can tell, she saw his story on TV and began writing to him."

Monty watched as his wife processed the information. It did not please her. "Another one," she said.

"Looks like it."

"What's the guy in for? Let me guess."

"Go ahead."

"Rape or murder, or both."

"Most likely. Serious violence of some sort. That's the impression I get. Inflicting his form of love on the powerless. I have a call in to a

Corrections Canada official. I'll check and see if he's called me back. Almost quitting time, but you never know."

He went to the phone in the kitchen and dialled his office number to check his answering machine. Yes, there was a message from Harold Lowther. Monty called him and gave him the spiel on what he was looking for, and why. Half expecting the runaround, Monty was surprised to hear Lowther say he had two possibilities in mind. There had been two incidents involving violence and injured guards, one at Renous just over two years ago and another at Dorchester ten months back. Two inmates had been disciplined following the Dorchester episode, but one could be eliminated from consideration; Lowther had recognized his name and knew he could barely write his phone number, let alone a series of letters of the kind described by Monty. Lowther didn't know the other inmate in Dorchester, or the one in Renous, but he would check into it, and call Monty when he had some news.

Monty thanked him for being so forthcoming to a member of the defence bar, and Lowther said, "No problem. It's simple, really. If your guy didn't do it, we don't want him. And if one of these other two did, we'd like to get him back inside sooner than later, before he kills again."

"Anything useful?" Maura asked when Monty returned to the living room.

"Sounds as if he can narrow it down. One of the letters referred to a riot, and the psycho was in the middle of it. This Harold Lowther is familiar with two incidents and is going to find out who was involved. He'll let me know."

"Good."

"Tell me," he said to Maura, "has anybody ever done a study of how many sexual predators have female pen pals and courtroom bunnies hanging on their every word? Studied what makes a person become the lover and admirer of convicted sex offenders and serial killers?"

"I'm not sure. If not, it's about time."

Monty spared Maura the details of the Podgis show he had seen, detailing just how far some of these courtroom bunnies and other panderers were willing to go to keep their men happy.

Maura said, "Jordyn's letters to him aren't available, I suppose."

"No. All we know of them is what he says in response."

"And that tells us everything we need to know, that he's a sadistic, paranoid, narcissistic, controlling psychopath. Why is that not obvious to anyone who reads these letters, including Jordyn?"

"Maybe it was obvious, and she liked him just the way he was."

"Don't make me sick."

"You just don't *understand him*, Maura, the way Jordyn did."

"Maybe at the cost of her life."

Brennan

Brennan was too agitated to concentrate fully on his work after searching the residence of the accused murderer, Podgis, and finding a photograph of Ignatius Boyle lying naked with a young woman who was presumably the victim of the murder. There was a part of Brennan that wished he had never broken into the flat, never seen the photo, never heard Boyle's unsatisfactory answers to his questions about the killing. Because now Brennan had to consider a possibility that pained him to the core: that poor, sweet Ignatius Boyle was a legitimate suspect in the case. And that the vile Podgis might be innocent. If he was, what in the hell were those depraved "confessions" about? But no, that did not necessarily follow. After all, there was incontrovertible physical evidence tying Podgis to the crime scene. Was it even remotely possible that the two men's lives had somehow intersected to the point where they acted together in committing this crime? What on earth could have brought two such disparate individuals together? The obvious link was Jordyn Snider. Boyle had been naked with her, and Podgis had the photo of them together. Had Podgis taken the picture? If so, when? Where? And, again, how did these people step into each other's lives?

Ignatius Boyle had been at the church the day of the debate on the Podgis show. He had encouraged Brennan to prevail over the forces of darkness and unbelief. To take on Podgis and win one for the Man Above. Boyle was no friend of Podgis at that time. And that time was a few hours before the broadcast. Less than twelve hours before the murder. It didn't make sense. What Brennan would normally do to hash out something like this was discuss it with Monty. But Monty was on the wrong side of this. The dark side. Or was he? Well, he was representing Podgis.

Brennan wondered, not for the first time, what kind of information Monty possessed about Podgis and his activities that night, and other previous troubles he might have had. How much did Monty know about Boyle? Were there other suspects as well? Monty could not reveal anything he had because of solicitor-client confidentiality. Brennan was in the same boat; he could not reveal to Monty the things he had heard from Podgis in the confessional. "Boat" might be an appropriate image; the priest and the lawyer were like the proverbial two ships passing in the night, when it came to knowledge about the murder of Jordyn Snider.

He would keep an eye out for Ignatius Boyle. Perhaps he could persuade the homeless man to come into the church. Boyle was a very devout Catholic. Would the magnificent interior of the church, with its statues and stained-glass windows depicting the angels and saints, and the presence of the Blessed Sacrament on the altar, induce in Boyle the desire to tell the truth? Brennan of course did not have the luxury of lounging about on the benches in the churchyard all day and night in the hope of catching the man when he came for his devotions. It would be a matter of chance, not at all an efficient way to make progress in an investigation, but he did not see what else he could do.

There was no sign of Ignatius Boyle over the next few days. Whenever Brennan had the opportunity, he took a peek out the window of the parish house or the choir school to see if he could spot his man. But no luck.

It was nearly a week before Brennan caught sight of Boyle again. On a Monday night when the priest was in his room basking in the creamy voice of Kiri Te Kanawa on his CD player, he looked out the window and saw his quarry shambling into the churchyard with his Roman missal in one hand and his pack of cigarette butts in the other. Brennan gently extinguished Kiri's voice and ran down the stairs and out to the yard. He thought it best not to draw attention to himself but to get good and close to Boyle before announcing his presence. He was just about to head over to him when he heard his name.

"Father Burke!" Shite.

Ignatius Boyle whipped around, saw Brennan, and hightailed it out of the churchyard.

Brennan turned to see who had hailed him. It was Urquhart, the fellow who did repair work around the church. He wanted a word with Brennan about cleaning and doing something to the furnace. The burner, the filter . . . something. Brennan could not remember ever looking at the furnace and had no interest in its maintenance; he told the man to go ahead and do whatever needed doing.

By the time he had dealt with that, Boyle was out of sight.

Well, Brennan was not about to let it rest. He took off at a fast clip in the direction Boyle had taken; he was determined to question the man again and get to the bottom of the connection between Boyle, Podgis, and Jordyn Snider.

Boyle had left the churchyard in the direction of Morris Street to the south, so Brennan sprinted to Morris and looked left and right. He had a split-second decision to make: which way to go? Left was the direction of the harbour. It was more likely Boyle had gone right, into the heart of the Halifax peninsula, so that's what Brennan did. He walked as fast as he could without breaking into a run. There, up ahead, was Boyle. Brennan slowed and moved into the shadows of the buildings as he followed his quarry west on Morris. He saw Boyle turn right on South Park; Brennan broke into a run until he got to the corner, then turned and resumed a walking pace. Boyle stopped for the light at Spring Garden Road and did not turn around. A man not plagued by any suspicion that he was being followed. Well, most people are not being followed, and Ignatius Boyle would normally be no exception. In fact, he was probably the least likely person to be pursued, having no possessions that anyone would want to steal. Boyle turned left on the north side of Spring Garden, walked the length of the Public Gardens to Summer Street and then cut through the Camp Hill Cemetery. Brennan made a little bow in the direction of the soaring column marking the grave of the great brewer Alexander Keith on his way through the graveyard. How far was this pursuit going to take him, Brennan wondered, but he stayed well behind Boyle and kept at it. Boyle did not stop until he reached a blue wood-shingled house on Yukon Street north of Quinpool Road. Only then did Boyle look about him. Brennan ducked out of sight behind an oil truck. When he peered out, he saw Boyle standing at the entrance to the house, leaning on the bell and pounding on the door. There had been a reference to Yukon in the notes in Podgis's closet. Podgis had this address.

After nearly a full minute of ringing and pounding, which attracted annoyed glances from a couple of people passing by, the door opened a crack. Boyle spoke to someone inside in an urgent whisper. Brennan strained to hear what was being said, but could not make it out. Boyle was admitted to the house, and the door closed behind him. Who was in there? Someone connected with Jordyn Snider? With Pike Podgis? Someone with a nostalgic taste for candid Polaroid photography?

Chapter 17

Brennan

Brennan, dressed in a navy sports coat, white shirt, and no tie, stood in front of the blue house on Yukon Street, treating the door with more restraint than had been shown by Ignatius Boyle the night before. It seemed long but it was probably only thirty seconds before Brennan heard someone shuffling towards the entrance. The door opened, and a woman of about seventy-five stood there glaring up at him through a pair of smudged eyeglasses. She had three sweaters layered on, all white, and still she shivered with the cold.

"Yes? May I help you?"

"Em, perhaps you can. I'm wondering if Mr. Boyle is here."

"Who?"

"Ignatius Boyle. This is the address he gave me."

"Ignatius!"

"Yes. Is he here?"

"I'd remember a name like that, so I can tell you the answer to your question is no. You must have the wrong address."

"It may be the upstairs flat . . ."

"The upstairs flat is occupied by three — "

"Maggie! Maggie!"

Brennan heard two very young voices coming from the top of the stairs, followed by footsteps and a crashing sound. The elderly woman looked upwards. "Take it easy up there, girls. You'll fall and hurt yourselves. I've warned you before about that landing. Now go back inside. It's not Maggie; it's me talking to a gentleman who's lost."

"Lost? We'll help him, Mrs. Lewis! We'll know the way!"

"No, no, he's just leaving."

But she did not succeed in hustling him off the property before two little girls came bounding down the stairs. One looked about ten, the other maybe eight. Both had dark curly hair and big brown eyes. They were wearing bibbed overalls made of denim with striped cotton T-shirts underneath.

"Are you lost?" the younger one asked.

"Well, it's more that I'm looking for someone and can't find him."

"So the other guy's lost."

"Could be." Brennan smiled at them.

"We'll help you. Come up to our house. You tell us what he looks like. We'll draw a picture, and you can nail it to a tree or a telephone pole, and people will see it and find him and you put your phone number on. That's what we did with our kitty."

"Oh, did you find him?"

"It's a girl! Buffy."

"Oh, I'm sorry. Did you find *her*?"

"Yeah!"

The older sister spoke up at that point. "But then she got sick and died."

"Oh, no."

"We had a funeral," the younger one said. "Buffy's buried in the backyard, and we have a picture of her out there. What does the lost guy look like?"

He looked uncertainly at Mrs. Lewis. She said, "Girls, why don't you go back inside and let this gentleman go look for his friend. I'm sure your sister will be home soon, and she won't want you out here gabbing with, well, with strangers."

"It's okay," the older child said. "If he does anything bad, we'll get you to call the police."

Obviously, the right thing to do would be to leave. But Brennan wondered if the girls knew, or had seen, Ignatius Boyle when he came to the house last night. There appeared to be only two flats in the place, one up, one down.

"How about this?" he suggested. "I'll come up and talk to you on the landing. I won't go into your apartment, because you don't know me and I don't know you. I'll tell you what my friend looks like, and you can go in and draw a picture if you like, and bring it out to me. Maybe Mrs. Lewis will leave her door open, so she can hear us in case she thinks of anything that might help. Does that sound all right?"

"Yeah, okay."

"Great!"

The girls were on side. Mrs. Lewis looked skeptical, as well she might. But it was a dead certainty that she would listen in, so she would know soon enough that he was harmless. She stepped aside, and he walked up the stairs to the landing.

"I'm Florrie and this is Celia," the younger girl announced. "She's one year, six months, two weeks, and two days older than me, but I learned to read at four and she didn't learn till she was almost six. She reads better than me now, though, because they have harder books in grade five."

"I'm pleased to meet you, Florrie and Celia. My name is Brennan."

"That's a nice name," Florrie said. "I don't know anybody else called that. I know four Joshuas and three Kaylas. But there's no other Florrie in our school. And no other Celia except one of the teachers and we don't call her that; we call her Mrs. Randall, because you have to be polite at school. I'll go in and get our drawing stuff and bring it out here."

"Sure. Or maybe I could ask you about the fellow first, ask whether you've seen him. You might have. He said something about coming to this street to see someone."

"I'm getting the papers and coloured pencils anyway, Celia," Florrie declared and stepped past her into the flat.

"So, what school do you go to, Celia?"

"Oxford."

"How do you like it?"

"It's good."

"What's your favourite subject at Oxford?"

"Math. The teacher sneaks me extra work from the bigger kids, in grade six."

"You must be very good at it."

"Well, you know . . . What do you work at?"

"I have a school. A choir school."

"So you're a principal?"

"I'm more of a music director."

"That sounds like more fun. We have music too."

"Brennan! What kind of music do you play?" Florrie called from inside.

"I do Gregorian chant, and something called Renaissance polyphony; that's where different parts of the choir sing different parts of the piece. Beautiful harmonies."

"I'm really good at music!"

"Florrie, that's bragging!" her sister said.

"Well, you were bragging to him about the math!"

"Oh, no! I guess I was." She looked at Brennan, the picture of guilt. "Sorry, I didn't mean to."

"I didn't think you were bragging; you were just stating a fact. Right?"

She grinned at him. "Right!"

He heard the banging of something that sounded like a guitar hitting the wall, and he winced. Out came Florrie with one hand clutching the neck of a guitar, the other arm barely enclosing a bunch of drawing supplies. She dropped everything on the floor. The guitar suffered another blow.

"I'll play something for you. But you can go first."

"No, no, I won't."

"Please? Sing one of your songs for us."

He decided on something short and simple, one of the most beautiful melodies this side of heaven: the Easter plainchant "Alleluia."

"Wow, that's really good!"

"Yeah," Celia agreed, "it is."

"Sing us another one."

"Well," he said, "this is a sad one but you can make up your own ending. It's about a cat that got sick. So if you don't want to hear it, I'll understand."

"No! No! We want to hear it, don't we, Cel?"

"Yes, please."

"All right. It's an old folk song I used to hear when I was a little boy in Ireland."

"Cool!"

Departing far from his standard repertoire, he launched into "Pussy Got the Measles."

"Pussy got the measles on the first day of spring, the first day of spring, the first day of spring. Pussy got the measles on the first day of spring, the poor, the poor, the poor wee thing." He revised the lyrics as he went along, so in this version the poor creature survived the ordeal.

"That is a great song! The other kids will be jealous 'cause I'll know it and they never heard it before. I want to learn it!"

"I'll send you the words and music."

"Great! Oh, here's the paper and pencils in case we need them to make a poster. Now I'll play you a song on the guitar."

"Lovely. What are you going to play?"

"What's the name of it, Celia?"

"'My Bonnie Lies Over the Ocean.'"

"It's got three chords in it. I know them all."

Florrie plunked herself down on the floor, cross-legged, and bent over the guitar, her face about three inches from her left hand as she formed her first G chord. She struck the strings and it sounded like hell.

"Oh, no! That's not it!" She looked crossly at the instrument, and tried again, louder this time. Same result. "But my fingers are right!"

"It's out of tune," Brennan said.

"Oh, no! That guy at the store said it was good!"

"He said we could bring it back if there was something wrong with it, Florrie."

"And there is. It's no good!"

"It's second-hand," Celia explained.

"There's nothing wrong with it," Brennan assured them. "Second-hand guitars are often the best. I'll tune it for you."

"Can you do that?"

"Sure, I can." He gently removed it from Florrie's grasp and played each string. He noticed she had her name printed on a yellow sticker on the back, Florrie Nelson. Then he closed his eyes for a second, found E in his head, and tuned the first string. He did the others in sequence, strummed it a bit, was satisfied, and handed it back. "Nice sound. It's a good guitar."

"Is it?" Florrie's eyes lit up.

"Take good care of it now. Don't drop it or bang it around."

"I never do!"

She got herself into position again, then played "My Bonnie," and her sister and guest applauded.

"Now let me ask you about this friend I'm looking for."

"Okay," they said in unison.

"His name is Ignatius."

"Wow!" the little one said. "Nobody at my school has that name!"

"No, I suppose not. He has grey hair that's a little bit wild-looking, and he usually wears a light tan-coloured coat. He may have — "

"That's the guy that was here," Florrie said.

"Yeah, that's him," her sister agreed.

"Oh, good, then I don't have the wrong house after all."

"No, this is the right place," Florrie agreed, "but he doesn't live here. He just came to see my sister."

Brennan looked at Celia, but she shook her head. "Not me. Our other sister."

"Older sister?"

"Oh, yeah, she's way older. She's like a mum."

"And this man came to visit."

"Yeah."

"Does he come here often?"

"No," Celia replied, "only a couple of times. But that was the first visit in a long time. I think she sees him other places, though. Even if he's old." She looked at Brennan, and a blush spread over her cheeks. "You're not as old as him. I don't mean old is bad."

"No, no, I understand."

The phone started ringing in the apartment, and Florrie leapt up to answer it. "I'll get it!"

Celia laughed. "I don't know why she says that. She always gets the phone. Nobody else even tries anymore."

"So who lives with you? Florrie, and your older sister? Anyone else?"

"No. Nobody else now. Our mum is in a special place. For wheelchairs."

"Oh. I'm sorry to hear it. What's your big sister's name?"

"Maggie." Celia leaned towards him. "She works with rats."

"Ah."

"Celia!" Florrie called from inside. "It's Maggie. She's gotta work late."

Celia said, "Sometimes she works late because the rats — "

Florrie came out then and relayed the rest of the conversation: "Maggie said to eat the rest of the waffles. They don't have to be heated up or anything. And she'll do the dishes when she gets home. And she said . . ." She glanced at Brennan, then looked quickly away. "She said we can't, uh, have anybody over. To visit. So we have to go in and lock the door."

"Good advice," Brennan agreed. "I'll be running along. Thank you for your help."

"You're welcome," said Celia.

"Maggie said you have to leave," Florrie told him, "but I told her you weren't bad and that you were looking for somebody. Except I couldn't remember how to say his name."

"Oh, that's all right. What did she say to that?"

"That's when she said we couldn't have anybody over, and we have to stay inside by ourselves. And she's going to make up some new rules about us answering the doorbell."

"I understand. She sounds like a very good big sister."

"She is!"

"All right, Florrie and Celia, I'm going now. It's been lovely to meet you. God bless you." He made a little, unobtrusive sign of the cross in their direction.

"Okay, bye, Brennan!"

"Bye!"

He went down the stairs and looked into the open door of the downstairs flat. Mrs. Lewis was standing just inside, making no effort to pretend she had not been listening. That came as a relief. Brennan was glad the little ones had somebody paying attention to the comings and goings in the house.

He nodded to Mrs. Lewis. "Thank you," he said.

Pike Podgis had made yet another appointment to see Monty in his office to ask yet again what progress he was making on the defence. Monty gave him a quick overview of the information he had uncovered, including the helpful evidence of Richard Campbell, who had heard male and female voices on Hollis Street the morning of the murder. Less helpful, in fact a dead end, was the information about Befanee Tate's boyfriend; he had not been out there knocking off Befanee's rival at the shrine of the saint. He had an alibi, as did Befanee herself. Much more promising was what Monty was learning about Jordyn Snider. It seemed she had more than one unsavoury acquaintance. Monty did not mention the letters she had received from the unidentified prison inmate. He wanted to know a lot more about that relationship before going public with it. And anything shared with Podgis tended to go public. If the letter-writer was still in prison, the correspondence was irrelevant to the murder case. Except for the light it would shine on the victim's character, and on the unsuitable male companions she might take up with after dark. But this category of person might have included Podgis himself. So Monty tried to reassure his client with "We are making progress."

Monty hoped Podgis would take a hint from the wrap-up: "Nothing more we can do in here this morning." But he suspected that his client had never taken a hint in his life. And sure enough, Podgis did not budge. Then the phone rang, and Darlene told Monty Father Burke was here. Should he wait or come back later?

"Send him in." Burke's presence might motivate Podgis to shove off.

Burke looked as if he had seen the dripping fangs of a serpent from hell when he caught sight of Podgis, but he took the other of Monty's two client chairs and sat down.

Monty did not let on that he was aware of any reason the three could not have a pleasant time in the same room together.

"Hi Brennan. What can I do you for?"

"I thought we might have a word."

"Sure."

"But I can wait."

Monty could almost feel a live current of hatred pass between the two men. All out of proportion on his client's part, surely. So out of proportion that he was planning to sue Burke for defamation. None of his lawsuits, against Burke or the Crown or against Monty himself, would see the light of day, but that was not the point. What Monty did not understand was the animosity Podgis displayed towards the priest. There was no question that Burke's testimony put Podgis in a bad light, suggesting he had a date planned with the victim, and making him look like a gross, ill-mannered boor. Humiliating for Podgis, certainly. But it seemed there was more than the resentment one might expect. As for Burke, well, Podgis was just the sort of ignorant, abrasive lout that would set Burke's teeth on edge. But the expression on the priest's normally impassive face was one of intense loathing, his dark eyes like death rays boring into the other man's soul. Monty wondered fleetingly whether Burke knew something about Podgis that Monty did not know. But how could he? Burke would not have any more information than these few strained encounters and the news stories provided. He had never even seen the television show until the night he made his brief appearance on the program himself. So that would not explain it. And it was not as if Podgis was one of Burke's parishioners.

Burke smouldered in silence but, true to form, Podgis had to hear the sound of his own voice and inflict it on everyone else.

"What would the Bar Society say, Collins, about my lawyer palling around with a key witness against one of his own clients?"

"Why don't you ask them? Give them a call."

"You're always such a smartass. Hard to believe you have any friends at all. Maybe that explains why you think you're stuck with this guy." He jerked his chin in Burke's direction. "Nothing to say, Burke? It's okay, you can speak freely here."

Again, nothing but eternal damnation coming from the eyes of Burke.

What was going on between these two? It was as if Podgis was needling Burke about something. Well, whatever it was, it was not doing anyone any good.

"All right, gentlemen, let's adjourn this convivial meeting *sine die*."

"What does that mean, smart guy?"

"It means 'without day.' We're adjourning, and no date has been set for another meeting amongst the three of us."

"That's not quite right, is it? We're going to meet again at my trial. Where the jury will catch on that this guy is out to get me, just like the police and the prosecutors. No surprise there, when you think about it. Church and state coming down on me, to silence me for good. Well, it's your job to make sure that doesn't happen, Collins. It'll be kinda hard for you to find clients if you fuck up and let them convict an innocent man."

"I'll never work in this town again, eh, Podgis?"

"You're an asshole, Collins."

"To respond in the words of our former prime minister, Mr. Trudeau, I've been called worse by better people."

"Mark my words: both of you will be laughing on the other side of your faces when this is all over."

Podgis heaved himself out of the chair and left the office.

Monty turned to Burke, but he too was out of his chair. "Where are you going? What did you want to see me about?"

"Nothing. Just lunch. But I've remembered something urgent, and I have to go."

"Where?" No answer. "Brennan, what is going on with you and him? You know what he's like. He's obnoxious to everyone he meets. What's so personal about this for you? You look at him as if he's the devil incarnate. I told you he's pathetic; he's not worth all this hostility on your part. So what is it?"

Burke did not say another word but left the room in Podgis's wake. Monty got up from his desk but sat down again when the phone rang. It was Tina. "Monty, Mr. Podgis just left. Does that mean you can see the insurance guy earlier than scheduled? I know he was wanting an earlier appointment if he could get one."

The claims handler for one of Monty's motor vehicle accident cases. "Sure, Tina, give him a call. I'll be back in five."

He went out through reception and pressed the down button on the elevator. When he arrived at the ground floor, he looked out the glass door and saw Podgis and Burke nose to nose on the sidewalk. Well, Podgis had his pugnacious face turned up, and Burke was looking down his nose, but it was a face-to-face confrontation any way you looked at it. Monty could not hear what they were saying, and he suspected that they would go quiet on him if he got in the middle of it. After a few seconds of this, the dynamics changed.

Burke leaned down to the shorter combatant and unleashed a torrent of words at his adversary. Burke was turned away from Monty so he could not lip read what was being said, but it was heated. The response from Podgis was strange. Rather than his regular mode of real or feigned outrage and loud remonstrance, he had affected an expression of amused incredulity. It was as if he were saying, "What on earth are you talking about?" In fact, Monty could read his client's lips at the end. He said, "What? No, of course not." His expression turned to one of pity, and he reached out and gave Burke a patronizing pat on the arm. Monty saw Burke tense up, and he half expected the priest to ram a fist into Podgis's gigantic mouth. But Burke restrained himself. Good thing for Podgis. If Burke chose to, he could reduce the man to rubble. Instead, Burke turned and walked away. The gloating expression returned to Podgis's face.

Monty went back to the office and met with the insurance man and other civil-litigation clients for the rest of the day. But one part of his mind was still on Pike Podgis. What was he up to?

Chapter 18

Brennan

Saturday, February 6, felt like a morning in spring. Brennan had
it in mind to pay a visit to Maggie Nelson and see what he could
learn about her acquaintance, Ignatius Boyle. He drove to Yukon
Street and parked, then saw the two little ones playing on the sidewalk. They both had on white ankle socks, black patent shoes, and
cotton dresses. Florrie's was red plaid and Celia's all white. Celia's
material had holes in it, but it was supposed to. What did Brennan's
mother call it? Georgette? Something-et. Eyelet, he believed. Both
girls looked as if they had been dressed by a grandmother from
forty years ago, or had perhaps got their outfits at a second-hand
clothing shop. Whatever the case, they looked sweet. They were
drawing pictures on the pavement with coloured chalk. When he
got closer he could see that the pictures were rooms in a house.
Smartly dressed dolls sat on the sidelines, waiting for their new
home to be completed.

"Hello, Florrie. Celia."

Two pairs of big brown eyes gazed up at him, then there was a
simultaneous "Hi!"

"How are the girls today?"

"Great! We're drawing a doll's house, but I had to erase part of what Celia did."

"How come?"

"Don't tell, Flor!"

"She drew a toilet and put a rock in it for poo, and a boy came along! So I scratched it out and told her off." Brennan tried to keep a straight face. "How would you like it if your sister did that, and a boy saw it?"

"I have sisters who I suspect would do much worse, if they could get away with it."

"Really?" Florrie asked. "Are they bad?"

"My mother had to take their chalk away from them. So you get the idea. Is your own sister home today? Maggie?"

"Yeah, she's in there."

"Do you think she might come out and talk to me for a minute?"

"I don't know," Florrie said. "Probably."

"I could ask her," Celia offered.

"All right. Would you do that?"

"Okay." She started towards the house, then turned to her sister. "Don't erase anything else."

"There's no more poo or toilets, so I don't have to."

Satisfied, Celia headed inside the house.

Florrie appraised her work, then filled in a barely noticeable gap in the deep blue walls of the house.

Celia appeared again. "Come on!" she urged the unseen person behind the door. She lowered her voice, but Brennan could hear. "He's really nice. He's not bad or weird."

He knew all too well that any man could come by the girls' home and pretend to be nice, and be very bad indeed. He hoped he would be able to reassure Maggie Nelson that his intentions were honourable.

Maggie stepped out from the doorway. In her late teens or early twenties, she had cropped brown hair and deep-set dark eyes in a face that would have been lovely if she were not so very thin. She wore a shapeless grey sweater that hung below her narrow hips. There was nothing remotely welcoming in her unsmiling face or her posture.

"Hello, Maggie."

"Hello," she said in a tone that did not invite further conversation.

"Girls, here's a couple of Loonies. You can go up to the store, but only if you promise not to cross over to the schoolyard."

"Okay!" Celia agreed.

But it wasn't enough for Florrie. "Aw! Let us go play in the schoolyard. That's what it's there for on Saturdays — a playground!"

Their big sister thought it over. "All right. If things look okay there."

"She means if there's no weirdoes or bad guys hanging around," the child explained to Brennan.

"Not just guys, Florrie."

"Or big mean ladies with guns and holsters!" Florrie made a gun shape with her hand, then pretended to comb her hair with it.

"It's not a joke, Flor. You have to be careful when you're out by yourselves. We've talked about this."

Florrie turned to Brennan again. "Maggie thinks there are some girls who are as bad as boys!"

"She's taking good care of you; that's all," he replied.

"Okay, get going. I'll join you in a few minutes. This won't take long."

The little sisters took off at a clip, and Maggie faced Brennan.

"You were here on Tuesday. You're here again. What do you want?"

"Well, I'll introduce myself and — "

"Go ahead, introduce yourself. But you could be anybody, and I wouldn't know the difference."

"My name is Brennan Burke. Father Burke, from St. Bernadette's church. Here, I'll show you my driving licence with my name on it."

She was looking at him closely. "No. I recognize you now. You were on the show with Asshole."

He laughed. "Right. That was me. And that was him."

"You walked off."

"Yeah. It wasn't long before I'd had my fill of him."

If he thought he had built up a bit of rapport with Maggie Nelson, he had jumped to conclusions a little too quickly.

"And now I'm going to walk," she said. "Whatever it is you want, I can't help you. Goodbye."

"Maggie, could I just ask you a couple of questions? I know Ignatius Boyle came here."

"And that's your business why?"

"Because I think he's in trouble."

"He's been living on the streets or in homeless shelters much of his adult life, as far as I know, so yes, you could say he's in trouble."

"Is he a friend of yours? A relation?"

She brushed past him and started to walk away.

"Maggie, please listen for a second. Then I'm gone." She turned to look at him with an expression that told him just how much of a nuisance he was.

"I saw a Polaroid photo of Ignatius."

She reacted as if she had been struck, but she quickly formed her lips into a sneer in an effort to cover it. "Yeah, right. He was a photographer's model in an earlier life."

"He was lying down. With Jordyn Snider." Her eyes widened; her lips parted. The fact that Ignatius Boyle had been photographed with the murder victim had come as a shock. Was there more than one photograph in play here? But again, Maggie recovered.

Her voice was strained, but she let Brennan know in no uncertain terms what she thought of him and his intrusion into her life. "You're sick. If you're not out of here in ten seconds, I'm going to go in and call the police."

"Why would Pike Podgis have that photo?" There was a quick intake of breath. This was clearly another unwelcome revelation. "Why would he have your street address?"

But Maggie had only one message that she wanted to reveal to Brennan: "I don't know what your problem is, but take your sick fantasies and get out of here. I don't want you near me or my sisters ever again. Or I'll have you arrested."

The only good thing about this scene on a public street in Halifax was that little Celia and Florrie were not there to witness it. The fact that their older sister considered him to be some kind of a pervert and a stalker was more painful than Brennan would ever have imagined. But her bravado was masking something else. There was something going on. And Maggie was in the know. And she obviously lumped him in with whatever other negative elements were at work in her life.

Brennan was not cut out for this. And he knew he could not come by and pester Maggie again; it just was not in him to persist with a woman who did not want him around. He had no idea how to proceed from here.

He got into his car and tried to banish the excruciating scene from his mind because he would be attending a much-anticipated concert that afternoon with his choirs, a recital by his favourite soprano in the world, Kiri Te Kanawa. He got nerved up just thinking about sitting there in her thrall. But a pang of mortification assailed him when he recalled what the infamous Befanee Tate had done with a letter he had dictated to the singer. The ghastly letter Tate had typed, with its horrendous spelling and punctuation. The memory caused his stomach to seize up with pain and embarrassment. Fortunately, the great soprano would be on the stage and he in the audience and, in the unlikely event that she had actually received the disgraceful document, she would not know that the man whose name was on it was sitting in the auditorium hanging on her every note.

Monty

Normie was nearly beside herself with excitement as they all took their seats in the Rebecca Cohn Auditorium for the Te Kanawa concert. All of the Collins-MacNeil family were in attendance except Dominic, who was with Maura's friend Fanny for the day. Tommy Douglas and his girlfriend, Lexie, were both musicians. They had a growing interest in opera, so they were in the right place today. Monty already thought of Lexie as his daughter-in-law but was wise enough never to let that slip out in conversation. The entire membership of the St. Bernadette's Choir of Men and Boys and the choir school were present in a block of seats at the front of the house, reserved early on through Maura's efforts. The schoolchildren wore their uniforms of blazers and white shirts, dress pants on the boys and kilts on the girls. The men were in suits and ties. This was an official outing. Brennan Burke was the only person present whose excitement approached that of Normie, though he seemed to have a case of the nerves as well. Immaculate in his black clerical suit and Roman collar, freshly shaved and scrubbed to perfection, he sat and stared at the curtain, willing it to part and reveal the heavenly vision. He was oblivious to everything and everyone around him.

Monty took the seat beside him, one in from the aisle. "That's not going to survive a case of the sweaty palms, Brennan," Monty said, looking at the concert program clutched in the priest's hands. Burke either did not hear him or did not care to respond.

At long last, the master of ceremonies came on and gave his introductory spiel, lauding the singer's achievements, and asked everyone to welcome Dame Kiri Te Kanawa, and the show was on.

She opened with "Dove Sono" from Mozart's *The Marriage of Figaro,* and she was in splendid form. Her voice was warm and lyrical, and, as if her talent were not enough, she was possessed of a radiant beauty that was even more pronounced in person than in her publicity photos. Monty kept sneaking glances beside him. Burke looked about eleven years old, so open and innocent and enthralled was his expression. His hands moved slightly, as if he were conducting every perfect note.

After two or three arias, Te Kanawa would address the audience with little explanatory notes or remarks in her soft New Zealand accent. About an hour into the show, she announced that she would be doing Mozart's "Laudate Dominum." That was a favourite of Burke's and of Normie's. Monty looked over at Normie, and saw her getting to her feet. The other students got up too, along with the men and boys.

Monty was so nonplussed that he realized he had not been listening to the singer's words. He tuned in and heard, "So please come up and join me."

What?

Then Maura was up too, motioning to him. "You're on too. That's why you've been rehearsing it." He joined the others as they scrambled from their seats. Maura leaned over. "Father Burke!" He looked at her, stunned. "Surprise! It's all arranged. You'll be given the sheet music when you get up there." This was happening, and Burke hadn't known about it! From the triumphant look on the faces of his wife and daughter, Monty concluded that they were somehow responsible for the arrangements.

Next thing Monty knew, he and the St. Bernadette's choristers were all onstage with the Mozart scores in their hands. Last to come was Father Burke. He looked as if he had ascended bodily into the heavens. And when Kiri Te Kanawa looked at him and smiled and said, "Father Burke, I presume?" he was no longer looking through a glass darkly but had come face to face at last with the Absolute. All he could do was gape at her. "Will you conduct us, Father?" He stood there nodding like an automaton, then snapped out of it and got to work.

The orchestra started up, and Ms. Te Kanawa sang the solo part of the exquisite composition. *"Quoniam confirmata est super nos misericordia ejus."* The choirs came in for the four-part harmony under her soaring lines, and the performance was superb.

The ovation was warm and sustained.

"Thank you for this, Father," the soprano said.

"I . . . I . . ."

"I wasn't led to expect you would be so bashful, Father!"

Laughter from the audience, and from the choir school members on the stage.

"Now would you be kind enough to sing this with me?" She produced a sheet of music and handed it to Burke.

His eyes were riveted on the page as if he could not believe what he was seeing. Then he cleared his throat and stood next to his idol and, taking their cue from the orchestra, they sang the "Sanctus" and "Benedictus" from Burke's own *Missa Doctoris Angelici*. She flew solo on the "Benedictus." The rest was a duet, and their voices were heavenly together.

When they finished, and the applause died down, she handed the music to him and announced that the piece was part of a Mass composed by Father Brennan Burke. Then she turned to him and said, "This is magnificent, Brennan. May I call you Brennan?"

"Oh, yes," he vowed, as if she had asked whether she could make love to him and only him every night for the rest of their lives.

The audience loved it.

"I'd like to sing this again someday, Brennan, and perhaps the rest of the Mass parts? I'll see what I have to do to acquire the performing rights."

He handed his music to her with a gesture that said, "It's all yours."

She looked out at the audience and said, "He needs a manager."

But he just shook his head.

"Thank you," she said then, "to all the talented singers from St. Bernadette's. Thank you, Ms. MacNeil. And thank *you*, Brennan."

She gave him a kiss on the cheek, and he floated from the stage, to affectionate laughter from the crowd.

When it was over, Monty and family and the slipped-the-surly-bonds-of-earth Brennan Burke all met back at the house on Dresden Row to celebrate.

"I have never seen you so happy, Brennan," Maura said. "*Have* you ever been this happy?"

"Did I even exist before now?" he asked, still looking like a young, fresh-faced boy who had given his heart to his one true love.

"All right, fill us in," Monty said to Maura as he poured wine for one and all, including his ten-year-old daughter. They stood in a circle in the living room and basked in the glory.

"I couldn't have done it without Normie," Maura said. The child grinned from ear to ear. "She tricked Brennan into practising the piece, saying it was for a sick friend. But going back a few steps, Monty, you showed me a copy of the mangled letter that Brennan's former secretary had sent off to Kiri."

"Oh, God," Burke said, his voice a wail of anguish.

"I did some research and confirmed that the address was the only correct thing in it, so it might actually arrive."

A mewling pained sound emerged from Burke.

"So I got in contact with her publicity person and explained what had happened. That Father Brennan Burke runs the choir school and the schola for traditional music. But that, unfortunately, he is functionally illiterate, can't even spell 'cat,' and has to be reminded to bathe once in a while — "

"No!" he cried out.

"Just kidding you, Brennan, dear. I told her what had happened with the secretary, how mortified you were, how much you love her music, and all that. And I wondered if she might consider making an appearance at the choir school, where the children might do a short piece for her and present her with a donation to her favoured charity, which supports young musicians in New Zealand.

"I figured I'd never hear back, but at least they would know that the letter was not the product Father Burke meant to send out."

"Thank you, angel of mercy."

"Then I got a note from the publicist, who suggested, instead of a visit to the school, a couple of pieces performed together at the concert itself. Which was good because I figured you wouldn't want her to see the circus going on at St. Bernadette's. I had sent along a bootleg recording of you singing with the choirs, Brennan. And a picture of you, a good one. Not sure which of those items might have turned the tide. But you should know that she was very keen on this and did it willingly, no pressure from this end.

"Normie got you practising the piece. I contacted the school and the members of the men's choir, and swore them to secrecy. It's a surprise to Monty as well, Brennan."

"Oh, yeah. I didn't see this coming at all," Monty agreed.

"Collected ticket money, and money for the donation, and made the reservations. And the rest is history."

"Oh, my God in heaven, it's so brilliant!" Burke put down his wineglass and threw his arms around her, squeezed her tight, and kissed her on the cheek. "If I were not pledged to Kiri, I would love you more than anyone on the planet."

"I'll take that as high praise indeed."

"And you!" He walked over to Normie, relieved her of her glass, picked her up and swung her around. "You little pet! Telling me about your friend with consumption. Perfect subterfuge. Thank you, thank you, thank you, Normie!"

He set her down and she stood there, beaming.

"Good job, Klumpenkopf!" Tommy Douglas said, and she didn't even flinch at the nickname, which her brother had bestowed on her because her curls were often clumps of tangles in the mornings.

She said, "I'm going to go and write a story about the big surprise in my diary!" With that, she left to scamper up the stairs to her room.

"Oh, and by the way," Burke said, "whenever I descend from the clouds, I'll make up whatever people put out for the donation."

"No, Brennan, don't even think about it."

"I will. But for now, I shall just revel in the memory."

"The most charming thing about it all, Brennan," Maura said, "is that there is one person on earth, your beloved Kiri Te Kanawa, who thinks you are not the stone-faced, hard-drinking, carnally knowledgeable, tough-arse renegade *we* know, but a shy, bashful, blushing, and holy priest of God."

"I just couldn't . . . what to say to her, I just . . . she is so . . ."

"Let's just leave him there stammering and have another glass of wine, shall we?"

It was agonizing for Brennan to come down from the heights to which he had ascended in the company of Kiri Te Kanawa. But he was brought back to earth when he recalled the disturbing behaviour of Ignatius Boyle, and the reaction of Maggie Nelson to the news that Pike Podgis was in possession of a photograph of Boyle and Jordyn Snider. Brennan was torn by the irony of the situation. When he was all but certain it was Podgis alone who had killed Jordyn Snider, he would have given anything to get out from behind the screen of the confessional, in order to reveal what he thought he had known about Podgis. Now that he knew Ignatius Boyle had a sexual history with the victim and therefore might have had a sinister connection to her death, could Brennan get him behind the confessional screen and protect him somehow? Brutal Ignatius's act had been, if he had a part in the murder, but at least in his case he had a life of hardship to perhaps explain his character and his actions.

And Brennan still wanted to find out more about the strange interlude in Boyle's life when he awoke with the ability to discuss theological matters in French. There would be nothing untoward about a priest conducting an inquiry into that phenomenon. But how would he begin? Monty had represented Boyle in the past, when Monty was with Legal Aid. There was likely to be information in the Legal Aid files that would help in Brennan's quest. But talking to Monty about Boyle, given the sensitive nature of what Brennan was learning about the unfortunate man, and Monty's interest in him as an alternative suspect, was out of the question. And Brennan would never be able to pry confidential information out of Monty even without those complications.

But he was not above asking Maura MacNeil, professor of poverty law at Dalhousie Law School, some general questions about the poor and disadvantaged citizens of Halifax. It was Monday and it was blues night. He knew Monty was out having a pub supper with his band, Functus, as a prelude to wailing on the harp late into the night. Trying not to feel too underhanded, Brennan dropped in on the MacNeil family on Dresden Row.

"Father, I am not worthy that thou shouldst come under my roof. Speak but the word and my soul shall be healed."

"Unworthy thou usually art. But you have earned yourself heaps of credit in heaven for your heroics in the Kiri Te Kanawa affair."

He spotted Normie in the living room. "Scots wha' hae wi' Wallace fled!"

"Father, that's not it! I keep telling you 'fled' would mean Wallace ran away. He didn't. It's 'with Wallace *bled*'! They fought with Wallace, and he was a hero."

"Oh, pardon me, Normie. I don't know why I keep getting that wrong."

"You're just teasing me because I'm half-Scottish, and you don't know how to speak Scottish!"

"I may be guilty of a wee bit o' tha. Sorrrry, lassie."

"You sound funny!"

"I can well imagine."

"I'm studying my Latin words for choir!"

"Good girl yourself, Normie. I wish more of the students were like you."

"I'm not always good, though, Father."

"You're well within the bounds, love, no worries. And thank you again for the concert surprise."

"Fafa! Fafa!" Little Dominic toddled over to see him, and Brennan picked the child up and kissed his cheek. It came as a relief, though Brennan would rather be burned at the stake than allude to it, when the little lad began calling him "Fafa" for "Father" instead of "Dada" as he used to during the darkest times of Monty and Maura's separation, when Brennan would occasionally help Maura out by looking after the children.

"Ah. Mr. Douglas." Tommy Douglas had come up from the basement den.

"Hey, Brennan. Great concert the other day."

"It was brilliant. Brilliant! How's your own music career progressing?" A bluesman like his father, Tom had put together a band called Dads in Suits. Brennan had not yet heard them, but looked forward to catching them sometime soon.

"It's going well. We have a gig coming up, St. Pat's high school dance. And we may be part of a show at the St. Mary's Boat Club; it's a charity event. We're waiting to hear."

"Good luck with it. And here's Lexie. How are you today, sweetheart?"

Tom's girlfriend, Lexie, was a lovely girl with long blond curls and wire-rimmed glasses that only served to enhance her beauty, like jewellery for her light hazel eyes.

"Just great, Father. I've got the choir doing a Healey Willan Mass now."

She was an accomplished organist and had taken the initiative of forming a small choir at St. Malachy's church. Brennan helped her out with sheet music from time to time.

"I'll stop by and listen. Willan has some very good music." Brennan had not been aware of the Anglo-Canadian composer until coming to Halifax, and he had become a fan. "And you have to love the way he described his provenance: 'English by birth; Canadian by adoption; Irish by extraction; Scotch by absorption.'"

"I know. Isn't it great? And we heard some wonderful music on Saturday, Father."

"Oh, yes. She was magnificent."

"Don't get him started on Kiri," Maura admonished Lexie. "He'll be useless for anything or anyone else for the rest of the day."

"We'd better clear out before he really gets wound up," Tom said, and the young couple said their goodbyes.

Normie made an ostentatious return to her Latin studies, and Dominic sat at her feet playing with a fleet of trucks.

Maura and Brennan headed to the kitchen and sat at the table.

"Drink, Father?"

"Ginger ale."

"She's a good influence on you, Brennan. Kiri, I mean."

"Well, you're not. So don't aggravate me. I might have to go back on the batter just to endure your insolence."

"What, I've used up my credit with you already? That was a short-lived indulgence."

"Right, right. I'm just not used to you being on the good side of the ledger."

"O ye of little faith."

"Thank you," he said when she placed a glass of ginger ale on the table in front of him, and returned to her seat "So, how are things?"

"Good, dear, good," she replied in a heavy Cape Breton accent.

"Any progress since I laid down the law in God's house in Dublin?" He was referring to the summer in Ireland, where he had launched his most recent salvo at the couple's separation and made a heartfelt plea that they resolve their problems and reunite their family once and for all.

He expected to be put off with a flippant reply, her usual mode of defence, but she surprised him again. "Things are going well, Brennan. Monty spends a lot of time with us here and, well, I'm hopeful. And of course, we both know it's not just Monty who's the sticking point. I'm the one who put the kibosh on things just as we were about to reconcile. But God knows, I didn't mean to." Her unplanned pregnancy, the birth of Dominic, and Monty not the father. She looked out at the dark-haired little boy in the living room. "It's difficult for Monty, and no wonder. I've often thought that if the situation were reversed, and he had a child by somebody else, I'd be just as resistant as he has been. There is blame enough to go around here, but everybody knows the baby is just an innocent party! Monty's making a real effort, and I do know he is fond of Dominic."

"I'm sure he is. What's not to like?" Brennan twisted around and gazed at the happy little fellow with his sister, then turned back to Maura, smiling at her.

"I don't know where you get the patience to deal with us, Brennan."

"That is the first time, and will probably be the last, that anyone has ever used the word patience in connection with my character."

"Get it while you can, Burke. You may never hear it, or any other compliment, from my lips again."

"I shall hold it in my heart and treasure it for the rare gem it is."

"So, what's happening with you these days?"

"Stalking the saints. Part of my job description."

"Sounds more elevated than what the rest of us do for our daily bread. What exactly do you mean?"

"I'd like to find out a bit more about Ignatius Boyle."

"Are you sure? It seems to me every time we find out about somebody, it's bad news."

You have no idea. She meant the indecency conviction. Imagine what she would say if she knew about the Polaroid photo of Ignatius naked with the young murder victim. Brennan could not think of a way that a young, beautiful girl like Jordyn Snider would willingly go with a scruffy homeless man old enough to be her father, and Monty's words came back to Brennan: "It's not a big step from a minor sexual offence to a more serious one." But, Brennan reminded himself, no matter what the shameful history of that encounter might be, the photo was in the possession of Pike Podgis, the one man with the blood of the victim on his shoes. So there was nothing to say Ignatius had been the man with the knife. Brennan tried to put all that out of his mind for the time being.

"Right now, it's Mr. Boyle's unexplained linguistic and theological abilities I'm interested in. How would I find out something about his family life? I've tried talking to him."

"Oh?"

"Yeah. But I didn't get too far."

"How come? Doesn't he want to talk about it?"

Brennan could hardly tell her that he had been interrogating Boyle in relation to the murder, after finding evidence in Podgis's apartment. After breaking in with the aid of a convicted burglar. Brennan began feeling the stress of his own furtive behaviour all over again.

"Brennan, are you all right?"

"Sure I'm grand."

"Aren't you always?"

"You said it. So, where would I look for background information on Ignatius?"

"Well, obviously, Community Services would be involved with him because he would be on assistance. Welfare, by another name."

"Would they talk to me? I assume all information is confidential. I should hope it is!"

"It is, of course. But if you're just trying to find out good stuff about Ignatius, such as considering him for sainthood, they might at least talk to you. You might ask whether he has ever taken a French course in an attempt to find employment. Even that might not be available to you, but they probably wouldn't kick you out of the office. His criminal record, though, might slow down his canonization."

"Mmm."

"Why don't you go in and talk to Lena Vanherk at Community Services? She's one of the workers there, and I've known her for years. Tell her I sent you. Hold on, I'll get you her card."

She left the kitchen, spent a couple of minutes with the children in the living room, and then returned with the business card.

Not one to waste time when he wanted something done, Brennan was sitting in the office of Lena Vanherk the following day. The social worker was a kind-looking woman in her mid-fifties, with an air of intelligence and competence. Brennan explained his interest in the linguistic phenomenon that occurred during the hospital admission of Ignatius Boyle. Lena told him what he had expected to hear, that all information was confidential.

"Sure, I understand that. Just thought I would ask. Have you any suggestions as to where I could look or how I could go about this?"

"I may be able to help you, Father. But don't get your hopes up."

His hopes went up instantly.

"We would have the names of family members, relatives of Mr. Boyle. I could ask around and, if one of them would be willing to talk to you, I could leave your number with that person. And leave it up to her or him to get in touch with you or not. That's the best I can do."

"That's great. I appreciate it. I'll write out my name and phone number." She offered him a pen and pad of paper, and he wrote the information down. "We'll wait and see what happens. Thank you very much."

"You're welcome, Father. Good luck."

Chapter 19

Monty

The Befanee Tate wrongful dismissal suit ended with a whimper, not a bang. On Tuesday, February 9, her lawyer called Monty and said Tate would withdraw the suit if Monty would agree not to go to court for an order forcing her to pay the costs the church had incurred in defending the action. It would not be worth anyone's while to make an application to the court for costs, so Monty knew his clients would be happy just to see the case go away. But there was a condition attached, and Monty spelled it out.

"We won't go for costs if she agrees to come clean with respect to her story about the Virgin Mary, and makes a public statement that she was wrong about it. She doesn't have to admit to fraud; she just has to say it wasn't really the Mother of God after all. Because there are poor, misguided souls still shuffling around out there who want to believe it. Bring her in, and let me hear her statement."

So an embarrassed Louise Underhill, solicitor for the plaintiff, brought her sullen client in to Monty's office for the final word on the St. Bernadette's Marian apparitions. Monty and Underhill exchanged a glance; Underhill all but rolled her eyes. "We have drafted a short release for the media, saying Ms. Tate was mistaken in what she thought she experienced."

Monty nodded. There was nothing to be gained by quibbling over the suggestion that she really thought she had experienced something.

Underhill handed him the printed statement, which consisted of two sentences: "Ms. Tate regrets that, in her enthusiasm for St. Bernadette and the Holy Mother, she mistakenly thought she had a genuine apparition of the Virgin. Ms. Tate apologizes for any inconvenience she may have caused."

Monty nearly choked over that, but he was well accustomed to keeping a poker face. He gestured for everyone to have a seat.

"Now go ahead, Befanee," Underhill said. "Tell Mr. Collins what happened."

Befanee sat with her eyes on the desk in front of her. Monty waited. Finally, it came: "When I started the job, Monsignor O'Flaherty took me all around the church and the choir school and where they have the Latin choir, and out to the statue of St. Bernadette. He asked me if I knew who she was, and I said I heard of her but couldn't remember what she was famous for. He said she seen the Virgin Mary, and Mary told her, Bernadette, where there was all this holy water with magical powers and stuff, and people got cured. And I said that was, like, totally awesome, and he asked me if I wanted to read a book about her. And he must'a been able to tell that I don't . . . I don't have time in my life to read much, because then he said there's a movie, and he showed me the poster in the office. It was a movie poster for *The Song of Bernadette*, and the actress got the Oscar for it. He said you could probably rent the video. But I didn't think nothing more about it till me and Gary, my boyfriend, were at Video Difference one night and we seen the video on the shelf. The girl that played Bernadette was really beautiful. Her name was Jennifer. And then later on Gary found out that even though she won the Academy Award, she wasn't even going to be in it at first. She was the girlfriend of this really big important Hollywood guy. He bugged the movie studio to put her in the movie and they did."

"So? Then what?"

"So me and Gary got thinking. If I said I seen the Virgin Mary and did a really good job about it, I might get on TV. And if I looked good and got famous, it would help my modelling career, and maybe even lead to an acting job."

"That's why you made the whole thing up."

"But I was planning to give all kinds of money to good causes when I started making money! And it's weird! Like truth is weirder than . . . whatever it is they say, because those ladies got cured. And the old guy learned French. So maybe she was really there. Mary. Maybe I was chosen to do this!"

"No she wasn't. And no you weren't. But anyway, give your statement to the press, that you were mistaken. And that's the end of it. Goodbye."

Monty made a call to St. Bernadette's to let the priests know the nuisance suit had gone away, but there was nobody home. He would tell them later. Soon there would be no more Befanee, no more pilgrims, no more Bernie Bear souvenirs.

From the fantasy world of Befanee Tate to the grandiose fantasies of Jordyn Snider's pen pal inside the prison walls. Two minutes after Monty had put the phone down, it rang, and it was Harold Lowther on the line, from Corrections Canada.

"Two candidates for your letter writer. Wayne Earl Stokes. He's in Renous for a sex killing. His second. Prior offences include an escalating series of sexual assaults. But he's still inside, and was inside on the date of the murder. Clayton Byner, however, is out on parole from Dorchester. He was in for aggravated sexual assault. Long criminal record. One of the letters said the guy's case was on the TV news? There was a big story about him being denied parole a while back, so that may have been when she saw him on the news. But he managed to pull the wool over the parole board's eyes this time. Wouldn't be the first time a clever psychopath put on a winning performance."

"This guy was out? Clayton Byner?"

"Yeah, he was out on parole in Dartmouth. Still is. So either one of these guys is a likely suspect as your letter writer. If it was Stokes, it didn't go beyond a paper romance. If it was Byner, he might have linked up with Jordyn Snider when he got out. Including maybe the night she was killed. So you'll want to turn those letters over to the police."

"I will indeed. Thanks very much, Harold."

"Any time."

Monty would copy the letters and give the originals to the police. He would have to wait and see what might develop from that.

For now, though, the settlement of the lawsuit by Befanee Tate put Monty in a good frame of mind. He looked at the rest of the office work he had set aside for the afternoon and decided to set it aside again, for tomorrow. He knew Maura was home. She had returned to teaching at the law school after her year of maternity leave, but she had set up a part-time schedule so she could be home with the baby on and off during the week. Monty thought it would be fun for Normie if he went over to the house, picked up Dominic, and walked him to the choir school to meet her after her last class. She loved to show off her baby brother at school.

So Monty drove to Dresden Row, parked and went to the house, greeted his wife, and was greeted in turn without any verbal abuse whatsoever. He got Dominic ready for his outing. He zipped the child into the bright red jacket that Normie loved; pinned to the sleeves were little woolen mittens with pictures of wolf cubs on them. Monty handed Dominic his currently favoured toy, a spotted wooden dog on red wheels, which Maura had had as a child in Cape Breton. Monty buckled him into his stroller, and they set off.

"Going to *school* in your *stroller* to see your big *sister*."

The little fellow made a series of S sounds, then turned them into a song, and pushed on the front of the stroller to get moving.

"Let's hope Normie doesn't have to *stay* in after *school* because she was *sassy* to the teacher, or because she has to *sing* the *soprano* parts of the *Stabat Mater*, eh, Dominic?"

"Baby sing!"

"Good singing, Dominic. You'll have your choice someday. The Rebecca Cohn Auditorium or the Flying Stag blues bar. Up to you."

"Da! Walk!"

"*What? Walk? Where? Why?*"

"Dom walk!"

"Don't you think it would be *smarter* to *stay strapped* in your *stroller* than have you *straying* all over the *street?*"

He carried on with the foolish talk till they got to the corner of Morris and Barrington. Dominic fiddled with the buckle and tried to get out of the stroller, so Monty decided to let him walk. He unsnapped the restraint and lifted the little guy out.

"All right. You hold on to the side here, and we'll walk the rest of the way. Hold on to the stroller."

Monty could hear a loud motor approaching, with an equally loud thumping of a car stereo, so he repeated what he said in case Dominic had not heard. A tractor-trailer was slowing to a stop for a red light. What was it doing there? Was it even allowed on this part of Barrington? Monty had no idea.

Dominic decided his spotted dog should have a walk too, and he put the toy on the ground and gave it a push. Monty bent to retrieve the dog, saying to Dominic "Keep holding" as he did so. He reached up to make sure he had a grip on the baby's clothes, but missed him. He looked up. Dominic was running into Barrington Street in pursuit of the dog on wheels.

"Dominic! Come back!"

At that moment, the light turned green. The eighteen-wheeler kept moving, and the driver geared up.

The baby vanished beneath the transport truck.

Everything from then on unfolded in slow motion. Monty launched himself towards the street. He reached out with both hands and grasped a rail running along the side of the trailer in front of the two rear axles; he managed to hoist his feet up, and he clung to the side as the vehicle banged along the street. Dominic was not on the pavement, so he must have been caught up somehow under the truck. Monty fought back waves of panic; he had to get under there. He let go with his right leg and pushed it under the flatbed. He hooked his foot into the underside of the deck, then let go with his right hand and managed to climb underneath, keeping himself braced against the steel ribs that ran across the underbody of the flatbed. There was the baby, suspended ahead of him, his red jacket caught on a metal bar of some kind. Dominic was screaming in unearthly terror, his eyes fastened on Monty, his hands reaching out for him.

For the first time in his life, Monty felt certain he was involved in something he could not survive. He would die under this vehicle. He would be jolted from his hold, the vehicle would turn, and he would be crushed beneath the wheels. But he had only one final objective: to keep that from happening to Dominic. He had to reach the little boy, keep him in place, keep him alive.

Monty was able to inch forward and twist around so that he was holding on with his right hand and foot; his left side was hanging towards the pavement. He managed to grasp the child with his left arm, and kept him pushed up into what Monty hoped and prayed was a safe place in the underbelly of the trailer. He shouted at Dominic, that he had him, that he would keep him safe. A loud bang sounded from the front axles as they went over a bump. Monty's left leg hit the pavement; he felt an intense burning pain in the side of his knee. Another jolt smashed his left elbow onto the ground, and he felt another searing pain. In an effort that nearly made him pass out, he kept holding Dominic up with his injured arm. All he cared about — the one last concern he would ever have — was that Dominic should live, and be unscathed.

The truck kept barrelling down the street; it showed no signs of stopping. The driver had no idea what was happening.

Then Monty heard yelling from somewhere, and the eighteen-wheeler lurched to a sudden halt. The door above them was wrenched open, and feet appeared on the pavement. Other feet appeared, and there was a cacophony of voices. Some of the people sounded out of breath; had they been running after the truck?

A man: "Did you see that? He let go of that kid!"

A woman: "Are you a parent? Do you think you can get through a day without having your hands free for a second? Shows how much you know."

Another woman, crying and saying: "You're all right! You're all right, sweetheart!"

A man: "You can let him go, sir. Let go now. He's not hurt. He's fine."

Monty was unable to move his left arm. He felt hands on him, and then the pain in his arm and leg made him cry out. He let go and fell to the pavement. He tried to keep himself quiet as kind hands eased him out from beneath the truck.

"Where is he? Please tell me he's all right. Where is he? Let me see him." He heard himself repeating the words, as if he was hysterical, but he could not stop.

"He's shaken up. He's scared but he's fine. Here he is."

They placed Dominic in the crook of Monty's uninjured right arm. The child screamed and cried, clinging to Monty's neck. Monty mumbled soothing words into his ear; he had no idea later what he said.

Paramedics and police arrived, and the driver and bystanders filled them in.

One man said to Monty, "You kept him alive at great danger to yourself. You're a hero, sir."

Monty just shook his head. "No. He's my son."

Brennan

Brennan had just come in from teaching a music theory class when his phone rang.

"Hello."

"Brennan!"

The MacNeil.

"Afternoon, Mrs. MacNeil. How may I — "

"Brennan, meet me at the hospital. Please! The VG."

"What's happened? Is everyone — "

"It's Monty. And Dominic. I'll see you here."

Monty and Dominic! What on earth? Brennan grabbed his keys and ran from his room. He closed his mind to the possibility that something terrible had happened to his closest friend or to the beloved little child, Dominic. He filled his mind with prayer and prayer alone. He got into the car, blasted out of the parking lot, and drove the few short blocks to the hospital in under two minutes. He parked illegally and ran to the entrance. Scarcely able to breathe, he asked for Monty Collins or Dominic MacNeil.

He was given directions and he headed for the room. A couple of people greeted him as he flew past them. He was unable to form words to respond. When he found the room he saw Maura MacNeil and Tommy Douglas standing just inside the doorway. Tommy had his arm around his mother.

Monty was lying in the bed, eyes closed, face scraped and bruised, his arm in a cast. Lying partly on top of him, his little arms curled around Monty's neck, was Dominic. His eyes too were closed.

Brennan looked to Maura and Tommy. Maura's eyes were swollen and red. Tommy looked as if he were barely holding it together.

"What happened?" Brennan tried to keep the panic out of his voice.

"He . . ." Maura started to speak, but was unable to get the words out.

"Tom?"

"Dominic ran out in front of an eighteen-wheeler. He got caught up underneath it."

Brennan looked at the child.

"Dominic's okay. Dad kept him from falling off, or getting caught in the — " Tommy, too, was unable to continue.

Brennan turned to the bed, reached out, and made a sign of the cross on the top of Dominic's head, and then on Monty's forehead. He began to pray. *"De profundis clamavi ad te, Domine . . ."*

When he finished the prayer, he turned back to Tom. "How did Monty keep Dominic from falling?"

"He went under the truck."

"It hit both of them?"

"No." Tommy cleared his throat. "Dad went under it on purpose. He jumped onto the side and climbed under while it was moving. To save Dominic. People saw it from the sidewalk. They said it was incredible. They didn't know how he managed to hang on himself and keep hold of Dominic. It was as if he . . . Dad probably knew going into it he might get killed. But he wanted to try to save the baby."

Nobody spoke for several long minutes. Then they were joined by someone new.

A big man in work clothes entered the room. It was clear to Brennan that nobody recognized him.

"I'm Al Hunt," he said quietly. "I'm the driver. I didn't know they were under there. I swear to God. I am so sorry. I didn't know. I had my radio on loud. I told the police everything."

Tommy looked at him. "It wasn't your fault. We heard all about it. The baby just ran out. We know that."

The truck driver looked at the two people in the bed and said, "He could have been killed. People were calling him a hero. But he was having none of it. He just said, 'He's my son.'"

Maura looked at the man. Her eyes filled with tears.

"Is he . . ." the driver started to ask.

"The doctor is on his way. He'll be here in a minute."

Everyone stood awkwardly at the bedside, in the hope of deliverance.

A doctor arrived with papers in his hand, and smiled at the group. "He's going to be all right, folks. Broken arm, serious friction burn to his leg. We're sending him to plastics to do a graft. A few scrapes and bruises. He's sedated, that's all. No head injury. He's going to be sore for a while, but you'll have him back in one piece." He reached over and ruffled Dominic's black hair. "Looks as if this little fella doesn't want to go anywhere."

"He won't leave him," Maura replied. "We tried to pry him away. He won't leave him."

†

Brennan said a Mass for Monty and his son, and returned to the hospital the next morning, accompanied by Michael O'Flaherty. Monty was lying as he had been the day before, eyes closed and bruises even more prominent. Michael took his uninjured hand and held it while saying a quiet prayer over him.

Monty's eyes opened, and he stared at his visitors. Recognition dawned a few seconds later.

"Fathers."

"How are you feeling, my lad?" asked Michael.

The patient tried to shrug, and winced with pain.

"Some things you can't shrug off, young man. Like what you did to save little Dominic."

"Is he really all right?" Monty asked. It was the first time Brennan had ever seen Monty look fearful. "I'm afraid maybe they're not telling me everything."

Brennan said, "He's A-one, really, Monty. Herself tells me he's in perfect health. He had nightmares last night. Well, you can imagine. But physically, he's fine. And they say you yourself will be back amongst us soon."

"Did they check his hearing? The noise under there . . ."

"Everything is fine. That's not your drinking arm, is it?"

"Would I put my drinking arm at risk, Burke?"

"Of course not. Please disregard what I said."

"I'll let it go. This time."

"You two," said O'Flaherty. "What a pair. Is there anything that would make you lose your cool?"

"It would have to be something serious, Mike. Eh, Brennan? Nothing serious ever happens to us clowns."

"Life's a circus. Just go to my churchyard if you don't believe me."

Monty brightened up. "No, no. That's over."

"What?" Brennan asked.

"I tried to call you. Whenever it was. We settled the claim. You don't pay anything, and I don't nail her with costs. All she has to do is make a public statement that she was 'mistaken' about the Virgin Mary, and it will all go away."

"Well done, Monty. Thank you!"

"Good work, Collins," Burke added. "Now what can we do for you while you're laid up in here? Anything?"

"We're not five minutes from the Clyde Street liquor store."

"Ale? Lager? Whiskey?"

"A shot of Irish would ease the pain. If your own pain-free, carefree life is any indication. Wouldn't mind some of that."

"*Fiat voluntas tua.*" Brennan turned to Michael. "Do you want to stay with him while I pop out on my errand of mercy, Monsignor?"

"Certainly, Father. You run along now."

Brennan left the room and walked the length of the corridor, careful not to look at any of the equipment lined up along the walls. He didn't want to know. Careful, too, not to catch a glimpse of any of the patients in the rooms. He was not a man for hospitals. He and O'Flaherty divided their tasks amicably: Father O'Flaherty visited the sick, Father Burke the imprisoned. Stone killers and armed robbers were easier on the head than bedpans, tubes, and bags of mysterious fluids being pumped into patients' veins. Or arteries. Whatever the case.

He crossed the parking lot, walked up South Park Street, then turned right towards the venerable Clyde Street liquor store. He bought a quart of John Jameson, and retraced his steps to the Victoria General.

When he was back in Monty's room, he picked up a glass from

the bedside table, held it up to his eye, and examined it for any sign of, well, whatever might get on a glass in a hospital. Again, he didn't want to know. But it appeared to be clean, so he poured a couple of fingers of the golden liquid and helped Monty sit up to sip it.

"Ah!" Monty sighed with pleasure. "That hits the spot. Miracle cure. No wonder you're always the picture of health, Father Burke."

"Father! What are you doing?"

The MacNeil.

"I'm just, em, administering this man's medication. He has to keep his fluids up. He is in need of — "

"He is in need of whatever the doctors say he is in need of, and I suspect that whatever it is, it's not supposed to be combined with alcohol!"

"Sure, it won't hurt him at all," Monsignor O'Flaherty stated for the defence. "In fact, not a word o' lie, a doctor actually prescribed a pint of Guinness a day for one of my parishioners in this very hospital. Vitamin G right there in the doctor's orders!"

"Well, you two quacks are in big trouble if it's not in the doctor's orders for *this* patient."

"Dada! Dada!"

Dominic had arrived, in the arms of his sister, and he began kicking and reaching out to Monty in the bed.

"He wants to see you, Daddy!" Normie said. "He's been asking for you all morning and all last night. Can he get into the bed with you?"

"Of course he can. Hello, Dominic, you little *sneak*!"

The little fellow burst into laughter and grinned at Monty. Normie tried to lift the baby up high enough to get over the rails of the bed. Michael O'Flaherty started to help, but Brennan gave him a little shake of the head, and directed his eyes to the child's mother. Maura leaned over, took hold of her son — their son — and gave him to Monty in his bed. Brennan saw husband and wife exchange a look. Dominic curled up on Monty's right side and smiled.

Brennan gave Michael the eye, and the two men withdrew from the room, leaving the family together.

Chapter 20

Brennan

Kathleen Boyle-MacIvor stood on her front porch and waited while Brennan emerged from his car and walked towards her.

"Father Burke, welcome. I heard your car turn in." She lifted her face to the elements. "Smells like snow."

"You can tell that?"

"Oh, yes. You wait. But I don't mean to leave you out on the stoop. Come in, come in."

Brennan had just driven an hour and a half northeast of Halifax, to the town of New Glasgow, after getting a call from the social worker, Lena Vanherk. Lena had made contact with Ignatius Boyle's Aunt Kathleen, and she had expressed her willingness to receive Father Burke at her little house on Highland Drive.

She was in her eighties, but her step did not falter and her handshake was firm. She was dressed in a green wool suit, with gold earrings and a chunky necklace. That day's *Globe and Mail* rested on the arm of her chair in the living room. She smiled at him, and he got the impression she was enjoying a private joke.

"I've been expecting you. For months now." He must have looked surprised, because she said, "Not you in particular. But I wondered how long it would take for someone to come around. Let me turn this off first."

He looked at the television in the corner. NHL hockey, a Leafs game. "You're a person of faith too I see, Mrs. MacIvor."

"Faith, hope, and charity, Father. I dedicate all those virtues to the Toronto Maple Leafs. Someday, someday." He laughed. "That's a tape. The games go too late at night for me, so I record them." She switched off the tape and the set. "Would you like a cup of tea?"

"I'd love one, if it's not too much trouble. Would you be having one yourself?"

"I would, and it's no trouble at all. You have a seat and I'll join you in a minute."

He sat on a chair across from hers and looked around at a room filled with well-kept old furniture, family photos, books, and news and sports magazines. Mrs. MacIvor returned bearing a tray containing cups and saucers, ornate silver spoons, a jug of milk, and a bowl of sugar.

"Thank you."

"You're welcome, Father. Now," she said as she took her place again, "you're wondering about Ignatius. So are a lot of other people, I gather."

"True."

"You're wondering whether he spoke French at any time in his life."

"Did he?"

"There was nobody French-speaking in our family. We lived in the north end of Halifax. My husband and I moved here to New Glasgow when he retired; he grew up nearby. But I'm a Halifax girl. We're like you, Father. Transplanted Irish on the Boyle side and on the Whelan side. Ignatius's mother was a Whelan. But you should know that Ignatius spent some time out of his home when he was young."

That struck a chord. "Right. He told me he had been in the hospital as a child, but he could not recall what condition he had. Ignatius blames his drinking for his problems with memory."

"He wasn't in the hospital, though he may remember it that way, I don't know," Kathleen said. "My brother Dermot — Ignatius's father — was troubled all his life. Troubled by drink and instability. He couldn't hold a job. Sad, but that's the way he was. His marriage to Doreen Whelan was turbulent, to say the least, and he finally just disappeared, leaving Doreen to cope with Ignatius and his sister, Irene. There were just the two children. Irene is dead now. Ignatius is the only one of his immediate family still alive. His mother was not a strong person. To put it bluntly, Doreen used to go on benders for weeks at a time. When she'd go on a toot, neighbours would go in and look after the children. Or they'd call family members in. There were a couple of times when Doreen was about to go off with one of her 'companions,' and neighbours saw her staggering down the street, towing poor Ignatius and Irene by the hand. Doreen deposited them, without asking first, with the Sisters of Charity at their convent in north end Halifax. My husband and I had five children of our own, and couldn't take Dermot and Doreen's children in. I wish we could have, but it was impossible. But I visited Ignatius and Irene during their stay at the convent.

"There were some French-speaking sisters there and one of them, Sister Marie-Hélène, was a great one for quoting the saints. That's where Ignatius would have picked up a bit of French. Whatever he said last fall never made the newspapers, but I suspect it would have been some lines from Sainte Thérèse de Lisieux or Saint Francis de Sales, the good sister's favourites among the sanctified. Ignatius would have forgotten all that in the ensuing years, especially with the drink, but everything we learn is still in us, isn't it? Buried in the deep recesses of our brains. Suffer a head injury and you can lose your recent memories, and recover your old ones. I've heard of it many times. No miracle in that."

"No."

"How is he otherwise, do you know?"

Brennan was not about to unload on her the recent woes of Ignatius Boyle. "He seems healthy enough. He's off the drink, he tells me."

"Well! There's the grace of God working in him, even if he is not exactly a miracle worker." She picked up her teacup and smiled. "I've been following the story, of course. And I know I should have contacted somebody — the press, the hospital, the church, I don't know who — but there's a bit of mischief in me, I guess. And I said to myself, 'Why not let poor Ignatius enjoy a bit of glory for once in his life?'"

The visit with Ignatius Boyle's lovely aunt made it even more distressing to contemplate what role the poor man had had in the death of Jordyn Snider. On the drive back to Halifax in lightly falling snow, Brennan made up his mind to try yet again to question either Ignatius or Maggie Nelson. They both knew more than they were letting on, and it was time for some answers.

So on Saturday morning he picked up the phone and called Maggie's number. A little girl answered. "Hello?"

"Hello, is this Florrie or Celia? It's Florrie, isn't it?"

"Yeah, it's me! I know you. You're Brennan. I remember your voice. Are you going to give me the song you promised?"

He scanned his brain to try to find the reference. "'Pussy Got the Measles'?"

"Yeah! Are you going to . . . Celia just butted in and told me I'm not being very polite. So I'm sorry for bugging you about the song."

"No, not at all. I did promise you and I am definitely going to give it to you. I'll put some guitar chords to it."

"Really? Wow, that will be great!"

He could not bring himself to use the child's eagerness for the music to engineer a visit to the house in the face of Maggie's resistance. "Tell you what. I'll put it in the mail for you."

"Okay! Celia! When a letter comes, don't open it. It's for me! Thank you very much, Brennan."

"You're welcome, Florrie. Is Maggie there by any chance?"

"Yeah, she's just outside. She doesn't have to work with the rats on Saturdays. I'll call her. Maggie! Phone! It's Brennan!"

So much for that. He steeled himself for a blast.

He heard the receiver banging against something, then heard Maggie. "You guys go out and make snow angels. I'll come back out in a minute, after I deal with this."

Deal with *him*, she meant.

"What were you saying to my sister?"

"The time I was there . . ."

"The time you wormed your way into my house and spent a whole lot of time with two very young girls. Right."

"Please believe me, Maggie. I have only the best of intentions. I am harmless."

"That's what they all say."

"Perhaps they do. But I assure you I mean no harm to you or to your sisters. I am only trying to find out what happened to the young girl who was murdered in my churchyard."

"And you think trespassing on my property and making promises to my little sisters that you have no intention of keeping is the way to investigate this murder? Maybe somebody should be asking where you were that night! Since you're so interested in young girls!"

"Somebody did ask and, in fact, I was probably the person closest to the murder scene, with the exception of the killer himself. So, yes, the police did question me, as you might expect. They know I'm innocent. And I am not 'interested in young girls' in the way you are suggesting. But I think you know that, Maggie. I am very concerned about Ignatius Boyle and the trouble he might have brought upon himself, with his relationship to the victim, whatever it was, and with that photograph. And his answers about the night of the murder are not at all satisfactory. I do not think Ignatius Boyle is an evil man, but I know there was something going on."

"And you want me to what? Help you frame Ignatius for the murder of Jordyn Snider?"

"Not frame him. Help me understand what happened between them. What is your own relationship with Ignatius?"

"I don't have a *relationship* with Ignatius Boyle!"

"I didn't mean to insinuate an improper relationship. I just meant: how do you know him?"

"You've insinuated enough. And none of this is any of your business. What?" She interrupted herself to respond to something happening off-stage. "Tell him to wait down there. No!"

There was a touch of panic in her voice. And was Brennan hearing things correctly? It sounded to him as if he heard Florrie saying to Maggie, "It's okay. He knows Brennan!" But Brennan would never know, because Maggie returned her full attention to him and told him yet again never to call, never to show his face, and never to contact her sisters again, or she would have the police on him. Then she slammed down the phone. Once again, he was made to feel like a stalker, a pervert, a creep who made phone calls to young girls.

†

Brennan had more luck on the phone Sunday afternoon. The MacNeil called, apologized for missing Mass in the morning, and he absolved her in good grace. She had called to give him the good news that Monty was out of the hospital and, although still looking a little battered, was feeling fine. He would be at work on Monday because how could he justify whooping it up at the Flying Stag Monday night if he had taken a sick day from work?

"He's playing at the Shag? How's he going to do that? Isn't his arm in a sling?"

"He's not going to play guitar, sing, or blow the harp. That is all going to be done for him by somebody else. Another band."

"So why is he going, if Functus isn't playing?"

"Because the whole show is to honour Monty for his actions in saving Dominic. The bar owner wants to do a tribute to him, so we're all going. And you too, we hope."

"Of course. Wouldn't miss it. That's grand of them to do this for Monty."

"Well, he's been bringing business in to the place for twenty-five years! But, more than that, they like him there. And the best is — *ta da*! The band for the night is Dads in Suits!"

"Tommy Douglas's band. Great!"

"Tommy is over the moon. They're having the show early to comply with the liquor laws, because the boys are still under age. Starts at seven, over by nine. See you there."

"See you there. Oh, I was nearly cavalier enough to hang up the phone without wishing you a happy St. Valentine's Day."

"Oh, Father, you shouldn't have."

"Well, I didn't. Send flowers or chocolates, or anything thoughtful like that. But on our next visit to Dublin, I shall take you and Montague to the shrine of St. Valentine, where relics of the great saint are kept and are venerated. Who says romantic Ireland's dead and gone?"

"I'll hold you to it. But, to give credit where credit is due, I believe you have successfully invoked the saint in your ministry to us even without a visit to the shrine."

"Maybe so."

"Brennan, about all that, bringing us together, I will never be able to thank you enough. I don't even know where to begin. You . . ." There was a catch in her voice, and then she stopped.

"No need, my pet. See you tomorrow night."

†

Brennan would not have thought it possible that he would be showing his face again at the Flying Stag after his all-too-memorable evening there six weeks ago. But he was very keen on the tribute to Monty, and this would be his first opportunity to hear Tom's band. It was quarter to seven, and he was in the process of shedding his clerical collar and substituting a sweater and jeans when his phone rang, and he picked it up.

"On my way," he announced.

"Father Burke?"

"Yes? Sorry there. I thought it was going to be somebody else."

"I have to speak to you."

"Certainly."

"Do you know who this is?"

Not until that moment, but now he knew. It was Ignatius Boyle.

"Uh . . ."

"It's Ignatius."

"Oh, yes, Ignatius. How are you?"

"Not good."

"I'm sorry to hear it."

"Can I talk to you tonight?"

"Yes."

"Meet me at the statue."

"Sure. Em, what time? Now?"

What was he going to do? He did not want to miss any of the tribute to Monty. But he absolutely could not miss whatever Boyle wanted to tell him. If the man was in the mood to talk right that minute, there was no guarantee he would be of the same mind at another time.

But Boyle surprised him. "When you answered, Father, you said, 'On my way.' I think I have caught you on your way to another commitment."

"Well, I . . ."

"That's all right. You have your ministry, and I respect that. We can meet at a time convenient to yourself."

"Are you sure, Ignatius? I don't want to put you off."

"No, no, Father, I'm not on a schedule of any kind. You just tell me what time. But it is important that we speak soon." Boyle's voice had taken on a nervous edge, and Brennan began to worry again that he might lose the opportunity.

He tested the waters by saying, "Ten o'clock at the statue?"

"That will be fine, Father. Bless you."

"And you, Ignatius. The blessings of God on you."

"Thank you, Father. Ten o'clock."

†

When Brennan arrived at the Flying Stag, the Collins-MacNeil family was already in place. The staff had put two tables together for the family, the members of Functus, and Maura's pals Fanny and Liz. And Brennan; there was a seat waiting for him, with a glass of draft settling nicely on the table in front of it. He would enjoy it, because it would be the only one for him tonight. Monty and Maura were sitting side by side; little Dominic was on Monty's knee. Monty's face was bruised and cut, and the arm was in a sling. But he had the look of a very happy man. Normie fluttered around the baby, smoothing his hair, adjusting his clothing, producing toys from her bag to amuse him. Constable Truman Beals, dressed down in civilian clothing, saluted them from across the room. The place was packed.

Tommy and his band were setting up, and Brennan could feel the excitement coming off of them. This was their first bar gig. Tommy was a smaller, but not much smaller, version of his father, with wavy dark blond hair and sky-blue eyes. The band wore dark suits, white shirts, black ties, and porkpie hats. They were not yet of age, hence the early show time, which would feel like the middle of the afternoon to the blues crowd. Brennan suspected the Stag was not too concerned one way or the other, as long as the band members did not openly indulge in any forbidden fluids. Brennan did not see Constable Beals coming for them, or for the bar staff, with handcuffs.

Oh, there might be a problem after all. Normie had a request:

"Can I have a beer too? That one looks good. It looks like apple juice." Her parents delivered the bad news. It was against the law to serve alcohol to a minor, and she had nine years to go.

"That's okay. I'll have what you drink when you're not drinking, Father. What's so funny?" she asked, as everyone in hearing range burst into laughter. The child's little face blushed pink. "I just want a ginger ale."

"You can have one, angel, and it's on me. So are the laughs. Make it a double," Brennan told the waiter.

Before the band's first number, the bar's owner got up in front of the microphone to say a few words. Brennan had never met Wayne Kovacs, but had seen him in the place on previous occasions. He was a big, burly fellow with a shaved head and a goatee; the sleeves of his grey sweatshirt were cut short, and his arms were festooned with tattoos. He looked well able to handle the day-to-day crises of a down-market blues bar.

"Evening, folks," Kovacs said. "I think we all know why we're here tonight. Not that we need a reason beyond the usual. But we do have a special reason to be here, and that's to pay tribute to a guy who's very well known to us at the Stag. How long have you been playing here, Monty? Twenty years? Twenty-five?"

Monty gave a little "could be" shrug.

"So we've got kind of used to Monty here. We know he's a good guy, and now we know he's a really, really good guy. I won't use the word 'hero' because I saw in the news that he doesn't get off on that word. And, well, when you think about it, what he did was not all that strange." Kovacs surveyed the room and nodded his head a few times. "I mean, come on, how many people in this room have ended up under a truck at some time in their life? Yeah, we've all been there, right?" Laughter around the room. "For one reason or another. Some of us are mechanics, working on and under trucks. Though I never got the impression Monty was all that mechanically inclined. If it's not a musical instrument, Monty can't work it. Am I right?"

Monty allowed as how that was all too true.

"Back in the bad old days, before our highly respected officers of the law — " he nodded in the direction of Truman Beals and his companions " — our boys in blue, started cracking down on drunk driving, and well they should, I can remember times when

Monty rolled out of here and couldn't get his car started. But maybe that's just because he couldn't get the key in the ignition. Anyway, mechanics. Other guys in here might have been under a truck, stripping it for, well, let's just call it redistribution. Say no more about that. And others of us have been just plain unlucky, winding up under the wheels of a truck that happened to be in the wrong place at the wrong time. Or we were so plastered, we fell under the wheels of a passing truck, and, well, that's just how it is. What can you do? Pick yourself up, take another drink, and write a twelve-bar blues about it.

"So that's the rest of us. But that's not Monty. Monty threw himself beneath a moving eighteen-wheeler, and clung on to parts of the undercarriage he would not even be able to name. He risked his own safety and his very life. What could have happened to him if he fell off and the driver made a turn, or . . . well, we don't want to think about the things that could have happened. He did it without hesitation. Why? He did it for his son. His little guy Dominic had run under the tractor-trailer, got caught up in the landing gear — that's the legs that come down when the semi-trailer's not attached to the truck part, Monty — so, yeah, Dominic was suspended from the landing gear, and Monty did what he did. And there's Dominic right there, not a scratch on him.

"I won't hold things up any longer. Everybody lift your glass in a toast to Monty Collins."

Everyone in the room joined the toast. "To Monty!"

"And now it's time for me to get out of the way. Because our band tonight is Dads in Suits, headed up by Monty's other son, Tommy Douglas Collins. And they are fuckin-A! Hit it, boys!"

The crowd welcomed the band with raucous applause, and Tom launched into "Born with the Blues." The boys were brilliant. Between songs, people came up to Monty and slagged him about the competition. Monty was beaming, particularly when Truman Beals came over and said a few words. Monty mouthed the words along with him; he had heard it before, and he looked as if no higher praise had ever been uttered: "Some of those tunes, not all, but some, if I close my eyes, that kid can almost pass for somebody who's not a blue-eyed little white boy."

At break time, Tom floated by on clouds of glory and accepted accolades from one and all. Then he said, "Gotta go." He looked around. "Where's the . . ."

Monty spoke up. "Brennan, any advice for my boy?"

"Yes, em, keep going past the first door, my lad."

"Why? What's the first door?"

Brennan was trying to find a suitable answer when one of the bar's regulars went rolling by and said, "That's the Honeymoon Suite. That's where *love* happens, boy!"

"*Honeymoon Suite* in the Flying Stag? What is he talking about?" Maura asked, looking to all appearances as if she knew she was not going to like the answer. "Tom, stay here."

"Brennan," Monty said, "fill him in, would you? You're more familiar with the place than I would ever be."

"Collins, why don't you meet me outside door number four?" Brennan pointed to the exit. "We'll settle this outside."

"No need for that now, Father, when a little blues can say so much. This is one of my own compositions, if you'll indulge me. I call it the 'Dirty Shag Blues.'"

"Mum, does that mean the carpet is dirty in that room?" Little Normie, God love her.

"You have no idea, dolly," Monty replied. "Why don't you . . ."

His imagination apparently failed him, but Fanny took up the slack. "Normie, I have some juice packs in the car. Why don't you and I and Dominic go out and get some?"

"Okay!" Normie took the little fellow by the hand and followed Maura's friend from the bar, but not before Fanny left instructions: "I'll expect a full report later, Maura."

Monty advised his son to go past the bar and proceed to door number three, and Tom went on his way. Monty then gave them all a song, "Dirty Shag Blues," thoughtfully dedicated to his dear friend and drinking pal, Father Brennan Burke:

> "Met my baby in the toilet
> In a place they call the Stag.
> Yeah, met my baby in the toilet
> In that place they call the Stag.
> Got down and dirty with my baby.
> I do anything for a two-bit shag."

"You dedicated that song to *Father Burke*?" Maura exclaimed. "What did you do to deserve that, Brennan?"

"Nothing. I swear on all that is sacred, nothing happened in there. I mean, it started to happen, but not through anything I did. She just got in there, and got down on her . . . I put a stop to it."

"Brennan, you're babbling."

"Yes, well, em . . ."

"I have never heard you so bereft of words, so inarticulate. Not since you were with Kiri Te Kanawa. I remember she left you speechless. Now it's this other person. From what I can gather, you had a brief but intense relationship with both women, one on the concert stage, the other apparently in the Honeymoon Suite of this dingy bar. Are you torn between the two, Brennan? Would you like to talk about it? No?

"One thing strikes me about your dilemma. Kiri is of course brilliant, talented, beautiful, and world-renowned. But your Honeymoon Suite sweetheart has one big advantage, from your perspective. She is *available*."

"No, all it was . . . I was standing by the sink, washing my shirt, and this one was there . . ."

"Spare us any further details, Father."

Brennan hissed in Monty's ear: "Make sure she knows nothing happened."

"I will. In time. Leave it with me, Brennan."

Brennan, having refrained from smoking up to then, lit up a cigarette, inhaled to the very pit of his being, then blew the smoke away from the table. He took a mouthful of his draft, his only draft, and turned with relief to the stage, where Dads in Suits were ready for the second and final set. Fanny returned with Dominic and Normie, treats in hand.

The band did a great job on some old blues standards, and then it was time for their big number. The culmination of a great night of music, the culmination of years of a family moving towards reconciliation. Tom and his sax man brought the house down with the Gary "U.S." Bonds song "Daddy's Come Home."

Maura did not even try to hide her emotions. Tears sprang from her eyes. She didn't bother to wipe them away. Brennan could see Monty struggling manfully to look pleasantly nonchalant.

"Why's Mummy crying?" Normie asked, concern written all over her sweet little face.

Brennan found he had to clear a lump from his own throat before he could answer. "Sometimes people cry when their feelings are so powerful they can't control them, even when they're happy, sweetheart. Your mum is really happy. Because, em, I think your dad is going to move back home with the rest of you."

"Yeah, he is! It's going to be great having him home again!"

"Yes, darlin', it is."

Brennan looked at Monty and raised his glass. Monty returned the salute.

Chapter 21

Brennan

Well over an hour later, at twenty after ten in fact, Brennan was sitting on the bench facing the statue of St. Bernadette. Alone. Trying to fight off the fear that he had blown it. He had changed into his clerical suit and Roman collar, donned his winter jacket, and had come to the bench well before ten. And there was nobody else in sight. By going off to an evening of *ceol agus craic*, music and fun, and by deliberately postponing his meeting with Ignatius Boyle, he had scotched the chance to learn what role Boyle had played in the life, and maybe the death, of Jordyn Snider. Brennan was convinced that Boyle had been on the point of confiding in him, perhaps confessing. And Brennan had failed him. He would wait anyway; he would sit there for another hour in the cold, but he feared it would be for naught, the opportunity lost.

He sat, and tried to piece together what he knew about the murder, in case he never heard another word that would help solve the case. Ignatius Boyle had been found unconscious two minutes from here the night of the murder, with blood spattered on him. Pike Podgis had been seen leaving here with the victim's blood on his shoes. The witness who saw him also heard other people in the street. Podgis had a photo of Ignatius Boyle and Jordyn Snider; he had the Yukon Street address. But nobody had the complete picture. If . . .

"Don't you even think about it! It's not going to happen!"

Brennan sat upright and listened. The voice came from behind him in Byrne Street, near the church. A young woman's voice. He turned around.

"Please don't!" She was almost crying.

"It's better this way! I can handle it."

Ignatius Boyle. And Maggie Nelson.

"I'm sorry I've kept you waiting, Father."

"Don't worry about that at all, Ignatius. Hello, Maggie."

"Hello."

She stood at one end of the bench, on Brennan's left. Ignatius was at the other end, on his right.

Maggie said, "We have something to tell you."

Ignatius took two steps and reached Maggie, putting one hand behind her head and the other across her mouth.

Brennan got to his feet and moved towards them, ready to pull Ignatius off the young woman, but Maggie twisted her head free and said, "It's all right, Father."

Brennan stared at them. What were these two people doing together? Maggie knew about the Polaroid of Ignatius and the young murder victim in a naked embrace; she had clearly not been surprised when Burke had mentioned it to her on their earlier meeting. So, knowing that, what was she doing with Ignatius Boyle, alone with him before they arrived here, in her house with him on past occasions as well? Had this man, disadvantaged and eccentric but to all appearances spiritual and kind, had he worked his way into these young women's lives, their confidence? What had Boyle said when he and Brennan spoke the first time, something about girls and their boyfriends? What was going on? There was something very disturbing at work here.

"He didn't do it," Maggie said.

"Podgis?" Brennan asked. He watched Ignatius, who was gazing intently at Maggie.

Maggie was shaking her head. "I didn't mean Podgis. I know you suspect it was Ignatius. It wasn't."

Why was she covering for him? What was the peculiar relationship at play here? Brennan fixed his eyes on Ignatius, who refused to meet his gaze.

Brennan asked him, "Ignatius, did you kill the young girl?"

It was Maggie who replied. "He didn't."

"Why won't he answer me then?"

"He wants to take the rap for this. Serve the prison term. He wants to protect me."

"Protect you from what? From whom?"

"I killed Jordyn."

†

That was all Brennan was going to allow her to say out in the open. Whatever evidence there was against Maggie Nelson, it was not going to be supplemented by anything overheard by unseen persons on a quiet night in his churchyard. Maggie was standing there, shell-shocked, as if she too had heard for the first time who had committed the murder.

Ignatius was shaking his head. "You don't have to do this, Maggie. I'll plead guilty to it. I can do the time. What have I got to lose? You have the little girls. What will they do without you?"

"No, Ignatius, please! You can't. I — "

Brennan put up his hand to silence them. "Maggie, I want you to come inside with me. Ignatius, you leave us now while I talk to Maggie. Do you have a place to sleep tonight?"

"Of course, yes, don't worry about me. Maggie, you talk to Father Burke. He will help you. And remember, my offer still stands."

Ignatius went off into the night, and Brennan gestured for Maggie to walk ahead of him into the parish house. They did not say a word until they were in his room with the door shut.

Then she turned to him and said, "I did it because of what she did to me. And what she threatened to do to Celia and Florrie."

He knew that whatever this was, it was going to be excruciating. He wanted to establish the groundwork first.

"Sit down now, Maggie. Let me get you a cup of tea."

"No, no, that's okay."

She sank into the chair on one side of his work table; he sat in the other.

"Maggie, are you a Catholic?"

"Yes. But I haven't been to Mass very much."

"That's all right. Would you like to make a confession to me?" If he could get her behind the seal of the confessional, where Podgis had been . . .

"Yes, I want to talk to you. But I'm still going to tell the police what I did."

"No. If you are going to tell anyone outside of this room, you are going to tell a lawyer, not the police."

She had started to tremble. "Okay."

"If you decide to go that route, I will take you to see a very good defence lawyer. Now take all the time you need, and tell me what you have to say."

She avoided his eyes as she began her story. "I knew there was a guy in the background. There always is. There's always a guy and, no matter how low he is on the food chain, no matter what kind of a bottom-feeder he is, there's a girl or a group of girls who want to go out with him. Girls who will go along with *anything*. They accept everything, they support everything, doesn't matter how horrible it is."

He could feel the table shaking from the trembling of her arms on it. Her voice was barely under control.

"He hid behind the curtain and pulled the strings. And the puppets danced along. They were there to do his bidding."

"They?" he asked quietly.

"Jordyn and her best friend, Jade. They tortured me. *Tortured* me. At the request of Jordyn's boyfriend. Because that's what he wanted to see. I didn't know who he was until a few months later, when I saw a story in the paper about this guy who raped a girl and beat her up. She was in the hospital for weeks. He got caught and went to court. The news story gave his name, Brandon Toth. And the story said there were two teenage girls who came to court to support him. And they giggled the whole time during the hearing. It was Jordyn and her friend. So I knew it was the same guy. He got sent to prison for eight years. Should have been eighty years. But anyway, he got his punishment and he's still in there. So all I had to do was punish his two helpers. His supporters. The courtroom gigglers. I hated them even more than I hated him!"

Brennan stayed silent. Anything he said, any stupid question, might only add to her pain. She was weeping by this time, and he longed to take her in his arms and comfort her, but he knew he had to let her get it out her own way.

"I hated them more because they should have been on my side. They were traitors. Traitors are hated by their own side even more than enemies are! Look how they get punished by their own people when they get caught."

Brennan had only to think of the dirty war in the North of Ireland to acknowledge the truth of this.

"They betrayed me and other girls everywhere by going along with this sex criminal. They didn't even have a motive of their own! It wasn't providing any sexual thrill for them. They weren't blinded by some kind of sick desire or anything like that. They knew it was wrong; they had nothing against me at all, but they did it anyway. They *went along*! Empty vessels to be filled with other people's poison."

Maggie did an imitation of an official courtroom voice.

"Why did you do it, Jordyn?"

"Uh, 'cause, like, he wanted me to. So I was, like, 'Okay! Tee-hee.' Fucking idiot." She looked out the window and said in a soft voice, "I despise people who *go along*."

"When did this happen, Maggie?"

"When I was sixteen. They invited me to a party in somebody's basement. It was outside the city somewhere. The other girl drove, and she went around so many twists and turns I had no idea where we were. And they covered my eyes when they dragged me out the next day, so I couldn't see the way back or where we were coming from. They tied me up. I tried to fight them off but the other girl was too strong. So they did things to me. I was crying and screaming with pain, and begging them to stop. But nobody heard me except them, and the guy who ordered the torture. Brandon. I guess he was in the house somewhere too. Listening or watching through a hole in the wall, I don't know. And the things they did were where my clothes would be over the injuries, so you couldn't see them after. There was sick stuff they did, and took pictures. I wanted to kill myself. And they knew it, and laughed about it. I think they wanted me to do it."

"This is dreadful. Maggie, I am so very sorry to hear what you went through."

"I still have nightmares about it."

"I'm sure you do. Did you report this? Tell your parents?"

"My father is dead, and my mother was really sick. She still is, and she spends all her time worrying about not being able to take care of me and Celia and Florrie. I couldn't bear for her to know that one of us had been tortured. But I couldn't tell anyway, and I couldn't call the police. Jordyn threatened me that if I told, the cops would believe her and not me, because her stepfather was a friend of the police. And if it went to court, she would get up on the stand and say I did all this with a guy and just blamed it on Jordyn to get myself out of trouble. And everybody would know all the details, and would know where the marks on my skin came from. And I would never have a boyfriend or a husband or kids, because any guy would know I was a sicko and a whore. Especially after another thing they did later. But anyway, I had to keep my mouth shut about it."

Brennan was heart-scalded by what she was telling him. How could anyone treat another human being in such a way? What was wrong with the world, with the human race, that such things could happen?

"But even with all of that, I might have been able to tell somebody. But not when she made the worst threat of all. Jordyn said she and her friend and some guys would hurt my little sisters. Do even worse things than they had done to me. If they were sent to jail, they would not be in there for long. And they'd learn all kinds of new ways to fight, and make sharp weapons out of things like nail files, and they'd come after Florrie and Celia and cut them up."

Her voice cracked on the last word, and she covered her face with her hands. Her whole body was shaking.

"When I showed up at school, they were right there waiting for me, making slashing movements with their hands to remind me that if I talked, they'd get Florrie and Celia. I pretended to go along.

"But I knew that if it took the rest of my life, I would get them back. It's not as if my hatred would ever go away. I figured it might be years or even decades before I could get my revenge. Then Jordyn popped up on television. Made an ass of herself at the Virgin Mary shrine. You could tell she was trying to muscle the other one out of the spotlight. Befanee. So Jordyn made herself into a public figure, seeking attention as always. And she'd get it. I could do away with her, and make it look as if some nut ball had done it, some creep who had seen her on TV. Jordyn had just succeeded in making herself a target."

She said it as if the story ended there. Brennan was not about to rush her. He rose from the table, plugged in his kettle, and made two cups of tea. When he returned to the table and placed her tea before her, she looked at the steaming cup as if trying to place what it was, where she was. Then she tensed and said, "What time is it? The girls. Mrs. Lewis goes to sleep at eleven. She doesn't babysit them, but she keeps her ears open, you know . . ."

"It's twenty-five past."

"They're alone. They'll be worried. I'm hardly ever gone at night, and they've sensed something wrong." Her eyes focused on him, and her expression deepened from agitation to horror. "I have to see them. Is this my last night? What's going to happen to them? They have nobody! My mother can't . . ."

"One thing at a time, love. This is not your last night. I'll take you home now to see to the girls. And whatever happens, I will make sure they are looked after. So we'll go, and you'll tell me the rest of the story after you get Florrie and Celia settled for the night."

†

Maggie preceded Brennan up the stairs to her flat on Yukon Street. Brennan carried a manila envelope he had snatched on the way out of his room. Not a word had been said in the car on the way to Maggie's home. She put her key in the lock and opened the door. Instantly there was the scramble of little feet in the apartment. A television voice was cut off in mid-bray.

"Florrie?"

The answer came through an exaggerated yawn. "Yeah?"

"Are you in bed?"

"Yeah. Well, kinda . . ."

"Celia?"

"Hi, Mag! Where were you?"

"Maybe she had a date!"

Florrie appeared then, in a long white nightgown, the hem of which was snagged in the waistband of her zebra-striped leggings.

Maggie eyed the leggings but made no comment. Celia came in, successfully transformed into a little girl all ready for bed.

"She did have a date!" Florrie crowed. "With Brennan! Ha ha."

"Ha ha yourself, you little brat," Maggie replied, and clasped her youngest sister in a hug. She put her arm out, and Celia came into the embrace. The young ones looked up at Maggie with faces radiating love and contentment.

Brennan knew the image of the little family was going to remain imprinted on his mind throughout a long and painful ordeal.

"What's that?" Florrie asked, pointing at the envelope when Maggie had released her.

"It's for you."

"'Pussy Got the Measles'!"

"Right. Lyrics and guitar chords."

"Great! I'm going to — "

"Not to be opened till morning."

"Aww!"

"And there's something for you in there too, Celia."

"Really?"

"What's she getting?" Florrie wanted to know.

Brennan had remembered Celia's interest in math, so he had grabbed a book of puzzles and games designed to illustrate the relationship between mathematics and music.

"You'll see tomorrow, after a good, long sleep."

"Do you have kids?" Florrie asked him.

"No."

"Were you the boss of your own family?"

"No, no. My big sister was the boss. Way it should be. And if Maggie wants you to go to bed now, that's what you're going to do. Right, girls?"

"Okay, okay."

"Good night then, little ones. God bless you."

"Thank you!"

"Yeah, thank you! See you tomorrow, Brennan."

Florrie reached up to put her arms around his neck, and he bent down to her. He gave her a hug, and she kissed him on the cheek. He planted a kiss on the top of Celia's curls. He did his best to put on a front of casual cheerfulness, as if tomorrow would be just another day.

Maggie dimmed the lights, took the girls by the hand, and put them to bed.

✝

When she returned, her emotions barely in check, she sat down with Brennan at her kitchen table, and they took up where they had left off.

"What happened that night, Maggie?"

She looked past him into the darkness as she spoke. "As if it wasn't convenient enough that Jordyn had become a public figure on TV, that Podgis freak announced he was coming to town. I've hated him for years, for all the shows he does exploiting people's problems and their pain. Pretending he is sympathetic when he is just using them for his ratings. Of course I despised myself every time I turned his show on, but I watched it anyway. Like a train wreck we can't stop looking at. What really nailed him for me was one particular show he did: girls who date guys who hurt other girls! How did he come up with that, you're asking? Easy. It goes on all the time." She peered at Brennan. "Don't believe me?"

"I'd believe just about anything, Maggie, unfortunately."

"I have a whole scrapbook of clippings I could show you. Ted Bundy, that serial killer in the States: he killed how many women? When they finally caught him, all these girls flocked to the courtroom to see him. And be seen by him. And all these other ones started writing him letters. There are other stories of grown women leaving their husbands to marry rapists and psychos who are in prison.

"So Podgis was on to another well-known fact of life. And he was coming to Halifax. To do a show making fun of all the poor, deluded people who were hoping to see the Virgin Mary. It was perfect. I was going to set him up."

She had succeeded. Podgis was on his way to trial for the murder. But this was evidence that her own crime was premeditated, first-degree murder. Brennan stayed silent.

"The setup began with a note to Jordyn's place, pretending it was from one of Podgis's minions. A public-relations person. Could Jordyn meet Pike after his show? He had seen her on the news and thought she could go far on TV. She had the looks and the personality. Blah

305

blah blah. Why not meet at the shrine itself? He could do a bit of a photo shoot there. Unfortunately it had to be late — midnight — because he had commitments till then, and he had an early morning flight. I didn't know when he would really be leaving, so I had to get it done that night. And I had checked out the shrine; everybody tended to clear out after suppertime.

"Then I made a call to him at the hotel, pretending to be Jordyn, asking if we could meet after his show to discuss my chances of getting into television. How about the shrine at twelve thirty? Sorry about the late hour, but I work at Tim's out in Bedford and I don't get off till twelve. I made myself sound dumb and flirtatious, like someone who would do anything to get on TV. As you can imagine, he jumped at the idea. So that was the plan. I would do . . . what I was going to do to Jordyn at midnight, then get him there half an hour later. I would hide and wait till he showed up, then call the police with an anonymous tip, then go home and scrub myself and wash my clothes and all that. But things got out of control. You read about these perfect crimes or conspiracies, someone orchestrating everyone else's moves. That's not what happens in real life.

"First of all, as soon as I got there and saw her, I changed my mind. Even though I hated her and had waited for years for this opportunity. I thought, 'I can't go through with this. I can't kill somebody! Even her.' She saw me and told me to get lost, because she was meeting somebody for a photo shoot. I started telling her what a horrible person she was, and she started making fun of me and telling me I would always be an outcast because of what had been done to me. She grabbed my jacket and tried to pull it away, and made a remark about the scars she had left on me. And I hit her, and she hit back. Then I said I was going to get her arrested for what she had done. And she told me she had a new boyfriend who was really tough, and she was going to send him to get me and Celia and Florrie, to make sure I kept my mouth shut. It was only then that I took the knife out and stabbed her.

"I couldn't believe how horrible I felt, even though it was her and she deserved it. I had finally paid her back. I thought it would be exhilarating. But it wasn't. And I couldn't believe how frightened I was, and how all my plans went straight out of my head. I went running off to see Ignatius. It was me that hit him and knocked him out. I didn't mean to!"

"How did Ignatius fit in with this, Maggie?"

"He is a sweet, kind man who's had a tough life and spent most of his nights on the street. They always find a room for him in the homeless shelter, and he goes in there and takes showers and all that, but he ends up taking off and sleeping outdoors. He's really religious and he would see some of us downtown, kids, and he'd try to help us. Counsel us to avoid drinking and drugs, and warn the girls to stay away from loser boyfriends. He was always good to me, and I liked talking to him. He's really smart, and he reads a lot. He used to drink and pass out. But even when he was drinking he was never bad or mean. Jordyn and them started giving me a rough time about liking him. And they said rotten things to him about me.

"Then, one night, they were driving along Spring Garden Road in somebody's van and they saw Ignatius sitting on the wall in front of the library. They stopped and invited him to come with them and get something to drink. They took him in the van and went to the liquor store and got all this cheap booze, and kept giving it to him until he passed out. Then they put him in the back of the van and took his clothes off. They drove to my house and came to the door, and threatened that they would all come in and do stuff to my little sisters if I didn't come out with them. Florrie came down to the door and they started playing with her hair and making creepy remarks that she couldn't understand. She started laughing, trying to go along with the jokes that she was too little to get. I was terrified, so I took her upstairs and locked her and Celia in the house, and went out with them."

Maggie looked suddenly exhausted, as if she had lived through the whole ordeal again. She looked about forty years old. She began to weep, and Brennan forced himself again to sit still and hold back from comforting her.

"I got into the car, and they told me to take my clothes off. I said no, and Brandon pulled out a knife and said he was going to break the lock of my apartment and get Florrie and Celia. I started shaking so much I couldn't get my clothes off, so Brandon took them off, and they all made gross remarks about my body and the marks from what they had done to me before. Then they pushed me over the seats into the back of the van, and that's when I saw Ignatius passed out. They started driving. I don't know where. I couldn't believe what was happening. I was shaking and crying, and they all laughed. They pushed me on top of Ignatius, and took a bunch of pictures. And I know they later showed them to a couple of their friends, and said I was getting it on with the homeless men. That's how vicious and trashy they were.

"You thought it was Jordyn in the picture, but it was me. I had long hair then, but I chopped it all off afterwards. People used to admire it. But I just wanted to disappear.

"Anyway, they showed Ignatius the pictures the next day and told him he had raped and abused me, and they had caught him. He nearly died when he heard it. He thought it might be true, because he was so drunk. But instead of taking off and hiding, he came and found me and called me to come outside. He was all upset. There were tears in his eyes. He said he was sorry, and if I wanted to get him arrested he'd wait for the cops to come. And I told him what really happened. That he hadn't done anything. He was unconscious at the time! But he still felt guilty about being with a teenage girl without our clothes on. And it wasn't his fault at all. He never took another drink from that day on. Not a drop.

"Later I found out he had to walk back to his place without his clothes from wherever they let him off, and two girls saw him on the street and called the cops. He had his hands in front of himself, down there, just to try and cover up. But they charged him with some kind of sex crime. Indecency or something.

"And the night that I stabbed Jordyn, before we got into the fight, she made a crack about me and Ignatius: our 'wedding picture.' And it came into my head that Ignatius was the only person who could connect me with Jordyn. The only person except for Brandon Toth and Jade, Jordyn's other friend who helped her abuse me. And they would keep their mouths shut because of how bad they would look if the story came out. I had never told anyone what happened, except Ignatius, because of the way they brought him into it. So I got paranoid. He was always writing little reminders and things on holy cards he'd get from various churches, and he stuck them all in his prayer book. He was always telling me I should keep a record of everything that happened, and lay charges against Jordyn and Brandon and the other one. But maybe he kept a record himself. I got scared when she said that about the picture.

"So I went completely off the plan to go straight home after . . . the stabbing. I never saw Podgis. And I never even thought about my other plan, that the police might suspect one of the kooks hanging around the shrine. All I could think of was that I had a motive to kill Jordyn Snider, and Ignatius Boyle knew about it. I didn't think he would turn me in, but I wanted him to destroy anything about that incident with him and me.

"There's a beautiful old white house on Hollis Street, made of wood. It was built in the 1820s. Around the back there's a staircase, a fire escape. It's kind of sheltered under there. And that's where Ignatius sleeps. By the time I arrived, I was out of my mind with fear. I blurted it out as soon as I woke him up. I told him I'd killed her. He wanted to know where I did it. He wanted the two of us to go and get the body and dump it somewhere nobody would find it. At least I was thinking straight enough to know that would have been impossible, and I didn't want to be seen anywhere near the churchyard. I took off, and he followed me and we kept arguing and he said he was going to go and take the body away somewhere. He started running up Hollis Street and turned on Morris towards the churchyard. And I ran after him and grabbed him and he turned around and I pushed him really hard and he fell and hit his head. And I left him there! I felt more guilty about that than about stabbing Jordyn.

"Anyway, I got home without anybody seeing me, and I got all cleaned up, and went to bed. But I couldn't sleep. And in the morning I heard they'd got Podgis for the murder, and I couldn't figure out how. I thought I must have hallucinated the whole thing."

"Podgis had her blood on his shoes."

"When I read about that in the paper, I sat for an hour without moving. He actually went to meet her. I really did set him up."

Maggie was wrung out after her terrible confession, and Brennan was wasted after hearing it. They were both silent for several long minutes. Then he said to her, "Maggie, I will do everything I possibly can to help you through this."

She looked up at him, her face swollen from crying. "Why are you being so good to me? I'm a murderer! And I knocked out Ignatius. And I treated you really bad when you came to the house, and when you phoned. I had to get you off the trail."

Brennan waved her protests away. "I'll take you to a lawyer tomorrow, and he'll know the best way to work things for you." What he did not say was that the lawyer would have his work cut out for him trying to get the charge reduced from first-degree murder. The fact that she had changed her mind when she got there, and only took the knife out after Jordyn grabbed her and they got into a scrap, would that help mitigate against a first-degree murder charge? He doubted it, but he had no idea. What if things could be finessed somehow so she could plead to manslaughter? How many years would she have to serve? This was all beyond his field of expertise. One thing he knew, though: "Do not tell anyone else, except your lawyer, what you told me tonight. Agreed?"

"I won't tell."

"Now, where is your mother?"

"She's in a special care home, because she has this spinal condition and she is in a wheelchair. I take the girls to visit her all the time. I get to live in this flat with Florrie and Celia because it was my grandparents' house and Mum owned it after they died. The government, or whoever runs the care home, takes the rent paid by Mrs. Lewis for the lower flat. Or something like that. Mum could get by in a ground-level apartment, and we're going to get a ramp built for the house and switch flats with Mrs. Lewis. But we can't afford to pay for the work yet. Plus Mum says she doesn't want me to spend my life looking after her. She says that is no life for a young girl, but I wouldn't mind. I've always said I'd look after her. I'd rather be home than out working with strangers anyway. It's no accident that I prefer working with rats in the psychology lab at Dal, right? Where they try to figure out why animals, human or otherwise, behave as they do."

Brennan nodded. He could see her point.

"I can't bear the thought of Mum finding out about this! It will kill her!"

"I promise you this, Maggie. Whatever happens to you, wherever you have to go, I will arrange it so Florrie and Celia and your mother will be close to you."

"You can't do that!"

"Ever hear what Prime Minister Trudeau said in the face of a challenge like that? 'Just watch me.' Wherever you go, I will go there and suss the place out, talk to the local priests and sisters, and find a place for your family."

"But that would cost money!"

"I will make it happen, pet. You can count on it."

"I can't believe you are being so good."

"I'm not good. Ask anybody who knows me! But I recognize the good in *you*, in spite of what you've done. You take care of your sisters. You love them. You fear for their safety. You were willing to spend your youth caring for your mother. You have committed the ultimate crime, the ultimate sin, of taking a life. But of course I know what drove you to it."

He stood up. "I'll go now. Don't do anything or talk to anyone until I come by for you in the morning. I'll call to give you a time."

She got up and went to him, stood on tiptoe, and put her arms around his neck. She clung to him for a long time, and he held her tightly, wishing damaged people could be healed by love alone. On his way home in the car, he thought of the "Song of Bernadette," the way Warnes and Cohen wrote about the damage we do to one another, and about healing and mercy. What kind of mercy could Maggie Nelson, killer and victim, expect to find in the courts of justice?

The following morning, after saying his Mass, Brennan went directly to Monty's office. Darlene, the receptionist, told him Monty was on his way to court with Podgis, for an application to vary. Vary what? Brennan wondered. Darlene caught his confusion and explained, "Mr. Podgis wants to vary his bail conditions, so he can go to Toronto next weekend. It's open court, no secret."

"Thank you, Darlene. I'll catch Monty over there."

"Water Street courts, not Spring Garden."

"Right. Thanks."

He left the building and headed down Salter Street to Lower Water, walked north till he reached the plaza in front of the big, square court building. There was Monty, just entering the courthouse, hobbling a bit on his injured leg, his left arm in a sling, a heavy briefcase weighing him down on the right. His client was at his side, not carrying anything. Well, what would you expect from a man who feels so little concern for others that he would exploit a murder for his own perverse amusement? Brennan increased his pace and caught up with them when they stopped inside the building's glass doors.

Podgis looked startled to see him. Startled and then hostile. Monty did not appear overly pleased, either. He gave his client an uneasy glance, then said, "Brennan. What are you doing here?"

"You'll want to know this," Brennan said.

"Excuse us, Pike. Let's step over here, Brennan."

Monty turned and walked past the reception desk to the end of the building, out of earshot of Podgis, who looked from one to the other with apprehension. Monty faced Brennan. "What is it?"

"I found out what happened that night."

Monty went completely still. He stared at Brennan without blinking. Finally, he spoke in a voice barely above a whisper. "What are you up to, Brennan?"

"I said I know what happened."

It was plain to see that Monty did not want to hear it. Last thing a defence lawyer wants to hear is what really happened that night, since it is usually his client who made it happen. Monty would not want to hear what was probably going to be surefire proof of Podgis's guilt, which would limit the kind of defence he could put to the court.

But Brennan pressed on. "He's innocent."

"What? Who's innocent?"

"Your client." Monty's eyes shifted to Podgis and back to Brennan. "Podgis didn't do it."

"*What!?*"

"I know who did it."

Monty said, quietly, "Ignatius Boyle."

"No."

"If not Boyle, then who?" Monty's voice quickened. "Was it Clayton Byner?"

It was Brennan's turn to be confused. "Who?"

"A psycho, a parolee. He was writing letters to Jordyn Snider from prison. I got a call yesterday from Corrections Canada, that the letters were from Byner, and he's out, so — "

"What's all this about letters?"

Monty just shook his head. "Never mind that. Tell me what you have to tell me."

"A young girl did it. I'm bringing her in. To you."

"A girl? What are you saying? I can't deal with this now, whatever it is. I've got to get up there with Podgis."

"Listen to me, Monty. A young girl by the name of Maggie Nelson killed Jordyn Snider. I've been speaking to Maggie."

"Who is this girl? Where did she come from?"

"Long history between Maggie and the victim. Maggie is going to turn herself in, but I want her to talk to you before she does anything."

Monty looked as if he had been tapped as a last-minute replacement for Stephen Hawking at the world theoretical physics debating tournament and was trying to formulate a Grand Unified Theory before he got to the podium. "If there's another suspect, I can't talk to her. I'd be in conflict while I'm representing Podgis."

Pitting one suspect against the other. True enough. "So who will I take her to see for advice? Give me another lawyer."

"Saul Green. Take her to Saul. I have no idea what's going on here, Brennan, but this had better be good. For now, I'm going in there with Podgis as if nothing has changed. After that, you're going to have a whole lot of explaining to do."

"You don't look any happier than I am, Monty, to find out that fucker, that ball of evil and spite, is not guilty. I can tell you this much: he didn't cover himself in glory."

With that, Brennan turned and left the building, not sparing Podgis so much as a sideways glance.

Chapter 22

Monty

"What did he want?" Podgis hissed at Monty when the lawyer returned from his conference with Burke.

Monty gave his client a long look, trying to imagine what Burke had been talking about, another suspect, and Podgis here, the accused, who had the victim's blood on his shoes. What on earth was going on? Until he knew, he would proceed as planned. He headed into the courtroom for the hearing on his client's bail conditions.

"What?" Podgis bellowed behind him.

"Never mind that," Monty said, not bothering to turn around. "We have a hearing to attend."

Podgis was even harder to handle after the hearing. The judge threw out the application and ruled that Podgis could not leave the jurisdiction for Toronto or anywhere else. As lawyer and client left the courtroom, Podgis grabbed Monty's suit jacket and tried to pull him around. But his fit of pique was not about Toronto or the judge's less-than-sympathetic attitude. It was about Burke.

"What did Burke tell you? I have to know! Don't fucking keep things from me, Collins!"

Monty turned and shook him loose. Beads of sweat stood out on his client's forehead. "Why do you assume it was about you? Pull yourself together."

†

But of course it was about him. And one would think it would be welcome news, though Monty had a contrary impression. When the truth emerged, and Monty was seated in the office for what he hoped was the last time ever with this particular client, there was no joy in Podgis. There was nothing but his habitual bombast and belligerence.

"Just to make sure you can't screw me around later, are we covered right now by the solicitor-client privilege?"

"Yes, we are."

"All right. Here it is. I got a call from a girl I thought was Jordyn. Said she wanted to meet me to talk about getting into television. How about meeting at the statue? Fine. She had to work late, so she said twelve thirty. But see, I always go early. Like a cop. Go and scope out the place first, watch the individual arrive. See what they're like when they don't know they're being watched. And I smelled a rat with this invitation to a midnight rendezvous."

"Sure you did."

"Believe me or don't believe me. I don't give a shit what you think. Anyway, when I got there a few minutes after midnight I saw these two girls eyeball to eyeball, talking into each other's faces. One of them had on a hooded jacket and gloves. That was the one we now know is Maggie. The other one, Jordyn, was dressed to kill. Or be killed. And they were going at it. I thought whoa, catfight! They had a lot to say to each other but most of it I couldn't make out. And they didn't say each other's names. All I caught was 'what you did to me.' That was Maggie. I always carry my tape recorder with me, pocket-size one, for interviews or whatever people might say. The two of them were at it for quite a while before I snapped out of it and thought of turning on the recorder. Jordyn grabbed Maggie, and then it got physical. A couple of punches were thrown. I caught Jordyn saying 'that old creep! Since you already have the wedding picture!' And Maggie answered, 'You did that. It wasn't real!' Then Jordyn said somebody was going to come and get somebody else, a couple

315

of other girls. I couldn't make out the names on my tape. And then I couldn't fucking believe it. Maggie's arm went up in the air and down on Jordyn. Jordyn let a scream out of her and went down. Maggie hit her again. Stabbed her, as we now know. Then she stood there staring as if she couldn't believe what she had done. She said, 'Oh my God!' I figured right then she knew she'd killed her. She turned, and I could see blood on her coat; not a lot, but some. Then she took off running through the churchyard. I stood there in the shadows for a bit; figured somebody might have heard the scream. But no lights came on; nobody came out. So, what to do? Follow the perp."

"And then what? Make a citizen's arrest? Call in the TV cameras?"

"Get the story. What are you looking at? That's what I do. I don't need any lessons in ethics from an ambulance chaser."

"I would have called the ambulance, not chased it."

"There was no life to save. So. I wanted to find Maggie, see where she would go. Maybe trail her to her house, find out who she was. I took off out of the yard and down Byrne Street."

"That's when Betty Isenor saw you."

"No, that was later. I was on Byrne Street twice. Anyway, I came out and looked and caught the tail end of Maggie turning the corner of Morris Street, heading down Hollis. I followed, staying in the shadows of the buildings. Gum-soled shoes, perfect footwear. I saw her cross to the west side of the street. There's this old white wooden house and she went behind it. By the time I got there, she was standing by the fire escape hollering at somebody. Turns out it was *Saint* Ignatius Boyle, living like a troll under the stairs. She knew where to find him. He had a plastic sheet rigged up over his sleeping bag and his pile of junk. So she's there, and he's like, 'Wha?' and she's bawling and crying and saying, 'I killed her!' Doesn't even say who. Doesn't have to. 'You've got to help me! If you have anything, get rid of it!'

"I was in the shadows watching all this and thinking, 'Who is this guy, a street bum, and why is she telling him what she did?' Then they started talking in low voices, and I couldn't hear them. Whatever he was saying, she must have got pissed off, because she left and started running. He burrowed around in his stuff, then came out and high-tailed it after her. He caught up to her on Morris Street. He was saying something like she had to go back to the churchyard, to the body, whatever, and he'd go with her. And she wasn't having any of it. She was flipping out. Looking all around her. I wanted to follow them, but I figured they'd spot me. And I wanted to check the body. So I pussyfooted out of there. I figure she gave Boyle a shove, and that's how he got knocked out. She had some of Jordyn's blood on her, so that must be how the blood got on the good saint's face. Anyway, I took a long, long way around and entered the churchyard through the back. Went to the body. I leaned down over her. Her eyes were wide open. No movement. Dead as a . . . Well, no life left in her."

"You don't know that. She may have been alive."

"You heard the evidence at the prelim. Incapacitated right away."

"You had not heard the evidence while you were still standing over her the night of the murder. As far as you knew, she might have been alive when you left right after the stabbing."

"The girl's reaction. Maggie's. She knew she had killed her."

"Yet you didn't call the police or ambulance."

A hesitation, then, "I hung around, describing everything into my recorder. I was hoping Maggie and the old guy would come and try to do something. Or somebody would find the body and call the cops and I'd get to see the investigation from the ground up. But I finally got spooked and wanted to get away, not be seen there. When I left that second time, that's when the nosy old bird in the apartment building would have seen me. She must have been still awake from hearing Maggie and Boyle hollering out in the street. I went back to my hotel room, all wound up. Kept pacing the room, turning the TV on and off. Thinking about the story."

"Of the murder you had just witnessed."

"Yeah. I finally fell asleep across the bed with my clothes and shoes still on. Then I was wakened up by a pounding on the door. The cops. The woman had seen me, and the hotel clerk had clocked me coming back in. The cops took the clothes I had on, and my shoes, and looked around a bit. But they missed the tape recorder, which I had stuck in the pocket of another jacket in the wardrobe. I got changed into the track suit I lounge around in, and off we went to the police station.

"So I looked good for the killing. But appearances are deceiving, right? 'Cause it wasn't me that did it."

Monty had never seen an innocent man so covered with guilt.

"When you got me out on bail, I knew I could solve the case. I knew this Ignatius guy was still in the hospital. I went behind the old house where he sleeps and rummaged through his stuff. Found a Polaroid of him and Maggie, naked together. Which we now know was a setup by some assholes who were harassing Maggie."

A bunch of assholes that included Jordyn Snider. Monty had read the letters she received from Clayton Byner while he was in Dorchester prison. She had been destined for a violent life, and a violent death. How many others, like Maggie Nelson, might have been victimized before Jordyn herself died the way she had lived?

Monty tuned back in to Pike Podgis as the curtains rang down on his latest performance. "When I saw the picture of Boyle and the young girl, I thought, *Whoa!* And there were some phone numbers and addresses with initials beside them. I went off on a few wild goose chases, wrong addresses, but I finally found out 'Yukon' meant Maggie lived in a place on Yukon Street. And I was ready to make my move when . . ."

When Burke beat him to it. How that must burn his client's arse, Monty thought.

"Oh, and tell your pal Burke not to lose too much sleep over the little clue I gave him about the Jeanie Ballantine murder."

"Jeanie Ballantine?" Like everyone else across the country, Monty knew about the girl who had been brutally murdered in Toronto. What did Podgis have to do with it? And where did Burke fit in?

"You look a little puzzled, Collins. I guess Burke really does keep his trap shut about what goes on in the confession box."

"Confession box! You went into his church? And, what? Had a sudden conversion to Catholicism, and then — "

"Yeah, I had a bit of fun with the good Father in there. He didn't take it in good grace, though, I have to say. He has a killer streak in him, did you know that? Must run in the family."

"What are you talking about?"

"He nearly killed me!"

"When? Where? What are you saying?"

"Ask him some time. Oh, and when you're talking to him, be sure to tell him the Jeanie Ballantine thing was a joke, on him. I didn't commit that murder either. I wasn't even in the country when it happened. But I covered the story when I got back to Toronto. And I pretended to Burke that I was the killer, just to get him wound up. Nah, I'm not a killer. But the notoriety sure was fun while it lasted. Gonna get a lot of program ideas out of this little episode in my life."

The repulsive man tried to put a brave face on it, tried to be flippant, but Monty could see the humiliation burning beneath the surface. Podgis had found himself in a position he could not possibly have imagined: a fantasy come true. Maggie's attempt to set him up had gone off the rails, as these things inevitably do. But it offered him a chance to be in the spotlight, a man wrongfully accused of murder, a highly public martyr who would then investigate the murder, "find" the real killer, and be the hero of the tale. Monty knew Podgis would never have admitted he was there for the murder, that he had it on tape. He would have claimed he had come upon the body after the fact, would maybe have stuck to his alibi story to explain walking through the churchyard. He would have loudly proclaimed his innocence to the arresting officers but not told them who had really done it. No, the evidence pointing to the real killer would have been acquired by his own brilliant detective work.

But he had reckoned without his nemesis, Brennan Burke, doing a parallel investigation and finding out the truth about Podgis's shameful role in the case.

Chapter 23

When it was all over, CBC Radio reported:

> "There has been a surprising development in the Pike Podgis murder story in Halifax. Hugh Donaldson has the details for us. Hugh?"
>
> "Surprising would be an understatement, Bill. There has been a stunning turnaround in the case. It is in fact no longer the Pike Podgis murder story. The charges against the talk show host were dropped today, and another person, a young woman, has pleaded guilty to manslaughter in the stabbing death of Jordyn Snider in the churchyard of St. Bernadette's on September twenty-fourth of last year. The person who committed the crime is Maggie Nelson, nineteen, of Halifax. Prominent defence lawyer Saul Green told CBC News that there are mitigating factors in the case. The two young women had a history, and Maggie was the victim of horrific abuse by Jordyn in the past. He did not give any details of the abuse or the confrontation between the two in the churchyard. He said Maggie Nelson

came forward of her own accord and surrendered herself to police.

"A reliable source told me that Crown and defence lawyers will likely present the court with a joint recommendation of ten years for a sentence. As is well known, Bill, with good behaviour, a person can be released on parole after serving only one third of his or her sentence.

"The story has captivated the attention of people across the country because of the notoriety of television personality Pike Podgis. From the moment of his arrest the morning after the killing, Podgis took every opportunity to make the claim that he was an innocent man, wrongfully accused of the murder, a victim of a miscarriage of justice. He vowed to fight the charges all the way to the Supreme Court of Canada, if need be. And it turns out he is indeed innocent of the charge. But here's the thing: it also turns out that Podgis knew from the very beginning what really happened that night. He somehow arrived on the scene while the murder was being committed, or soon afterwards. It is clear now that Podgis had enough information to learn fairly quickly who the real killer was. So his case was never going to the Supreme Court of Canada, not even to the Supreme Court of Nova Scotia, and he knew it! Why he didn't present his information to the authorities immediately, and provide some clarity for Jordyn's family, is anybody's guess. The Crown prosecutor's office would not comment on whether any charges might arise out of Podgis's presence on the scene or his failure to assist the victim, if those facts are borne out. So Pike Podgis, martyr to the criminal justice system, is now Pike Podgis with a lot of explaining to do!

"But that's not the end of it, Bill. You may recall the religious debate on the Podgis show the night of the murder. Podgis came to town to do a show on the claimed sightings of the Virgin Mary at St. Bernadette's church. The debate was between an atheist, Professor Robert Thornhill, and a believer in God — though not a believer in the claimed sightings — Father Brennan Burke of St. Bernadette's. But it was a circus, and minutes into the broadcast Father Burke walked off the set in disgust. And the word is out that it was Father Burke who investigated the killing on his own and found out the truth of what happened. He came to court to support Maggie Nelson, and our sources tell us he has plans to travel to Kingston, Ontario, where Maggie will likely be serving her sentence. He will be making arrangements for Maggie's mother and sisters to rent a place close to the women's prison. So the priest, who is no admirer of Pike Podgis, has been instrumental in freeing him from the murder charges. Father Burke has refused comment, and has turned down all requests by reporters for interviews.

"So that's where it stands now, Bill. We'll be following the story in all its twists and turns."

Bruce MacKinnon's cartoon in the February 22, 1993, *Chronicle Herald* showed Podgis in a theatrical pose at the top tier of a grandstand, empty except for him and a television camera aimed up at him from below. Podgis was shown in profile, chest puffed out, arms extended, mouth grotesquely wide open. The words "wrongfully accused!" and "miscarriage of justice!" came blaring out of his mouth. Sticking out of his back pocket was a reporter's notebook with "Real Killer!" printed on it. A speech balloon coming out of the notebook said, "Wrongfully accused, schmongfully accused! He's had me in his pocket the whole time!" On the grounds beyond the grandstand, a smaller picture showed two people on a bench in the shadow of the statue of St. Bernadette: a young girl with her head down and a priest bent towards her in a gesture of comfort, holding her hand in his.

Acknowledgements

I would like to thank the following people for their kind assistance: Pauline Cameron, Joe A. Cameron, Joan Butcher, Rhea McGarva, Tommy Parsons, Judge Pat Curran, Fr. Paul Glynn, and Frances Larkin Reynolds. Also thanks once again to my editors.

This is a work of fiction. Any liberties taken in the interests of the story, or any errors committed, are mine alone. St. Bernadette's is a fictional church and Byrne Street a fictional location. I have placed it perpendicular to Morris Street on the north side, between Hollis and Lower Water.

At ECW Press, we want you to enjoy this book in whatever format you like, whenever you like. Leave your print book at home and take the eBook to go! Purchase the print edition and receive the eBook free. Just send an email to **ebook@ecwpress.com** and include:

Get the eBook free!*
*proof of purchase required

• the book title
• the name of the store where you purchased it
• your receipt number
• your preference of file type: PDF or ePub?

A real person will respond to your email with your eBook attached. And thanks for supporting an independently owned Canadian publisher with your purchase!